Before It Was Us

MARIE FOX

To anyone wondering if good is good enough:
you deserve a love that sets your soul on fire.

Prologue

My name is Paisley Hamilton, and I have a good life. But some days, that's entirely the problem. Because how do you know if good is actually good enough?

I know, I know, I've heard it all before. The grass isn't always greener. Be grateful for what you have. Blah, blah, fucking blah. But why does wanting something beyond the comfort and predictability of our everyday lives somehow makes us selfish or ungrateful?

No one ever warned us how hard adulthood *actually* is—okay, maybe they did, but let's be honest... we probably weren't listening.

Sure, we might know the basics. Graduate college. Land the "big girl job." Pay the bills. File our taxes (probably incorrectly). And wake up at five in the goddamn morning for the rest of our lives. We work to live and live to work, but what about the moments in between?

No one prepares us for the *other* stuff—the thoughts and feelings that live within us so deeply that even *we* aren't aware they are there, settling in like houseguests we can't get rid of even after it hits nine o'clock. And who wants company that late?

All of these questions and worries get pushed aside by the daily mundane, and we continue through our days completely content with the way our lives are going simply because we aren't aware of the possibility that there could be more.

Or maybe we are, and we're just too afraid to think about it because we've been conditioned to ignore it.

So instead, we wake up, go to work, scroll through social media, see yet another engagement announcement, another picture-perfect baby reveal, another cozy holiday family photo, and we compare ourselves to these people we probably haven't even seen since high school. We assume everyone is still madly in love with their high-school-sweetheart, thrilled about parenting three kids under five, and effortlessly nailing the whole happy, fulfilled adulthood thing.

But what if settling isn't the answer? What if maybe, just maybe, good really *isn't* good enough?

The truth is, we don't let ourselves wonder if the grass *could* be greener. We've been told so many times to stop looking, to stop questioning, to be happy with what we have, that we stay safely behind the fences we've built, and we don't let ourselves acknowledge what's beyond them because that means facing all of the ways our lives might be falling short.

That is until the universe throws something our way that shakes us awake, that rattles the foundation of the life we thought we wanted, and then suddenly... we do.

"When you're happy, you enjoy the music;
when you're sad, you understand the lyrics."
Frank Ocean

A Note on Music

Each chapter of *Before It Was Us* is accompanied by a song
chosen to match the tone and emotional arc of the story.
You can listen along by scanning the Spotify code on this page or
by searching for the *Before It Was Us* playlist on Spotify.
Listening isn't required, but it's encouraged for a deeper, more
immersive reading experience. Let the music carry you where
words sometimes can't.

Songs referenced are the property of their respective artists.
This playlist is shared for listening enjoyment only.

Chapter One

♫ "Landslide" — Fleetwood Mac ♫

PAISLEY

The relentless pounding in my head is the first thing I notice as I attempt to flutter my eyes open—which, by the way, is a huge fucking mistake. The curtain in the hotel room is slightly ajar, and the sun is peering straight through the glass and directly into my soul, punishing me for taking so many shots last night.

I, on the other hand, blame Charlie for my inebriated decisions, given that *she* was the one who kept buying trays on trays of pickle shots. Yes, *pickle shots,* because apparently bars in Wisconsin think $2.00 shots of pickle juice and cheap-ass vodka make for a stellar good time. Unfortunately for me, tipsy Paisley agrees.

Simply thinking of the smell of those shots is almost enough to send me over the edge and running for the bathroom, so I shove the memory from my mind and begrudgingly roll over in bed. And there she is, the Shot Queen herself, lying next to me sleeping as soundly as a damn baby. Her blonde hair is strewn across the pillow, and last night's mascara is smeared down her cheeks.

"I'll get you back for this, you little bitch," I whisper toward her, only half-joking, and she stirs slightly.

"Paisley? You're alive?" Maddie's voice startles me from across the room.

"Unfortunately," I respond, my mouth full of cotton. "What the fuck were we thinking last night? We are way too old for this, and people definitely weren't lying when they said once you turn thirty, hangovers hit different." I attempt to rub the sleep from my eyes as a yawn escapes my lips.

"Well, technically, you're not thirty for another six days. But you're right, we are one hundred percent too old for this," Sarah chimes in. I didn't even notice her sitting up in the other bed, but she looks about as good as I feel. Terrible. And maybe still a little drunk?

I attempt to get up to use the bathroom, and as soon as my feet hit the ground, whether I'm still tipsy or not is no longer a question. Because I most *definitely* still feel the remnants of what I consumed last night. The room spins slightly as I come to a stand, and I almost lose my balance. Luckily, I'm not far from my arch nemesis that is the window, and I grab onto the windowpane to steady myself.

Maybe we should have booked the hotel for the entire weekend instead of one night like we debated before coming. We could have locked ourselves in, pulled the blackout curtains shut—all the way this time—and ignored the rest of the world while we slept our hangovers away until we felt better tomorrow morning. But with school starting on Monday, I wanted to be home early tomorrow to meal-prep and get mentally prepared for my first week back at work. I'm sure I'll be happy with my decision once I wake up in my own bed in the morning, but at the moment, I'm regretting that decision.

Past Paisley: two.

Current Paisley: zero.

"Anyone up for some breakfast?" Maddie asks as I reach the bathroom. The mention of food does not help my queasiness, but I know I need to get something into my stomach.

"Uh, sure," I agree. "Just give me a minute to go to the bathroom and brush my teeth. Oh, and wake Charlie up. That bitch doesn't deserve to sleep in after all the shots she bought last night."

Charlie drives us home because I am still far too nauseous to focus on the road. Typically, with my car, I'm a huge control freak—okay, maybe not *only* when it comes to my car, but that's not important right now—and I rarely let anyone drive it. Not even my husband Ethan, which is why I usually am the one to burn through my mileage anytime he and I go anywhere. But I figured having someone else drive today was a safe bet in case I needed to demand her to pull over and let me hurl.

I'm still thinking about ways to get back at my so-called best friend. I specifically remember telling Charlie and the others to *not* let me take any shots last night. And that lasted, what? All of two minutes? I turn my head and glare daggers at her.

She must sense my eyes drilling into her skull because she jumps in to defend herself. "Oh, no you don't, Paisley Hamilton. Don't you dare look at me like that. I might have been the one to *pay* for the shots, but don't forget that it was *you* who suggested them."

"Yeah, after I explicitly told you not to listen to me. You can't trust a drunken Paisley. She's always out to get me," I rebuttal, rolling my eyes.

Maddie and Sarah collectively snort from the backseat. "That may be true," Maddie says. "But you're putting a lot of faith in your drunken group of friends to listen to you."

"Yeah," Sarah jumps in. "And besides, it's not like you're the only one feeling the effects of last night. But hey, you can only get drunk for the last time as a twenty-something-year-old once. Might as well go out with a bang."

I groan and rub my hands down my face, partially in annoyance and partially in dread about hitting the next decade of my life. "I know, but I was hoping to be at least a somewhat productive member of society the rest of the weekend. We go back to school first thing Monday morning, and I wanted to get into my classroom for a few hours tomorrow before being bombarded with meetings all week."

"Oh, quit being such an overachiever," Charlie pipes up, a smile pulling from her lips. "You work too hard, anyway. You need to focus more on doing things you *enjoy*. Plus, tomorrow is our last day of summer. Let's go to the beach or something instead. Fuck work."

I look at her with resistance. "Yeah, that sounds great. But you know if I don't get my shit together tomorrow, I'll be stressed about it all week. I have to get that furniture put together that I ordered for my classroom, and you *know* we will be bombarded with meetings all week during in-service and I won't have any time to do it. Then guess who will be the one who gets to deal with a crabby Paisley?" I give her a menacing smirk.

"That's right!" Maddie bursts out from the backseat. How does she have so much energy? "I keep forgetting you two work together. I'm actually a little jealous. It must be nice to have someone to waste your prep period with." She lets out a sigh and stares wistfully out the car window.

Maddie is also a teacher, but she works in Minnesota rather than Wisconsin, so she doesn't go back for another week, giving her ample time to recover from last night. But given she teaches elementary school and not high school like Charlie and me, she probably needs it more than we do.

"Fine," Charlie says, ignoring Maddie's comment. "You're right. I'm already dreading going back to work with the Giggle Squad. I don't need to add a grumpy-ass Paisley to the mix."

That draws Sarah's attention to the conversation, which surprises me because I thought she was passed the fuck out back there. "The Giggle Squad? Did I miss something?"

"Oh, it's just this group of women—"

"And their husbands!" Charlie interrupts me, her eyes still trained on the road.

"...and their husbands," I nod slowly and continue, "that we work with. The best way to describe them is that they're like the group from *Mean Girls*, except instead of teenagers, they're grown-ass women. Super cliquey, always look like they're judging anyone who walks past them—you know the type."

"Cliquey how?"

"Have we really never mentioned any of this to you guys?" I question, and Maddie and Sarah both shake their heads. "God, I don't even know how to explain it. They just aren't very... friendly or welcoming? And kind of—"

"Bitchy," Charlie finishes for me again.

"And you're not?" Maddie asks cheekily. Charlie takes one hand off the steering wheel and reaches toward the back seat attempting to poke her.

"Hey, easy!" Maddie yelps.

Charlie retreats. "I'm serious! I remember one time last spring, I said hi to Bethany Davenport in the hallway, and she looked at me like I asked her for her social security number." She rolls her eyes. "God for-fucking-bid."

"Oh, damn," Sarah chimes in. "Sounds like she'd be fun at a party."

"Oh, come on. She's not *that* bad. Maybe she's just... super introverted or something," I say, trying to defend her.

"Who is this Bethany, anyway?" Sarah asks, leaning in as if the drama between our high school staff is the most interesting news she's heard in months. Considering she's a county social worker, I doubt that's the case.

"Our assistant principal's wife," Charlie explains. "She works for the entire district, but she pops into the high school often enough to silently judge us. But she's married to *thee* Briggs Davenport," she mocks, "and I'm sure she just relishes in the clout."

"He's got a lot of power or what?"

Charlie jumps in before I can answer. "Oh God, yeah. Working in a small town, it's not hard to impress the community. Especially when you're such a prominent member of the district. But honestly, I don't know if he enjoys it as much as his wife does. He always looks like he's a single email away from a breakdown. You can tell he's over it, and he's mastered the face of permanently looking pissed the fuck off."

"That's actually so true." I laugh. "Whenever he comes into my room to observe me, he looks like he's simply bothered by my *existence.* And he doesn't even have to say anything—just stares at me with these piercing eyes like, *is this lesson over yet?* He's kind of... intimidating."

"Yikes," Sarah says, grimacing. "But I'm sure he can't be *that* bad."

"Nah. He's a little grumpy, but I think Pais is just intimidated by him because he's hot as fuck," Charlie suggests before she casually takes a drink of her water.

"Is he? Huh, hadn't noticed," I lie. I *definitely* noticed—three years ago when I got the job at Stonebrook. But she doesn't need to know that. I would never live it down if she did. "And even if I *had*, which I haven't, that's not the reason. I mean, he's like super smart and overqualified for his position. He has a PhD for Christ's sake. It *is* intimidating. But his whole vibe is so... *intense.* Like would it kill him to smile every once in a while?"

"Suuuuure," Charlie says, not sounding convinced.

"And then there's Bethany," I continue, changing the subject off Davenport and his attractiveness. "She's just as pristine. Always so put together. Never a hair out of place. They're like the golden couple of our community—just not the warm and fuzzy kind."

"Sounds more like ice and steel," Maddie mutters.

Charlie laughs. "If so, then Davenport is definitely the steel. He's too hot to be the ice. Right, Paisley?"

Heat crawls up my neck as she looks at me. "Stop it!" I swat at her and bite my lip to hold back my smile. "I never said I thought he was hot!"

"You didn't have to," Charlie says. "You're not blind. Davenport *is* hot. Especially when he wears those glasses—he kind of has that sexy professor vibe going on. If I wasn't totally obsessed with John, I would maybe take a whack at him," she says, winking.

"Jesus fucking Christ," I mutter under my breath. "You're ruthless."

"Maybe," she says, laughing. "But anyway, the Davenports aren't even that bad. Their friends Carli and Joe, also founding members of the Giggle Squad, are even worse. They literally walk with their noses in the air."

"I don't think you're using the term 'literally' correctly there, babe," I mock. "But anyway, all this talk about school is making my headache worse. Let's just focus on getting home in one piece."

The rest of the drive is mainly silent, with me dozing off and on in the passenger seat, and by the time I finally stumble through my front door, I'm barely holding myself upright. The water I forced myself to drink on the ride home is sloshing around in my stomach with every step I take, and I make a mental note to *never* get that drunk again, knowing full well I'll break that vow but hoping that I won't.

As soon as I open the door, our tortie cats, Cheeto and Sebastian, come running to greet me, chirping at me like they always do as they nuzzle against my leg. I close the door behind me and notice the house is extremely quiet, which tells me Ethan must be out. Probably with his dad somewhere. I texted him before we left the hotel, letting him know I would be home in a couple hours, and he never replied. With fall only a few weeks away, I assume he's most likely tending to the land we bought a couple years ago.

The land we bought with me under the impression that we would build our forever home on but that has only been used for hunting since.

As a result, we bought this house instead, and now, whenever I broach the topic of building on our forty acres, Ethan either brushes it off or makes a comment about how it's "too good" of a hunting spot to disrupt it with new construction.

The worst part? I don't even hunt.

I kick my shoes off by the door and beeline directly for our bedroom. All I want to do is collapse into bed and let the world disappear for a while. I just need to wash the smell of the shots from last night off me first.

After a good, long nap, maybe I'll finally start that book Maddie has been begging me to read. I've always loved romance novels—I mean I *am* an English teacher—but apparently this one is completely *racked* with smut. Like, not able to read in public for fear of what it will do to me kind of smut.

I usually only read *those* ones when Ethan isn't around. I read a series about a group of sex club owners a couple months ago, and when I read him a steamy passage that piqued my interest, he was utterly shocked that anyone would read something like that. Like I'm indulging in something that's forbidden.

I wonder how he would feel if he knew about the box of toys I keep tucked away in the closet for when he's not home. I wish I felt comfortable enough to tell him, to share some of my fantasies with him, but I don't know how he would react, and I'm far too embarrassed to bring it up now after being together for almost a decade. What would he think of me?

Oh, well. What he doesn't know won't hurt him.

Besides, as much as I enjoy *reading* those kinds of books, I know they are unrealistic anyway. I mean, come on, no one actually comes *that* often when fooling around. Right? There are no women out there who are overcome with the need to rip a man's clothes off from the mere sight of him. That kind of desperate, all-consuming passion is saved for the books and the books alone.

Pure fiction.

Stepping into the room, I'm surprised to see Ethan sitting on the end of the bed lacing up a pair of boots. He's dressed in his usual Carhartt jeans and a simple beige t-shirt, and his brown hair is slightly tousled. He looks up at me as I enter the room, and his green eyes are dull with dark circles around them, telling me he probably didn't sleep well last night.

"Hey. I was just heading out."

"Heading out where?" I ask, trying to hide the exhaustion from my voice. I'm not sure why I feel guilty for having a late night with my girlfriends, but that always tends to happen when I get back from being away from him.

"Walking through the woods with Dad. We're gonna set up some trail cams before it gets too late in the season. I thought maybe you could come with us."

I slump against the doorframe. The last thing I want to do is traipse around the woods in the bright sun and warm weather while I'm hungover.

"I'm not really feeling up to it today. Charlie bought us one too many shots last night," I say with a chuckle, attempting to lighten the mood. "I think I'm gonna chill here and try to sleep off this hangover."

I walk over to the dresser and pull out a pair of black leggings and an oversized blink-182 tee I can throw on after my shower. Ethan's eyes follow me, his eyebrows knitting together in what appears to be frustration.

"Paisley, the weather is beautiful, and you go back to work this week. I thought it would be nice to go and get some fresh air together."

My instinct is to roll my eyes, considering it's not really "together" when his dad *always* has to tag along with us, but I bite my lip to keep myself from commenting on that.

"I know, I just..." I rub my temples, carefully selecting my next words. "I'm just really tired, Ethan. And a little bit nauseous. The last thing I want to do is walk around for miles outside in the hot sun."

He stands up and shifts his gaze from me before changing the subject. "So you had fun last night, I take it?"

"Yeah, I guess," I mutter. The truth is I had a ton of fun, even with the result of this hangover, but I get the feeling that's not what he wants to hear.

He scoffs, so quietly he probably doesn't think I hear it, but I do.

"Ethan, it was my birthday weekend, and I wanted to spend time with some friends I rarely see anymore. I'm sorry if that upset you, but I didn't do anything wrong."

He walks toward the door, readying himself to leave. "I just thought we would spend your birthday weekend together, that's all." My heart squeezes as I sense his disappointment. Maybe he's just upset that he lost time with me. "But I guess setting up trail cams isn't as exciting as getting shitfaced with your friends."

"That's not fair," I say, and that remorse I was experiencing a second ago is quickly replaced with defensiveness. "I always go out and do those kinds of things with you, and we're celebrating my birthday with dinner next week just the two of us."

"Yeah, whatever," he mumbles and starts into the hallway. "I'll be back later. Enjoy your nap."

I'm still standing by the dresser when the front door slams shut behind him, and now I'm not sure whether my nausea is coming from the cheap vodka running through my bloodstream or from the mix of emotions I'm feeling.

Fuck the shower. I crawl into bed instead, not even bothering to change.

Chapter Two

♫ *"Against the Wind" — Bob Seger* ♫

BRIGGS

"Did you finish setting up the chairs?" Bethany calls from the garage, her voice floating toward the lake.

"All done." I load the last of the Coors Light into our Yeti. "That should be it, unless you have a secret checklist hiding somewhere I don't know about."

"Ha. Ha. Very funny," she mocks as she walks down the hill to join me. "That's everything then?"

"Just have to grab the stakes for the kids to make s'mores when they get here. You know Lance's offspring would have aneurysms if they couldn't roast a marshmallow."

"Be nice," she says, playfully slapping me on the arm as she shifts her attention to the fire. "Oh, good. You got it started."

"Yeah, figured that way we don't have to worry about it later. It's still a little warm now, but it'll cool down fast. Now I can focus

14

on what really matters." I stretch my hands out in front of me and lace my fingers together like I'm warming up. "Whooping Aaron's ass in beer darts."

She smiles. "Sure, you do that. Just don't get too drunk. We have lunch with my parents tomorrow afternoon, remember?"

Not sure how I could forget, considering we've had the same Sunday routine for the last decade.

"Well, guess we'll see how good I am at darts today then. Might have to push it to dinner." I wink at her, but judging by the look on her face, she isn't very amused.

"Briggs, do not make us have to cancel. I'm going to go grab the stakes," she says dryly, and I throw another log onto the fire.

When I look up, our neighbors Aaron and Amber are heading across the yard. I met them a few years ago at an antique auction when they were visiting Amber's parents up here in the Frozen Tundra. Aaron and I have been close ever since, making a few trips each year to see each other. They only recently moved from New Mexico to Wisconsin. When the lot across from us went up for sale, they jumped on it immediately and started building, even before having jobs figured out up here.

"Hey, buddy. Fire looks great," Aaron says as he grabs a beer from the cooler and hands one to me.

"Thanks, man. It's good to unwind a bit before school officially starts up on Monday." I clink my icy cold can against his before bringing it to my lips.

"No doubt," Aaron replies, taking a swig of his beer. "We appreciate you putting this together. Always nice to spend some time with friends after a long week of work."

Aaron eventually found a position working as an underwriter for an insurance company, and although my job as assistant principal isn't my dream career by any means, I sure as hell don't envy him sitting in a cubicle all day long, especially when the nice days of summer are fleeting.

I glance over and see Amber on the patio talking with Bethany. From across the lawn, I can see *The Last Hurrah!* scrawled across the front of my wife's shirt in big, bold letters. I chuckle under my breath.

"I swear, they treat every weekend like a bachelorette party." I shift my attention back to Aaron. "If I had a dollar for every *last hurrah* they've had, I could probably fund an actual vacation."

"You're probably right about that, but you know Beth isn't very fond of traveling anyway."

Trust me, I know. Whereas I love visiting new places, Beth would rather spend her time off staying in Stonebrook or on our annual vacation to South Carolina with her parents. Don't get me wrong, the beach is nice, but why continue going to the same exact location when there's an entire world out there waiting to be seen?

Before I can respond, we're interrupted by a four-foot tall miniature Aaron tugging on his sleeve. "Dad, Dad, Dad!" he says, exasperated. "Can I drive the golf-cart around the yard?"

"In a minute, bud," Aaron says back to him. "Go play in the treehouse for a little while."

"Pleeeeeeease!"

"Maybe in a bit," he tells him. "We're gonna eat soon."

"Fine!" he explodes angrily, and he storms off to play in the treehouse with his sister.

From the look of it, Adison doesn't want anything to do with her brother, but before a tantrum can break out, Amber yells across the yard and tells her to be nice to him.

Damn. They definitely have their hands full with those two. Not envious of that, either.

Lance and Cortney show up next, with Lance hauling a cooler and a bag of chips while Cortney juggles a bag of marshmallows in one hand and their toddler in the other, somehow balancing everything on her ever-growing pregnant stomach.

I wave them over, pushing the thoughts of kids out of my mind, which is never easy to do these days with so many of them around. Every couple we hang out with has at least two, and though I'm happy for them, it's hard to relate. Having children isn't something I've ever wanted—not really, anyway. And when Beth and I first started dating, we were in agreement on that.

Lately, though, I'm not so sure.

"Hey, we brought supplies." Cortney holds up the bag of marshmallows. "Can't have a fire without s'mores."

Lance sits his cooler down next to the Yeti and gives me a nod. "You ready to lose at beer darts tonight, Davenport?"

"You wish," I fire back.

"Hey, I want in on this," Aaron jumps in.

We each grab a chair from around the fire and move them farther over in the yard to form a circle. Sometimes we up the ante by playing *across* the fire, but the wives usually aren't too happy about that, given the riskiness of, you know, burning our hands to a crisp.

We make a pitstop at the coolers and each grab a new beer since the game requires them to be unopened, and as I do, Joe and Tyler's vehicles both pull into our yard. Their wives, Carli and Stephanie, have been friends with Beth since we started at Stonebrook High, but we all get along pretty well. I wouldn't exactly call Joe and Tyler my *friends*, but because we work together at the school, we always have plenty of conversation to fall back on. They're good dudes, but outside of our careers, we don't have much in common. I suppose that's true for pretty much anyone I work with, though, now that I think about it.

Then again, I guess most adult friendships are based on proximity more than anything else.

"Hey, Briggs!" Tyler shouts as he walks over with some cheese curds and beef jerky. "Thought we'd add to the pile." He reaches into the cooler and pulls out a Sprite.

"Much appreciated," I say, taking the food and adding it to the growing collection on the picnic table. "How ya been?"

"Been good," he answers, shrugging. "Counting down the days until we're back to the daily grind next week."

"Tell me about it." *The daily grind.* That's all life is once you're approaching your forties, isn't it? Work. Routine. Counting down minutes to get to the next break. It's like I'm living to work and working to live, never feeling truly fulfilled through any of it.

Technically, since I'm the assistant principal, I started back at work a few weeks ago. Beth, too, because she has a district position. But we've only been working a few days a week, and it's much different work when students aren't around.

Joe and Tyler join their wives over on the patio, and I walk back over to the chairs we set up for beer darts, each with a can positioned on the ground in front of it. Aaron is already seated, holding a metal dart. He has one eye squinted and his lips pursed as he concentrates on his target. My can.

"Hey, hey, wait a second! Let me sit down before you take out my foot," I holler, rushing to my lawn chair.

"Well, hurry your ass up!"

I move the beer up a few inches and put my feet on either side of it, hopefully out of harm's way. I've played enough times to know that once people start drinking and darts start flying, there's no saying one won't go rogue and draw some blood. That's what adds to the fun of the game.

"Watch out!" Aaron shouts as he tosses a dart my way. Luckily, Aaron misses my Coors entirely, and the dart plunges into the soft soil, a good foot in front of the can.

"Nice one," Lance mocks, giving him a sarcastic nod.

"Hey," he says, rolling his shoulders to loosen them. "I'm still warming up. And I'm coming for you next." He points his finger in Lance's direction threateningly.

I pick up the dart and wipe off any remaining dirt. I pose my hand in front of me, zeroing in on Aaron's beer. With one swift motion, I lunge the dart forward, and it plunges perfectly into the bottom of the can, tipping it over and spraying beer everywhere. Aaron quickly grabs it and covers the hole with his thumb.

"You know what that means," I taunt.

Aaron nods and pushes his thumb through the space the dart already created, making the hole even bigger. He puts the can up to his mouth, tilts it to the side, and cracks open the top to shotgun it. He downs the liquid in a few big gulps and tosses the can to the middle of our circle.

"One down!" he celebrates, and he reaches into the cooler to grab another.

Once the game started to wind down, with Aaron the clear loser after having to shotgun two beers and drink another four, we decided to call it quits and threw the burgers and hotdogs on the Pit Boss. The kids ran around the yard for a bit and were able to make some s'mores, and the rest of us sat around the fire casually talking as the sun set.

Now it's getting dark, and Bethany is in the house doing some dishes while I finish packing up and putting the food away.

"Man, we need to plan a guys' night," Larry suggests as he snaps a lid on the leftover potato salad. He leans in a little closer and somewhat whispers, "I love those kids more than anything, but I need some time to unwind, ya know?"

"Tell me when, and I'm there," I offer, and I give him a slap on the back. "Maybe we can hit up the bowling alley in a couple weeks and grab some drinks."

"Sounds good, buddy." He nods, and I wave to Cortney across the lawn as she peels one of their sleeping kids off her shoulder and carefully fastens him into his carseat. After gently shutting the car door, she waves back and climbs into the driver's seat of their Ford Escape.

"Drive safe," I yell in their direction and sit in the chair next to Aaron. Just as I do, my phone buzzes.

I'm tired and heading to bed.
Tell Aaron I said goodnight. Don't
stay up too late.

I run my hand through my hair and blow out a breath, slipping the phone back into my pocket. Aaron notices my reaction and raises an eyebrow. "Everything good?"

"Yeah. Just Beth reminding me not to 'stay up too late.'"

It's pretty common for Bethany to comment on my actions when I'm hanging out with the guys, and it gets exhausting. I wish that sometimes she would let me have a *little* freedom to unwind without her worrying about what other people will think or about how it will affect the next item on our lifelong to-do list. It's like she's always holding me to some invisible standard she set for us in her mind.

"She never stays up with us, does she?" Aaron responds, his tone carefully neutral.

"Nah," I shrug, taking a sip of my beer. "It is what it is, though."

As the fire burns lower, Aaron takes that as his cue to head back to his house. "Well, thanks for hosting, bud," he says, standing up from his chair.

"Anytime."

He claps me on the shoulder, and when I look up, his face is serious for once. "You sure you're okay, dude? You seem a little off tonight."

"Yeah, tired is all," I say, forcing a slight smile. "Not ready for the week to start. See you later this week?"

"Definitely."

He walks across the yard, and the fire slowly dies beside me. At this point, I should probably head in, too.

But I don't move. Instead, I sink deeper into my chair and give myself a minute alone to breathe.

Chapter Three

♫ "Can't Stop the Feeling" — Justin Timberlake ♫

PAISLEY

"Goddamn it." I survey the stacks of boxes cluttering my classroom, realizing I *definitely* should have come in a few days last week instead of convincing myself today alone would be enough time to get everything done.

Last spring, I told my principal David that I wanted to implement flexible seating, and he approved my ordering of all new furniture—high top tables, bean bags, a couch for my reading corner. Sounded great at the time, and I'm still excited about it, but staring at all these items packed up in boxes and waiting to be put together right now is making me think otherwise.

This is going to take fucking hours, but I came ready to do some manual labor. I figured no one else would be crazy enough to come in on their last day of summer vacation, so I tossed my insanely thick and long brown hair (thanks, Mom, for passing down that gene) into a messy bun and threw on some athletic shorts paired with an oversized t-shirt. It's one of my favorites and has a picture of a ghost reading a book with the word *booooooks* written above it. Not necessarily my cutest attire, but it is appropriate for the task at hand.

I take a sip of my iced caramel latte, letting the caffeine hit my veins, and turn on my JBL speaker. Scrolling through the playlists on my phone, I stop at one that will motivate me to get some work done for the next couple hours. Early 2000s throwbacks it is. Perfect.

I start with the bean bags, because how hard could those be? I probably only have to pull them out of the box, though the box they came in looks awfully small to be hosting pre-stuffed bags. Oh, God, I hope I don't have to personally stuff the—wait, are they *actually* filled with beans, or is that just what they're called? Either way, I hope I don't have to fill them myself.

I tear open the box, hoping to see a fluffy, ready-to-go bean bag, but instead find a large, lumpy sack of what looks like white beads and an empty, deflated cover.

"Oh, you've got to be fucking kidding me," I mutter to no one.

I take out the instructions, knowing damn well what I'm already in for, and my gaze immediately lands on a cheesy picture of a person smiling while pouring the beads into the cover as if it's the best thing they've ever done.

I sigh as I pull the bag out of the box and flatten it on the ground so I can locate the zippered opening. I start the recommended process, and it's extremely tedious: pour, stop, shake, pour some more. After what feels like an eternity (but was probably only like 20 minutes), I'm finally finished with all three bags.

While filling them, I noticed one had a small tear in it, but I didn't want to go through the hassle of sending it back. So instead, I found some duct-tape in my room and patched up the hole. Sure, maybe it doesn't *look* the best, but hey, it works. We're gonna start the year off with some character in Mrs. Hamilton's classroom.

I drag the three bags to the back of my room and set them up on the rug next to the bookshelf. After I have them situated, I put my hands on my hips and assess my progress.

"There," I say, pleased with the result, and give one of the bean bags a pat. "The students are going to love you during silent reading time."

Okay, I *really* need to stop talking to myself. Or, in this case, to inanimate objects. Good thing no one is here to witness it; otherwise, they would probably think I'm losing it before the kids have even arrived.

Time to tackle the high-top tables next. I rip open the box and begin taking out all the needed parts, but when I read the instructions, it clearly mentions that everything needs to be assembled with the allen wrench. I rummage through the box, and yep, just as I feared. No allen wrench.

"I swear if I have to go out and buy one of these things now..." I say to my empty classroom, silently chastising myself for lasting all of two minutes before talking to nobody again.

I look at my watch. *3:02.* The hardware store in town is still open, and it's only a few minutes away. But I'll be damned if I have to spend my own money on a wrench that was *supposed* to be included already.

I let out a groan as I stand in the center of my classroom, debating my next move. I guess I'll have to bring a wrench with me from home tomorrow and finish working on these after our staff meetings, even though I was hoping to have it all set up when I got here in the morning so I could focus solely on lesson planning in the afternoon.

I slump in a chair, frustrated, and take another sip of my coffee. With no immediate solution in sight, I take a break from the furniture and work on organizing my bookshelves instead.

I reach for my phone to turn up the volume, and the telltale beat of Justin Timberlake's "Can't Stop The Feeling" blasts loudly through my speaker. Unable to help myself, I immediately start singing along, grabbing my Phillips screwdriver as a makeshift microphone. I move toward my box of books, and as I sing, I also dance—albeit poorly—twirling around to place each book back on the shelf, exaggerating each movement and sway of my hips for my imaginary audience.

I slide a book into its spot and then spin back over to the box, doing a little shimmy as I bend down to grab the next one and belt out another verse.

"*So just imagine, just imagine, just imag—*"

"Nice moves, Hamilton. But I think you might need a bigger stage."

The sound of someone's voice forces me to jump and drop both the book and the screwdriver I'm holding.

"Jesus Christ!" I yelp, spinning around to see none other than Briggs freaking Davenport leaning against my doorframe, with what appears to be a smile starting to form. Heat immediately flushes my cheeks. How much of that did he see?

"You scared the crap out of me," I tell him as I grab my phone to turn down the volume. "How long have you been standing there?"

"Not long enough." He chuckles. "What is that, early 2000s pop?"

His smile catches me off guard. It's something I haven't seen much before—or at least haven't really paid attention to. But as he's standing in my doorway now, in a pair of simple black shorts paired with a plain white long sleeve, I realize that Charlie was right. Briggs Davenport is *definitely* hot. Grumpy, sure. But also hot. And he totally knows it.

I mock glare at him, feeling even more flustered now. "Hey, everyone needs a guilty pleasure. Besides, JT is a legend."

He shakes his head slightly. "No judgment here. I just didn't expect anyone else to be here today. When I heard the music, I figured I better come check it out. Sounded like a stray cat might've been dying and was in need of some help."

"Um, *rude,*" I say, pretending to be more offended than I actually am. "And sorry for all the ruckus. I didn't realize anyone would be here, either." I pause for a moment, biting my lip in further embarrassment. "What *are* you doing here anyway? Shouldn't you be out on your boat somewhere?"

He shrugs. "Mandatory preparation for tomorrow's meeting per David's orders. What are all the boxes?"

Of course. Leave it to David to make Danvenport come in during the summer when he's out having margaritas on the golf course.

"Furniture, books, desk supplies. I wanted to come in early to get my room set up, so when we start this week, I can focus on curriculum and making copies."

"Oh, yeah. You're trying flexible seating this year, right?"

Great, I'm sure he's already thinking about all the 'behavior problems' it's going to cause.

"Oh, um, yeah…" I say quietly, avoiding eye contact.

"That's great. I'm looking forward to seeing how it turns out."

"Look, I know you—wait, did you just say *great*?"

He grins, but he looks sincere. "Yeah. The last district I worked at had a few rooms set up like that, and the students loved it."

His response surprises me, but I try to backpedal. "Oh, okay. Yeah, I'm excited, too. I think they'll like it." I look over my shoulder toward the boxes with the high-tops. "But I don't think anyone will be seeing it any time soon. I'm missing the tools I need, so I'll have to wait until tomorrow to finish putting them together."

"What kind of tools?"

"I think just an allen wrench. I came prepared with a screwdriver, but the box was *supposed* to have a wrench in it." I roll my eyes to show my annoyance.

Davenport squints his eyes slightly, then nods. "I've got a key to the janitorial closet. Should have what you need in there."

"Seriously? That would be great." I smile at him. Then I add, "I guess you're not just a grump who is good at glaring at people. You're actually useful, too."

His lips part slightly, and I immediately shoot a hand up to cover my mouth.

"Oh God," I say, though it comes out muffled. "I'm sorry. I didn't mean to—"

I'm interrupted by his laugh, a *genuine* laugh, and whoa. His *smile.* It's wide and effortless, and his teeth are insanely white, especially against his tanned complexion, which I'm assuming comes from hours spent outside this summer. His lips are full and perfectly shaped, and most definitely kissab—

"Don't worry about it," he assures me, and I shake my head subtly to refocus my thoughts.

The fuck, Paisley?

He turns on his heel in the doorway and calls over his shoulder. "Come on, I'll show you."

Chapter four

BRIGGS

"So do you have a key for every room in this building?" Paisley asks as I open the janitor's closet.

"That I do," I tell her. "But luckily, they all open with this master key. I would hate keeping track of all the keys for the different departments and wings of the school."

"The only downfall would be if you lost it. Could you imagine how much it would cost to replace *all* the locks in this building?" Her brown eyes are wide and full of imaginary horror.

"About ten thousand bucks is what I've been told. Trust me, I've been worried about that since I started here." I push the door open and turn on the light, scanning the room for the toolbox.

"Ten *thousand* dollars?" she repeats, her voice rising in astonishment and her eyes growing even wider. "Damn. It's true what they say. With great power *does* come great responsibility."

"Who says that?" I ask as I rummage through the shelves in the room.

Rather than following me into the closet, she stays by the door and holds it open. "What do you mean who says that? Um, Spider-man? Duh."

"Never seen it," I say nonchalantly. "Marvel movies haven't ever really been my thing."

"Well, yeah, they're not really mine either, but I at least know the story of Peter Parker." She looks at me as if she's waiting for me to defend myself. "Peter Parker is Spider-man, by the way."

A slow smile spreads on my face. "Yeah, I gathered that much."

Her cheeks turn slightly pink at my comment, and she begins to fidget with a ring on her finger. "So if you're not into Marvel, what kind of movies *are* you into, Dr. Davenport?"

"The classics." I finally find the toolbox buried under a pile of rags, and I open it to search for the allen wrenches.

She mulls my answer over. "The classics, huh? So a little *Rear Window* action is more your thing?"

"Actually, yeah." I pause. "The movie, I mean. Not the whole spying on my neighbors from my bedroom window."

She laughs at that, her shoulders becoming more relaxed, and the sound is playful and endearing. "Okay, that's fair. I can support some love for Jimmy Stewart."

I nod in approval. "I didn't realize you had such extensive movie knowledge." I continue rummaging through the toolbox, moving aside hammers and screwdrivers until I finally find what I'm looking for.

She shrugs. "My brother was a huge movie buff. When I was younger, we would spend weekends watching different films and binging Chinese food together. He was over a decade older than me, so he threw in a lot of the classics."

I notice her face drop slightly, but I don't read too much into it.

"Got 'em." I hold up the wrenches triumphantly toward the door. "This should solve your high-top table crisis."

Her eyes light up again, and she squeals with excitement. "Yessss! Now let's just hope it doesn't take me more than an hour or two to put them together."

"How many do you have to assemble?"

"Only two," she says casually with a lift of her shoulder. "Oh, and a couch. Easy-peasy."

"That's going to take you all night. Especially with those impromptu dance sessions you're so fond of." She side-eyes me for my comment, but I smirk and continue. "Want any help?"

Beth is still at her parents' place from our lunch this afternoon, and if I go home now, I'm sure I'll get roped into going back over there. Might as well play the part of a helpful assistant principal instead.

"Oh, no, I couldn't possibly ask you to do that..." she says, hesitantly. "Besides, didn't David give you a to-do list for tomorrow?"

"Already did it," I assure her. "I don't have anything left to do. If you let me help, you'll be done a lot quicker."

She shifts on her feet, clearly not sure if she wants to accept my offer or not. After a few seconds of silence, she finally sighs in defeat. "You're right. It will take me forever by myself. I guess if you don't mind…"

"I don't." I shut off the light and gesture for her to walk back to her classroom, and I lock up the janitor's closet behind me.

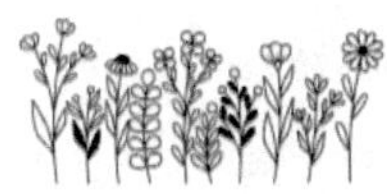

It's been an hour, and we've successfully assembled both of the high-top tables and are now working on the couch. The work has been surprisingly enjoyable, not only because it's a break from my usual administrative duties but because I've realized Paisley Hamilton is easy to be around. Even though we've worked together for a few years now, I've never spent much time around her other than when I've observed a few of her lessons. She's got a positive energy that's somewhat infectious, and her passion for teaching and for the students is obvious; I can tell by the way she's been rambling on about what made her want to try flexible seating and how excited she is about the new curriculum she's trying out this year.

Listening to her talk makes me think about how I lost that excitement when it comes to my job—but to be honest, I'm not sure I've ever really had it to begin with.

"Thanks again for staying and helping me," she says, pulling me from my thoughts. "This would have taken an eternity by myself."

Right as I'm about to answer, the electricity surges and the lamps in her classroom all flicker simultaneously. Paisley's head shoots up from what she's working on.

"Did you see that?" she asks, a slight panic in her voice.

I huff out a laugh. "It would have been hard not to."

She gives what appears to be an involuntary shudder.

"Relax. It's probably old wiring, not poltergeists."

"Easy for you to say," she says. "It reminds me of the time I was studying abroad in Europe and had an encounter with a ghost."

I raise an eyebrow, intrigued. "Well this sounds like a story I need to hear."

She sets the screwdriver down, her messy bun flopping to one side as she settles in to tell me about it. "In college, I studied abroad in Scotland for two months for student teaching. I stayed with the sweetest host family in this quaint little town outside of Edinburgh, and they lived right down the street from this old-timey bookstore. It was my favorite place. Probably still is, despite the creepy paranormal experience I had. I would go there almost every night. Grab a coffee, bring a book with me. There was this one particular chair that was by the fireplace where I would always sit."

She pauses for a moment, reflecting back on her time abroad and reimagining it.

"Anyway, one night I was there later than usual because I was working on a lesson for the following day. There was hardly anyone out at that hour, and it was silent in there besides the faint jazz playing over the speaker. Then, out of nowhere, the music cut out and the lights flickered."

I give her a look, not completely convinced.

"Yeah, yeah, I know that alone isn't a big deal," she retaliates. "But when I looked up from my laptop, I saw books falling off the shelf like someone was literally ripping them down." She pauses, picking the screwdriver back up and tightening a screw on the couch frame. "But no one was there."

I look at her quizzically while I align another piece of the couch. "Are you sure it wasn't someone playing tricks on you?"

She shakes her head and reaches for another screw. "I'm sure. I wondered the same thing, being an American tourist and all, but I sat there waiting for thirty minutes—mainly because I was too afraid to move—and no one else came or went from that side of the bookstore. Right before closing time, I finally got enough courage to get up and walk to the front where the old owner was quietly reading."

She hands me the screwdriver, and I work on the next section of the couch while she continues.

"I told him about what I saw, fully expecting him to tell me I was crazy, but he just shrugged and said, 'Yeah, this place is haunted. Didn't you know?' as if we were having a casual conversation. Like, okay, thanks for the heads up? But he assured me that their 'resident spirit' was harmless and that he simply liked playing pranks on people once in a while, especially tourists." She shakes her head and chuckles as she recalls the conversation. "Lucky me."

"So did you ever go back?" I ask, tightening the last bolt on my side.

"I did, actually. Given the owner's response, it seemed like it wasn't anything to worry about. But after that, I always made sure to leave before it got dark."

"That's crazy," I say, passing the screwdriver back to her. "But I can do you one better."

She looks at me incredulously. "Oh yeah? How?"

"When I was in grad school, a group of us took a trip to Paris. I always wanted to visit the Catacombs, so we scheduled a tour at the latest possible time."

"Excuse me?" She sets down the tool and stares at me deadpan. "You went to the catacombs at *night?* And *willingly?*"

I grin while I stand up and take a step back to inspect our work. "Well, yeah. I've always been a little adventurous. I wanted to get the full experience." I shrug nonchalantly. "When we got there, it was already getting dark, and before we got into the tombs, the guide warned us not to wander off. You would think that wouldn't have to be stated, but apparently it happens more often than you'd expect."

Paisley looks up at me from where she's sitting on the floor, a mix of intrigue and horror crossing her features. "You didn't."

"I did. But not on purpose."

She rises to meet me, her interest officially piqued. "You're really going to stand here and tell me you got lost in the Catacombs?"

She takes a seat on the couch to test its stability and rests her hand in her palm as she leans forward to hear the rest of my story.

"Not lost, exactly..." I pause, rubbing my neck as if the memory still makes my skin crawl. "We were in a group—a *big* group—and we were packed in like sardines when we started. But by the time we got to one of the deeper tunnels, we had to spread out a bit. I... I thought I was following the guide, but it was so dark in the small tunnels."

Paisley's eyes shoot open. "You mean you got *separated*?!"

"Yeah. That underground system is *huge*. And you don't realize how easy it is to get turned around and disoriented until you're there. Everything looks exactly the same. Low ceilings, damp walls, narrow passages. Somewhere along the way, I turned a corner and was by myself."

"Okay, you win already." She throws her hands up in defeat, her body shivering at the thought of being stuck there alone.

"That's not even the worst of it," I tell her as I gather the tools to return them to the janitor's closet.

"It gets *worse?*"

I nod. "At first, I wasn't too worried about it. Figured I could retrace my steps and catch up to the group. No big deal. But then I started hearing sounds. Footsteps. Like someone was behind me."

"Was there? Someone behind you?"

"I thought so at first. But then I realized the steps weren't really in sync with mine. They were too loud. Too heavy. Too *close*. And then when I turned around, no one was there."

"Shut up."

"I kept walking, thinking I was paranoid. I mean, I was in the Catacombs, after all. They're bound to play tricks on your mind, right? But every time I stopped, they stopped. And when I started walking again, they followed."

"You're lying," she says adamantly.

"Swear on my PhD."

"Did you ever find anyone? How did you get out?"

"Eventually the tunnel I was in led to another, and I could hear the guide speaking, so I followed his voice. Once I made my way back to the group, the footsteps just... vanished. As if they were never even there to begin with."

"Are you sure it wasn't an echo or your mind messing with you?"

I shake my head. "I've thought about that a lot, actually. But the air in the Catacombs is thick. Stifling. And something about it just didn't feel right. I can't say for sure, but I would bet a lot of money that I wasn't actually alone in that tomb."

She shudders, clearly unsettled. Then she stands up, brushing off her hands. "Damn. And here I thought you were just a boring, data-diving, assistant principal."

I smile, picking the allen wrench off the floor. "Maybe now. But I was young once."

She rolls her eyes. "You're still young. Aren't you only like thirty-five?"

"Thirty-six," I correct her.

"Oh, excuse me," she says sarcastically. "So did you go anywhere else in Europe while you were over there? Or only Paris?

"I went to Tuscany for a week. No horror stories from there, though, except maybe the hangover I got from all the wine I consumed."

She laughs heartily as she throws some of the trash away in the nearby recycling bin. "Sounds like me yesterday. I'm sure the wineries there were beautiful, though."

"Rough day, huh? But yeah, they were. Super idyllic and 'picturesque' as people say. Do you go to a lot of wineries?"

"Not as many as I would like," she says, her energy dropping a bit. "Ethan's not really into wine. He's more of a beer guy."

"Makes sense. You know, when I was in grad school, I actually thought about opening a speakeasy style bar. One of those hidden, prohibition-style places where you need secret directions and a password to get in."

"Okay, that actually sounds so fun," she exclaims. "I would *totally* go to that. Did you come up with a name for it?"

I blink, a little surprised I still remember this, and nod. "I did. I wanted to call it 18th Amendment. Kind of like a nod to the reason those kinds of places existed in the first place."

"Wow, I love that. Did you ever look into it seriously?"

"Not really, no. Grad school took up most of my time, and then Bethany and I moved to Stonebrook right away for our jobs. After that, life just kind of... took over."

"I get it," she says, nodding, and her eyes drift to the clock on the wall behind me. "Well, looks like it must have been faulty wiring tonight. No poltergeists for us." Her mouth tilts up at the corners, and I can't help but notice how easy her smile is. "Seriously, though, thank you again for staying late to help."

"No problem. It was nice to do something different for a change."

"Glad you feel that way," she says, looking up at me with her big, brown eyes. Her irises are so dark that I can barely see her pupils, giving them a mysterious and almost foreboding look. "See you bright and early tomorrow morning?"

"Sounds like a plan. We're meeting at ten for PBIS after our all-staff meeting," I remind her. "Not that you wouldn't remember. I just know it's your first year on that committee, so thought I would let you know in case you didn't get the calendar invite."

"Appreciate it. I'll be there. Have a good night, Dr. Davenport." She flashes a smile my way again, and something about the way she says my name makes my stomach tighten.

I swallow nervously and clear my throat, brushing it off. "You, too, Mrs. Hamilton."

Chapter five

PAISLEY

I glance at my Apple watch as my house comes into view. *5:28.* Twenty-eight minutes for three miles? Not bad considering I took a pretty big hiatus from running the last few weeks of summer. But with school starting today, I wanted to start on a positive note, and getting a run in before the sun comes up is always the perfect way to do that.

I approach my driveway and remove my headphones and stumble over to the grass to do some stretches. In college, I never used to take the time to do so after a run, but ever since I turned twenty-five, I knew I needed to start taking care of myself a little more than I had been. And with turning thirty this week—*thirty? How is that even possible?*—it's probably more important than ever.

I look back at my watch. I still have enough time to make breakfast for Ethan before he leaves if I hurry. Things are still a bit tense between us after my weekend shenanigans with the girls, so maybe this will help alleviate some of that.

I move around the kitchen as the sun peeks through our bay windows and the cats are already sunbathing. Those windows were my favorite part of this house when we decided to buy it last May, along with the open concept and skylights. The kitchen itself, though, irritates me off every time I step foot into it, which happens to be a lot considering I'm the one who does all the cooking.

It has this old, weird 80's vibe going on—and I'm not talking about the cute 80's style with the bright colors and big hair. No, it's extremely outdated and looks like the people who lived here before us ran out of renovation money when they got to this room.

I dollop the last of the pancake batter onto the griddle just as Ethan shuffles into the kitchen.

"Morning," he mumbles, immediately reaching into the fridge and grabbing an energy drink. Would this man *please* drink some water before pumping his veins with caffeine and sugar?

"Good morning," I say cheerfully while sliding a plate of pancakes and bacon on the table for him. "I thought I would surprise you with your favorite today before I head to school."

"Thank you." He takes a sip of his Red Bull before sitting down.

"Do you have a lot of jobs today?" I sit across from him with my own plate of food.

He nods. "Yeah, we're framing a house out in Eagle River, so I'll be there most of the day. But I also have to check on the crew at the commercial site downtown. One of the guys said there's an issue with the blueprints, so I need to sort that out before they pour the foundation."

"Think you'll be home late?"

"Hard to say. Shouldn't be too late, though. Do you have a lot of meetings today? Or what's on the agenda?"

"Yeah," I say, sighing. "I'm hoping I get at least some time in my classroom, but we have a staff meeting this morning. Who knows how long that'll take. Then I have a PBIS meeting and another meeting with the English department later. Plus an IEP meeting this afternoon. I'm sure I'll be braindead by the time I get home."

The mention of PBIS triggers the memory of putting furniture together with Davenport last night, but I push it out of my mind. I'm not thinking about him. Not thinking about his smile. And definitely not thinking about what Charlie said.

"Well, we can order takeout for dinner," he says as he grabs my hand across the table.

"Sounds like a plan." Some of the tension between us subsides, and I give his hand a squeeze.

Ethan looks down at his phone to check the time. "Shit. I've got to go. I told the crew to be in Eagle River by 7:00 today, and it's a forty-five minute drive. Thanks for breakfast, though, babe."

He gets up from the table and rushes to the closet to grab his work boots. I peer down at his plate, barely touched, and a pang of disappointment floats through me.

"See you later!" he shouts from the doorway.

"See you—" The door clicks shut before I can finish. "—later."

I sigh, directing my attention back to the food in front of me. I quickly finish my breakfast before hopping in the shower. But once I get out, I realize I somehow manage to be running late.

My 8:00 AM meeting starts in forty minutes, and I have a thirty-minute drive to school. I quickly run a brush through my hair and blow dry it slightly.

"Guess we're going curly today," I say to myself in the mirror.

I apply some foundation and swipe on a bit of mascara and lipgloss before rushing to my closet. I throw on the dress and earrings that I thankfully picked out last night. I have just enough time to brush my teeth, fill up my water bottle, and grab my coffee before fleeing out the door.

I might be late, but I'm never too late for coffee.

As I run to my car, however, I spill said coffee all over my arm while trying to juggle my computer bag and gigantic water bottle. Fumbling with my keys as they find their way to the ignition, my heart rate picks up.

And of course, I get stuck at *every* red light in town because why the fuck wouldn't I? First of all, our town literally has less than 1,000 residents, so why the actual hell do we need *three* stop lights? A little excessive if you ask me.

Once I get onto the highway, though, it's smooth sailing.

For a minute, anyway, until the car in front of me decides to take a leisurely drive at seven-fucking-thirty on a Monday morning. I can't wait to be one of those old people who has nothing better to do than drive down the roads in the morning delaying everyone else's morning commute.

When I finally arrive at the school, I'm still extremely tense. Luckily, I actually remembered to grab my key fob this morning and am able to get in the back door and hopefully slip in unnoticed. I check the time as I swing open the heavy metal, still juggling my water and coffee mug, trying not to spill again.

Yep, definitely late.

I forgo stopping at my classroom like I normally would to drop my things off and head straight to the library instead. Hopefully, everyone is still gorging themselves on breakfast donuts and catching up on their summer vacations, so I can casually walk in without drawing attention to myself. Besides, it's the first day of school—they can't expect us to be on time, right?

I rush through the library doors and immediately spot Charlie and Leah sitting on the couch in the back of the room, a spot saved in the middle of them for me—a true godsend. As I sink into the cushion, my heart slows for the first time all morning.

Hot damn. It's only the first day back, and I already need a nap.

Chapter Six

BRIGGS

I roll over and glance at the clock. My alarm isn't set to go off for another hour, but I've been staring at the ceiling for what feels like forever, unable to fall back asleep. With it being the first day of school, I tossed and turned all night, and that conversation I had with Paisley Hamilton yesterday about my old speakeasy dream added to my restlessness.

On my right, Bethany is still fast asleep. Her ash blonde hair is tied up in a top bun, and she looks peaceful as her chest rises and falls beside me. Not a care in the world—or at least that's how it seems.

A heaviness settles into my chest. When did we drift so far apart? To anyone on the outside looking in, it wouldn't appear that we have. In college, we were nearly inseparable when we were surviving our graduate program together. Our time was filled with endless readings, late-night study sessions, countless hours of research, lengthy dissertations. All memories that seem like a different lifetime now.

Maybe that's the problem. Maybe grad school was the glue that held us together, and over time, that glue has slowly started to come undone.

Once we earned our PhDs, proposing felt like the natural next step, so that's what I did. But since then, it seems the only thing we have in common is work, and I find myself feeling more like we're roommates than spouses. But I suppose that's normal after you've been with someone for so long.

I sit up in bed and rub the sleep from my eyes as my mind drifts back to my conversation with Paisley. My dream of opening that speakeasy is something I haven't thought about—and especially haven't talked about—in years.

I grab my glasses from my nightstand and walk to the bathroom to brush my teeth, reflecting on when I got the idea for the bar in the first place. I was sitting in the library, surrounded by books and articles on psychometrics, ethics, and cognitive assessments. *Yawn.* It was late, and Bethany and I were each trying to finish final projects, fueling ourselves with a generous amount of stale library coffee.

I remember mentioning the idea of opening a bar to Beth, but she laughed it off. Told me I was a few weeks away from earning my doctorate degree and it wasn't the time for "pointless dreams." Said it would be a waste of energy and money and that I needed to focus on finding a career—a *real* career, as she put it—to find some stability.

I knew she didn't mean any ill-intent, and to her, I'm sure it seemed like I was just overwhelmed and drowning in final assessments.

She was probably right.

I sigh quietly as I turn off the water and tip-toe out of the bathroom to head downstairs. How would my life have turned out differently had I actually followed my crazy idea instead of continuing down the path of school psychology and administration?

Am I thankful for the career I have now? Sure. Am I happy to have a sense of stability and a roof over my head? Of course. But do I enjoy what I do every day? Not even fucking close.

But does anybody?

Once I get to the kitchen, I turn on the coffee pot and pull a mug out of the cabinet before grabbing a pen and notepad from a nearby drawer.

Truthfully, working in administration isn't all it's cracked up to be. Paisley may have not taken me seriously last night when I said assembling furniture was a nice change of pace from my usual duties, but I was serious. I've been working in this position for ten years, and my psychology degree isn't even being put to use. What a fucking waste.

Instead, the majority of my days are taken up by monitoring the halls for students who are skipping class and checking footage to see who the latest culprit is for the vandalization in the bathroom. Last spring, I walked into the stall to see "Dr. Dickhead" written in big black sharpie and had to spend the afternoon watching which students used the bathroom on that side of the school to figure out who did it.

The sound of the coffee gurgling and filling the pot draws my attention away from my thoughts, and the antique clock my grandpa left me when he died a few years ago ticks rapidly in the hallway. He always knew how much I loved old antiques, so he made sure to leave most of his treasured belongings to me. Unfortunately, many of the items didn't match Bethany's "aesthetic" for the house, so most of them ended up in the garage.

But man, a lot of those things would look fucking sick in a speakeasy bar.

Maybe getting these thoughts down on paper will help me focus on something else, which is probably important with school starting this morning. So after pouring myself a cup of coffee and tossing a bit of sugar in it, I sit on a stool at our island and start scribbling on the notepad.

18th Amendment
1950's Style
Red leather booths
Jukebox in corner
Antiques
Unique cocktails
Jazz music

"You're up early," Bethany says, her voice still heavy with sleep as she reaches into the cupboard for a coffee mug. I was so lost in my thoughts I didn't even hear her come into the kitchen.

"Yeah," I reply, trying to sound casual. "Just had some ideas I wanted to get down on paper."

She raises an eyebrow, glancing at the notepad. "Sounds ominous," she says sarcastically. "What kind of ideas?"

I take a deep breath. "Do you remember that old vintage speakeasy I used to talk about wanting to open? Well, I've been thinking about it again, and I think it could be really great. I could use some of the antiques that Grandpa Levi left for me to decorate, and—"

"A speakeasy?" Bethany frowns, pouring herself a cup of coffee. "What about your job at the school? We have plans, remember? Saving for a bigger house, getting a vacation home in Florida, starting a family..." she drifts off, waiting for my response.

I inwardly cringe, trying not to show my discomfort. Since when are we preparing to start a family?

"I know," I say, trying to keep my voice steady. "But I've been feeling restless. Like I'm not living the life I truly want, you know? Like something is missing. Being assistant principal isn't exactly what I envisioned myself doing forever. While it helps pay the bills now, it's not what I want to do for the rest of my life. This speakeasy is something I've dreamed about for a long time."

She takes a sip of her coffee, her expression unreadable. "And what if it doesn't work out? That's a lot of money you'd be putting on the line." She sets her mug back on the counter and sighs with exasperation.

"We could take it slow," I suggest. "I can start looking around at buildings for lease or for sale, see if there's even anything available that I'm interested in. Then we can budget. It's not like we're hurting for money, Bethany. We're living quite comfortably," I remind her, signaling to the house around us.

She turns to face me and crosses her arms. "I just don't see how it fits into our future, Briggs. We need stability. A savings. We've discussed this already, and it's best that we both stay working at Stonebrook."

"I'm not saying we have to do it right away. Just... think about it. We could make it work," I urge.

She shakes her head, looking frustrated. "I don't understand why you can't be content with what we have. We have good jobs, a house, a plan for the future... why risk it all for some bar?"

I swallow hard, tamping down the frustration and anger brewing in my stomach. "Because it's not just *some* bar, Bethany. It's my *dream*. And I'm tired of putting my dreams on hold."

"Well, what about my dream, Briggs?"

The hint of anger and sadness in her voice makes me wonder if there are things she hasn't been telling me, either. She turns back to face me and stares for a moment, and the silence between us grows thicker.

"Forget it. I need to get ready for work." She storms out of the kitchen, leaving me alone with my thoughts yet again.

As I watch her walk away, my heart sinks and my shoulders droop, guilt pooling in my stomach.

Bethany wants stability. And I should, too. But lately, I've started to wonder if stability is the same as fulfillment. Because if it is... why do I constantly feel like something's missing?

I walk into the media center for our morning meeting, and it's already full of staff members catching up on the past few months and grabbing donuts from the front counter. They are all chatting loudly with big smiles on their faces, and everyone seems eager to be back.

I would rather be anywhere else.

David and his secretary, Helen, are at the front of the room, working on getting their presentation set up. I give them a head nod and walk to my usual spot in the back corner, hopefully out of sight enough that no one tries to talk to me. I prefer to lie low in meetings and fly under the radar most of the time. I like the staff—most of them, anyway—but I've never connected with many of them. Seems like we don't have a ton in common. Or maybe I've just never taken the time to get to know them since I never planned to stay here as long as I have.

Because Beth works for the district and not solely the high school, she doesn't have to attend these meetings, so I take an empty seat in the back of the room near the computer monitors by myself. Scanning the room, I spot the brown-noser of the school, Catherine, sitting at the table closest to David, right up front and center as always. I grab my phone from my pocket to put it on silent when there's a squeal of excitement not too far from where I'm sitting.

Charlie, our school librarian, is sitting on the gray couch near the rows of books in the back of the room, and next to her sits Leah, one of our history teachers. "Hamilton! Get your behind over here!" one of them shouts across the room.

I divert my attention to the double doors where Paisley Hamilton walks in looking a little frazzled, carrying her gigantic water bottle and attempting not to slosh her coffee all over the carpet. Unlike yesterday, her hair is let down, and her long, dark locks fall past her shoulders in waves, bouncing as she heads toward the couch.

She's wearing a white, flowy sundress with yellow daisies scattered all over it, and her matching daisy earrings swing back and forth as she sashays over to Charlie and Leah. She somehow manages to look both chaotic and professional, and the corners of my mouth twitch up into a smile.

Her quirky style intrigues me probably more than it should. I've seen her hundreds of times before today, but right now there's something different about her.

Maybe it's the fact that I'm dreading this meeting while her enthusiasm is impossible to ignore. Or maybe it's the way she carries herself, a tiny bit disheveled but oddly endearing? Or it could be the way she has interacted with every person she has walked past in this library, greeting them or offering them a smile, genuinely excited to be here.

She gives Charlie and Leah each a quick hug and attempts to smooth down her dress as she sits, her petite frame looking even smaller under the pile of notepads she pulls out of her bag and stacks onto her lap.

My mind fleets back to the argument Beth and I had this morning. When she came back downstairs after we each had a chance to calm down, things between us were back to normal, and we didn't broach the topic of the cocktail bar again. Maybe she's right; maybe the speakeasy *is* a risky idea. It probably wouldn't work out anyway. At least not right now.

When David starts to discuss the district goals for the year, I realize I'm still staring in Paisley's direction. He cues Helen to flip through the poorly designed slides on the Google presentation she clearly threw together right before this meeting, and Paisley shifts on the couch and adjusts her dress. She leans over and whispers something to Charlie and Leah, attempting to hide her giggle while David drones on.

My eyes focus on her, and an unfamiliar feeling zips through my stomach. Jolted, I shift my gaze back to the front of the room and force myself to concentrate on what David is saying. I have bigger shit to deal with right now than this sudden interest I have in my colleague.

Besides, there's no way I'm attracted to Paisley Hamilton.

Is there?

Chapter Seven

♫ "Unwritten" — Natasha Bedingfield ♫

PAISLEY

The bell echoes through the hall as I walk into my room and close the door behind me. It's the first official day with students, but it already feels like I've run a fucking marathon. Three days of back-to-back meetings that could have been emails, countless reiterations of policies we've heard over and over again, never-ending yapping from superintendents and board members who have never actually set foot in a classroom, and incessant reminders to "take care of ourselves this school year"—all while the one thing we actually need is time in our classrooms to prepare for the students who always, without a doubt, arrive before we're ready.

Exhausted is an understatement.

"Good morning, cl—" I start to say, but a ginormous burst of color hovering above my desk catches me off guard. There's a sea of pink, purple, and yellow helium-filled balloons floating around, one of which has **HAPPY BIRTHDAY** scrawled across it.

I divert my gaze from the swarm of colors and look at my group of juniors and seniors, most of whom I've had in English courses multiple times since they first walked through the doors of Stonebrook High as freshmen.

"Oh my gosh, what is this?" I grin, one hand lifting to cover my mouth to hide my smile.

Three of my Velcro students—that's what I call them since they barely ever leave my side, even during my prep and lunch period—wave me forward. One of them signals to the card sitting on my desk and motions for me to open it.

Happy birthday, Mrs. H! We are so excited to have class with you again this semester! We love you!

"Surprise!" Collin, another student I've had since he was a gangly, awkward fourteen-year-old, shouts, and my heart constricts. Tears threaten to escape my eyes, but I *refuse* to let myself cry on the first day of school, even if it is for good reason.

A lot of people question how I can teach high school, saying they could never deal with the hormones and attitude, but it's moments like this, when I get a glimpse of the selflessness and compassion under their hard exteriors, that make my job so rewarding. Plus, now I have a gigantic floating reminder letting everyone know it's my birthday.

And although I usually don't like to be the center of attention, my birthday is an exception. Because, hello, it's my *birthday*. Even if I am thirty now.

"I can't believe you guys remembered," I gush to them. "Especially on the first day of school! You are too sweet to me!"

I give a few of them hugs as the rest of the students grab the syllabus from the front table and settle into their seats for class.

Still, as I stand here feeling all warm and fuzzy, a small ache is lodged deep within my chest, and anxiety attempts to spool out.

Something about hitting the next decade in my life makes me think about everything I *thought* I would have accomplished by now and still haven't. Married at twenty-three, kids by twenty-six, dream house and career by thirty. Instead, I'm two years into my marriage and shudder at the thought of having kids. No way am I ready for that, and Ethan *definitely* isn't ready to be a father.

As far as the dream house goes... Well, we purchased our home a little over a year ago, but it's definitely not where I imagine us being forever. Unfortunately, this is an area of contention for Ethan and me. He's perfectly happy remaining in Stonebrook for the rest of his days with his parents ten minutes down the road.

But I want to travel, to see the world, to do... *something*. I love teaching, truly I do, but this can't be all there is for the rest of my life.

I take a deep breath and push those worries out of my mind for now, looking at the group of half-asleep teenagers in front of me.

"Alright, earthlings!" I say to them with more energy than they're probably ready for. "Who's ready to learn?!"

I swear I can hear the entire building let out a collective sigh as the last bell of the day blares through the halls. I walk out of my classroom to say goodbye to the remaining students filing out of my room and lean against the cold, brick wall.

"One day down, 179 to go," I joke to Nicole, the science teacher whose classroom is across the hall.

"But who's counting?" she quips back, and I chuckle. "Any big plans tonight for your birthday? I hope Ethan plans on spoiling you."

"Yeah, we're going to get dinner at my favorite restaurant, and I'm going to treat myself to a big ol' bowl of pasta and drown my sorrows."

I'm only half serious. Nicole knows I'm being melodramatic, so she laughs.

"I have the night off from Tumbleweed, so I'm taking advantage of it."

"So you decided to keep waitressing during the school year, huh? I know you were contemplating being done at the end of summer with how chaotic school gets."

Having her room across the hall from mine, Nicole often falls on the receiving end of my venting sessions. I consider myself a pretty positive person, and I always try to keep an air of encouragement and optimism at school—especially around the students—but some days when four o'clock rolls around, I need to let it out to someone who understands before I go home. Nicole's been teaching for twenty-two years, so she's heard, and experienced, it all, and sometimes it's nice to have someone to bitch to who will simply listen instead of trying to offer advice. Teacher trauma bonding or whatever they call it, right?

"Yeah, I thought about being done at the end of August, but the extra money is so nice to have. Ethan works late most nights anyway, at least until winter, so if I'm not working, I end up sitting on my ass and feeling bad about my lack of productivity."

"Paisley, you work harder than most people I know, and definitely harder than any other teacher in this school. Some nights you *deserve* some rest and unproductiveness. You have to give yourself a break sometimes," she reminds me.

"Yeah, yeah, I know. I promise I'll remember to slow down and not overwork myself this year," I answer, waving her off. "Anyway, I better grab my stuff and head home. Eth and I have reservations at 5:30. He's taking off from work early so we can leave as soon as he gets home. See you tomorrow?"

"Sure thing. Another day, another half dollar." She smiles. "Have fun at dinner. And happy birthday, again!"

I shuffle back into my room to turn off the lights and grab my things. Snagging my bag off my chair, I loop the tangled rainbow mess of balloon strings around my wrist and wobble to the door looking fucking ridiculous. How the hell am I going to get these into my car?

The hallway smells like a mix of dry-erase markers, gym socks, and body odor. Yep, there's no mistaking school is back in session.

And no, fourteen-year-olds have still not discovered the importance of deodorant.

The balloons bob with every step, drifting up and tugging lightly against my wrist like they're ready to pull me to space. I'm trying not to let them whack me in the face, but it's a losing battle, and I stifle a laugh as the last of the straggling students glance my way, some of them laughing and some of them side-eyeing me like I'm a weirdo.

As I'm juggling my bag and trying not to bash anyone with my balloons, Davenport stands at the end of the corridor, supervising the halls with his arms crossed, looking thoroughly unimpressed with everything. His glasses are perched on his nose, making him look even more serious. Or hot. Ugh. Both.

He glances up, and his eyebrows lift slightly when he sees the parade of colors floating behind me. He's wearing a pair of navy-blue chinos and a maroon long-sleeve, and I realize, yet again, that Charlie was right—he *does* have a sexy professor vibe going on. Goddamn it.

"Look at you. You're like a damn bird in a China shop." He smirks.

"Please," I say, rolling my eyes with a grin. "If I were a bird, I'd be one of those angry seagulls that dive-bombs people for their sandwiches."

He chuckles, crossing his arms, and my eyes instinctively drop to where his sleeves are rolled up, exposing his forearms. They're strong and tan, and a hint of ink peeks out from beneath the fabric. He has a tattoo?

"Yeah, I could see that."

I snap my gaze back up to his face and shrug. "Gotta survive somehow. Everyone's out for themselves these days. Birds included," I say, confidently.

"Whatever you say, Hamilton." And there's that fucking smirk again.

"You're a smart man, Davenport," I quip, feigning assertiveness as I angle my arm to keep the balloons from drifting into his face.

His gaze flickers up, and his expression shifts as he catches sight of the big bolded letters emblazoned across the top balloon.

"Oh, shit. It's your birthday?"

"Yup." I pop the *p* for dramatic effect. "The big three-oh."

He chuckles again, low and warm, giving a nod of respect. "Well, happy birthday, Paisley. Here's to a year of new experiences."

"Thank you," I say quickly. The way he's looking at me makes heat creep up my body, so I promptly shuffle toward the parking lot with all of my balloon soldiers in tow.

As Ethan and I walk into The Copper Vine, his hand finds the small of my back to usher me inside. While he and I have never been overly intimate, he has always done a great job of showing his affection for me and making me feel loved.

"Hamilton, party of two," I say to the young, blonde hostess standing near the podium of menus.

She motions for us to follow her, and Ethan grabs my hand in his and leads me to our table. The space is a cozy little bistro we both like with low lighting and rustic wooden tables, and it always smells faintly of fresh bread and roasted garlic. It always fills up extremely fast, so I made our reservation weeks ago to ensure we would get a table tonight.

We're barely settled into our booth by the window and near the fireplace when he's already ordering a bottle of wine. Moscato—my favorite.

When the bottle arrives, he pours both of us a glass and raises his to mine. "To you." He smiles. "Happy birthday, Pais."

We clink glasses and fall into easy conversation. I'm finally starting to unwind from the chaos of the day when I notice the small, velvet box he pulls out from under the table and slides across to me. My heart pitter-patters, though I'm not quite sure what I'm expecting. I've always preferred giving gifts to receiving them because I worry I won't look as excited as I feel, and then I think if I try to *act* excited, it will seem ingenuine. The whole situation of getting a present stresses me out, really.

I open the box, and a thin silver bracelet gleams back at me, dainty and elegant.

"You like it?" he asks, looking pleased with himself. It's kind of cute how excited he is.

I run my fingers over the bracelet, trying to keep my expression in check. It's beautiful—don't get me wrong—but it's not really *me*. I've never worn bracelets much; besides my Apple watch and occasional hair tie, I actually don't like the feeling of anything on my wrist. I usually don't even leave my sleeves down and prefer to have them rolled up to my elbows.

I'm much more of an earring girl. It's kind of my "thing," you could say. Okay, maybe no one *else* knows it's my thing, but I'm trying to make it be. I love wearing fun, spunky earrings and hearing my students comment on how silly they are. I guess I thought that after years together he might know that, but how would he? It's not like I outwardly talk about my love of earrings, or about my lack of love toward bracelets.

Ethan is looking at me expectantly, waiting for my response, and I realize I've been having a conversation in my mind for far too long. I smile, not wanting to disappoint him.

"It's beautiful, Ethan. Thank you," I say, closing the box and setting it carefully beside my glass of wine.

I look up, catching his grin, and feel a bit ashamed for wishing he'd gotten me something different. I should be appreciative and not so greedy. *Jeez, Paisley. Quit being such an ungrateful brat.*

"You deserve something nice," he says, leaning back in the booth. "I don't say it enough, but I'm lucky to have you, babe."

I squeeze his hand across the table, letting his words sink in. It's moments like these that make me feel grateful. Obviously our relationship isn't *perfect*, but whose is? Marriage is about compromise and sacrifice, and I'm lucky to have someone who loves me. A lot of women aren't so fortunate.

Our meals arrive, and I dive into my chicken parmesan almost before it's placed on the table. Ethan talks about his plans this weekend to go back to the land to finish setting up for hunting season and asks if I can come with him this time since I won't be hungover like I was on Sunday.

I nod, swallowing my bite. "Yeah, it'd be nice to get some fresh air after a long week of school." I pause, waiting to see if that will encourage him to ask about my first day back with students, to see how my day went. When he doesn't, I add, "The kids surprised me today. Bought me a card and some balloons. It was really sweet."

"Oh yeah?" He smiles, still focused on his steak in front of him. "That was nice of them. Reminds me, I had to deal with Devon being late again today..."

As he continues to talk, I glance at the box again, and it reminds me of the weekend we got engaged.

I had been telling him for months—years, even—that I was a size four and a half. Hell, we even went to a jewelry store *together* to try on rings and get sized. While we were there, I tried on a few different styles because he wanted to know the kinds I liked, even though I knew exactly what I wanted before we got there.

I was never one to dream about my wedding day or anything, but I knew when the time came, I wanted something simple. I showed him a beautiful three stone trellis, exactly like the one my grandma had gotten from my grandpa, and let him know that's the kind I liked most.

Yet when the time came to propose, he pulled out a size eight halo ring, and I could barely even wear it for pictures without it flying off of my hand. I had to send it in to be resized the next day and didn't get it back for three weeks. When I asked him about it, he said that he had bought the first ring he looked at and didn't even think about the size.

I know it's not a big deal, and I'm sure if I said this out loud to anyone they would think I'm being a total bitch, but it was yet another example of a time he didn't listen to what I wanted or consider my own interests. Of course I was extremely happy to be marrying him, but something about it just didn't feel… right.

Not that I've ever admitted that to anyone.

And that's how I feel now, looking at this velvet box staring up at me. I want to appreciate it, and I do, but part of me can't help but feel like I'm right here beside him, and yet he doesn't even see me.

Maybe he never really has.

Chapter Eight

BRIGGS

I'm pulled out of my trance for the third time today as the bell shrieks and a flood of students comes rushing into the corridors.

"Dr. D! What's up man?" Justin, one of our varsity basketball players, shouts as he walks toward me with his hand out for a high five.

"Oh, just livin' the dream. How are your classes going so far?" I slap my hand to his to return the gesture.

"Dude, they're so easy. Senior year is going to be a breeeeeeze," he replies as he mimics shooting a ball.

I shake my head and give him a pat on the back. "Glad to hear it. Looking forward to your final season this winter?"

"For sure. Can't believe it's my last year playing, but we're gonna crush the Buffalos this season!" He flexes his arm for emphasis.

The Buffalos are our rival team and have been for as long as Stonebrook has been around, way before I got here, but I've always been one for tradition.

"That's right we are. I heard we have some pretty good freshmen comin' up to varsity this year, too, which will be good. We should have a strong team." I look around and notice the waves of students thinning. "But hey, you better get to class. Don't want to be late!"

"Alright, alright, alright. Have a good one, Dr. D!" he calls out as he shuffles down the English and science hallway.

I slowly start walking the opposite direction to my office when a familiar laugh echoes toward me. And sure enough, Paisley Hamilton is standing outside of her classroom door talking animatedly to a student who is heading into her class. My feet stop moving before I even realize it. I glance down at their betrayal, then back up, watching as Paisley throws her head back in laughter, completely at ease. It catches me off guard, but frankly, it's the best sound I've heard all day.

It's contagious. Intoxicating.

Her long, chocolate brown hair is pulled into a ponytail that swishes back and forth every time she moves. And hell if it isn't the perfect length to wrap a fist around. It also accentuates her neck, pulling my attention to the book earrings she's wearing today that match her green dress hanging perfectly above her knees—long enough to be appropriate for school but still short enough to pique my imagination.

As if she can sense me staring, Paisley's gaze flicks up and lands on me. She smiles and waves, tucking a stray hair surrounding her face behind her ear. I nod curtly in return but feel myself smile without even trying to. And then the bell rings, so she ducks into her classroom.

"Good afternoon, humans of earth!" Her voice floats down the hall in my direction.

Then, with the thud of her door closing, my brain finally decides to communicate with my feet to move again, and they lead me straight back to my office with a tight, heavy weight that has settled into my chest.

I put the last slice of cheese on the burgers when Bethany saunters into the kitchen.

"Smells delicious. Looks like dinner's almost ready?"

"Just about." I pull out two plates from the cupboard and set them on the counter next to the stove. "Waiting for the cheese to melt and then we should be good."

She takes a seat at the table and rests her chin in her hand, watching me as I finish preparing the food. I can feel her eyeing me like she wants to say something, but I don't prompt her. After another minute, I turn off the burner and slide the patties onto the buns I already put on our plates.

"Still thinking about that bar idea?" she asks randomly. Her voice is light when she speaks, but when I turn around and look at her, she's scrolling on her phone, seemingly uninterested in this conversation. The topic hasn't come up since I mentioned it before school started up again and she squashed the whole thing.

I take a deep breath before answering. What should I even say? *Yes, I've been thinking about it nonstop? It's the only thing that seems to bring me any semblance of joy lately? I hate my job and can't wait to get out of it and do something that actually makes me feel like I have a purpose?*

Because although all that's true, I don't think it's exactly what she wants to hear.

"Yeah," I respond dryly. I walk over to the table with our plates in hand and slide one of them in front of her. "Do you want a glass of wine?"

"Sure, that would be great." She sets her phone down and lifts up her fork to take a bite of broccoli. "So?" she asks, urging me to continue.

"I've been looking into it more, actually. I really think it could work. We would just have to find a location with the right price. Not sure if there's much near Stonebrook, so I might have to widen my search area."

I place her glass of Merlot on the table, and she finally looks up at me, her expression guarded. "You always do this, though, Briggs. You get an idea in your head and fixate on it for a while, then move onto the next thing. I'm sure the excitement over this silly bar will fade, too."

Her words sting more than they should; I don't want to admit it, but she has a point. I do have a tendency to get caught up with big dreams and ideas—but this speakeasy isn't something I thought up on a whim one random night. It's a vision I've had since I was twenty-six years old, and ten years later, I still have the same vision I did then. It had just gotten buried for a while.

"I'm serious about it," I tell her as I set my own fork down with a little more force than necessary. *Keep your emotions in line. Arguing won't help anything.*

Bethany's gaze narrows. "I just don't understand, Briggs. You have a good job at the high school. You have stability. Why throw that away for something so... uncertain?"

Frustration creeps into my shoulders, and I attempt to tamp it down. But this isn't only about the bar—it's everything else that's been building up over time.

Like the way she never really listens to what I need or want. The way I can never seem to get her attention for more than five minutes without her phone buzzing or her friends calling. The way she doesn't listen when I say I'm miserable with my job and am dying for a change. The way she didn't even thank me for this damn dinner I made.

"I'm not throwing anything away," I remind her, my voice low but firm. "I'm just not happy settling. I want more than this. More than going through the motions, watching life pass me by. You know what I mean?"

She takes a sip of her wine and sets it down with a soft sigh. "I'm not asking you to settle, Briggs. I just don't get why you think something new will fix things."

I open my mouth, but the words stick in my throat. I want to tell her that it's hard to fix things when you aren't even sure what's broken. That I'm staying in this job for her, for our future, for the "stability." But if I'm being honest with myself—and I think it's time that I am—I constantly feel like I am simply drifting through life, disconnected from everything. From her. From myself.

Our days are spent surrounded by her friends and family, and we never have time alone anymore. She is always planning events with them while I'm left trying to keep up, not even interested in what we spend our time doing.

"You're right. You don't get it." My voice is a little softer now. "Because it's not only about the cocktail bar or about being unhappy with my job. It's about..." I trail off and run a hand through my hair, trying to collect my thoughts. "It's about feeling like I'm not really *here* anymore. Like I'm not even part of our life, Beth. It's always about what *you* want, or what your friends want, or what your family wants. But what about what *I* want? When do I get a say in how my life plays out? When do we get time to figure out who *we* are, just the two of us?"

She stares at me for a long time. For a moment, I think I see a flicker of remorse in her eyes. Or maybe sympathy? Pity? Who knows. It's gone before I can recognize it.

"You're being dramatic," she says, the words sharp, signaling our conversation coming to a close. "We have a good life, Briggs. Isn't that enough for you?"

I don't say anything after that, and we eat the rest of dinner in silence, all the while thinking she could be right. Maybe everything *is* fine. We have our routine, our friends, our jobs.

But is that enough?

Chapter Nine

♫ *"Autumn Leaves" — Ed Sheeran* ♫

PAISLEY

A gust of wind slams me in the face as I push through the doors to the parking lot, bringing the scent of fall with it. I love this time of year, and the leaves are finally starting to don their autumn colors. Unfortunately, that means winter's not far off, and I'm not ready for 4:00 P.M. sunsets and negative thirty degree temperatures."

Stardust Distillery is pretty packed when I arrive for our staff get-together, but it's been a long week, and I am more than ready for a drink or two. It's *always* busy here, but it's obvious why—the inside space is modern but rustic at the same time, and it has garage doors that open to a beautiful deck area in the back that illuminates with Edison lights whenever the weather permits, like tonight.

As I round the corner and head straight to the deck, I immediately spot Charlie, Leah, and one of our math teachers, Miranda, at a nearby picnic table.

"You made it!" Charlie exclaims, as if I didn't see her literally five minutes ago when I told her I would meet her here. "Ready for a drink?"

I slide onto the bench next to Leah. "You have no idea."

I wave the bartender over and order myself a cranberry gimlet with lemonade—hold the martini glass, please; those things are a bitch to drink out of—and glance around to see who all made it here tonight. As I peer over Leah's head, I spot our principal.

"Ugh, don't you wish we could have a staff event *without* David? I mean, I know he's the one who plans them, but—"

"Correction," Miranda cuts me off, "you mean his little minion Helen plans them. David wouldn't know his ass from his elbow without her being there to remind him."

"True, " I agree. "We should just plan one. A *real* happy hour where we only invite the people we actually like." I take a sip of my drink and welcome the immediate release of tension in my body.

Okay, to be fair, our principal isn't actually *that* bad. He's just old and his ideas are outdated, and who wants to hang out with their boss outside of work?

I glance over to the admin table again, where Bethany Davenport lets out a sharp and shrill laugh, but her hubby sitting next to her looks like he would rather be getting a root canal. Normally, I would make a comment about how grumpy he is, but I can't really blame the guy on this one. I would be bored as fuck having to converse with that group all night, too.

"God, she's such a nightmare," Charlie mutters, following my gaze. "I don't know what Davenport sees in her."

"I'm not sure he does, either," Miranda says casually. "Did you guys know I started at Stonebrook the same year as them?"

"I don't think I knew that," I answer. I don't know why I *would* know that. I don't know Davenport at all, other than his tendency to get lost in the Catacombs, apparently.

She nods. "Yep. We started the same year as Owen from the history department, too. The following spring, Owen got married, so we all went to the wedding. Davenport brought Bethany, and he looked... miserable. Like he wanted to drink and dance and have fun but couldn't."

"I could see that," Charlie nods. "She definitely seems like the fun-sucker in the relationship. I wonder what he would be like without her around."

"That's what I'm trying to tell you! If you would just let me finish," Miranda chastises her with a laugh. "As I was *saying*, the next year, another colleague got married, and Bethany didn't come with him that time. He was a completely different guy. Joking around, dancing, acting like we were all *friends*. Way different than he even is at school. It was kind of bizarre."

"Maybe it's because of his job. Probably thinks he needs to be serious all the time to 'maintain order,' and all that jazz," Leah suggests, adding air quotes around her words.

"Maybe," I say slowly. "But I couldn't imagine working with my spouse every day. I mean, I love Ethan, but if I spent every minute at home with him *and* every minute at work with him, I would feel like I was suffocating. I would need a break. My own space. My own *life*."

"God, yeah," Leah agrees. "I would hate it if I had to work with John all day."

The other girls nod in agreement, and our conversation shifts to venting about our week at school. But my mind lingers on Miranda's comment... because if even the Davenports are that good at putting on a show, then what does that mean for the rest of us?

"Hey," I say, lifting my empty glass. "I'm out. Anyone need a refill? This round's on me."

They all say yes, obviously, so I walk toward the bar, my maxi skirt blowing slightly in the breeze. Just as I finish ordering our drinks, someone sidles up beside me.

"Thirsty tonight, Hamilton?"

I turn and find Davenport, a slight smile pulling at his lips. He's in a black sweatshirt and a backwards snapback, and goddamn it, why does that work so well for him?

When I don't answer, he nods toward the bartender. "That's a lot of drinks for one person," he says with a wink.

And for the first time, I actually notice the color of his eyes. They're bright blue—feels like I'm lost in the middle of the damn ocean blue—but the black he's wearing pulls out tiny flecks of gray. They're kind of mesmerizing.

I smile cheekily at him. "If you think I can drink all those myself, then you must think very highly of me."

"I do," he says without missing a beat, and my heart falters for a second. "But that isn't the reason."

I tap my nails on the bar top trying to ignore the heat crawling up my body. "Are you always this charming, or is the autumn air messing with your head?"

His mouth lifts into that slow, sexy smirk, and he shrugs. "Maybe it's just the company."

That catches me off guard, but I recover quickly and give him a onceover. "Something is different about you tonight, Davenport. Not in a bad way," I add quickly. "Just different. Less... grumpy assistant principal who scowls-at students who are late to class and more..." I pause, searching for the right word.

"More what?" He's standing close enough that my body can feel the warmth of his presence.

"...human?" I offer, biting my lip as I smirk.

That gets a full-blown laugh out of him, and he tosses his head back in amusement.

"I don't hear you laugh very often," I say casually.

"Guess I don't always have a reason to."

God, this man is cryptic. There's a beat of silence between us, and for a second, our eyes lock.

"Besides, I try my best not to laugh in public. Ruins the whole asshole vibe I have going on."

"You're right. Better not let the students ever hear it. Your credibility would be totally shot."

He slides his empty glass forward on the counter, signaling to the bartender he needs a refill, and I notice the ink poking out from his rolled up sleeves.

"So... is there a story behind the tattoo? Or should I start brainstorming crazy stories about you belonging to a biker gang?"

His eyes crinkle slightly as he smirks again. "Definitely a biker gang."

"You know what? I could totally see it."

"I see you went with pumpkins tonight," he says, quickly changing the subject.

I reach up instinctively and fiddle with the clay pumpkins swinging from my ears. "I'm surprised you noticed."

"Hard not to. You wear a new pair almost every day. I especially liked the skeleton ones you wore earlier this week."

My fingers freeze. He's been paying attention? To me?

I know it's stupid. They're just earrings. Tiny, seasonal, quirky pieces of jewelry I throw on in the morning to make myself feel a little more like me. My students love them and notice them all the time, but I didn't expect Davenport to. The fact that he's been paying such close attention does something to me. And whatever that something is, it seems dangerous.

"Those are nothing. You should see my lineup for the Christmas season. I have a whole collection."

"Can't wait to see them," he tells me, and I actually believe him. "I used to collect things, too. Not earrings, obviously."

"Obviously," I repeat. "Oh, let me guess! You have a secret collection of fun-themed socks?"

He shakes his head and chuckles. "No. Good guess, though. Antiques. I got a lot of stuff from my grandpa, and I would go to flea-markets and buy some clocks and other items to fix up and restore, back when I had more time before I moved to Stonebrook. Still have a few in the garage, but I don't really do much with them anymore."

"Why not?"

He shrugs. "Beth hated how they clashed with the house. And once we moved here, life kind of got in the way. Dreams got shelved. You know how it goes."

I open my mouth to reply, but the bartender returns with my drinks before I can. Briggs nods at the counter. "That your whole table's order?"

"No, they're all for me, remember?" I wink.

Smirking again, he pulls out his wallet and slides a card across the bar before I can stop him. "I've got it."

"Seriously?" I protest. "I said I would buy this round."

He shrugs. "They don't have to know. Consider it assistant principal's honor."

I give him a timid smile. "Well... thanks." I grab the tray of drinks and turn to leave, pausing and looking back over my shoulder. "Oh, and Davenport?"

"Yeah?"

"Have you ever thought that maybe it's time for some dreams to be dusted off?"

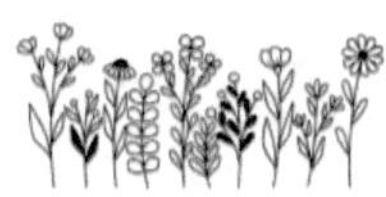

As the night wears on, I relax more than I have since school started a couple weeks ago. I really should do this more often.

Taking a sip of her third Old Fashioned, Charlie leans in, a mischievous glint in her eye. "You guys won't believe what I overheard in the library today."

Here we go. Charlie always gets all of the student gossip. Working in the library, she supervises kids who have a free period or who come in for work time. The kids typically do more talking than working, and Charlie has mastered the skill of eavesdropping—although with these students, she barely has to do so. They openly tell her pretty much everything these days.

"You know Julia, right? Well apparently, she hooked up with Jace, and Tommy found out about it,"

"You're kidding!" Miranda interrupts. "They've been dating for like three years, haven't they?"

"Yep," Charlie answers. "But not anymore. I guess he called and dumped her ass immediately. The kids say she keeps calling him and trying to get him back, but he doesn't want anything to do with her. Drama!" She shakes her head slightly and laughs under her breath.

"Jesus," Leah chimes in. "Honestly, though, it's for the best. Tommy was planning to stay in the area to go to college because of her. I was like, dude, do not change your life path for a freaking girl in high school. Maybe now he'll change his mind."

"For real," I agree. "I tell kids all the time how I regret staying so close to home for college. I wish I would have taken those years to explore and spend some time outside of Wisconsin to find out what I truly wanted to do with my life. To figure out who I was. And seriously, no one should make decisions based on a high school relationship."

The girls continue to talk about the other gossip Charlie picked up this week, but my phone buzzes on the table and displays Ethan's name.

I walk over to the grass to take the call. "Hey, babe."

"Hey. Just wondering where you are."

"We're still at Stardust," I reply. "Kind of lost track of time. It's been a long week."

He pauses. "Yeah, I figured. Just thought you'd let me know. I've been waiting for dinner."

My heart drops to my stomach. "I'm sorry. I finished my drink a bit ago, so I'm going to have a glass of water and then head out. I'll be home soon," I promise.

"Well, guess I'll just have cereal," he snaps. "But hope you're having fun."

The familiar sting of resentment rises in my chest, but I push it down, forcing myself to stay calm. "I'll be home soon," I say. "I love you."

"Love you, too."

I hang up and close my eyes for a second, trying to shake off the returned tension in my shoulders.

I sigh and sit down at the table. "Hey, guys. I think I'm gonna finish my water and then head home."

"It's because Ethan called you, isn't it?" Charlie asks, knowing all too well that whenever I'm out for too long without talking to him, he acts the same way.

"Well, he did call, but I'm also tired, and we have a long day tomorrow," I respond tersely. She's not entirely wrong, but I don't want them to think badly of Ethan.

After closing my tab, I give them each a hug goodbye and head to my car. I pass by Davenport, who is now back at his table, and for a fleeting moment, our eyes lock again and my stomach flip-flops.

I smile and force myself to shift my gaze, pushing down whatever *that* was, but as I trudge through the gravel lot, there's a small part of me that can't help but wonder what it would feel like to be with someone other than Ethan.

Chapter Ten

BRIGGS

Mornings at Stonebrook High are always the damn same. Half-awake teenagers fueled by Mountain Dew and Bubbl'r, fluorescent lights screaming at me, and lockers slamming way fucking harder than they need to. But that's all background noise at this point. I've grown used to it over the years.

I tug at the cuffs on my shirt, letting out a slow breath through my nose as I supervise the students heading to their first class.

"Walking! No running!" Miranda, one of our math teachers, shouts down the hallway. I swear, even though our school is small and easy to get from class to class, these kids act like they are racing to avoid a meteor shower or zombie apocalypse.

I walk toward Miranda's voice, and a student—definitely a freshman by the size of him—flies around the corner, his half-zipped backpack flapping wildly on his back, threatening to toss out his materials with every step.

"Woah, woah, woah, easy there," I say to him, stepping into his path and pressing my hands gently to his shoulders to slow him down. "Where ya headed?"

"Sc...i....ence," he huffs out between gulps of air.

I suppress a smile, giving his shoulder a quick pat. "Well, you have plenty of time. Just slow down before you run someone over, all right?"

"Sorry, Dr. Davenport," he mutters between taking off again, this time at a half-hearted jog, his backpack still bouncing.

I shake my head and laugh under my breath as I continue my stride and settle into the intersection of two hallways. David approaches from down the corridor once the bell rings, a red folder in his hand.

He raises it toward me as he approaches. "PBIS conference, the week after Thanksgiving break. I'm roping you into this one."

This one? Is there anything he doesn't rope me into?

I take the folder, glancing at the dates. It's right at the beginning of basketball season, but I'll have to make it work. "Are the other team members already aware, or do I need to talk to them?"

David smirks. "Yep, I let them know earlier today. Charlie and Stephanie said they could make it. Hamilton practically jumped on board before I could even finish my sentence. You know, for this being her first year on the committee, she sure is stepping up to the plate already."

I shrug, trying to stay professional. I'm not sure why Paisley Hamilton has been such a topic of conversation around me lately. I went the last three years with hardly having to interact with her, and now, she's... everywhere.

"She's sure got the passion and energy for it," I say, keeping my voice even.

David nods. "Oh, by the way, Joe was looking for you earlier this morning. Said he had some questions about tryouts. You ready for some more glory days?"

I let out a dry chuckle. "If by glory days you mean working with kids who think they're Lebron James but are actually more like baby giraffes learning to walk, then sure, can't wait."

David laughs and claps me on the shoulder before sauntering down the hallway back toward our offices. I exhale slowly and shove the folder under my arm before heading to make sure no kids are skipping class and hiding in the bathroom.

The *thunk* of my coffee mug hitting my desk sounds like a bomb going off, and it might as well be with the way this day has dragged on. I let my head fall back against my black leather chair and stare up at the hideous dropdown ceiling for a second before pulling up Google calendar and scanning the never-ending list of things I'm apparently supposed to give a shit about.

Somewhere between approving a field trip and signing off on a maintenance request, I catch my reflection in the monitor—my blue eyes are shadowed, my hair is in dire need of a trim, and the stubble on my face has gotten to a length that Bethany hates.

My computer dings with an incoming email. And then another. And then another.

Urgent: Cafeteria Vendor Issues
Student Complaint—Follow Up
Policy Update (Action Required)

I pull off my glasses and pinch the bridge of my nose. None of this really matters, does it?

I used to care more. I think.

A decade ago when I earned my doctorate degree, I thought I was going to make a difference. I mistakenly thought a big degree in psychology would lead to something more than talking to parents who insist their kid didn't cheat on a test. But to tell you the truth, I'm not sure I even cared then.

I never imagined working in a school. I actually *hated* school when I was a teenager. The monotony of everything. The entitled kids whose parents thought they "deserved" more than the others. The assholes who only cared about sports and not about actual people.

And yet, somehow, I ended up here. Beth got offered a job in the district, and before we knew it, we were buying a house in Stonebrook and building a foundation. The assistant principalship opened up, and even though I didn't have my admin degree at the time, they offered me a job—contingent on my earning one. It was easy to do, just an online course that took a couple months, and the district paid for it.

And now, here I am. Pretending to give a shit about things that don't actually matter in the grand scheme of life.

A quick knock on the door interrupts my thoughts.

"Hey, Briggs?"

My hands drop from my face, and I glance up to see Joe poking his head in. He teaches P.E. here at the high school, and his face is flushed like he just got done running laps.

"Yeah?" I say, sitting up straighter.

He steps inside, looking half-apologetic. "You might want to get to the gym. We've got two seniors about to kill each other over a girl."

I shake my head. Of course it's over a fucking girl.

I smell the sweat permeating the air before I even step through the double doors. The majority of the class is huddled in the corner of the gym on the other side of the bleachers, most likely talking about the incident currently happening in the middle of the floor. I scan the room and spot the two boys at center court, faces red, shoulders squared, fists twitching at their sides. It's clear that if I don't intervene soon, this will surely escalate and police will have to get involved.

"Hey!" My voice slices through the tension like a blade. Both heads snap toward me. "What are we doing, gentlemen?"

I stride across the gym floor until I get closer to them. It's quiet enough to hear the squeak of my shoes against the polished wood.

Neither of them answers.

"I asked a question. What. Are. We. Doing?"

"Tommy started it," one of them mutters.

Jace, I think his name is. He's short, and I tower over him as I come to a stop in front of them.

"Oh, really?" I say, tilting my head. "Is that the defense you're going with? Tommy *started it*?" I pause in front of him, close enough that he shrinks back a little, though I'm not even raising my voice. "Tell me something, kid. When you fill out college or job applications in the future, is *I blame other people* going to be one of the strengths listed on your resume?"

His mouth opens to say something and then shuts as fast as it opened. I can see his eyes calculating whether he should respond.

"That's what I thought."

I turn to Tommy next. He's taller, but his gaze falters the second I look at him. "And you." I point at him, my finger coming close to his chest without actually touching him. "I expect better from you. And you're about to get into it with him over... what? A *girl*? Newsflash, buddy. She's not impressed. No one is."

Again, I'm answered again with silence.

Good.

I let the words sink in for a few seconds, and then I soften my posture, but only slightly. "Here's the deal. You're going to shake hands, like adults, and then we're walking straight to my office where you'll explain to me, in great detail, how I get to spend my morning dealing with *this* instead of, oh, I don't know, literally anything else."

Neither boy moves. I step even closer, my voice lower.

"Or... we can let this play out." I shrug. "You throw a couple punches, make fools of yourself. And I walk to my office alone and call the police, resulting in both of you leaving the school in handcuffs today. What'll it be?"

I see the two make eye contact with one another, and in an instant, two hands shoot out like puppets on strings. They shake, begrudgingly, muttering apologies under their breath.

"Good choice." I nod as I point toward the gym doors. "My office. Now."

They trudge toward the double doors, heads low, and I can't stop the smirk that pulls at the corner of my mouth.

"Hell of a show, Dr. Davenport."

I glance over my shoulder to find Joe leaning against the wall, arms crossed, clearly enjoying himself.

"Yeah, well," I say, sliding my hands into my pockets and offering him a sarcastic wink. "Somebody's gotta keep 'em in line."

Chapter Eleven

♫ "Boot Scootin' Boogie" — Brooks & Dunn ♫

PAISLEY

"Oh, shit—sorry!" I holler from across the food warmers as the plastic cup of green flakes clatters onto the cooking line.

Tony, one of our cooks, glares at me over the mashed potatoes and ribs sitting between us on the metal warmer. I can tell by his expression that he is clearly having a worse night than I am, and I am currently his bane of existence. I clench my teeth and grimace at him.

"Sorry," I say again, this time whispering

"For fuck's sake!" he bellows, turning to face the head of the line, Mike. "I'm taking my five minute break. Fucking waitress spilled parsley all over everything."

He motions to the counter now glittered with herbs, and my stomach drops in both shame and annoyance. I've worked at Tumbleweed for almost four months now, and I know he knows my name. He's just dehumanizing me to be an asshole and to make me feel worse. I hate that it's working.

I look at Mike. "It was an accident," I say timidly, feeling a burn behind my eyes.

Parsley is scattered around the tins of food, and I hope I didn't ruin anything. The restaurant is swamped and the kitchen is already behind on their orders, so Tony's impromptu break is only going to set them further behind. All thanks to clumsy fucking Paisley.

"It ain't your fault, sweetheart," Mike reassures me. "Things happen. Besides, Tony's dumb ass knows better than to leave uncapped herbs sitting up on the warmer where all the plates are. He's just being dramatic. You go back and check on your tables. We've got it from here." He offers me a small smile and returns to cooking the steak on the grill in front of him.

I grab the plate of ribs and potatoes, along with the ribeye that accompanies it, and head toward table twenty-two where my regulars, Darlene and Buck, sit.

When I first became a server at the beginning of the summer, I wasn't sure how much I would like it, but turns out, it's exactly what I need to get some time out of the house and to unwind after working with teenagers at school. I also love meeting all kinds of people, like these two. The biggest downfall is getting scheduled with a human hemorrhoid like Tony.

The only other drawback, which isn't nearly as bad as working with dickhead cooks, is that Tumbleweed is a western-themed restaurant, hence the name. And although I can get down with some country music and throw on a pair of Wranglers and a cowboy hat from time to time, I wouldn't say I'm exactly *country*.

As I approach Darlene and Buck, they are holding hands over the table, staring into each other's eyes like it's their first date. I've always admired how in love they still seem to be with one another even though they recently celebrated their fiftieth wedding anniversary.

"Here you go, love birds," I comment, setting down their food in front of them. "Can I grab you anything else?"

"Oh, thank you, dear," Darlene responds, picking up her fork to begin eating.

Buck gives me a little squeeze on my arm and smiles up at me. "I think that's all for now, but we'll let you know if we need anything."

"Sounds good. Enjoy!" I beam, and I saunter over to the POS system to make sure all of my tables are up to date.

After refilling a few waters and checking in on my other customers, I finally get a minute to breathe. I lean against the host stand and peer over at Darlene and Buck. He is still holding her hand, and he lifts it to his mouth for a kiss. Seeing them like that, so in love, I can't help but wonder what happens if you marry the wrong person. Do you still get that kind of ending? That kind of love?

"Out in the country past the city limits sign…"

I rub a hand down my face and groan. *Ugh, not again.*

But much to my dismay, Brooks & Dunn's "Boot Scootin' Boogie" is blaring through the restaurant speakers.

I check to see if I'm close enough to make a dash for the bathroom to hide, but the rest of the servers are already filing past me and forming a line. Damn it.

Oh, yeah—did I forget to mention the horrendous line dancing they make us do to "liven up the place" here? Add that to the list of reasons I should have quit at the end of summer. *Hello*, I am *not* a line dancer. I do not aspire to *be* a line dancer. I am in no way, shape, or form *good* at *being* a line dancer.

But still, I oblige most of the time, because the guests really do seem to love it. Darlene and Buck are already clapping along, huge smiles on their faces.

Jade, another server, grabs my wrist and pulls me along to the dance area with her. Once we are all in alignment, the music gets even louder, and we fall into step. I allow myself to get lost in the music and energy for a minute, and I actually find myself laughing along with the others, my long braids swaying back and forth to the rhythm of the music.

"We look absolutely ridiculous, you know," I say to Jade, laughing.

"Of course we do, but that's half the fun!"

Over her head, I catch a familiar figure sitting in a booth at the other end of the restaurant. My brain lags for a second, and I can't quite place who it is. I squint, trying not to lose the beat, and peer past the pillar beyond the dance floor.

Something about the way he sits, the broadness of his shoulders...

And then we shift to the left, and I wind up staring at none other than Briggs Davenport, who is clearly on a date with his wife.

Hoping he doesn't notice me—because oh my God, *embarrassing*—I hide behind the pillar the best I can. But when the tempo changes and Jade grabs my arm to do-si-do, I'm shuffled out into the open, vulnerable and very, very much in his line of sight.

And when I glance up at him again, he's not just *looking* at us. He's watching us. Watching *me*.

And he looks pissed.

My whole body heats up like I just downed a bottle of tequila, and I am now painfully aware of how tight my jeans are and the fact that I'm flailing around like a fish who just got dumped on the shore.

Fuck my life. Forget about being embarrassed.

No.

I am absolutely fucking mortified.

Chapter Twelve

♫ *"MakeDamnSure" — Taking Back Sunday* ♫

BRIGGS

I try to ignore the knot tightening in my chest as Bethany laughs, her fingers tracing the stem of her wine glass.

For some reason, I'm too aware of her every movement tonight and of the space that seems to continue to grow between us. I wonder if she can feel it, too.

Dinner was my idea. I was hoping it would help me feel more connected to her and help me shake off whatever this doubt is that's been creeping up. I thought that maybe sitting across from each other with no distractions would remind me of how strong our relationship has always been.

But the restaurant is loud with clinking glasses and conversations, and I'm finding it hard to focus. We used to come to Tumbleweed all the time, but we haven't been here in probably a year.

The smell of steaks and fresh bread permeates the air. There's a grandiose bar in the middle of the room, and since it's Saturday, it's pretty packed. There are barely any empty tables, and the waitresses are all running around like crazy. I scan the room out of habit, and my eyes catch an elderly couple leaning in close to one another, holding hands while eating their meals.

Bethany sits back in her chair, sipping her wine as she talks about work and a baby shower she has next weekend. She and her mom will be shopping one day this week to pick up a gift. I listen, or at least try to, nodding when it feels right. But I'm half here and half somewhere else, my mind wandering to the smallest things, like the sign hanging on the wall behind her with the picture of a cowboy on a horse next to the words "Don't sell your mule to buy a plow."

If I decide to go through with this bar idea, I will need to start looking at some antique shops and vintage sales for more decor. I have some from Grandpa Levi, but not enough to fill an entire space.

"Hey," I say after a pause in conversation. "I, um, wanted to show you something."

She lowers her glass of red wine, her face turning more serious. "What is it?"

I pull my phone out of my pocket, the screen lighting up as I open the web browser I had saved from earlier this week. I look at the picture on the screen—a small brick building, slightly worn and rundown. It popped up on my Zillow the other night, and I thought it might be worth a shot. It's the kind of place you'd miss if you weren't looking.

But I have been.

My heart rate picks up a little, and I turn the phone toward her. "I found this space. It's for lease. It could be the perfect building for the speakeasy…" I trail off, hesitantly.

She leans in, tilting her head to get a better look at the screen. "How much is it?" she asks, her face giving nothing away.

"I'm not sure of the logistics yet. I'd have to reach out to the realtor and crunch some numbers. But it's been sitting vacant for a while now, so there might be a little bit of wiggle room. What do you think?"

She sighs, quietly enough that I barely hear it. "It looks like a lot of work, Briggs."

"That's okay. I like work," I say with a smirk, attempting to lighten the mood.

"Well, I suppose you could reach out to them and see what they have to say. But I would hold off on making any rash decisions before we have all the facts."

"Okay. I'll keep you updated on what they say," I assure her, and she nods in response. My heart slowly returns to its normal rhythm.

The remaining tension between us is cut quickly when the music volume heightens and guests start clapping. This has always been one of my favorite parts of Tumbleweed, but Bethany has never been as big of a fan. She finds it silly and a bit tasteless, but I think it's entertaining.

I watch as the servers shuffle to their spots, and my eyes land on a waitress who looks familiar. Do I know anyone who works here? I don't think so, but it has been a while since we've come. As the music picks up and they start to dance, my eyes follow her, and it doesn't take me long to recognize that long brown hair and those flushed cheeks.

Based on the heat rising up her face, she clearly isn't very comfortable being the center of attention, but with the way her body is moving, you wouldn't ever know it. The change in her body language is like a flipped switch—the sweet, innocent teacher I see every day has faded, and in her place is someone more relaxed, more... *sexy*.

Her smile is wide, and I'm instantly drawn to it. And then there's the way her body moves with the music, the way her hips sway to the beat and draw attention to her ass.

Oh, fuck. Her *ass*. I try to look away, but it's impossible.

My eyes are glued to her. Those tight black jeans cling to every curve, and with each shift, I notice details I never have before—how the fabric molds to her like a second skin, how it accentuates what I didn't even know she had. She moves with confidence, like she's completely unaware of the effect she's having on me.

Probably because she is. She doesn't even know I'm here.

I've seen her in flowy dresses at school. Casual. Modest. Wholesome. But this is different. The tight black shirt she's wearing hugs her chest, and her breasts shift with the beat of the music, sending a rush of heat through my body.

What the hell is happening to me?

Her body is a fucking temptation. Watching her feels like an itch I can't scratch, and I hate the fact that I can't tear my eyes away. A knot forms in my chest even bigger than before.

What the fuck, Briggs?

I shove my thoughts about her down, swallowing hard, my stare turning icy cold. My jaw tightens, and I will myself to look at Beth across the table instead.

"You okay?" she asks, her voice light but her eyes narrowing.

I grab my drink, my fingers locking around the cold glass so fucking hard I'm surprised the damn thing doesn't shatter.

"Yeah, um, I'm fine," I say through gritted teeth.

Frustration churns in my chest. Burning. Unwanted. Impossible to ignore.

It's not Paisley's fault. She isn't doing anything *wrong*.

But seeing her like this, seeing her *move* like that, highlights everything I've been missing. Everything I'm not supposed to want. Everything I *can't* want.

But goddamn it, I think I do.

And I fucking hate myself for it.

Chapter Thirteen

♫ "Shallow" — Lady Gaga & Bradley Cooper ♫

PAISLEY

After what feels like an eternity, the music finally fades and the dance ends. I shake off any remaining humiliation and try not to let it bother me. After all, the Davenports are the ones encroaching on *my* territory, so I shouldn't have to be the one to feel awkward.

And by the look of it, Davenport was equally unhappy to see me, or he's at least back to his grumpy old self. Not sure what got up his ass since our last interaction, but I'm not going to expel any more energy trying to figure it out.

Or at least I'm going to try not to.

I scurry over to Buck and Darlene's table to see if they're ready for dessert, still hyper-aware of Davenport sitting nearby. I'm not sure how I didn't notice him before, but now that I know he's there, I can feel his gaze burning into the back of my skull.

I walk back into the kitchen to warm up some bread pudding when Jade corners me by the soda dispenser.

"Paisley. Do you know that fine piece of a man sitting out there?"

I shift uncomfortably on my feet, hoping to God she's not referring to whom I think she is.

"Um, not sure who you're talking about..." I answer, pretending to be busier than I am. This damn microwave is taking forever.

"You mean you *didn't* notice the guy out there who was watching your every move while you were boot scootin'? Please. He literally did not peel his eyes off of you during the entire dance, and he hasn't since. Does he come here often or something? I think I would remember him."

I roll my eyes, realizing she *is* in fact talking about the exact person I'm trying not to think about. "Ohhh, you mean Davenport." I shrug, feigning nonchalance. "He's my assistant principal at Stonebrook High. And he's here with his *wife*, so I think you misinterpreted his staring. Dude looks more angry than anything."

"Ah-ha! So you *did* notice him watching you." Jade smiles and raises her eyebrows at me, making more of this situation than there is. "And hot damn, I wish my principal looked like that when I was in school. I would have gotten in trouble a lot more often," she adds with a wink.

"Okay, first of all, he's the *assistant* principal. My actual principal is still old and gray, so keep your panties on. Secondly, I'm sure you got into plenty of trouble regardless. And third, if you mean I noticed his icy glare drilling holes into me, then yes, I did. Not sure what I did to piss the guy off, but he seems less than pleased to see me. Now if you would excuse me, some of us actually have *work* to do."

"Whatever you say, girl," she responds, huffing out a small laugh. "Anger. Passion. Call it what you want, but that man has a thing for you. Mark my words."

"Uh huh, sure," I dismiss and wave her off.

I walk to the back of the kitchen and step into the freezer to grab the carton of ice cream to go with the bread pudding. The cold air is refreshing on my heated cheeks, and I allow myself a minute to breathe and let my shoulders drop. Maybe if I stay here long enough, the Davenports will be gone before I re-emerge with Buck and Darlene's dessert.

Unfortunately, I don't wait quite long enough because as soon as I saunter out of the kitchen, the two of them are walking to the door, directly in my path, and literally impossible to avoid.

Do I say something? Or pretend I don't know them? I mean, I don't *really* know them. Davenport is simply an acquaintance, and do you really have to say hello to acquaintances? Probably not, right? And I barely know Bethany. I would be surprised if she even knew my name. Maybe if I walk slowly enough, they won't—

"Paisley."

Damn it. There it is. His voice—deep and smooth, with a hint of annoyance behind it. Still, my name coming off his lips does sound kind of... hot?

"Didn't know you worked here."

"Oh, heyyyy!" I trail, acting surprised to see him and not entirely sure what I should call him. *Briggs* sounds too personal, but *Dr. Davenport* sounds too professional—or like I'm some school girl with a crush. So instead, I draw out the "hey," which ends up sounding awkward and unfinished. "Um, yeah. Part time gig." I lift one shoulder, and the heat is already fighting its way up my face again.

Fuck me sideways. Where's a freezer when you need one?

Thankfully, Bethany chimes in, saving me from further unraveling. "You're a teacher at Stonebrook, right?"

But before I have a chance to say anything, Davenport answers for me. "Yes," he says, his tone clipped. "One of our best."

One of our best? Huh. That's news to me. I didn't know Davenport had any sort of opinion about what type of teacher I am. A grin spreads across my face at the praise without my permission.

"Oh, um, thanks," I mumble, trying to brush it off, but the compliment makes me feel weirdly self-conscious and unsure how to proceed. This whole interaction is a little awkward, to be honest. There's some weird tension in the air, and I don't know how to get out of it.

Bethany, oblivious, shifts her focus back to me. "So, do you like it here? Must be a good change of pace from the classroom, right?"

I nod, my confidence returning a little. "Yeah, it's definitely different, but it's nice to get out of the school routine every once in a while. I only work a couple shifts per week, but it's fun to be a little less... teacher-like, I guess."

I glance at Davenport to see if he's even listening to me, but his eyes bore into me and his expression is unreadable. Maybe I'm imagining it, but there's something in the way he's looking at me, just like he did the other day, that makes my heart pick up a little. It's intense, like he's staring right through me but also sees all of me at the same time.

"I'm sure it's a nice break," his voice cuts in, sounding entirely uninterested in this conversation and like he can't wait for it to end.

What happened to the guy who helped me put together furniture or that I talked with at the distillery? It's like that playful side of him never existed. What the hell did I do?

The tension between us thickens, and my nerves jangle, my stomach tightening. Jade was so far off with her observation—the only thing this guy feels for me is contempt.

Bethany seems to finally pick up on the strain in the air between us. "Well, we should get going. It's getting late." She rests her manicured hand on her husband's arm and offers me a tight smile. "Nice to see you, Paisley."

"Yeah, you too," I reply, a little too quickly and obviously distracted.

Davenport turns to leave without so much as a goodbye, his movements quick and decisive. It feels as if he's rushing to get away from me, and he's gone because I can even fully process the interaction.

I turn on my heel and head straight back to the kitchen to find myself a freezer.

Chapter fourteen

♫ *"Dream On" — Aerosmith* ♫

BRIGGS

"Dr. Davenport?" Mrs. Gordon's voice cuts through my thoughts. "Any additional input?"

We're sitting in a meeting that could put even the most caffeinated teacher to sleep. A senior has been skipping class again, and now I'm supposed to "make him understand the importance of responsibility." But here's the deal: if students haven't figured that out by seventeen, then no amount of "talking to" from the assistant principal is going to get them to that point. They don't care. I don't care. The school system's a broken record of punishing kids for things that no one's really sure how to fix.

And also, where the fuck is David? How did I get roped into this again?

Damn. Paisley's right. I *am* a grump.

Paisley. The thought of her makes my body tense. It's been almost a week since our encounter at Tumbleweed, and I feel bad for how I acted so coldly toward her. She's probably back to thinking I'm a total fucking dick, which I deserve.

Mrs. Gordon clears her throat next to me.

I throw a look her way. "Yeah. We've been here before," I mutter, tapping my pen against the table. "Another warning. If he doesn't shape up, we escalate. Eventually, it will lead to a truancy case in court. Then a fine or community service. Simple as that."

"Understood," she confirms, scribbling something down. Probably something super profound, like *Davenport is an asshole.*

She's not wrong.

We finish wrapping up the meeting right when the bell rings, and I stop in my office to grab my things before heading out for the day.

I'm driving north right after school today to check out that building I mentioned to Beth last weekend. Luckily, the place is only about thirty minutes away, and when I pull up to the place, I grin. It's old, like 70's nostalgia meets forgotten corner store old, but I can work with that.

I step out of my car and stand in front of the building for a moment. The windows are dusty, and the door looks like it hasn't been opened in years. I wouldn't doubt if that were the case. I've been living a half an hour from here for a decade, and I never even knew this building existed.

I shut my door and give it a longer look, trying to envision opening up the bar here. I close my eyes for a second and imagine the velvet curtains and vintage lamps before opening them again.

And you know how sometimes a place can make you feel like it's meant to be?

Yeah, this doesn't feel anything like that. But maybe I'm wrong. The posting online didn't have much besides the exterior, so I'm not exactly sure what to expect.

"You must be Briggs?" a quiet, mousy voice says from behind me.

I turn to find a woman, probably in her forties, who can't be more than five feet tall. She pushes her thick rimmed glasses up on her nose before extending a hand for me to shake.

I reach out and meet it. "Hi, Nancy, yeah. Thanks for meeting me."

"Oh, of course. I'm sorry we had to wait a few days. I was out of town and just got back yesterday. Shall we go inside?"

She unlocks the front door and ushers me into the open space on the other side of the threshold. The smell of stale air and dust smacks me right in the face, but this place has got character, I'll give it that. The floors are beautiful and appear to be original wood although they creak with every step I take. The windows are small—almost too small—and the layout is all wrong for what I had pictured in my mind.

I step further into the main room, my boots tapping against the worn hardwood. The floorboards groan under my weight, like they're protesting my presence.

Unlike the windows, the space is actually bigger than I expected—maybe too big to get that quaint, cozy feel I'm going for—and I don't feel the excitement I thought I would. I take a slow breath, the air heavy with dust.

I run my fingers along the counter. The surface is scratched and dented, and the counter's warped. All things that can be fixed, but all things that require a lot of time and money.

I feel like this place would be one of those home renovation shows where the host keeps saying, "It's got potential" while they tear down walls and throw money at the project, and you're like, *eh, kind of looks like a lost cause to me.* But instead of the Property Brothers, it's Nancy staring at me expectantly, and I try my best not to let my disappointment show. She gives me a few more minutes to look around, and I use this opportunity to pull out my phone and text Beth.

Checked out the place. It's not gonna work. Needs too much work and the vibe isn't right. I'll keep looking.

Straight to the point. No need to sugarcoat it. I'm sure she'll be happy to hear that, anyway.

After thanking Nancy for her time, I let her know I'll be in touch if I have any further questions, but I know I won't. This place is all wrong for what I had in mind.

My phone buzzes in my pocket with Beth's response.

Maybe it's just not meant to be?

The words sit on the screen, sharp and simple, and they sting more than they should. I let out a breath and shove my phone back into my front pocket. She probably means well, or maybe she doesn't. Either way, I'm not ready to deal with it right now.

What I am ready for is a drink and some time to think, and that's exactly where I'm headed.

PAISLEY

Our living room lights illuminate through our bay windows as I turn onto our road. When I pull into the driveway, the grass that hasn't been mowed in a few weeks and the cracked window in the downstairs living room that still hasn't been replaced tempts the sour mood I've been pushing down all day to return.

I put my car in park and sit for a minute, letting the silence wash over me. My drive home from school is a half an hour, and I didn't even turn on my radio today. I do that sometimes when I have a long, exhausting day—like when students are too loud and I leave feeling overstimulated.

But today wasn't loud. It wasn't even really a *bad* day. It was just *that* day. A day that comes back around every single year but that I still haven't grown used to.

Do people ever get "used" to grief? Or do they just learn to live with it?

I called my mom at the start of my drive to check in and see how she was doing. We didn't talk long; just long enough to make sure she was holding up okay. But after that, the rest of my drive was silent.

I stayed late at school to clean up and organize my classroom, not that it even needed it. It was mostly for a distraction, so I would have less downtime at home to sit in my thoughts.

But it didn't work.

It never does.

I hate how the grief still creeps in every year, no matter how much I try to push it down. And the worst part is that I don't even think Ethan remembers.

When he left for work this morning, he didn't even acknowledge the date, didn't even realize that something was off with me. Just kissed my cheek and left like any other Friday.

I've been telling myself all day that he's probably waiting for the right time to bring it up. But deep down, I know he won't.

It's not that I can really blame him. I don't talk much about it, so it's probably on me that he doesn't remember.

Sighing, I kill the engine and step out of my car into the cool evening air, my body already exhausted. Thank God I don't have a shift at Tumbleweed tonight. I don't have the energy to plaster on a smile and pretend I'm happy to be there. All I want to do is throw on some sweats, crawl into bed, and mindlessly watch trash TV.

Maybe Ethan will have dinner ready so I don't have to cook tonight, but I know the possibility of that is zero to none.

I open the door and, sure enough, find him lying on the couch playing video games. Cheeto and Sebastian come running over to me, meowing like they haven't seen a human in years. After one glance at the cat dish, it's clear he hasn't fed them, either.

"Hi, my babies," I say to them, reaching down and giving them each a scratch. "Are you hungry?"

They meow again in response, and I set my bags down and walk over to their food dish.

"Hey, Pais," Ethan says, not bothering to look away from the TV.

"Hey," I say emphatically. "How long have you been home?"

"A little over an hour, probably."

"And have you done anything productive since then?" I know I shouldn't be taking my aggression out on him, but my bad mood from today is still seeping through.

Ethan merely shrugs and continues playing his game.

"Babe," I say, more serious now. "I really need your help sometimes. It would be nice to be able to come home to a nice meal once in a while."

"Well then you better get cooking," he says with a laugh, obviously trying to make a joke.

It doesn't land well.

"I'm serious," I say. "You could cook once in a while, too, you know."

"But you're such a good cook. I would just ruin everything I try to make," he rebuttals, trying to pacify me. "Besides, my job is so grueling every day. The last thing I want to do is come home and cook."

I finish filling the cats' dish and take a long, deep breath, trying not to snap. "I know that, Ethan." I turn to face him. "But I work hard, too. I might not be doing manual labor all day, but teaching is just as exhausting."

He pauses his game and looks at me briefly. "I know. I'm sorry. I'll try to help out more, okay?"

Before I can even respond, he resumes his game and continues playing with no sign of getting up. Instead of pressing the issue further, I let it go. I know that at this point, anything I say will fall on deaf ears, anyway.

So, like always, I walk into the kitchen like I'm unbothered, pull the ground beef out of the fridge, and mindlessly begin making dinner.

We eat in tense silence, and it leaves me feeling even more exhausted, both mentally and physically.

I feel like I keep trying to fix something when I don't even know what part of it is broken. I know—I *think*—something feels off between us, but maybe this is how everyone feels after being together for so long? You always hear about the honeymoon phase and how after it fades, things change. I guess that could be true.

Call me crazy, but I always thought that if you were with the right person, that stage of the relationship would never end. I mean, yeah, things can get difficult at times, but I always hoped that kind of passion and fire would never dissipate. But maybe that's the difference between lust and love. Maybe this is just how things always are. How they're supposed to be.

After cleaning up the dishes, I shoot a text to Charlie and ask if she's up for meeting me at the bar. Forget about trash TV—what I need right now is a drink and some girl time.

She says she'll be there in fifteen minutes, so I grab my wallet and keys off the counter. Ethan has resumed playing his video game after dinner, but he hears the jingle of my keys and looks up.

"Where are you going?"

"Oh, Charlie asked if I could meet up with her for a bit," I lie. If he knows it was my idea, he'll get upset about it. "She got into a fight with John and just needs some girl time. I shouldn't be out too late, but don't feel like you have to wait up for me."

"Okay, well tell her I say hello. Drive safe."

I contemplate kissing him goodbye, but that's something we never do anymore, either.

Damn. How long *has* it been since we've even kissed each other?

I'm standing outside the door of Shooters when I get Charlie's text saying she can't make it.

Of fucking course she can't. Usually, Charlie is the one I can count on to lighten the mood when I'm feeling down, but she's *also* the friend I can count on flaking out of almost anything. Hate to love her, but I can't say I'm surprised.

Maybe I should get back into my car and go home. What kind of girl needs to go sit at a bar and drink alone?

This one does, my inner voice answers. What's the harm in one drink? If anything, it will give me some time to cool off before heading back, and maybe then Ethan and I can have another go at our conversation from earlier.

I open the door and scan the bar. Shooters is a classic dive, but I've always liked it here. The dim lighting offers a little privacy when I don't want to be bothered, and the bar itself is a long, polished wooden counter that runs along the right side of the room.

I walk through the bar and find an open stool near the end of the bar while "Dreams" by Fleetwood Mac spills out of the speakers. It only takes a minute or two before the bartender notices me, and the next thing I know, a gin and tonic is sitting right in front of me, condensation already dripping from the glass. I squeeze the lime into the liquid and lick the remaining juice from my fingertips.

With my first sip, my shoulders relax immediately. I know I'll need to sip it slowly since I'm driving, so I look around and take in the walls that are adorned with an eclectic mix of memorabilia—old concert posters, neon beer signs, random trinkets scattered everywhere.

After a few minutes, I sense a figure standing next to me and look over to see a man, probably mid-forties, take a seat on the stool beside me. He has slicked-back hair that glistens unnaturally under the bar lights, and his shirt is unbuttoned a little too far, revealing a tuft of curly chest hair and a gold chain that screams midlife crisis.

"What'cha drinkin', sweetheart?" he motions to me, looking past my glass and at my chest.

A chill creeps up my spine. Already with the pet names? Never a good sign. I'm not worried about him doing anything since we are literally in the middle of a busy bar, but you can never be too safe.

"Gin," I say curtly, hoping he catches the vibe that I'm not in the mood to socialize.

"Well, a girl like you is too pretty to be drinkin' all alone." He leans in closer than I prefer. "How about I buy your next round? We can get to know each other a little better?"

I shake my head, trying to offer a polite smile. "No, thanks. I'm good," I reply, turning my attention back in front of me.

"Aw, come on. It's one drink. Maybe a dance or two. What d'ya say?" He stands up from his chair, his arm outreached, inviting me to take his hand.

I sigh, my patience wearing thin. "I appreciate the offer, but really, I'm just here to relax. Alone."

I take a sip of my drink, hoping that will be the end of it, but he leans in again, undeterred by my rejection. What the fuck is with this guy? I'm not interested. Get the hint, dude.

"Come on, baby," he says, his voice dropping to a low, suggestive tone. "Don't be like that. Nobody likes a prude. I promise I know how to show a lady a good time. So how's about that dance?"

"She said she's not interested. I think it would be in your best interest to leave now," a firm voice says from behind me.

I turn to see Davenport, standing tall and glaring at the man, his hands tense at his sides.

"Hey, man, I was jus' talkin' to her," Sleazeball says, his hands raised with his palms out in a placating gesture. "No need to get all protective." The man grins slightly as if to mock him while his eyes travel down to the wedding band on Davenport's finger. "What are you, her husband or somethin'?"

Davenport steps closer, his tone low but unmistakably stern, with a seething intensity in his eyes like the one I saw at Tumbleweed last weekend. His jaw ticks as he inches toward the guy. With his height, he towers over Sleazeball and has to look down to speak. "I think she made it clear that she's not interested in talking. Leave. Her. Alone."

Sleazeball pouts slightly, clearly not used to his manhood being put on trial. Rolling his eyes, he addresses me. "Your loss, sweetheart. If you change your mind, you know where to find me." With a final wink, he backs off and heads to the other side of the bar.

I turn and look at my assistant principal standing before me. Jesus, talk about whiplash. How is this the same guy who basically tried to set me on fire with his glare at Tumbleweed? Because now he's going all protective mode like Jacob from *Twilight*.

My cheeks flush at the thought of it being *me* he wants to protect.

"Um, thanks... for that," I say, still recovering from Davenport's rollercoaster of personalities. "But I could have handled him on my own, you know."

"I have no doubt you could have. But you shouldn't have to," he remarks, his eyes softening.

"Well, thank you," I say again. His eyes are a darker shade of blue than normal, still filled with intensity, though they are no longer narrowed like they were only a minute ago.

"Don't mention it," he says, waving it off. "Have a good night, Paisley." He turns on his heel and starts to walk away. Without thinking, I grab his arm to stop him, and a zip of charged energy radiates between us so strongly my breath catches. I instantly retreat my hand like I've just been burned.

"Hey, wait. Where are you going?" I ask him, ignoring whatever the hell *that* just was. "Why don't you stay and have a drink here? No need to act like we don't know each other, especially with you being my knight in shining armor and all," I joke, a soft smile playing on my lips.

"Are you sure? You seemed pretty set in not wanting to be bothered," he comments, raising his eyebrows.

"Yeah, not bothered by Mr. I Use Too Much Grease In My Hair." I chuckle. "But I don't mind if you join me. I can't promise I'll be very talkative, though, so as long as you don't care that we sit in silence."

"I actually prefer it," he says, his face remaining serious as he takes a seat in the now vacant barstool next to me. He motions to the bartender, and he must come here often because suddenly there's a Captain Coke sitting in front of him without even having to ask. I laugh under my breath and take a sip of my drink, my eyes trained ahead of me.

"Something funny, Paisley?" he asks, and hearing him call me by my first name sends a jolt of butterflies through my body.

"You must come here often." I nod my head toward his drink.

His face registers what I am alluding to. "Not all that much, actually. The bartender is a buddy of mine. He knows what I like." He shrugs, taking a sip of the amber liquid.

"Got it," I say, directing my attention to the television in the corner of the bar. It's not actually on, but with nowhere else to look, I stare at it nonetheless and try to appear distracted. I search my brain for something else to say, *anything*, but all I can focus on is this weird magnetic pull between us.

"So," I finally manage to get out, "I gotta ask. Did I do something to piss you off last week? Because when I saw you at Tumbleweed last week, you acted like I just killed your dog."

He takes a sip of his drink and huffs out a breath, and I can't tell if it's more of a laugh or a sigh. "No. You didn't do anything."

I grab my drink off the bartop and glance at him out of the corner of my eye, not fully buying what he's selling. "Could've fooled me. I thought we were passed the whole grumpy scowling phase."

He runs a hand over his stubbled jaw. "I'm sorry. I was just dealing with some shit that day. Seeing you threw me a bit."

"Threw you? Looked more like you wanted to throw me. Directly into traffic." I smirk.

He laughs at that. "I could never. Traffic is too unpredictable. I'd have to think of something more guaranteed, like hurling you into the sun."

I bite my lip to hold back my smile. I much prefer this playful, witty version of Davenport than the one who looks like he's a minute away from ripping out his own eyeballs.

"I could never be so lucky. Could you imagine the tan I would get?"

He shakes his head, but I can tell he's amused. "So," he says more casually, "what *are* you doing here drinking alone, anyway? Not that I'm judging. Seems a little out of character for you is all."

"Oh? And what would be *in* character for me, Dr. Davenport?" I study him, our eyes locking for a brief moment.

"I don't know, reading books and baking bread? Wine days with your girlfriends? Cute little date nights with your husband?"

My stomach drops at the mention of Ethan, bringing attention back to the reason I'm here in the first place. He must sense the change in my mood because he shifts in his seat uncomfortably.

"Sorry, I didn't mean to—"

"Oh, no, don't worry about it. You're actually not that far off." I smile and try to lighten the mood again. "I do spend a good amount of time reading, but that's an easy one, considering I'm an English teacher. And yeah, I *do* like to bake in my free time, but that was a lucky guess. As for the wine..." I pause, thinking of a good reason for why I am so predictable. "Well, who doesn't like wine?"

Davenport chuckles. "Good point." He nods in approval. "But still doesn't explain why you're sitting at the bar all alone on a Friday night." He moves his mouth a little closer to my ear and lowers his voice slightly. "And by the way," he says, the heat of his breath on my neck causing goosebumps to erupt down my arms, "you know we're not at school, right? I think Dr. Davenport is a little formal for this environment, don't you?" He winks, and my *God*, does it do something to my stomach. I do my best to hide my reaction, hoping he doesn't notice.

"I could ask you the same question," I deadpan. "So tell me, *Briggs,*" I emphasize his first name, "what are *you* doing out all alone tonight? Did you run out of data reports to analyze?"

"You don't actually think I spend my time reading data charts for fun, right?"

"Well... do you?"

He pauses. "Not on Fridays," he says, a soft smile pulling at his lips. "But it's not unusual for me to stop and get a drink by myself. I like the time alone to think, and Shooters is a nice, dark atmosphere where I'm usually not bothered. Besides, they play good music here."

"That they do," I say, waving over the bartender for a refill. "I was supposed to meet Charlie here," I offer. "But she bailed on me right as I was walking in. I figured I would grab a drink before heading home so it wasn't a total waste of a drive."

The bartender sets my refilled drink down, and Briggs motions toward it. "Looks like that drink turned into two."

"What can I say? I'm enjoying the company." I knock my shoulder into his, and my face immediately burns. *God, why am I so awkward?*

Changing the subject, I quickly ask, "So what is it that you come here to think about, anyway?"

Briggs glances down at his drink, swirling the liquid thoughtfully. "Oh, you know, the usual existential stuff," he says with a hint of sarcasm. "Should I have taken a left turn at that stop light rather than a right? Did I miss my calling as a lumberjack? What if I actually peaked at seventeen and never even realized it?"

"See, I *knew* you were the brooding type."

He chuckles again, but it's a bit more subdued this time. "Maybe. But there's a lot you don't know about me, Paisley."

There he goes using my first name again. Why does that make my body tingly?

"Okay," I challenge. "Tell me something about you I don't know, then."

He pauses to think for a minute and stirs the ice in his drink. "I almost took a job out of state after grad school. I had spent my entire life in the Midwest, and the idea of living somewhere else excited me. I had the offer. My bags were packed. But the day I was supposed to leave, Beth couldn't stop crying. So I stayed." He says it matter-of-factly, his voice void of any emotion.

Unsure of what to say, I decide to share something about myself in return. "I miss sleeping in my childhood bedroom," I say softly, my solemn mood returning. "When I was eight, my brother painted a galaxy on the ceiling for me. It had planets and glow-in-the-dark stars and everything. It smelled like paint for weeks, but I loved it." I smile softly at the memory. "He was ten years older than me, so when he moved out for college, it still felt like I had a piece of him with me every night. But two years later, we had a house fire and were forced to move. I don't think I've slept that well since."

Briggs takes a sip of his drink and lets out a sigh before responding. "My best friend used to joke about how I never got tired," he says eventually. "He would always talk about how I was a big dreamer while he was the realist. During high school, we would stay up late playing video games and talking about the future. Where we would live, the lives we would build. He was certain I would get out of Wisconsin and start something new somewhere else. But life didn't quite turn out the way we imagined."

I nod in understanding. "I get that. I mean, I never thought I'd be sitting in a bar, talking to my assistant principal about life's disappointments on a Friday night. But here we are."

"Your assistant principal, huh? And here I was thinking we might actually be friends." He flashes a smile my way and then leans back in his chair, his gaze turning more distant. "You know, when I was younger, I had all these plans. I thought by now I'd have it all figured out, and everything would be perfect."

I want to ask more, to learn more about what isn't "perfect" in his life. From where I'm sitting, it looks like he *does* have it all figured out. Great job, great friends, great wife. But I don't want to pry.

"Tell me about it," I mutter sarcastically instead, taking a sip of my drink. "Sometimes I wonder if I made the right choices. If things could've been different, maybe better somehow."

He looks at me, his eyes softening. "Yeah, I wonder that, too. But I guess all we can do is keep moving forward and try to make the best of what we have."

There's a moment of silence between us before I respond. "Do we, though?"

Briggs turns and looks at me, subtle confusion crossing his features.

"Have to make the best of what we have, I mean. Why not make what we have better? Or even different?"

He nods slowly and wets his lips, his tongue dragging over the bottom one—and yep, my brain almost short-circuits. That *shouldn't* be hot. But now my face is on fire again, and I quickly take a sip of my drink to distract myself.

"Guess I've never considered that."

"I feel like I'm considering it a lot more lately."

He nods but doesn't say anything, and the words hang between us for a few minutes.

"So, tell me," he says, breaking the silence. "What's your biggest *what if*?"

I think for a moment, swirling the liquid in my glass with the straw. "Hmm, good question. I guess... what if I had taken more time to discover myself and figure out what I truly wanted in life before settling down? What if I had followed my heart instead of always trying to follow the status quo?"

He tips his head in agreement. "Yeah, that's a good one. And what is it you truly want?"

"See, that's the problem," I answer. "I'm not sure I know anymore." I pause, but he doesn't say anything in response. "What about you? What's *your* biggest *what if*?"

He takes a few seconds to answer. "What if I had prioritized my happiness over the happiness of others? Maybe if I had put myself first, things would be different."

I stare at him for a moment, analyzing his expression, trying to gauge what he's not saying. With a shrug, I respond, "Maybe they still can be. Different, I mean. It's never too late to put yourself first."

He sighs. "The same goes for you. It's never too late to change the narrative."

"Maybe you're right." I offer him a coy smile. "Well, I already overstayed my one drink, so I better get going." I reach for my wallet to grab a twenty, but Briggs moves his hand and stops me.

"Don't. I've got it."

"But that means I owe you two now."

"I'm looking forward to it."

Chapter Sixteen

♫ *"Wicked Game" — Chris Isaak* ♫

BRIGGS

Rusted gears and tarnished hands stare up at me from the Craftsmen workbench in my garage. A few days ago, Grandpa's old clock in our house stopped ticking, so I figured now would be a great time to get back into my old hobby. But the harder I've tried to focus on fixing it, the louder the thoughts I've been trying to drown out become.

I didn't plan on stopping at Shooters tonight. All I wanted was some time to clear my head and to consider if moving forward with this damn speakeasy idea is truly what I want. For a second, I thought about just driving by and heading home to talk it out with Beth, but when I saw the bar sign illuminating the sky, something urged me to go inside. Call it fate or instinct or just terrible fucking luck; either way, I yanked my keys out of the ignition and walked toward the door.

I just didn't know that waiting on the other side of that door was Paisley fucking Hamilton.

The sight of her caught me off guard. Again. Shooters is the last place I thought I would see her—but go figure that after successfully avoiding her all week at school after our little run-in at Tumbleweed that I happen into the same tiny dive bar as her. Maybe the universe is trying to tell me something.

Or just making me feel like a jackass. That's more likely.

Because when I noticed that guy leaning toward her with that smug-ass grin on his face, I don't know what came over me. His voice was low enough that I couldn't hear it across the room, but I didn't need to. I've learned over the past few weeks that Paisley's mood is pretty easy to read, and I recognized the look on her face immediately. It was the same one I've seen from teachers in parent meetings when they're humoring someone they don't want to deal with.

For a second, I thought maybe he was her husband. I mean, I've never actually met the guy, so for all I know, it could have been. He never comes to any staff outings with Paisley; she always shows up with Charlie and Leah instead. But when the man, who was obviously drunk based on his inability to stand without wobbling, leaned in close to her, I could somehow sense her body stiffen, like some kind of strange telepathy was happening between us. And before I could register what was happening, my hands curled into fists at my sides while the whole bar blurred in my peripheral, and suddenly I was hovering over the guy.

I shake off the memory and tighten my grip on the screwdriver, testing one of the screws anchoring the clock's motor.

It refuses to budge. If I keep cranking too hard, it'll strip the damn thing. My shoulders tense in frustration, and I toss the tool onto the bench, the clang of it ricocheting through the garage.

Goddamn it, this was supposed to help.

I lean back on the stool and run a hand through my hair while scanning the garage around me. It's filled with stuff I've harbored over the past twelve years we've lived here. Some of it I brought with me, some of it I've collected since. Trophies from sports growing up, vintage beer cans from antique shops, an old baseball cap collection I got from my grandpa. Antique license plates are scattered on the walls, and the vintage cooler I picked up at a flea market a few years ago sits under a sheet, untouched. Dreams and projects I told myself I'd get to someday, now just taking up space.

Damn, am I depressing or what?

I close my eyes, and an image of Paisley from earlier tonight comes into view, unwanted and uninvited. The way her big brown eyes stared up at me through her thick lashes. Her dark, chocolate hair, curled and cascading down her back. The wetness on her lips after she would take a drink from her gin and tonic. What those lips would look like wrapped around my—

No. I won't go there. I *can't* go there.

I try to shake the image of her from my mind, but it refuses to leave. Her smile. Her laugh. The softness to her voice. It's infuriating. It's magnetic. It's...

Wrong.

My eyes snap open, and guilt drags its claws down my chest. She's married. *I'm* married. And yet, when I think of her—when I picture those big doe eyes looking up at me—it feels like the first deep breath I've taken in years.

Fuck. What the hell is wrong with me?

My pulse pounds in my ears as I stand, pacing the small space as if I can outrun the thoughts chasing me.

This isn't who I am. I made vows. I've spent over a decade trying to be the kind of man—the kind of *husband*—Bethany deserves. Reliable. Predictable. Steady. *Faithful.*

But maybe that's the problem. Maybe I've been holding so still, so careful not to step out of line to live in this perfectly curated life she's built for us, that I forgot how it feels to actually *want* something. To want *more*.

But why does "more" have to look like Paisley fucking Hamilton?

"Fuck!"

I remove my glasses to rub my hands down my face in frustration. Because it's not just her. It's everything. Even my job—my steady, respectable job as Beth loves to remind me—feels like I would easily be replaced. I had hoped that eventually I would get to the point where I felt like I was doing what I was supposed to be doing, that I was where I'm supposed to be, but day after day is just one long stretch of beige.

And now, out of nowhere, after years of knowing her, Paisley comes into my life like a huge burst of color, impossible to ignore. How does that happen?

I need to get her out of my head. I need to forget the way she looked tonight. The way she made me *feel*.

I sink onto the cooler in the corner, my head in my hands. I sit there for what feels like hours, letting the guilt and longing wage war in my chest until I'm too tired to fight it anymore.

At some point, the garage door creaks open, and Bethany steps inside. She's wearing yoga pants and an old college sweatshirt, her hair pulled into a tight ponytail that doesn't have a single strand out of place. She looks at the mess on the workbench and sighs.

"Are you still messing with that thing?"

"Almost got it figured out," I lie, standing up to assess the damage. "What's up?"

She leans against the doorframe, arms crossed. "I was going to watch a show. You coming in?"

It's not an invitation so much as an expectation, and we both know it. I walk toward her, brushing a kiss against her cheek as I pass. She doesn't lean into it, and I try not to show my disappointment.

Inside, the living room feels colder than the garage, even though the fireplace is roaring. We sit on opposite ends of the couch, the silence broken only by the sound of some HGTV show Bethany picked. *House Hunters,* maybe? It's some young couple, probably in their early twenties, looking for their "forever home." I try to focus, but I can't ignore the distance between us, both physically and emotionally. It's a stark contrast from the magnetic pull I felt last night at the bar.

I slide closer to Bethany and place my arm behind her on the back of the couch. She doesn't acknowledge it, but she doesn't move away from it, either.

Maybe if I try to create a spark between Bethany and me, it will help re-center my attention on what matters. My marriage. My wife.

I slide in even closer to her and rest my hand on her knee, sliding it up the soft fabric of her leggings. She freezes for half a second before gently pulling my hand away.

"Not tonight," she says softly, her eyes trained on the TV screen. "I'm really tired."

I nod like it doesn't bother me, but it does.

"I think I'm going to go to bed," she murmurs a few minutes later, standing up and disappearing down the hallway before I even have a chance to say goodnight.

I sit on the couch a while longer, staring at the TV screen. None of this is Bethany's fault. She didn't ask for any of this—for me to feel like I'm sinking, to feel like I'm wasting my potential going through the motions, for me to be haunted by thoughts of someone else. But she doesn't even see it. She doesn't see *me*.

Or maybe she does, and she's just as good at pretending as I am.

After mindlessly watching yet another couple find their dream home, I trudge upstairs to bed. When I get into our room, Bethany is already asleep. I slide into bed next to her, but sleep evades me. I lie there staring at the ceiling, the silence heavy around me, and it doesn't take me long to realize why. Because when I close my eyes, it's not my wife I see.

It's *her*.

And that scares the hell out of me.

Chapter Seventeen

♫ *"I Wanna Dance With Somebody" — Whitney Houston* ♫

PAISLEY

I stroll into the media center Monday morning with an iced Apple Crisp Macchiato and an Americano in hand. There's no better way to start the week than with coffee that *actually* tastes good rather than the shitty K-cups we keep in the staff lounge.

I hand Charlie her drink and look around the library. It's newly decorated this school year, and it's such an upgrade compared to when I first started at Stonebrook. Rather than the rusty pink colored walls, they are now a soft gray, and Charlie replaced all the worn chairs with sleek, modern ones. In the back of the room, there's a gray couch sitting on a fluffy, white rug where students hang out throughout the day. She also ordered some of those Japanese style pillows—the ones used in lieu of chairs—that surround a coffee table. Definitely chic. And so definitely Charlie.

On the other side of the floor-to-ceiling window at the back of the room, the brown leaves lay scattered on the grass. We've been blessed with a warm fall this year, so even though Halloween is only a couple weeks away, we haven't gotten any snow yet. Instead, the sunshine glinting through the window warms my face and sparks an idea.

Either that, or it's the caffeine hitting my veins. I can't be too sure.

"Hey!" I say abruptly, startling Charlie. "You know what I've been thinking? We need to do something fun around here—something to get the students excited and out of their slump."

Charlie takes a sip of her coffee and eyes me suspiciously. "Like what?"

"Well, Halloween is only a couple weeks away, and you know I *love* the fall," I start calculating. "And you and I are both on the PBIS team, so we could plan something as some sort of incentive..." I trail off, my brain already thinking of a million possibilities.

"Oh, oh, oh!" Charlie interrupts. "What about... a Fall Ball?"

I snap my fingers and point at her. "Yes! We could deck out the gym with autumn colors. Orange, red, black, maybe even some green and purple for some Halloween vibes."

Adrenaline is already pumping through my body. I've always been the type of person who, when I get an idea, I *run* with it. Full steam ahead. Some might say I'm impulsive; I would say I'm passionate.

"I love it! And we can have a mix of classic but also modern fall decor. Some twinkling lights strung up everywhere, and—oh! A photo booth!"

"With cool props! Like some old school flannels, scarves, maybe some witch hats…"

"Yessss," Charlie nods enthusiastically. "What about the music? Maybe some classic fall hits and traditional Halloween songs? Throw in a few new ones to get the students pumped up, too?"

I nod rapidly. "This is going to be great. Maybe we could even have a costume contest! And a prize for best costume? Ooo! Or different categories! Like most creative, funniest, scariest…"

Charlie smiles. "I *love* that! And fall-themed snacks! Caramel apples, pumpkin spice *everything*, hot apple cider—"

"A hot chocolate bar! With marshmallows and chocolate syrup!"

We're definitely getting ahead of ourselves, but we have to find the fun in teaching somehow, right?

Charlie claps her hands together. "Eek! This is going to be so much fun, and the kids are going to love it. But…" she pauses, a thought clearly occurring to her.

I furrow my eyebrows at her change of tone. "What?"

"You know we're going to have to run all of this by Davenport first." And just like that, the simple mention of his name causes my stomach to cinch. Why does that keep happening? "I know he's usually on board with things that boost student morale, but you know how he is about safety and structure."

I sigh. She's right. Although David is the one who technically approves these kinds of events, Briggs is in charge of any and all student activities and is the one who organizes them. Plus, he's in charge of the budget for PBIS, so if we want to use the funds for that, he'll have to be on board.

I take a sip of my macchiato. "True. He'll probably want to make sure everything is in order before he gives us the go-ahead. But we have a solid plan! And we'll pitch it to him in a way that shows how great this will be for the students."

And he said himself that we're friends now, so...

Wait. *Are* we friends now? Or do I need to remain professional? I don't entirely know how to proceed from here.

I swear, no one ever taught me anything about being an adult.

"Yeah, okay." Charlie agrees. "I think once he hears how excited we are, and how excited the students will be, he'll see the value in it. Let's just hope he's in a good mood when we bring it up," she jokes, though there is a hint of nervousness in her tone.

I smile reassuringly at her, though my mind flashes back to the whiplash in his demeanor lately. "Don't worry. We'll get him to agree. This Fall Ball is happening."

"I think we should push it to November," Briggs says to us as we sit in his office after school. "I like the idea, but the end of the month is kind of pushing it, especially with budgeting and getting information out to students and parents. That way, it can be an end-of-trimester celebration in addition to a Fall Ball, and it'll give you guys more time to plan."

Charlie lets out an audible breath that I didn't know she was holding. "That will work. By then, the first trimester will be over, and it will give the students something to look forward to as we trudge through November."

"And it will still be fall, so we can still go with the autumn decor," I add, my nervousness finally leaving my body slightly.

We came in to pitch the idea about twenty minutes ago, and luckily Charlie has done most of the talking. Normally, I'm extremely confident in my position at the school—I lead entire PD presentations to the whole staff without faltering for Christ's sake—but lately, Briggs's presence has been throwing me off my game. It's ridiculous. I'm gregarious by nature, always quick with a witty comment, but whenever I'm in the same vicinity of him now, it's like my brain short-circuits. Words get stuck in my throat, and I wind up thinking about how his voice dips when he's serious or how his stupid Stonebrook Eagles t-shirt fits him perfectly in all the right places. It's annoyingly distracting.

"I suppose the costume contest would be a little irrelevant at that point, though." Charlie's voice pulls me out of my reverie.

"Probably for the best," he insists. "I've never liked encouraging students to dress up for Halloween."

And there's the brooding administrator I'm used to. I refrain from rolling my eyes.

"Trust me," he continues, "I love Halloween as much as the next guy, but when I did my internship during grad school in another district, we had multiple students show up in actual lingerie thinking it was appropriate. Those were some awkward conversations for the admin."

"You're lying," I say adamantly. There's no way students actually did that. Who would have the nerve?

"Wish I was. But believe me, some students give zero fucks."

Charlie's eyes widen, and she looks at me, speechless.

"Sorry," he interjects. "That wasn't exactly professional." He pauses. "But it *is* true." The corner of his mouth pulls into a smirk as he looks in my direction, and my damn stomach betrays me again.

I laugh awkwardly, shifting the conversation back to the ball. "Well, what about the other stuff? Are you okay with the autumn-themed snacks and hot cocoa bar?"

"That shouldn't be a problem," he says, slipping back into his usual role of assistant principal. "I'll have to run this by David and get full approval, but then we can talk logistics and start planning. Paisley, you have prep third period, right?"

"Right."

He knows when my prep is?

Duh, of course he does. He's the assistant principal. I'm sure he knows everybody's.

"Why?" I eye him curiously.

"Just so I know when to stop by your room if we have anything to discuss. I think we can use PBIS funds for this because it's connected to the end of the trimester, and since you both are on the PBIS team, that works out well."

"That's what we were thinking!" Charlie exclaims, but I'm barely paying attention anymore. I'm still far too distracted by how hot Briggs looks today. I watch his lips move as he mutters something to Charlie, and an unexpected sensation zips through me, even stronger than when I touched his arm at the bar.

"Paisley? Did you hear us?" Charlie nudges my shoulder.

"What's that?" I mumble, slightly overwhelmed by my body's reaction.

"Davenport said we need to get a proposal together so he and David can look it over."

"It doesn't need to be anything too specific," Briggs assures us. "Just a basic plan for the ball and a list of items we will have to purchase."

"Okay, we c-can do that, " I say, stuttering as I shift back to the present moment. "When do you need it?"

And why is there a lump in my throat keeping me from speaking?

"By the end of the week should be fine. That way we can make sure everything is ordered in time."

Charlie and I nod in confirmation, and after saying goodbye, we saunter out of his office and back toward the other wing of the school where my classroom is. Charlie is rambling beside me, already brainstorming ideas for what we need to include in the proposal, but I'm struggling to focus on her words. My thoughts keep drifting back to the moment I just had in Briggs's office.

The flutter in my stomach is gone now, thank God, but what the hell caused it in the first place? I'm sure it's mainly the adrenaline from pitching the idea and getting it approved. That's all. What else could it be?

I glance back down the corridor where Briggs's office is, as if somehow I will find the answer there.

"Paisley, you okay?" Charlie asks.

"Yeah, I'm good," I reply, shaking my head slightly and forcing a smile. "Just tired. I'm going to grab my things and head home. We can pick this up tomorrow?"

"Sounds good. Come see me on your prep!" she calls out, already heading the other direction.

I grab my things and push my way through the double doors to the back parking lot. But as the crisp fall air hits my face, I know I'm anything *but* good. I don't think I've been truly *good* for a while now. It's just taken me this long to realize it.

Chapter Eighteen

♫ *"Wonderwall" — Oasis* ♫

BRIGGS

I stop outside Paisley's classroom and take a deep breath. *Keep it professional, Davenport. Short and to the point. In and out.*

I knock lightly on the doorframe, peeking my head in, and see her hunched over her desk with her laptop open in front of her and a stack of essays at her side. Her hair is in a side braid today, and a short strand hangs in front of her face, tempting me to push it behind her ear. Her earrings, which are little pencils today, sway as she moves her head to read the paper in front of her. She's biting the end of her pen, ever so slightly, as if she's extremely concentrated on, or pained by, the essay she's reading.

I clear my throat as I step into the room, and she looks up, startled at first, but then breaks into a smile. It's bright and effortless, and probably her default, but it knocks the wind out of me slightly.

"Oh, look what the cat dragged in that the dog doesn't want," she says, and then her cheeks immediately turn crimson. "Oh my gosh, I'm sorry. That was rude." She shakes her head and buries her face in her hands. "I was just kidding. The dog would totally want you. I mean, why wouldn't it? You're—uh, never mind." She takes a deep breath to refocus herself as I try to bite back the laugh forming in my throat. "To what do I owe the honor, Dr. Davenport?"

I smile and hold up the manila folder in my hand like a peace offering. "Don't worry, I've never been a big fan of dogs anyway. But I'm here on business, I'm afraid. Sorry to disappoint."

"Boring." She rolls her eyes, mockingly, and pushes her chair back, stretching her legs out in front of her and coming to a stand. "You need the Fall Ball proposal, I'm guessing?"

"You would be correct," I confirm, dropping the folder onto her desk as she pushes her laptop aside. "Figured I'd save you a trip."

She turns around and bends over the smaller desk behind her, and goddamn it if my body doesn't react to the sight. Ruffling through a folder of papers, she pulls one out and turns back around to hand it to me.

"I think my brain melted a little putting this together."

I take the sheet from her and glance at it quickly, noticing the entire breakdown she has compiled for the dance. Chuckling slightly, I look up at her. "You and Charlie work fast."

"Yeah, well," she says, tucking that loose strand of hair behind her ear and smiling sheepishly. "We wanted to make sure we had time to smooth-talk you in case you tried to change your mind."

I lift the folder off the desk and place the paper inside, keeping it open. "That's what this is, huh? Smooth-talking?"

"Not my finest work," she says, her smile widening. "But you should see Charlie work a room. That girl could make *anyone* say yes to her."

I laugh, even though I don't agree. Charlie is attractive, sure, but she's definitely not my type. I think she comes off a little… abrasive? The polar opposite of Paisley. I was surprised when I learned they're such close friends, to be honest.

Whereas Charlie needs to be loud to command attention, Paisley has no problem doing that without even saying a word. Positive energy radiates from her, and I have no doubt she could work any room she steps into.

But for some reason, she doesn't seem to realize that.

I scan the proposal, zeroing in on the section titled *Vendors*, and change the subject. "Alright, so… decorations, table rentals, a DJ? Ambitious for a first-time dance that's only a few weeks away. Not sure if I'm more impressed or worried."

"Go big or go home," she shoots back. "We're asking for a little extra budget to make it happen." She bites her lip in what I assume is nervous anticipation.

I raise an eyebrow, half-skeptical. "Extra budget, huh? And what's your pitch for why I shouldn't shut that idea down immediately?" I cross my arms and look at her intimidatingly. I have no doubt most of these ideas will get approved, but I might as well have a little fun with her.

She leans forward, placing her hands on her desk. Instinctually, my eyes scan down to her chest. Her shirt isn't very low-cut, but at this angle, I can still slightly see her cleavage, and a familiar sensation builds in my groin. I shift on my feet and force myself to look up and meet her gaze instead.

"Be real, Briggs," she says, her face turning serious, and I inwardly smile at her use of my first name. "Our school morale sucks. You know it. I know it. The kids know it. We barely have any events to celebrate the students; our pep rallies are a joke and only praise the 'popular' kids. I mean, just look at our sporting events... the attendance was at an all-time low last year. The kids are bored and disengaged." She pauses for a moment, trying to collect her thoughts. "If we can give them something good, something that feels worthy of showing up for... I don't know." She shrugs. "Maybe they'll start buying into other things, too. Maybe it'll help them see the value in everything else we do here."

I hold her gaze a beat too long, and suddenly, it feels like she's pitched the idea to me, and I don't mean just the Fall Ball. I can literally *see* the passion for what she does in her eyes. Her passion for these kids. For actually making a difference in their lives, even if she knows it might be a lost cause. I shift my gaze and look down at the folder in my hands. *Professional, Briggs. Focus.*

"That's not a bad argument." I flip the page over. "But a *photo booth*? Really?"

"It's not as ridiculous as it sounds," she says, defending herself. "We can rent one for two hours, and students can take home those cheesy little strips. It's a cheap keepsake."

"Cheap being relative," I say, pointing to the price.

She sighs dramatically. "Look, if you want to be the person responsible for saying no to the one fun thing we put on the list, be my guest." A soft smile tugs at her lips. "Just know I will personally tell every student in the entire school that you hate joy."

"That won't look great on my evaluation," I deadpan, and she laughs. "But we have a budget we have to work with, and at the end of the day, David has the final say. So we can tell kids *he's* the killer of joy."

"Well," she says, moving closer to look at the proposal. As she does, her scent floats toward me, and I realize this is the closest we've ever been. Her smell is soft and warm, like coconut mixed with something else. Vanilla? It's subtle, but it lingers in the air, teasing me. "If you're vetoing the photo booth, at least leave the popcorn machine. Charlie's really excited about it."

I step away from her, putting some distance between us to help myself think straight. The smell of her is intoxicating. And distracting. And surely clouding my judgment.

"Alright. I'll consider the popcorn machine."

Her eyes widen, triumphant. "Really?"

"As long as you promise not to let Charlie turn it into a fire hazard. We don't need another homecoming fiasco."

"Those pizzas never even saw that fire coming." She grins. "I'll personally supervise the popcorn situation. Scout's honor," she promises and salutes me. Instantly, another blush of pink starts creeping up her neck, and it draws my attention to her chest yet again. I shoot my gaze back up and nod, closing the folder with a hard thud.

"I'll take a closer look at it this afternoon and run the numbers. If I have questions, I'll come find you."

"You know where I'll be," she says easily, though something that looks like excitement flickers in her expression.

"And really, this is impressive, Paisley. I'm not sure if you're told this enough, but you're an amazing teacher. The kids are lucky to have you."

The red in her cheeks deepens even further, and she bites her lip, which makes the sensation I felt earlier return. They are pink and full, much different from Beth's. I linger on the comparison for a millisecond, and then the thought makes my stomach tighten and I immediately hate myself for thinking it.

"Thank you," she says quietly. "That means a lot."

"You're welcome. And hey, this might actually turn out to be a good dance," I comment to break some of the growing tension between us.

Her lips twitch into a smile, and she rolls her eyes again. "Wow, don't be so enthusiastic about it, Briggs. You'll scare the kids away."

"We could only be so lucky," I say with a wink.

She groans dramatically. "Oh, whatever. Now get out of here before you change your mind about anything."

I smirk, lingering for just a second too long. *You're making this worse, Davenport.*

"See you later, Paisley."

"Later, boss," she calls, settling back into her chair at her desk as I walk out of her classroom.

Shoes are already squeaking on the floor as I step into the gym for basketball tryouts. On the first day, we typically start with warm-ups and conditioning drills to assess the players' fitness levels, and from there, we evaluate fundamental skills related to the game. Dribbling through cones, partner passing, layup lines, shooting exercises.

That's all we will get through today before moving onto scrimmages tomorrow, which lets us observe the players' teamwork, hustle, and ability to perform in live scenarios. The third day, we tell players where they stand. Luckily, Stonebrook is a D5 school, so we usually don't ever have to cut anybody, but we do have a varsity team, junior varsity team, and a C-squad. That way, students at least get to play the season, even if it's not necessarily on the team they were hoping for. I'm happy about that. Being assistant principal, I'm already the bad guy most of the time, and regardless of how much of an ass people might think I am, I'd hate to crush these kids' basketball dreams, too.

Once all the players are in the gym and Joe and I are prepared, we start running some drills. I blow my whistle, commanding everyone's attention. The gym is quiet with anticipation to start.

"Suicides. Half-court and back. If you're not tired after two, you're not running hard enough." The kids stare at me, as if they are waiting for further direction. "What are you waiting for? Get moving!"

They work their asses off for an hour, and by time we finish the conditioning drills, they are tired and out of breath. We take a short water break, and Joe sidles up next to me. He places his hands on his hips and tucks a clipboard under his arm while he observes the students chugging their waters. In my opinion, the dude always looks like he's trying a little too hard.

"Good group this year. I think we have some real contenders for varsity."

I nod and swipe the sweat from my neck. "Once they learn to pass, maybe," I say with a soft laugh.

Joe laughs in response and turns to me, changing the subject. "Hey, Carli said Beth's hosting the girls this weekend. I think she's already Pinteresting charcuterie boards and margarita recipes."

I raise an eyebrow. I had no idea Beth had any plans with the girls this weekend, much less at our place. Why didn't she tell me?

I force a small smile to hide my unease. "There always something going on with them," I say, the words sounding almost rehearsed.

Luckily, Joe doesn't sense the shift in my demeanor and continues by nudging me in the side, which almost feels like an actual jab. "Must be nice having a wife who's always putting stuff together. She's definitely a go-getter. You're a lucky man, Davenport."

"Yeah, that I am," I agree, but why doesn't it feel true?

The kids start shuffling around the gym again, re-energized from their water break, which shifts our focus back to them.

Thank God. I glance at Joe, who is watching with pure pride in his eyes.

"Man, this really is the life, isn't it? Coaching, teaching, being around these kids. Making a difference. Best job in the world. I don't know why anyone would want to do anything else."

My stomach tightens at his words. I do enjoy coaching the kids and getting away from the monotony of the other aspects of my job, but I don't totally agree. I've been realizing more and more lately that I *do* want to do something else. I want to open that damn cocktail bar. But, much like Beth, I doubt Joe would understand that. To him, our job is everything. And why throw that away for something so risky?

Joe slaps me on the shoulder and starts walking to center court. "Alright, here we go again! And hey," he calls back toward my direction, "tell Beth to save me a plate of that cheese Carli whips up, would ya? Doubt the wife will let me snag any beforehand." He winks.

"You got it," I say, another fake smile plastered across my face.

Tell *Beth*? Why doesn't Beth tell *me* anything? I stare down at the floor for a moment, but before I can ruminate on it too long, Joe's whistle forces my attention to shift. It's really not that big of a deal. Beth has had the girls over dozens of times before, and it's not like we usually tell each other everything. So why is it bothering me now?

The rest of the tryouts go by quickly, and before I know it, I'm jangling my key in the front door and pushing it open.

"Beth? I'm home."

I'm met with silence. I walk toward the kitchen, which is pure darkness except for the faint glow of the night light by the kitchen sink. I flip on the overhead light and glance around.

The dark walnut cabinets, the granite countertops, the hardwood floors—we chose all of this. When we moved in, there was a lot of work that needed to be done, but we couldn't beat the price, so we jumped at the opportunity to buy. There were a lot of aspects of the house that we loved but also some that we loathed, especially the once-white countertops that had aged into a dingy yellow and the linoleum floors that squeaked when you walked across certain areas.

Bethany had wanted to hire a contractor, but I insisted I could do it myself. And I did. I spent months working on it, primarily during the summer when I had the time. But those summer days turned into nights after school, and I spent many weekends sanding, painting, and laying the flooring. Every detail is exactly how I wanted it. Or at least how Bethany wanted it. At the time, I thought I agreed.

But as I stand here now, running my hand along the cool countertop, it feels almost... sterile? Like a showroom kitchen in an HGTV show, pretending to be more perfect than it actually is. There's no character. No *life*.

I shrug off my jacket and place it on the back of a stool before dropping my keys on the countertop. The sharp clink echoes through the space, and I notice a piece of paper lying on the counter covered in Beth's familiar handwriting.

Out with the girls. Don't wait up!

I place the note back down and walk toward the fridge. When I open it, it lets out a low creak, and I push past Tupperware containers and bottled water to find a beer in the back before walking into the living room.

I collapse onto the couch and let the weight of my body sink into it as I catch sight of the leather-bound notebook sitting on the coffee table. I pick it up and open it, looking at the writing scrawled on the page. *18th Amendment.*

I trace my finger over the ink, closing my eyes for a moment and allowing myself to daydream while I finish my beer. I imagine rows of glinting bottles behind the bar, backlit by the soft glow of Edison lights. A jazz musician is set up in the corner, playing live music for the customers who are huddled into velvet booths drinking specialty cocktails with clever names like The Midnight Principal or The Volstead. The vision feels so tangible I can almost smell the faint trace of bourbon and hear the quiet conversations of the crowd.

Then my phone buzzes in my pocket, and I'm brought back to reality. Closing the notebook slowly, I place it back on the table and check the message from Joe.

Great tryouts today! This is going to be OUR YEAR!

I begin to type a reply, but my fingers hesitate. Instead, I drop the phone on the cushion beside me and open the notebook again.

Chapter Nineteen

♫ *"Slow Dancing in a Burning Room" — John Mayer* ♫

PAISLEY

I wipe the sweat from my forehead and look around at my progress in my yard. I was able to dig up the majority of the pallets that were left from the previous owners, with the exception of one stubborn fucker that refused to budge from the weeds and packed dirt despite my best efforts.

Regardless, I'm pretty damn proud of what I've accomplished this morning. There was a lot of sweat, and even more swearing, along with an unfortunate amount of splinters, but for the first time in days, I was able to focus on something without my thoughts distracting me.

When we moved into this house, I imagined this flat area on our hilltop turning into a beautiful garden. But like a lot of things lately, that kept getting pushed off. Ethan kept promising we'd borrow his parents' four-wheeler to clear it out, but that day still hasn't come.

So I gave up on waiting. I threw on a sweatshirt, blasted some music through my headphones, and did what I could on my own. Turns out it served as some much needed self-care.

Ethan got home about forty-five minutes ago. He was off doing something with his dad on our land again, and when he pulled in and saw me sweating my ass off, I thought maybe he would offer to help.

But he didn't. Just gave a wave and went inside.

Typical.

Look, it's not that he's a bad guy. I know he loves me, and I know he appreciates me in his own way. But it's hard to feel appreciated when the to-do list never ends and is always mine to tackle. Between school, errands, bills, the cats, the laundry, the groceries, the meals, I'm so tired all the damn time. I figured if I handled the inside of the house, maybe he'd take care of the outside. But here I am, still doing it all.

When I get inside, the dishes are still in the sink where I left them this morning, and the laundry in our bedroom hasn't been touched. The sound of a movie playing on the basement TV floats up the stairs.

"Hey, Eth," I call down. "I am really struggling today and am stressed out about everything that needs to be done." I try to keep my voice level so the annoyance doesn't shine through.

"Okay, so why don't you take a break and relax a little?"

I steady my breath to keep my growing frustration at bay. "Because I want this stuff to get done so we don't have to worry about it tomorrow when we have to prepare to go back to work this week. I really could use some help," I answer.

Rather than a reply, his movie continues to play. He doesn't even bother to answer me, and I don't bother repeating myself. Instead, I head to the bathroom and step into the shower to get the dirt and debris off my body. I turn the water as hot as my skin will tolerate, watching the steam rise and fill the air as it surrounds me, The heat chases away the tension while I close my eyes and rest my forehead against the cool tile.

I finish my shower in a daze, skin tingling, my thoughts still heavy. There's still so much cleaning to do, but the yardwork and the shower has left me drained. A quick nap won't hurt, right? I can rest my eyes just long enough to get refreshed and set an alarm with plenty of time to finish what I planned to accomplish today.

Sliding under the covers, I allow the warmth to envelop me and let my eyes fall closed until my mind starts to drift, pulling me deeper.

When I open my eyes, I'm standing in the middle of a room, but it's not my room. I think I'm in Stonebrook High, but the scent of bourbon and something like mint fills the air while the golden glow from the afternoon sun peaks through the window.

I glance around and see a mahogany desk in front of me. I think I'm in the main office. But why?

I walk through the door and into the hallway. Overhead, the lights are dim, different from the usual fluorescent bulbs that flood the halls. I move quickly down the corridor, hoping to find someone to help me understand why I'm here.

What time is it, anyway? Why are there no clocks?

I turn the corner toward my classroom, and there he is. Waiting for me. He's wearing his usual work attire—an olive green sweater, navy chinos—and he's watching me with that damn smoldering look he always has. But something seems different here. His blue eyes are a little darker. More dangerous. It feels like I should be afraid, but I'm not.

I know he sees me, but he doesn't say anything. Instead, he continues to stare at me from down the long hallway in a way that feels too intense. His eyes bore into me like he can see right through me, and it makes me feel... exposed. Like he knows everything I'm thinking.

I take a step toward him, but my legs aren't moving right. It feels like there is lead in my shoes. The hallway is impossibly long, and the more I walk, the farther away he gets.

His lips curve into that little half-smile that drives me insane. He doesn't say anything, but I can feel the air thicken with tension. The space between us seems to stretch and compress simultaneously.

By the time I finally reach him, it feels like I've been walking for hours. I'm exhausted.

His hand lifts to push a lock of hair behind my ear, and his movements are slow and deliberate, like he's not sure if I'll flinch away from or lean into his touch. But I don't do either. I don't move at all. I can't. I'm stuck.

And then his fingers brush my face. Just a feather-light touch, but it's enough. Heat rises in me, a flush spreading down to my toes. His fingers linger on my skin, and my pulse skips. Fast. Erratic.

He leans in, his breath warm on my ear. "Paisley. What's going on?"

I open my mouth to speak, but nothing comes out. I feel like there's something I am supposed to tell him, but all I can focus on is how close he is, how warm his breath is, how good he smells. He's so close I can feel the heat of his body, and it makes my pulse quicken more.

Unable to respond, I look up at him. His eyes are dark. Wanting. Waiting. Like a predator hunting his prey. His fingers move down to caress my arm, and a bolt of electricity zips through me. He slides his hand down to my wrist and pulls me closer.

I know I should pull away, but I don't. I can't.

I'm still stuck.

He lowers his voice, barely above a whisper now. "Do you know what you're doing to me, Paisley?"

The words hit me like a jolt, stirring something deep inside. I don't know if I want to pull away or pull him closer.

His lips brush my neck, and my breath catches. He's so close. His other hand glides down my back, sending a shiver through me. I try to speak, but my voice is lost in the space between us, swallowed by the tension.

His lips brush my ear, soft and teasing, and it's like the world has narrowed down to only the two of us.

I lean in, ready to feel his lips on mine, to taste them, to consume them, when suddenly I'm pulled away. A sound, an echo, something that sounds like a school bell, cuts through the moment.

And in an instant, everything disappears.

Chapter Twenty

♫ "Witchcraft" — Frank Sinatra ♫

BRIGGS

"Before the month was over, the spell she cast over me was gone, and I never made that same mistake again." Paisley looks up at the ninth graders sitting in front of her as she reads the end of the text.

The story is about a teenage boy who has a crush on the girl who lives next door. One night, he gets the chance to take her on a date, and he sacrifices reeling in the biggest bass he's ever hooked to impress her. In the end, she isn't worth it, of course. Sheila Mant doesn't care about the fish. She doesn't even pay enough attention to know about it. She doesn't care about the boy, either. And by the end of the story, he knows it.

I sit at the back of Paisley's classroom, watching the students shift in their seats. As the assistant principal, part of my job is to observe teachers a few times a year. Even if we know they're damn good teachers—like Paisley—we still have to do it to check a box for the state.

When David told me I would be the one observing her this time around, my stomach instantly tightened. I wasn't sure it was a good idea, but how could I tell him that? To David and everyone else, Paisley and I are merely colleagues. Two people who have worked together for a few years and are barely friends. I'm the only one who knows it's becoming more than that.

"If the story revolves around the topic of sacrifice," Paisley says to the class as her eyes shift briefly in my direction, "then what is the author trying to tell us about that?"

The students turn and talk with one another before Paisley calls them back to discuss as a group.

One student raises his hand to share. "Um, well, I think the author is trying to say that love requires sacrifice."

"Are you sure?" Paisley challenges him.

"I think so..." he says hesitantly.

"Well, let's think about it this way," she says as she strides across the front of the classroom. Her floor-length skirt sways with each step. "If Wetherell wants us to believe that love requires sacrifice, wouldn't the boy have been happy in the end?"

"I guess so," the student answers.

"So then why does he regret his decision?"

Another student raises her hand to answer. "Because he realized that love wasn't worth it. Or that he was never truly in love in the first place."

"Precisely," Paisley says. "The boy doesn't just regret losing the fish; he regrets giving up a piece of himself. Something he *did* love. And for what? The fleeting approval of someone who never saw him in the first place?"

Many of the students nod in realization and begin scribbling words down in their notebooks. I'm still sitting in the back, a little mesmerized. I've seen Paisley teach before, and I've always known she's a fucking great teacher, but watching her now, it's different. The way she challenges students, the way she gets them to really think, the way she owns the room and holds the attention of almost every kid in here... it's impressive.

And really, really, fucking sexy.

As Paisley continues facilitating the discussion and asking kids to find evidence in the text, I think about the last line of the story. *I never made the same mistake again.*

Am I making a mistake? Am I sacrificing everything I've spent years building for something temporary? Are these feelings that I'm developing for Paisley a simple infatuation?

Maybe.

But it's not just about Paisley. It's not even entirely about Beth, either. It's about me. About the goals and dreams I've given up and forgotten about somewhere along the way. The sacrifices I've already made.

I've spent years sacrificing pieces of myself in the name of stability. And if I let these dreams slip away again, will I regret it?

Paisley finishes her lesson and reminds the students about their upcoming assessment on their independent reading books. When the bell rings, I say goodbye to a few of them and hang back until the rest are out of the classroom.

When the last student walks out of the door, Paisley swivels around to face me.

"Enjoy the show?" she teases, her smile bright and warm. It causes the tension in my shoulders to soften a little.

"You put on quite the performance, Hamilton," I say with all the seriousness I can muster.

She smiles even wider. "Good to know at least one member of my audience was captivated," she quips, walking over to her desk and organizing a few of the papers from class into folders. "What did you think of the story? Did you like it? Or am I boring the youth of America to death?"

I shrug. "I think you've got 'em hooked. Pun intended." I wink. "It's a good story."

She looks up at me. "It's one of my favorites to teach. I think the message is so deep. Timeless. The idea of giving up a piece of yourself for something—or someone—you think you want..."

Her gaze meets mine, and her words hang in the air between us.

"Yeah. It kind of makes you wonder what you would have done in that situation, I suppose."

Paisley tilts her head, studying me. "Do you think he made the wrong choice?"

I shift my weight and glance down at my feet. "I think the fish mattered more than the girl ever could."

She chuckles, but it's hollow. "I agree. But it's easy to say that when you're not the one making the choice in the moment. Hindsight's twenty-twenty, right?"

"True," I admit, looking back up at her. "And I guess sometimes the risk might be worth taking."

At that, she smiles genuinely. "Won't know until you try. But anyway, I'm assuming you're sticking around so we can hash out some details for the ball?"

"You'd be correct," I confirm, moving closer as she searches for a clipboard on her desk.

"Let's start with the playlist," she says excitedly.

And then we spend the next thirty minutes planning for everything we can think of. I approve the music playlist a PBIS student had emailed her (after taking a few of the extremely explicit songs off the list), we make sure we have all the decorations we need, and we argue over the necessity of having a balloon arch. By the time we're done, she's laughing at my insistence that no one, absolutely no one, under the age of eighteen cares about themed centerpieces.

"You underestimate what teenage girls care about," she tells me, placing the clipboard back on her desk. "But I'll take your word for it."

"Good. You should," I say with a grin.

She tosses her pen down next to the clipboard with a dramatic sigh. "Okay, my brain is officially fried. Let's take a break."

I glance at the clock. "But we're almost done."

"Yeah, but where's the fun in that?" She hops onto the edge of her desk, swinging her legs. "Let's play a game. Rapid-fire questions. No overthinking. No judgment. You in?"

I chuckle, shaking my head. "You're ridiculous, you know that?"

"I'll take that as a yes."

"Fine. Go ahead."

She grins. "Okay. Favorite movie?"

"*Grumpy Old Men.*"

"Ironic," she teases. "Mine's *The Hangover.*"

That answer pleasantly surprises me. I didn't take her as one to have such a raunchy sense of humor.

"Favorite holiday?" she continues.

"Halloween," I say without a second thought.

"Even with the worry of students showing up in lingerie?"

I nod. "I can get past that. It's the best day of the year."

"I can't fault you for that," she says. "Halloween was my brother's favorite holiday. We always went all out for it." A flash of something crosses her face that I can't quite discern. Sadness, maybe? But I don't focus on it too hard.

"Worst costume you've ever had?" I ask her.

"Oh, God. I don't want to say. It's extremely embarrassing," she says, biting her lip like I've noticed she does when she gets nervous.

"Well, now you have to tell me."

"You can't tell anyone."

"Scout's honor."

"Okay, when I was in like... eighth grade, maybe? My friend Elizabeth and I decided we were 'too old' to dress up, so we didn't get any costumes. But when the night came around, we realized we really wanted to go trick or treating, so we had to find something in our houses to wear."

"What, did you have to wear an old costume that was too small, or?"

"Just, shh." She waves me off. "Let me tell the story."

I put my hands up in surrender. "Okay, okay. I'll be quiet."

"Thank you," she says, a huge smile spreading across her face. "So, I didn't have *anything* to wear. All I could find was this hideous striped shirt hanging in my closet."

"Let me guess," I interrupt, "you went as Fred—"

"Briggs!" she orders, but she's giggling.

"Shit. Sorry. Continue."

"So I put on the striped shirt and shoved a pillow on my back under the shirt so I could be... a snail. A fucking *snail*. Then I took this bright, shimmery blue eyeshadow and painted my entire face with it. It was *hideous*. And the worst part was that all night, everyone thought I was a hunchback."

I try to contain myself, but I burst out laughing at the thought of a young Paisley walking around town dressed like a fucking mollusc.

"Hey! We agreed on no judgment!" she says, swatting my arm. Then more sheepishly she adds, "And I told you it was embarrassing."

"Oh, no, not at all. I actually think that's kind of adorable." A hint of pink flushes her cheeks. "Besides, as a huge Halloween buff, I could never fault someone for celebrating the holiday, no matter how ridiculous they may look."

She laughs and waves me off. "Okay, my turn. Biggest fear?"

I hesitate. "Failure."

Her expression softens slightly, but she keeps her tone light. "Elaborate."

"Later," I say, deflecting. "Your turn."

"Being stuck," she admits, her tone quieter. "Or always wondering if good is really good enough."

We lock eyes for a moment, and a look of understanding passes between us.

"Okay, lighter topic," she says quickly, breaking the tension. "If you could only eat one food for the rest of your life, what would—"

"Pizza. Easy."

"Predictable."

"Delicious."

She laughs, and it's such a genuine sound, I can't help but smile. "Touché. Your turn."

"Favorite snack?"

"Definitely salt and vinegar kettle chips."

"Really?"

"Really. They're amazing."

"Never had 'em."

"Well, you're missing out. I'm also a granola bar *fiend*. I have a whole drawer of them."

"Good to know."

"Yours?"

"Chex Mix."

"Honorable choice."

"All right," I say, leaning back onto a desk and crossing my arms. "Hendricks, Sawyer, Jacobson. Fuck one, marry one, kill one. Go." A slight smile pulls at my lips knowing I'm testing the line of appropriateness.

Her eyes snap to mine in disbelief. "W-what?"

I arch a brow. "Come on, Hamilton. You're telling me you've never sat in a faculty meeting and considered who would be the best in bed?" The incredulous look on her face makes me grin wider, so I keep going, fully leaning into it. "Sure, Hendricks has probably been teaching math here since before the prohibition, but that mustache could sure give someone a ride. And maybe Jacobson's sex drive disappeared forty years ago, but I bet he makes a hell of a meatloaf..."

She finally bursts out laughing, shaking her head like she can't believe this conversation is happening. "Good Lord," she mutters, more to herself than to me, but I can tell she's entertained. "How dare you forget about Mr. Sawyer? You know that man probably has all kinds of stories to share from the Great Depression. I bet he could even put Hemingway to shame."

"You're probably right. But you're avoiding the question." I wink at her again.

She rolls her eyes but finally plays along. "Fine. I'd marry Sawyer. He's seen it all—wars, economic downfalls. Shit, he probably even has a bunker somewhere for a future apocalypse. That kind of experience and expertise could come in handy."

"Solid choice. And?"

"Adios, Hendricks," she continues, clearly trying to hide her smile. "Only because I can't spend the rest of my life wondering what he might be hiding in that mustache."

That coerces a genuine laugh out of me. "Fair point. So that leaves..."

"Jacobson. Fuck him, obviously," she says, smirking. "The man probably has a stash of little blue pills in his pocket. And since he teaches culinary, I assume he could spoil me with lots of snacks afterward. I might be young, Davenport, but I'm not an idiot."

Something about the way she delivers her answer, so confident and unfiltered, sends a jolt of heat straight through me. "Wise choices, Hamilton. But poor Hendricks," I say, shaking my head. "Guy never stood a chance."

"Oh yeah, a real tragedy," she deadpans. "Okay, your turn."

I wave her on. "Give me your best shot. And don't hold back. I like a challenge."

"Charlie, Miranda, Leah. Go."

I groan, running a hand over my face. Should've seen that coming. "Damn. You're ruthless."

She shrugs, taking a sip of her coffee. "You said you like a challenge."

"Alright. But this stays between us. Got it?"

"I'll take it to my grave." She crosses her heart with her finger.

"Kill Miranda. Not really my type."

She gasps mockingly. "Damn, that was fast. You've thought about this before."

I ignore her comment. "Marry Leah. She has the personality I would get along with best, I think."

"So that leaves…"

"Charlie. Probably too wild for me to handle long-term, but…" I glance at her, letting a smirk play at my lips. "The students don't call her 'Ms. Moody with the Booty' for nothing."

Her mouth drops open. "You've checked out her ass?!"

"Oh, come on. I *am* a man, Paisley. And it's not exactly like she's trying to hide it. How could I not?"

A flicker of curiosity crosses her expression, like she's wondering if Charlie is the type of woman I'm attracted to, so I step closer to her. "Don't worry. She's not really my type."

She tilts her head at that. "Oh? And what exactly *is* your type, Dr. Davenport?"

I hesitate for half a second, my gaze deliberately sweeping down her body before meeting her eyes again. "I like more of a girl-next-door-vibe."

She snorts, shaking her head subtly. "Got it. So you want someone who brings you a lasagna when you move in but then secretly drinks all your beer while you're at work?"

"Precisely."

"Then I'm surprised you ended up with Bethany." Her hand shoots up to cover her mouth. "Oh my God. I'm sorry. I shouldn't have said that."

I let out a breath of amusement. "Don't worry about it. That's a fair assessment."

It's actually something I've been wondering myself these days. Why did I end up with Beth when she was never really what I wanted?

I take a step back again and sit on top of a nearby desk. "Beth is actually the opposite of who I thought I'd end up with."

"So how *did* you end up with her?"

I answer honestly. "We met in grad school and were friends for a really long time. We had a lot in common, given we both were getting our doctorate degrees, so we spent a lot of time together. The day came where I felt like I needed to take the next step in my life, and it felt natural to do it with her."

She nods, her expression softening. "I get it. Something similar happened with Ethan and me."

I eye her curiously. "Yeah?"

"Yeah. Although I'm not sure we even really had much in common when we were in college." She laughs, but it sounds empty. "He was fun to be around and made me feel comfortable. We got along well. Things were easy between us. But I wouldn't say our goals or values have ever really aligned."

My chest tightens slightly in familiarity. "But you married him anyway," I say quietly.

She shrugs. "I did. And things are good. Isn't that all people ask for?"

"I'm starting to ask myself that same question," I murmur. But before she can press, I change the subject. "Next question. If you weren't a teacher, what would you be?"

Her body language shifts and becomes more relaxed. "Oh, that's a simple one. Travel writer. I'd go to all the places I've always dreamed about going and write terrible, overly romanticized blogs about them. Not sure if that would make me any money, but I would figure it out."

"That actually suits you."

"I think so." She smiles. "I always thought it would be fun to travel the world and work odd-jobs at each place I visited. Maybe stay in each location for a couple weeks, exploring and working, then hop on a plane or train to the next one."

"That sounds amazing, actually."

"Yeah. I read a book about it once." She shrugs. "If only I didn't hate flying."

I laugh. "That *is* problematic."

"I could get over it, I bet. But okay, what about you? If you weren't an assistant principal, what would you do?"

"I... I don't know. Lately, I've been thinking more and more about that bar idea."

"18th Amendment?" she asks, excitedly.

"Yeah, that's the one."

"So you're serious about it then? You've thought more about it?"

"More than I should, probably," I admit.

Her eyes light up. "Briggs! That's so exciting! Tell me more!"

I shrug, feeling oddly self-conscious for the first time in, well, forever. "Um, it would be almost like something out of a vampire movie. Dark, moody. Wall sconces. Lots of wood. The smell of mahogany and tobacco all around. A mysterious lady in red in the corner, singing. A place people could go to lay low, unwind. A place people would feel like they belong."

"I love that," she says dreamily. "You should totally do it."

"It's not that simple," I say, shaking my head.

"Why not?" she challenges. "Big risks, big rewards, right? Aren't you the one who said sometimes the risk could be worth it?"

Damn. She's good.

"Maybe," I say finally.

She grins. "Let me know if you need help. I'll keep an eye out for spaces."

"Thank you."

"Anytime," she says, hopping off the desk and grabbing her mug. "And hey, don't think this lets you off the hook for helping with balloon arches."

I laugh, shaking my head. "We'll see."

But I know she's right. I'll do whatever it takes to help this dance succeed—because at this point, I'll find any excuse to be spend more time with Paisley Hamilton.

Chapter Twenty-One

♫ *"Collide" — Howie Day* ♫

PAISLEY

The school is eerily quiet as I sit alone in my classroom, the only sound a faint hum coming from the lamp on my desk. I almost never have my overhead lights on; the bright fluorescents trigger my migraines, and studies have actually shown that lighting can affect students' concentration and learning. With teaching ninth graders, I will do literally anything short of selling one of my kidneys to dull down their squirrely behavior, and the warm glow from the lamps definitely helps. Most days at least. We're awfully close to the end of the trimester and the Fall Ball is quickly approaching, so the kids are getting stir-crazy.

Typically, I refuse to stay after school to work. Teachers put in enough time on things as it is, and if I can't get it done during my contract hours, then it can wait until tomorrow. Unfortunately, though, the end of the trimester is next Friday. My prep hours this week and next have been commandeered by meetings, and this stack of essays isn't going to grade itself, no matter how many stars I wish upon.

Sometimes I actually like grading essays, especially if they are written by the upperclassmen in my Honors English course. But, alas, freshmen aren't up to Fitzgerald's level quite yet.

It doesn't help that all forty-three essays are on the same topic: analyzing the development of a character from *Lord of the Flies*. Yawn. Who assigned this book anyway? Fucking Past Paisley out to get me again.

The clock ticks loudly, and I look up to see it's already 4:22. Damn, time goes by quickly when I'm in the throes of teenage angst and run-on sentences.

I stretch my arms above my head. At this hour, caffeine probably isn't the best idea, but a cup of coffee might help me power through a few more papers before heading home to the bath that awaits me.

As I stand up to head to the staff lounge, the next essay up to grade catches my eye: Power and Fear in *Lord of the Flies*.

Maybe there was a reason I had the students read this book after all. Life really *is* like what those kids in the novel faced on that island, isn't it? Sure, our situations aren't literally life or death like theirs, but damn, sometimes it feels like it is.

Life is full of unexpected turns, and even though we're not stranded, sometimes it seems like we are all just trying to simply *survive.* The pressures of society, the expectations, the fear of failure—it's just as intense as the boys' fight for dominance and safety on that island.

The only difference is that we can decide to change our path and get ourselves out. So why do most of us choose to stay stuck instead?

Is that what I'm doing? Staying stuck? Settling?

I shake my head. That's far too serious of a thought for right now, so I peel my ass off my chair and grab my lanyard off my desk.

Once I get to the staff lounge, I push the door open with one hand and am met with a heavy thud.

"Oh my God, I'm so sorry!" I shout out as I carefully ease the door open the rest of the way and reveal the solid form I bumped into.

Who would be here this late?

I step into the lounge, and papers are scattered across the floor—and, as the universe would have it, Briggs is squatting down to pick them up. He's dressed sharply in gray slacks paired with a black long sleeve that complements his dark hair and olive skin. His stubble is the perfect amount of well-maintained mixed with ruggedness, and he looks hot as hell. Figures.

Suddenly, the dream I had the other day flashes in my mind— the one where he was looking at me like he wanted to fucking devour me and was brushing his lips across my skin. I hadn't ever let myself think about him that way before, but ever since that damn dream, I can't seem to *un-think* it.

His steel blue eyes meet mine, and damn, they are *striking*. He looks momentarily surprised, but I think I see his irritation dissipate when he realizes it was me who body slammed him with the door.

"Don't worry about it," he says, still gathering papers from the floor. "I guess I should have moved out of the way for the door." A playful smile tugs at his lips.

I smile in return and kneel down to help him. "Seriously, it's my fault. I came blasting through here like a woman on a mission." I pause. "But to be fair, I kind of was. Caffeine was calling."

"Caffeine? At this hour? Sounds like you have a long night ahead of you. What are you doing here, anyway?"

"Oh, I'm sorry, Dr. Davenport." I press a hand to my chest, feigning offense. "Am I not allowed to stay in my classroom to work after school?"

"You're definitely allowed. I'm just not sure why you'd want to." He chuckles, shaking his head slightly as he begins to stand.

I extend my arm out to hand him the papers I've gathered, and he grabs them and adds them to his stack. "I'm trying to get caught up on grading. End of tri grades are due soon, and I'm losing all my preps this week to meetings. One of those being another meeting with you to finalize details of the dance," I tease playfully. "Life of a teacher. What about you?"

"I get it. I don't envy any teachers, especially ones who have to grade all those essays you do." He's holding the stack of papers in one hand, and he uses the other to comb his fingers through his hair. "I actually should be at basketball practice, but we have benchmark testing coming up next month, and I need to get some things in order, so Joe agreed to run practice while I got some paperwork squared away for that. If I wait to do it during the school day, something always comes up, and I don't end up getting to it. Life of an assistant principal." He smiles as he mocks my earlier statement. "It's easier to do it when no one is here and there are no distractions." He takes a second and looks me up and down. It's brief, but I catch it. "At least not many, that is."

"Yeah, I know what you mean," I reply, suddenly nervous. Why am I blushing *again*? This guy is going to start thinking I have a freaking skin condition. "I don't normally stay late, but I have a stack of essays a mile high, so duty calls." I shrug and walk toward the Keurig by the fridge. Reaching into the drawer below it, I pull out a caramel coffee K-cup and put it into the machine. I grab a red mug with the words *Stonebrook Eagles* etched into it from the cabinet and set it under the drip spout. Remembering Briggs is still in the room staring at me, I ask, "Want any?"

He shakes his head. "Nah, I've hit my quota for the day on caffeine. But thanks." He pauses. "So... I should get back to my office. Have a good night, Paisley."

"You too," I say, but he's already gone.

When I open the door to the parking lot, I'm hit with the cool evening air. It's refreshing after being stuck inside the school for almost twelve hours straight. The soft, fading daylight is blending into an evening hue of cool blue and soft gray, and the last hint of sunlight is dipping below the horizon. It's nights like this, the picturesque, quintessential autumn evenings, that remind me why I love living in Wisconsin. Someone needs to remind me of that in a few weeks when mounds of snow cover the ground.

I toss my bag in the back of my SUV and settle into the driver's seat. The fading sunlight filters through the windshield, casting long shadows inside the car. I turn the key in the ignition, but the only sound is a series of clicks. The dashboard stays dark, and the engine refuses to start.

"No, no, no," I whisper to myself. "You have got to be fucking kidding me."

I glance at the dashboard and attempt to fumble around with some settings, only to notice the headlights are still switched on. My heart plummets, and I slump into my seat as I realize I must have left them on all day. The battery is completely dead.

With a resigned sigh, I pull out my phone and try to call Ethan, but his voicemail greets me instead. He sends a text immediately following my call telling me he's still at work and can't answer.

I stare at the message, and a tightness blooms in my chest. I knew there was a possibility he was still at work, so it's not like I expected him to come rescue me, yet irritation still threatens to rise.

Great. Just fucking great. I sit for a minute in the dwindling daylight contemplating my next move. I knew I should have paid for AAA. My parents and sister live too far away. I could call a friend from school, but it's right around dinner time, and I would hate to interrupt, especially because they all have kids to wrangle.

Then it hits me—I still have the staff phone list from the beginning of the year. It's a small school with less than thirty staff members, and I remember that everyone's number was included. I quickly grab my phone from my bag and log into my school account, pulling up the file. I scan the list, searching for the name of the last person I thought I would call, hoping he might still be inside the building.

I dial Briggs's number, and while it rings on the other side of the line, I realize I'm holding my breath. Why didn't I call his school number to get a hold of him?

I guess this way, if he's not in his office, he might still answer? Unless he never picks up numbers he doesn't know. Then I have no idea what I'd do. Or what if he already left the school and I'm calling him while he's at home? This was a terrible id—

"Hello?" A voice on the other end answers, low and warm and unmistakably his.

Shit. He picked up. I freeze, completely unprepared despite having just played this scenario out in my head. "Oh, uh, hi," I stammer. "Briggs?"

"Yeah, Briggs here. And this is...?"

"Oh, crap—yeah, that would probably be helpful information." I let out a soft, idiotic laugh. "Um, it's Paisley. I'm so sorry to bother you. I'm wondering if you could do me a favor?"

Chapter Twenty-Two

♫ *"In Too Deep" — Sum 41* ♫

BRIGGS

An unknown number lights up the screen of my phone in the passenger seat as I turn down the road to my house. With all the spam calls I get, I typically don't answer calls from numbers I don't know, but something urges me to pick up, so against my better judgment, I do.

"Hello?"

There's a pause on the other end—too long to be one of those damn telemarketers—before a familiar voice speaks. "Oh, uh, hi... Briggs?"

I recognize her voice immediately. I straighten slightly in my seat as my pulse quickens. I'm surprised she's calling me, though not entirely displeased.

"Yeah, Briggs here." I try to sound as casual as I can. "And this is?"

There's another pause, followed by that soft laugh I've been trying not to think about all fucking week. Earlier tonight, in the staff lounge, I felt that same magnetic pull I've experienced every time I'm in the same vicinity as her lately. And as she was getting her coffee, I noticed things I knew I shouldn't, like the way her shirt slightly lifted as she reached into the cupboard for a mug or the way her hair fell when she leaned toward the Keurig. And that smile when she turned and offered me a cup... it almost made my guard slip for a half a second. In that moment, I knew I had to get the hell out of there—because I realized for the first time ever that I couldn't trust myself to be alone with her.

"Oh, crap—yeah, that would probably be helpful information." My lips turn up at how flustered she sounds, despite my best efforts to stay neutral. "Um, it's Paisley. I'm so sorry to bother you. I'm wondering if you could do me a favor?" She sounds even more bashful than she did a second ago, and it's kind of endearing.

"Paisley?" I repeat, not because I don't believe it's her, but because I need to give myself a second to get my fucking thoughts straight. "Sure, what's going on?"

"Uh, this is really embarrassing..." She pauses. "But I apparently left my headlights on this morning, and now my car won't start. I think my battery is dead."

"Is it turning over at all? Like any lights on when you turn the key? Or is everything dead?"

"It doesn't do anything when I turn the key. Just clicks. I'm hoping it's only the battery and not something more serious. I'm not really good at this stuff, I guess," she explains, sounding a little sheepish.

"Okay. Do you have jumper cables?"

"Yeah, I have some in the back that I keep just in case. I guess that doesn't really help me when I don't have another car here to help me out, though, huh?" She laughs nervously.

I can tell she feels slightly uncomfortable calling me for help, which begs the question of why it was *me* she called. Doesn't she have a husband who should have noticed she wasn't home yet?

As if reading my mind, she continues. "I tried calling Ethan, but he's still at work, and it would take him a while to get here. I was hoping you were still at the school and would be able to come to the back parking lot to help me before you head home. Unless you've already left?" Her voice is laced with a tinge of desperation.

I could tell her the truth, which is that I left about ten minutes ago and am only five minutes from my house, but I don't want to leave her all alone in the parking lot when it's going to be dark soon. And if I told her the truth, I know she would tell me I don't have to come.

Yeah, that's not happening.

"Oh, that makes sense. I'm actually just... finishing something up in my office and was going to head out once I was done," I lie. "I can be out there in about ten minutes. You said you're in the back parking lot?"

"Yes! Thank you so much!" she squeals.

Once we hang up, I pull my car over and shoot a quick text to Bethany letting her know I'll be home a little later than planned. Then I turn my car around and drive back to the school.

"You're a *lifesaver*," Paisley tells me as I'm peering into the hood of her car. It seems like it's only the battery, which I'm thankful for. I'm pretty handy with vehicles, thanks to my dad making sure I was prepared for the real world as I was growing up, but I'm still no mechanic. "I'm glad you were still here when I called. I'm so sorry to bother you with this."

"Don't worry about it," I reassure her. "Would you mind grabbing the jumper cables from your trunk?"

"Oh, yeah, duh." She laughs and rolls her eyes at herself. "Those would be helpful."

As she walks to the back of her Kia, I hop into my Dodge Charger and pop the hood. The sun is setting rapidly, so I'm glad she didn't have to sit here waiting for Ethan alone in the dark.

"You know, I do know how to jump a car," she says with a little sass in her voice as she hands me the jumper cables. "I'm not *that* helpless. I just didn't have a spare vehicle lying around tonight."

"Oh, is that right?" I smirk.

"Yes, it is right! I learned how when I was in high school. It's kind of cheesy, but... I just remember that black is a dark color, and when we are in a dark place, we tend to be negative." She shrugs her shoulders. "Ergo, the black cable goes on the negative, and that leaves the red for the positive."

"A mnemonic device, huh? I can definitely tell you're a teacher," I say. It comes out a little mockingly, but I don't intend for it to.

Chuckling, she nods. "Oh, definitely. You should know all about that, though, Mr. Psychologist," she teases. "Or, should I say *doctor?*"

With a slight laugh and shake of my head, I respond, "That's right. I do." Then, leaning in a little closer and speaking a bit more quietly, I add, "but I also like hearing you teach it to me."

She shifts on her feet and tucks a lock of hair behind her ear, exposing her earrings. They are little coffee cups today with pumpkins on them. "But, regardless, I will never turn down a man willing to do the work for me." She smirks, and her cheeks flush slightly.

I take the cables from her hand, and our fingers brush. She jerks her hand back so slightly that had I not already been focused on the electricity between us, I would have missed it entirely.

Clearing my throat, I move back toward the hood of her car to connect the cables and forget the feeling that just erupted in my body. Once I have them attached, I motion for Paisley to get into my Charger and start it.

"How long do we need to wait for?" she yells over my running engine.

"We'll just give it a few minutes. Once yours gets started, you are generally good to go. Just don't turn it off anytime soon."

In the middle of my sentence, her phone rings, but I can't identify where the sound is coming from. When she pulls it out from her bra to look at it, I shoot her a quizzical look.

"Oops, sorry," she addresses, shrugging innocently. "No pockets."

"Got it." I purse my lips and nod, averting my gaze.

She flips over the phone, and I see Ethan's name scrawled across the screen. For some reason, that causes a lump to form in my throat.

"It's Ethan calling me back. I'm just going to send a quick text to let him know I got it figured out."

And I'm not sure why, but the mention of him causes my stomach to tighten, and the thought of her going home to him makes me grit my teeth slightly.

As she texts him, I let her know she can try to turn over her engine. It starts instantly, and her car hums to life.

"Yes!" she shouts from inside the car. "Seriously, thank you so much. How can I repay you?" She hops out of the driver's seat and walks toward me.

"I'm sure you'll find a way," I say as I walk back toward the hood of the car, and again it comes out more flirtatious than I mean for it to. I hope she doesn't notice as much as I do. Or maybe some part of me hopes she does.

I reach toward the engine and disconnect the cables. Before shutting the hood, I walk toward the driver side so I can hand them back to Paisley, but she's rounding the car at the same time, and we literally run into each other... for the second time tonight.

"Shit, I'm so sorry," she apologizes. "Jesus, I'm a fucking klutz today." A hint of red creeps up her cheeks, clearly embarrassed to have collided directly into my chest. To be honest, it's kind of cute how frazzled she seems to be as a result.

"Sweet, innocent, Paisley Hamilton. That's quite a mouth you have there," I tease. We're still standing close, mere inches apart, and her breath is warm against my neck.

"Oh, you have no idea," she rebuttals, and again, that damn fluttering sensation works its way down toward my groin. When I raise my eyebrows at her, she realizes what she implied and shoots her hand up to cover her mouth.

"Oh, God," she scrambles, taking a step back. The space between us widens, and I miss the heat of her body already. "That's not what I meant. I just... I mean I tend to... I just swear a lot, okay?" she rambles, the words flying out of her mouth before her brain seems to have time to process them. "I mean, obviously not at school. No, that wouldn't be appropriate. But I'm quite different in my personal life than I am within the school walls. Not that you need to know that, but—"

"Paisley," I say, putting my hands on her shoulders to stop her before she has an aneurysm right in front of my eyes. "I'm just giving you a hard time. It's all good," I huff out.

"Ugh, I'm so embarrassing," she responds while rolling her eyes, but the flush in her cheeks slowly begins to fade. "Anyway, thank you again for doing this for me. I'm glad you were still at school. Otherwise, I don't know who I would have called."

I hand her the jumper cables and move back to the hood to close it before returning to face her. "It's not a problem, really. I was happy to help."

"Okay, well, um, see you tomorrow then?" she asks, a little awkwardly, clearly not sure how to end our unlikely exchange.

I look down at her big brown eyes, and I realize that the thought of seeing her in the morning makes me actually look forward to coming to school tomorrow for the first time in a while. As she gazes up at me, her hair falls softly across her face again. Instinctively, I reach out, gently brushing the strands behind her ear like my body has been begging me to every time I've seen her lately. My touch lingers for a moment longer than necessary, and tension rises between us. I pull my hand away, my heart pounding in my ears. Our eyes lock, and a sort of intensity flashes in hers. It's a fleeting moment, but it's enough to make me realize I'm not the only one who feels whatever this is between us.

I shift on my feet, putting some space between us, and run a hand through my hair. "See you tomorrow, Hamilton," I say abruptly, and I turn on my heel toward my car.

Running from Paisley is apparently becoming a habit. But I need to get a handle on this situation before I'm tempted to do something I know I shouldn't. So as she waves goodbye from the parking lot, I quickly climb into my car, heart still racing, and slam the door. Then I head home to Bethany where I belong.

Or at least where I'm supposed to.

Chapter Twenty-Three

♫ *"Feel So Close" — Calvin Harris* ♫

PAISLEY

"You *WHAT*?" I scream into the phone, anger bubbling up inside me.

"We, uh... we double-booked our DJ, ma'am," the voice on the other end repeats.

I take a steadying breath before I respond. "So... you're telling me that I have a Fall Ball happening exactly one week from today, with over three hundred students looking forward to it, and I have to somehow find *another* company in this tiny town to DJ it with this short of notice?"

There's a brief moment of silence on the other end while this imbecile obviously tries to collect her thoughts. "Well, um, yeah, I guess that's what I'm saying... I'm sorry, ma'am, but your refund should be issued to you by the end of the day Monday."

A refund. Ha, as if that's helpful at the moment. "Great," I say, sarcasm lacing my words. "Looking forward to it."

I hang up the phone without so much as a goodbye and instantly feel guilty for my rude behavior. But I don't have time to feel bad about it for long. I have bigger fish to fry, like finding a new DJ in the next seven days who happens to be free the Friday before Thanksgiving break.

I look down at my desk and see a stack of essays, and I'm thankful I stayed late the other night to get most of them done. My eyes drift for a half a second to the window, and a snapshot of Briggs jumping my car flashes in my mind. The feel of his body so close to mine. The way he brushed my hair behind my ear and stared into my eyes. God, what was that? And why can't I stop thinking about it? What is actually wrong with me?

Nope. Not today. Not going down that road right now. I shake it off, dragging my attention back to my phone. I don't have time to think about that today—because instead of grading, now I'm spending this entire prep period searching for a new source of music for this damn dance.

I grab my coffee mug and tunnel down the hallway in dire need of caffeine. Once I fill my cup with some caramelly goodness, I stride back to my classroom in a rush. Stupid DJ. Stupid dance. Stupid coffee that just burnt the hell out of my tongue when I took a sip of it too soon.

I'm so distracted as I barrel back toward my room that I don't even acknowledge the other people in the hallway. Normally I'd stop and chat with the kids I pass, but poor Collin says hello to me and doesn't even get a wave. Sorry, kid. I'll make it up to you later.

Right now my brain's stuck in a never-ending loop of things to feel stressed about. DJ, Fall Ball, end of trimester grades. Briggs.

Damn him. Why did he have to look at me like that? And why do I *care?* Yoo-hoo, remember Ethan? Your husband? *Get it together, Paisley.*

I'm so wrapped up in my internal monologue that my heart almost leaps out of my chest when someone grabs my arm. It's not rough or anything, but it's firm enough to pull me out of my fog.

"Paisley? What's wrong?"

The voice is low. Concerned. And familiar in a way that makes me feel things I definitely should not be feeling. I blink up, and there he is, staring down at me with those stupid blue eyes that see straight into my soul.

"Are you okay?" he speaks again, urgency dripping from his words.

It takes a minute to come to the present moment and register what he's asking, bogged down by both my own thoughts and the instant heat that rises when I see him.

"I... yeah," I say, even though it's obviously a lie. My voice falters just enough to give me away, and I know he notices. His hand lingers on my arm for a second too long, like the other night, and when he lets go, it's like losing balance all over again.

"You don't seem okay," he says, softer this time. "What's going on?"

With a big sigh, I relent. "It's this dumb dance. You know that DJ we had lined up? Well, apparently they double-booked and aren't going to be able to make it. The ball is a week away, and we have no music. So now I have seven days to find an alternative, on top of end of trimester grading, and the IEPs I have to attend next week, and working at Tumbleweed all weekend, and…" I trail off, turning my head away from him, feeling suddenly embarrassed. "I know it's stupid to get so worked up over something so trivial."

"Hey," he says, pulling my attention back to him. "You have a lot on your plate, and it can get overwhelming. I get it. Don't ever say that your feelings are stupid. They're completely valid," he reassures me, a softness in his voice that tells me he means it. "What can I do to help?"

I laugh slightly, but it's hollow and doesn't make its way to my eyes. "Nothing, unless you know any good DJs around here who would be free with a week's notice."

He takes a second to respond, and I can tell he's actually thinking about it.

"I was just kidding," I say. "I'll figure it out."

"Actually…" he responds, ignoring my last comment. "I used to DJ weddings as a side gig. It's been a few years now since I've done it, but I'm pretty sure I still have all the equipment lying around my garage somewhere. I bet I could dig it out."

"Are you serious?" I ask, hope blooming in my chest.

"As a heart attack. I can't promise I'll be as good as whoever you had lined up, but as long as we have some lights and music, right?"

"Briggs…" I say, feeling both appreciative and guilty at the same time. "You really don't have to. You already have a lot on your plate with supervising everything."

"Oh, I know I don't *have* to. I want to," he counters. "Besides, it's for the kids, right? I mean, we can't have a Fall Ball without any music. Now *that* would be criminal."

"Oh my God, you're really not joking?" I open my eyes wide, some of my frustration dissolving.

"I'm really not."

Relief and excitement crash over me at once, and before I can think twice, I'm squealing like an idiot and jumping up and down, my coffee sloshing in my cup and threatening to spill all over the floor.

"Briggs, you're the absolute *best!*"

My arms are around him before I even realize what I'm doing. It's instinct, pure adrenaline and gratitude driving me. For a split second, I lean into the warmth of his body and breathe in the smell of him. Fresh mint and bourbon fills my senses, sharp and sweet all at once, and I allow myself to relish in it for a moment too long.

But then reality comes crashing down, and I freeze. What the hell am I doing? This is *not* appropriate. My arms drop like they're on fire. I quickly step back, my face burning hotter than the coffee in my cup.

"Uh, sorry... I, um, I don't know why I did that..."

His eyes lock onto mine, and I swear the air between us thickens. His smile is still there, but it's more intense now. More hesitant.

"Don't apologize," he says curtly, his voice low.

It's commanding. And sexy.

I nod, swallowing the lump in my throat. I know he feels it too because his gaze dips, just for a second, like he's debating whether to say something more.

After what feels like an eternity but is probably only a few seconds, he finally speaks, breaking the silence and separating some of the tension between us. "You sure you're okay?"

"Yeah," I manage. My voice is unsteady, along with my legs. I'm not sure how I'm going to walk back to my classroom without them turning to complete jello.

"Good," he says simply.

I force myself to smile, trying to shake off whatever the hell just happened. "Seriously, though, you might have just saved this dance from being a total disaster. I owe you."

"It seems that's becoming a habit," he says, still eyeing me a little too closely. "But don't worry; I'm sure you'll find a way to make it up to me." He winks at me, and I swear I almost self-combust.

Lord, help me. How am I going to spend an entire night at the dance with this man?

Chapter Twenty-four

♫ *"Over My Head (Cable Car)" — The Fray* ♫

BRIGGS

The house smells like cinnamon and sugar as I step through the front door. Beth took the day off for her annual baking day with the girls, which always leaves us with too many cookies we don't know what to do with. Usually, she brings them for the basketball team or donates them to local businesses as a catalyst for the holiday season, neatly packaging them in tins with perfect bows on top.

She loves doing things like that—things that make people smile, but also things that make *her* look like the kind of person who has everything together. The kind of wife who bakes from scratch, hosts game nights, shows up with homemade treats instead of grabbing something from the store. But sometimes, I wonder if she does all of this because she *wants* to, or if it's simply part of the perfectly curated image she's been painting of our life together for the last decade.

She's curled up on the couch with a blanket draped over her legs and the glow of the TV flickering across her face when I walk in after practice. She's wrapped up in something on her laptop, and she doesn't even look at me as I enter the room.

Before, I welcomed this—the independence that came with our marriage—but lately, I find myself wishing she would care just a little more.

"Hey," I say softly as I sit on the couch next to her.

She closes her laptop and starts right away. "Oh my God. You should have seen the cookies Carli made today. They turned out *so bad.* She accidentally grabbed the powdered sugar instead of the flour, and we had to throw the whole batch away."

I smile. "I can only imagine what those would have tasted like."

She shakes her head, laughing. "Not good. But anyway, I saved you some of mine. They're in the kitchen. Not my best batch, but they're still pretty good."

"I'm sure they're great. So did you guys bake all day like usual?"

Beth picks up the remote and absentmindedly starts flipping through the Netflix queue.

"Mm-hmm. They left about an hour ago. It was me, Cortney, and Carli. Oh, and Stephanie. But Steph mainly drank wine and ate the batter out of our bowls." She laughs again.

I huff out a quiet chuckle, but it feels forced. I lean back into the cushion and run my hand through my hair. "Sounds fun. I'm glad you had a good time."

Beth finally selects a show on the TV and sets the remote down beside her. "It was. I always forget how much I love baking days with them. We should have everyone over soon, by the way—Carli and Joe, Cortney and Lance... maybe Aaron and Amber, too? How about sometime over break next week?"

She's already pulling out her phone to look at the calendar before I even answer her, and a heavy weight settles into my chest because that sounds like the absolute last thing I want to do. Can't we ever just have some down time?

This is normal for us, though. Or at least it used to be. Planning events, filling our schedules, never having time to ourselves or making space for our relationship in between. It wasn't until recently that I noticed she never really included me in the planning or asked what I wanted to do.

It wasn't until recently that I realized I cared.

She hasn't even asked about my day today. She's so preoccupied with her world—in this "perfect" world she's created for us—that I don't even think she knows I'm no longer invested in it.

"Can we look at the schedule later?" I ask her. "I need to head out to the garage. " I stand from the couch, and she looks up at me.

"What for?" She gives me a onceover for the first time since I've gotten here.

"I've gotta dig out my old speakers and mixer. I told PBIS that I would DJ the dance."

"You? DJing? How'd you get roped into that?"

I shrug, already moving toward the kitchen. "Paisley mentioned that the DJ backed out at the last minute. Figured I would help out."

Beth lets out a small laugh. "Did she know you used to DJ weddings?"

"Not at first," I say, grabbing my coat off the hook. "Pretty sure she thought I was kidding."

"Well, I hope your equipment still works. It's been sitting out there forever. Just don't bring back any of your cheesy wedding mixes."

I chuckle under my breath. "Hey, those cheesy mixes paid for a lot of beer and textbooks, if I remember correctly."

Beth smirks. "Fair."

I lean over and plant a kiss on her cheek. "I'll probably be out there for a bit."

Beth nods, already turning back toward the kitchen. I open the door and step outside, leaving the scent of cinnamon and sugar lingering in the air behind me.

The following Monday, I walk into Paisley's room for our final meeting before the dance this weekend. I came in here to finish going over the logistics, but based on the binder she gave to Helen this morning to pass on to me, she's already thought of everything and this meeting is now more of a formality.

Her door is already open when I approach, so I step inside and hold up the binder.

"You color-coded," I deadpan.

She looks up from the papers spread across her desk, a smile playing at her lips already. "Are you surprised?"

"Not even a little bit." I smirk at her and stride towards her desk. "David made a good choice putting you on the PBIS team. You're the perfect person for the job."

"I try." She waves me off, like she's not used to receiving compliments, but a blush creeps into her cheeks nonetheless. "We should still go through everything, just in case."

I nod and flip open the binder, taking a moment to scan the information. She's got a sketch of the gym set-up, names of the supervisors for different areas on rotation, a list of items we still need to get before Friday, and so much more. It's extremely thorough. And extremely impressive. This must have taken hours.

"You really love this stuff, don't you?"

"I really do."

"It shows."

She glances at me. "You don't think it's too much?"

"Nah," I say without hesitation. "I think the kids are going to love it."

She exhales. "I hope so. What if no one shows up? It is the day right before break. The last thing kids are going to want to do is come back to the school and—"

"Hey," I interrupt before she can spiral further. "That's not going to happen. I've already heard students saying how excited they are. Even some of our varsity players were talking about it in the locker room the other night after practice."

"Really?" Her eyes light up beneath her lashes.

"Really. But Paisley..."

"Yeah?"

I shake my head subtly. "You work too hard sometimes. You deserve a break, too, you know."

She looks down at the papers scattered on her desk and bites her lip. "I'm not sure if the word break is in my vocabulary."

"How *are* you doing?" I ask, and I genuinely want to know the answer. "I know you have a lot going on between the end of trimester and the ball. Throw your waitressing shifts in there and whatever plans you might have for Thanksgiving, and you have to be exhausted."

She shrugs one shoulder. "I'll survive. Besides, you're the one who's going to be running the show on Friday. Seriously, Briggs, thank you again for stepping up as a DJ."

"I'm supposed to DJ?" I feign confusion.

She swats at my chest. "Stop that right now! Don't even pretend."

I put my hands up in surrender. "Okay, okay. You're right. I'll have to run home after school on Friday to load up my equipment, but I should be back by five to unload and run a sound check."

"I hope you know how much I appreciate it."

"It's really not a big deal. I'm looking forward to it," I tell her. And to my surprise, I mean it. Ever since working on this dance with Paisley, it's like some of her passion and enthusiasm for her job has seeped into me. I still don't love being an assistant principal by any means, but seeing how much Paisley loves what she does has made my job a little more... enjoyable?

"Me too. And looking forward to it being over." She laughs. "I never knew it was this hard to plan a dance. There's so much to consider."

"Speaking of, is there anything else we need to cover?"

She pauses for a moment. "Actually..." she begins, "there is one more thing I wanted to run past you, but it's not exactly about the dance."

I close the binder and look at her. "Okay. What is it?"

She pulls out her phone and swipes open a tab. "I found a space I wanted to show you. It's about an hour away, which I know might not be ideal, but I saw it and couldn't help but think how perfect it would be for 18th Amendment. I reached out to the owner and—"

"You found this for me?" I interject, staring at her. Her brown eyes shine as she smiles and nods her head excitedly.

"Why?" I speak again before she has a chance to even respond.

"Why not?" She lifts one shoulder nonchalantly, clearly not aware of how big of a deal this is to me. "Ever since you mentioned how serious you were, I've been casually looking at spaces. I can tell how passionate you are about it, Briggs. I think maybe you just need a little push. And besides, I think 18th Amendment could be really great."

She moves to my side and centers her phone in front of both of us. As she starts swiping, a hint of coconut wafts through the air.

"I reached out to the owner, ya know, to feel it out before I brought it up to you. She's eighty-seven, and it's been in her family for generations, but she has no one to leave it to. I told her about your idea, and she loved it, Briggs. She's willing to give you an amazing deal on the space."

She hands me the phone and nods at me in encouragement to flip through the photos. The space is *exactly* what I envisioned for the bar—an old warehouse style building, brick exterior, the words *1918 Automobiles* sketched in paint on the outside, large, arched windows...

I swipe to another photo and see the inside space is industrial with concrete flooring and exposed brick walls. Although it's old, it's clearly been taken care of. Paisley must see my wheels turning and points at the screen.

"You see that door there in the back of the space? It leads down to a basement—one that's similar to the floor you're looking at, minus the large windows. It would be perfect for—"

"The speakeasy," I say as I continue flipping through the pictures. "No one would expect it to be there. When you first walk in, it's just a big, open space, but once you get through that door, it would lead to a beautiful, moody cocktail bar. Just like in the prohibition."

"Exactly," she says as she hops up onto her desk.

"It definitely has character."

She nods enthusiastically. "I thought you'd see that, too. It needs a little work, but the owner won't be around much longer and would love to see it turned into something special before she passes. She's willing to let it go for a good price. I told her I would have you call and set up a time to view it. That is, if you like it."

Her enthusiasm lights something inside me on fire. The way she's looking at me right now—like she truly believes I can pull this off—is a major contrast to Bethany. Never once have I truly felt she believed in me. At least not like this.

"Paisley," I start, my voice thick with appreciation. "I don't even know what to say. You really think this is a good idea?"

Her smile widens, and she hops off her desk and moves closer to me. "Of course I do. You're so capable, Briggs. You've got the vision. And the passion. And the drive. I believe in it. I believe in *you*."

"Thank you," I say softly. I hand the phone back to her. "Okay, I'll call and set up a time to see it. On one condition."

She looks at me quizzically. "What?"

"I want you to come with me."

Her face shifts, her excitement slowly changing to hesitation. "Briggs, I don't know if that's a good idea. What if someone sees us together? Wouldn't that seem... weird? How would we explain?"

"By saying that you're a wonderful, compassionate person who found the space for me. But don't worry. You said the place is an hour away. No one will see us."

She bites her lip, thinking.

"I want your opinion on it," I press. "You're the one who found it, Paisley. You believe in this. You believe in *me*. Don't you want to see it in person?"

Her eyes search mine, and I can feel the exact moment she gives in. She exhales softly before speaking.

"Okay. You're right. But we should drive separately. Just in case."

I nod, disappointment building in me. I know she's right, but it fucking sucks that she is.

"Deal."

Chapter Twenty-five

♫ *"Fast Car" — Tracy Chapman* ♫

PAISLEY

My hands grip the wheel tightly as I pull into the gravel lot. The old brick facade looks even better in person than in the pictures, and although it's going to need some work, it looks promising. The faded *1918 Automobiles* lettering stretched across the side sets up the perfect vibe for the speakeasy style bar Briggs has in mind, and the fact that *I* am the one who found it—that *I* get to be the one to show it to him—makes my heart flip with pride.

I cut the engine to my Kia and lean forward, peering through the windshield at the large, arched windows. Speaking of windows, I *really* need to clean mine. I can barely see the building through my windshield.

I move my head to a cleaner spot of the glass and examine the exterior further. It still has its original brick, though the reddish color is worn and faded from the years it's been sitting here vacant. The doors look original, too, like ones you'd see in a 1950s movie.

God, he's going to fucking love this.

The crunch of tires pulls my attention to my side mirror, and the simple sight of Briggs's car pulling into the lot makes my pulse race. I quickly push my door open and step out into the frigid air, goosebumps immediately erupting on my arms—though I can't tell if it's from the cold or from the image of Briggs getting out of his vehicle. His door swings open, and *fuck me,* he looks good. He must have changed after practice tonight because he's not in his usual work attire. Instead, he's wearing dark jeans and a black Eddie Bauer jacket with a backwards baseball cap. Slight scruff lines his jaw, and I swear it should be fucking illegal to look as hot as he does right now.

Shit. I'm screwed, aren't I?

His gaze finds mine almost instantly, and then it happens— the same thing that always happens when we are in the same space together lately. A slow, unspoken shift in the air. One that feels like we're the only two people who exist, even though we shouldn't be. And even though I'm standing outside with all the fucking oxygen I might need, simply being in the same vicinity as him makes it harder to breathe.

I walk over to his Charger casually, trying not to appear as giddy as I feel. My gaze shifts from him to the building and back to him again in an attempt to read his expression.

"So? What do you think? First impression?"

"Paisley..." He pauses for a moment, taking in the building. "This... I can't believe you found this for me."

"I know. Is that weird?" I say, suddenly aware that I went from zero to one fucking hundred. "You just sounded so excited about it. But also kind of hesitant. I thought maybe... I don't know. I thought maybe you needed a nudge?" I shrug. "I was only casually looking. I didn't plan to find anything. It just kind of fell into my lap. Almost like it was meant to be."

He smiles at me but doesn't say anything right away.

"No pressure, though," I backpedal. "If you don't like it—if it's not everything you envisioned—don't pretend it is for my benefit. I want your full and honest opinion, Dr. Davenport." I press my lips together and give a sharp, official looking nod, which I instantly regret because of how ridiculous I probably look.

He lets out a small laugh and rests a hand lightly on my shoulder, giving it a slight, reassuring squeeze. The gesture catches me off guard, especially standing here in the middle of a public parking lot. I know we're far away from Stonebrook, but we're not *that* far away.

"Thank you," he whispers.

"Wanna see inside?" I ask, gesturing toward the building.

But before he can say anything, the front door creaks open, and an adorable elderly woman—who might actually be older than the building—steps out, clutching a thick coat around her frail frame.

She slowly steps down the stairs, but Briggs rushes over to her, offering a hand to assist her.

Be still, my fucking heart.

"Well, thank you, young man," she says, her voice strong despite her age, and I instantly recognize it from our phone conversation the other day. "You must be Mr. Davenport."

"That's me," Briggs replies as he helps her take the last step. "And you must be—"

"Josephine. But you can call me Jo. Nobody has called me Josephine since 1972, and I don't plan to bring it back now."

She looks up at him and winks, which elicits a grin from Briggs. "Fair enough, Jo. This is Paisley." He motions to me, and I move closer to the two of them. "She's the one who found this place and put us in touch."

"Oh yes, dear." She nods and takes my hand. Her skin is warm, soft, and fragile. It reminds me of my late grandma. "Sharp eye, young lady. This place has been in my family for generations, but I don't have anyone left to leave it to." Her lips press together, and for a second, a flicker of sadness crosses her features. Then she clears her throat and releases my hand, waving us inside. "Come, come, let's get out of the cold."

Briggs nods, and Jo staggers back up the steps, using the railing to assist her this time. He motions for me to walk in front of him, and as I pass him to take the first step, his hand, warm and solid, presses into the small of my back. Just for a second, but long enough to send a shiver straight down my spine.

We step into the space, and I watch as Briggs takes it all in. The high ceilings, the exposed beams, the massive open floor plan with the original concrete. Then his eyes land on the door in the back corner. The one that leads to the basement.

"This goes down?" he asks, already walking over to it, not even waiting for Jo to lead the way.

She nods. "Same square footage as up here, just without the windows. It used to be storage, but it's been empty for years. It needs some work, dear, but it should be sound."

Briggs exhales slowly, nodding as he processes. "A hidden cocktail bar," he murmurs quietly. "It would be completely unexpected." He looks over to me as he continues to envision it. "You walk in, and it looks like this—industrial, open. But once you get through that door..."

I walk toward him slowly. "You like it."

He looks at me, a slow smile spreading across his face. "No, Paisley. I fucking *love* it."

I laugh. "But you haven't even seen everything yet."

"Don't need to. I can already tell there's something good about this. It feels... right."

He pauses on that last sentence, and something tells me he's not just talking about the building.

Jo's voice cuts through the electricity between us. "Well, I'd sure love to see it turned into something special before I go. So tell me, young man, what exactly do you want to do with this place?"

Briggs straightens slightly, shifting his stance so that he's facing Jo as he speaks. He talks excitedly, outlining his vision for the space he's clearly been picturing for years.

Briggs has always been confident, and I've seen that plenty of times in his role of assistant principal, but this is a whole other level. The ambition in his voice is obvious. Briggs is a fucking go-getter.

Whereas Ethan is content to simply exist, to stay stagnant in a job he hates, in a town that offers nothing, and in a house that will never get fixed, Briggs *makes* things happen.

And *that* is the sexiest fucking thing about him.

I swallow thickly as I listen to him tell Jo about the plans he has for the space, my pulse hammering in my ears.

Because I can picture it. I can picture *him*, behind the bar, sleeves rolled up, tattoo exposed, smile wide as he's making a drink for a customer. I can picture myself here, walking in after a long day of teaching, sitting at the counter, telling him about my day.

And the vision of what life could be like with someone other than Ethan hits me so hard that my knees begin to shake. I turn away from the two of them to hide the tears welling in my eyes—because *how* would that ever happen? The simple thought of it is insane, and how terrible am I for even thinking about it?

"I'll tell you what," Jo tells him. "Like I told Paisley here, I'll give you a good deal. You remind me a lot of my late husband. He was a dreamer, too."

Briggs smiles warmly. "Thanks, Jo. That means a lot. Really."

They move to the side to go over numbers while I give them some privacy. And after getting the full tour of the place—including the basement, which was just as perfect as Briggs had hoped—we finally step out into the crisp Wisconsin air and head to our cars.

Briggs opens my door for me, but before I climb in, I glance up at him one more time. "So... does this mean you're officially considering it, Dr. Davenport?"

Briggs smirks, tilting his head slightly, his eyes locked on mine. "I'm officially considering a lot of things, Mrs. Hamilton."

My heart stumbles in my chest at his words. Excitement spreads all the way through my body, from my chest to my stomach, reaching between my legs, and all the way down to my knees.

Oh yeah. I am *so* fucking screwed.

Chapter Twenty-Six

♫ "Yellow" — Coldplay ♫

BRIGGS

"I think this might be the place," I tell Beth as we sit down for dinner. "It's exactly what I've been looking for."

"Oh yeah?" she asks, although nothing about her says she is interested in what I'm saying right now. She's sitting on the couch eating dinner while mindlessly staring at the TV, and it's almost as if her response is more of a reflex than an actual question.

"Yeah. It's exactly what I pictured. Old original brick, concrete floors, basement space that can be renovated. I can't believe I found something like that."

She looks over to me then. "How *did* you find the place anyway? I thought you decided to take a break from looking."

"Oh, um, Paisley actually found it and mentioned it to me." There's no reason to lie about how I discovered the place. It was just a colleague helping another colleague out. Nothing wrong with that.

At least there wouldn't be if that was all that was happening between Paisley and me.

Beth is still looking at me, her fork paused in the air. "Paisley? Like Paisley Hamilton?"

"Yeah. She saw the listing and showed it to me the other day. I had mentioned the idea to her at one point, and she thought I would like it."

I realize too late I probably should have mentioned that I had told Paisley about it beforehand. That, or kept my mouth shut about it altogether.

Beth turns and sets her pasta bowl on the coffee table in front of us. "I didn't realize you and *Paisley* were so close."

The way she says Paisley's name, with such disdain, gets under my skin. Paisley has been nothing but supportive.

I keep my voice even, trying not to give my emotion away. "It just happened to come up in conversation. She must have been able to tell how excited I was about the idea, so when she came across the listing, she sent it my way."

Beth scoffs at my comment, shaking her head slightly. "Well, that was awfully thoughtful of her."

"Why do you say it like that?"

She shrugs. "I don't know, Briggs. Maybe because I've barely heard a word about this bar thing in weeks, and now you're suddenly all excited again because *Paisley* found a place for you?

Sorry if I'm not thrilled my husband is confiding in another woman about his dreams."

"Well it's not like anyone else cares about my dreams!" I erupt, standing up and pacing the floor in front of the couch.

Beth just stares at me for a moment. I take a deep breath and run my hand through my hair.

"I'm sorry." I turn to face her. "I've been looking, Beth. It's not like I stopped caring about it after we discussed it. I just hadn't found anything worth pursuing until now."

She leans back on the couch and crosses her arms, looking at me incredulously. "You mean until Paisley helped you find it." She says that as a statement, not a question.

And what am I supposed to say to that? Yeah, I *did* need Paisley to help because she's the only one who seems to fucking care about anything I want these days?

When I don't answer right away, she continues. "Whatever, Briggs. You're too busy with work and basketball season right now anyway. Maybe this isn't the best time to throw yourself into another project."

It's my turn to huff out a laugh at that. Because this isn't just about the bar. And it sure as hell isn't about Paisley sending me a Zillow link. This is, yet again, about the fact that she doesn't *see* me. Not in the way I need her to at least.

"This bar is happening," I say quietly. "With or without your support."

She exhales through her nose, picking her plate back up as she stands. "Alright, Briggs. Do what you want. But when it doesn't work out, don't come complaining to me about it."

Paisley is already in the hallway when I walk down her wing the next morning. She's leaning against the doorframe of her classroom, talking to Nicole.

She's wearing navy dress pants with a golden yellow sweater today, and the color complements the complexion of her skin perfectly.

"Good morning, Nicole," I say as I walk past them. "Mrs. Hamilton." I nod at Paisley.

Her lips part like she is going to say something, but then she closes them and just smiles at me instead.

I keep walking, forcing myself to focus on anything other than the way her fingers are tightening around the edge of her coffee cup, when a loud *thud* down the hallway pulls my attention away.

It's a sound I know well. Not one I've heard often, but one that you're conditioned to listen for when you're in the position I am at school.

It's the unmistakable sound of a body hitting a fucking locker.

Picking up my pace, I jog around the corner at the same moment two kids are about to swing at each other.

Where the fuck is David? Why is it always *me* who has to put out the fires around here?

"Hey!" I yell down the hallway. "Knock it off!"

Both of the boys' heads snap up in my direction, and Luke Amundson has one fist clenched in the air while the other grips Caleb Turner's shirt. Working in a small school, it's easy to know the majority of the students, which works in my favor most of the time.

Acknowledging my presence, Luke brings his fist down to his side, opting to shove the kid back into the locker instead. The students around them gasp, and one student pulls out her phone to start recording.

"Amundson, *enough*!" I shout as I get closer. "And you—" I point to the girl with the phone in her hand, "put that away and get to class. *Now*!"

The surrounding students scurry down the hall as I wedge myself between the two boys. I grab Luke's shoulders, forcing him back a step. His chest is heaving, his jaw is tight, and I can *feel* the anger radiating off of him.

"Both of you. My office. Now."

Caleb glances down the hallway, clearly nervous, looking like he might bolt. As if he has anywhere to go. I jerk my chin toward the direction of my office.

"Did I stutter? Move!"

By the time both of them are sitting in front of me, the adrenaline has begun to wear off, leaving frustration in its place. This is not how I wanted to start my Friday. Damn days around here can't just be easy, can they?

Luke slouches in his chair, arms crossed, glaring at the floor like he's going to try to fight that next. Caleb keeps shifting uncomfortably in his seat next to him.

I lean forward, resting my elbows on the desk, rubbing my temples.

"Start talking."

Neither of them speaks.

I let out a deep breath. "Amundson, you *know* you can't be out there throwing punches in the middle of the damn hallway. What the hell was that?"

He exhales through his nose, the tension in his shoulders loosening a bit, but he still doesn't say a word.

I look at Caleb. "And you?"

His jaw tenses. "I wasn't—" He stops, shaking his head. "I didn't mean to start anything."

"Bullshit," Luke spits out with a dry laugh. "Fucking *bullshit.*"

"Alright, *enough*," I snap. "Amundson, you're one of my players. A *varsity* player. You're on the PBIS team, for God's sake. Does 'positive behavior' mean nothing to you? You're supposed to be a leader around here, not throwing people into lockers and spending the morning in my office. What's going on?"

His knee bounces under the desk as he side-eyes Caleb.

"He was talking shit about my sister."

I glare at Caleb, who is now looking down at his hands.

"Yeah? And?" I say to Luke. "You think slamming him into a locker or beating the shit out of him is going to fix that?"

He shrugs.

"Look, man, I get it. You're pissed. You want to stand up for your sister. I would feel the same way. But let me tell you something—reacting like this isn't the way to fix anything. It makes you look like a guy who can't control himself."

His shoulders drop a little more. "Yeah? Well? What the hell else was I supposed to do?"

"Take a step back. Assess the situation. Determine if the consequences that come with your actions are worth a couple cheap shots. I know it's easier said than done, but that's part of growing up."

He doesn't respond.

"And you," I address Caleb. "You got anything to say?"

He shifts in his seat again, and his voice is barely above a mumble. "I didn't mean to piss him off. I was just telling him what some other guys were saying."

Luke tenses again, but I shoot him a daring look before he can say anything.

"Amundson, get to class. You're benched for the game tonight."

"But—"

"Don't test me. You're lucky I don't suspend you. The only reason I'm not is because I was able to break it up before any damage was done. You'll sit for tonight's game. *At least*. And if I see anything else like this from you once we return from Thanksgiving break, consider yourself out for the rest of the season. Now get to class."

He nods tightly as he stands, and then he walks out.

"Am I—" Caleb hesitates. "Am I suspended?"

I shake my head. "Not this time."

He visibly relaxes.

"You're lucky he didn't get a punch in," I tell him. "And in the future, don't be an asshole. That's all I'm gonna say."

He nods, and when he finally leaves my room, I drop back against my chair.

Fuck, this job exhausts me. Drains me in ways I don't always have the patience for. But for the first time in a long time, I don't feel completely empty being here, even when I have to deal with teenage drama.

A month ago, dealing with something like this would have ruined my entire day. But right now, I don't know… I almost feel like I actually give a damn.

Chapter Twenty-Seven

♫ "Kiss Me" — Sixpence None the Richer ♫

PAISLEY

"Is that balloon arch falling over, or have I been staring at it too long?"

I glance up from the table of refreshments and squint at the arch Charlie is gesturing to with a roll of tape in her hand. "Um, definitely leaning. Kind of like you at the bar a few weeks ago."

"Hey! Can't a girl let loose once in a while? Besides, *I'm* not the one who had to drive home. It was perfectly fine for me to have a few glasses." She tosses the tape on the table next to me in defeat, still looking at the arch. "I swear that thing looked fine ten minutes ago. Tell me again why we signed up for this?"

"Technically, we didn't sign up for it. We created it," I remind her. "And because we love what we do. Plus, it'll totally be worth it to see the kids' faces. And everything will look fine with the low lights. Forget about the balloons—the kids aren't coming for the decorations anyway."

"You're right," she smirks. "I'm sure the kids will be *coming* for something diff—"

"Okay, gross. Stop!" I swat at her. "These are teenagers for God's sake. Have some class!"

"Oh, like you don't know kids are gonna be trying to sneak off to the bathroom to hook up during the dance."

"Either that or vape," I concur. "But that's why we have staff here. To *supervise,* remember? It's kind of our job."

"Supervise, or babysit? Feels the same these days." She looks back at the balloon arch and grimaces. "Are you sure I shouldn't try to fix it?" she asks, rethinking her decision.

"Maybe just check to make sure it's not going to topple over and kill anyone. Otherwise you'll be the one explaining to David why a junior got smothered by balloons at the dance."

"Good point. I thought Davenport was taking charge of the dance, though. Will David even be here?"

Davenport. Right. Briggs should actually be back to the school any minute to unload his DJ equipment.

"Oh, you're right," I respond, acting as though Briggs being at the dance tonight hasn't been at the forefront of my mind all week. "Well then, you'll be the one to explain to Br—er, Davenport— why a teenager died by balloon arch."

Charlie smirks, then winks. "You know, for a guy who dresses like he's ready to host the evening news, he's not as intimidating as he tries to be."

"Try telling that to the freshman who got caught cheating in Miranda's class last week," I joke, even though it actually happened. My juniors told me all about it.

"Fair. But you seem to handle him just fine," she says, a little too casually.

My stomach tightens. If she only knew.

Because *handling* Briggs Davenport lately feels a lot like trying to pretend I didn't stand inside a building with him a few nights ago and hear him talk all about his goals and visions and dreams while I stood there picturing an entire fucking life with him.

Oh wait, that's exactly what handling him feels like. Because that's exactly what happened.

And I've promptly avoided him ever since.

We haven't really talked since we checked out the space together—at least nothing beyond formal emails and quick check-ins about the dance—and I have no idea what he intends to do about the bar.

And frankly, it's none of my business.

I give Charlie a pointed look, brushing off her comment even as heat creeps up my neck. "Speaking of things that need handling—the balloon arch?" I remind her, shooing her away before she can dig any deeper.

Because I am absolutely *not* prepared to unpack any of that. Not here. Not now. Maybe not ever.

"You're deflecting," she says, grinning, and she's right. "Face it, Paisley. Davenport has always been a grump. But ever since planning this dance with you, he's been a lot more... tolerable. I've even seen him *smile.* Are you telling me that's just a coincidence?"

"Are you telling me you're okay with teenagers getting trampled by balloons? We only have a couple more hours until kids start showing up, and we still have to run the sound check and get changed. Move it or lose it."

I wave her away, but my mind is still stuck on what she said. Is that really true? *Has* he been different lately? Sure, I've noticed that when he's around me, but I didn't know other people were noticing it, too. That can't be because of me, can it?

"Oh, I'm sure you'll have no problem helping Davenport set up the sound system. But whatever you say," she mocks, and she bounds back to the arch.

Rolling my eyes, I finish stacking cups near the water and lemonade dispensers and take a quick sweep of the gym. Twinkle lights glow along the walls, the inflatable pumpkins stand by the entrance, and the balloon arch that Charlie is now wrangling with again—her DIY solution after Briggs vetoed a real photo booth—looks surprisingly good. A few PBIS kids are near the door hanging the rest of the streamers, and a couple others are stocking marshmallows in the tins for hot cocoa.

I exhale and examine our progress. The floor is mostly clear for dancing, the tables are moved along the perimeter of the gym, and somehow, despite surviving on nothing but caffeine this week, it all looks... *good*.

Well, as good as a high school dance can look on a tight budget.

But in the midst of feeling proud of what we've accomplished in such a short amount of time, my brain apparently doesn't get the memo and immediately goes rogue and drifts straight back to Briggs standing in that bar.

Because of course it does.

Fan-freaking-tastic.

"Mrs. Hamilton, if he asks me to slow dance, I'm actually going to die."

I look over at Bella, one of my freshman students, who's half hiding behind the popcorn machine. Her wide eyes are trained on a boy I don't know across the gym, who is currently attempting some weird dance with his friends.

"I'd prefer if you didn't, so I don't have to do the paperwork," I say with a grin. "But if you do, could you at least die somewhere far away from the snack table? I just restocked the cookies."

She snorts but doesn't take her eyes off the boy. "Do you think he will?" she asks, both hopeful and nervous.

I tilt my head, pretending to consider. "Well, he'd be stupid not to, don't you think? You look beautiful tonight, Bella. I love your dress."

Her cheeks flush, and she bites back a smile. "Thanks, Mrs. H.," she tells me, and then she scurries off toward her friends.

I laugh and shake my head, trying to remember what it felt like being that young. It was only fifteen years ago, but it feels like a different lifetime. I watch as they enter the dance floor and notice more kids starting to trickle in. It's only about seven-thirty, and most students probably won't show up until around eight, but there's a good turn out so far.

My eyes continue scanning the gym and are quickly pulled to the one spot I've been avoiding all night. The DJ booth. Briggs is standing to the side of his equipment, talking to a group of kids while a Beyonce song plays out. Of course, he looks hot as fuck, which I've been noticing a lot more lately, thanks to Charlie and the way he looks at me every time we are in a room together. Per usual, though, I blame her the most. Ever since she brought it up a couple months ago, I haven't been able to stop thinking about it.

All of this is her fault, really.

The glow from the party lights catches his steel blue eyes, making them pop even more, even from across the gym. He's wearing black slacks and a white button up that accentuates muscles I hadn't noticed were there until now.

Okay, *fine*, maybe I have, but how could I not?

The black pants fit him just as nicely, looking like they were tailored specifically for his legs... and his ass. He stands tall, his posture relaxed, but there's something about him that commands attention.

I'm standing here staring at him like a damn creep when his eyes lock mine, and intensity builds between us instantly. My stomach does that weird fluttering thing again, and my throat is as dry as the Sahara Desert as I try to swallow down my embarrassment of being caught staring.

"Um, Paisley?" a voice says in my ear, though it sounds like it's a million miles away.

"Hmm?" I ask, not really interested in what whoever it is has to say.

"Um, we have a little bit of a problem."

That comment grabs my attention, and I turn to find Charlie, who *definitely* just noticed me drooling over Briggs. "What's up?" I ask, trying to brush it off and sound casual.

"He's hot, I know," she comments, instantly calling me out. "But you can make googly eyes over Davenport later. Right now, we have a situation."

"Well then spit it out, for fuck's sake," I say, quietly enough so the students nearby won't hear. "What happened? Did someone spill the punch?" I scan the room to identify the problem.

"Not punch," she says, her eyes wide. "Vodka."

Chapter Twenty-Eight

♫ "Scared to Start" — Michael Marcagi ♫

BRIGGS

We're only an hour into this dance, and it already smells fucking terrible in here, just like every other dance I've had to chaperone—which has been a lot over the past ten years, considering David never wants to do it and pushes it onto me like I don't have anything better to do with my Friday or Saturday nights.

Okay, maybe I *was* the deciding factor of whether this dance actually happened or not, but I knew how important it was to Paisley, and I wanted to make her happy.

So here I am, spending the first night of my Thanksgiving break with horny teenagers who are dancing way too close for comfort. Not only that, but I somehow roped myself into DJing this entire fucking thing.

There's a group of basketball boys standing near my booth talking my ear off. I'm half listening, half scanning the gym to see if anything is amiss, and that's when I see her. Staring at me from across the room.

God. Damn. She looks beautiful.

Her eyes lock with mine, and for a moment, I forget to breathe. Her hair cascades down her back in waves, her dark eyes intense with the heat building between us already.

Charlie walks up to her and pulls her attention away from me, and Paisley's whole demeanor shifts in a millisecond. Her face drops and her shoulders stiffen, which means something must have happened. If I've learned anything over the past few weeks, it's that Paisley Hamilton is easy to read—and impossible to ignore. The way her cheeks instantly turn red when she's embarrassed, the way she bites her lower lip to hide her nerves, the way she tilts her head slightly when she's genuinely listening to what you're saying, the small sigh that escapes her lips when she's stressed or overwhelmed.

Paisley trains her eyes back on me and starts moving in my direction, irritation now lacing her features. I know I should be worried about what she's about to tell me, but all I can focus on is the sway of her hips and that tight black dress clinging to her like it's got a goddamn personal vendetta against every ounce of self-control I have left. The velvety fabric glides over her curves all the way down to the floor, but that slit in it... *fuck.* It's high, teasing, and flashing just enough leg to make me question everything I stand for. It's simple, elegant, and technically appropriate for a school dance... but the way it's fucking with my mind should be illegal.

As she walks, her hair trails around her shoulders, and her earrings sparkle in the cheap twinkle lights strung around the gym. I've never seen her dressed like this before. Or maybe I have, and I just never noticed.

How haven't I noticed?

Seeing her dance at Tumbleweed a few weeks ago was one thing, but tonight she's someone entirely new to me, and I'm stuck between wanting to stay the hell away from her and wanting to risk everything I have. Because whatever that dress is doing to me, it's not just dangerous. It's absolutely criminal.

She continues moving toward me with purpose, her heels clicking on the gym floor, and with every step she takes, my heart pounds louder in my chest like it's trying to escape. My head's screaming at me to pull it together, to stop staring at her like a man starved, but my body isn't listening. And by the time she reaches me, I'm a fucking goner.

This is bad. *Really* bad.

"Briggs," she says as she approaches, her voice low and cutting right through the shitty pop music blaring from my speakers.

"Paisley," I manage, hoping she doesn't hear the way her name sounds like gravel in my throat.

She glances around, checking to see if anyone's close enough to overhear. Her body leans in, not touching me but close enough that it feels like she is. "We've got a problem. Two boys snuck in some vodka. Charlie said they went into the bathroom."

Figures. I could have seen this coming.

"Vodka?" I say, trying to play it off, but my eyes keep drifting to her mouth. "Not even whiskey? Guess they've got no taste."

Her lips twitch, almost into a smile, but she maintains a seriousness in her tone. "What do we do?"

I force myself to drag my eyes off her and toward the bathroom. "I'll go in there and check it out. Then I'll confiscate it and call their parents. If they're already trashed, I might have to get the police involved, but if they're not, I can get away with having their parents come pick them up without causing much of a scene."

"Okay." She nods. She's all business when I'm anything but. My brain's in a fog, and all I can think about is how good she looks in that dress and how she's so close I can smell her coconut-vanilla scent and how much I shouldn't want her but I do.

I've been an assistant principal long enough to learn two things: never question kids together who have gotten in trouble, and never sugarcoat anything. Once we're in my office, away from everything else, there is no time for pleasantries.

Which is why Tommy is sitting in front of me but Carter isn't. He's sitting in the office, being supervised by another teacher, while Tommy and I have this conversation. I'll get to him next. The only way to get to the bottom of what's actually going on is to separate them so they crack.

Damn, forget about the cocktail bar. Maybe I should join the FBI.

"Tommy," I start. "What the hell were you thinking?"

"It's not a big deal," he mutters back to me, barely looking up. "Everyone sneaks in booze to these things." His voice is quiet, much different than the normal 17-year-old I see on the basketball court during games and at practice.

He's been on the team every year of high school, and generally, he steers clear of trouble. Recently, though, there's been a change. There was that altercation with Jace earlier this month, him skipping class a few days ago, and now this?

I cross my arms and lean back in my chair, analyzing him. "You're not everyone. You're better than this. What's really going on?"

His jaw tightens and his shoulders stiffen slightly. "Nothing. Can't you just take the flask and let me go back in?"

I shake my head, exhaling. "You know I can't do that, Tommy. Best case scenario is I send you home with your mom. Worst case is the police get involved. You're the deciding factor on what happens here."

Tommy's gaze is glossy, but I don't think it's from alcohol. He shifts his attention from me and fidgets with his hands as he looks toward the door. It looks like he wants to say something but doesn't know how.

"Tommy, I know the last few weeks haven't been easy," I tread carefully.

He freezes for a moment before snapping his attention back to me. "What do you mean?" he asks, an edge in his voice.

"I heard your dad got out last week." I don't sugarcoat it. The kid deserves honesty, not condescension.

I still remember the first time Tommy got in trouble his freshman year three years ago for snapping at one of our teachers and flipping a desk in her classroom. It seemed out of character for him compared to his behavior records, so I decided to look a little more into it. Apparently, the teacher made an off-hand comment about his dad, and I spent a long time in my office with him trying to get to the bottom of it. After a while, he broke down, telling me about his dad's struggle with drug addiction.

I filled in the rest myself afterward; apparently, Rick has been in and out of jail for drug possession, starting when Tommy was eight. He's gone through treatment multiple times. The first time, Tommy's parents were still together, and his mom called the cops to have him arrested and brought to treatment. Tommy and his sister were home at the time and watched through the living room window as their dad was shoved into the police car.

Since then, Rick's been in and out of rehab, but he always falls back into old patterns. He'll be clean for a few months, sometimes even a year or two like when Tommy was in middle school, and then get wrapped back up with the wrong crowd, starting the cycle all over again.

After a few years of the constant instability, Tommy's mom finally left, and his parents have been divorced for five years now. She works two jobs just to keep their family afloat, and I can imagine the pressure Tommy feels to be the "man of the house" now that his dad is no longer in the picture.

Tommy's face twists in front of me, a mix of anger and sadness contorting his features, as if he's fighting off tears. "So what? That doesn't have anything to do with this."

"Doesn't it?" I press. "I know how hard you've worked to keep things together for your mom and sister. Between school, basketball practice, and your part-time job, that gets to be a lot. Add the confusion and anger of your dad being released into the picture, and I know how tough that must be on you. But you can't let that pull you down. You're better than that."

He looks away from me and is silent for a few minutes. Instead of pressing further, I give him time to process.

"You don't get it, Dr. Davenport," he finally says, his voice cracking. "He keeps promising he'll change, but he never does. I'm so fucking tired of hoping things will be different. I can't do it anymore."

My chest tightens, and helplessness knots in my stomach. For a moment, I'm not sitting in my office talking to Tommy. Instead, I'm sixteen again, staring helplessly at a friend whose problems ran deeper than I ever even knew. That same feeling of helplessness rushes back to me now, but I shake it off and ground myself in the present moment.

I've been working with teenagers long enough to know kids like Tommy. They try so hard to rise above the shitty hand they've been dealt only to be sucked down the same path as their parents. It's a cycle that's almost impossible to break.

I lean in closer, softening my voice. "You're right. I *don't* get it." I pause for a minute. "But I do know one thing. You are not your dad, Tommy. You are not his mistakes. And it's his loss to miss out on a kid as great as you."

Tommy blinks rapidly, refusing to let any tears fall. "It doesn't matter. People still think of me as just his kid. Like I'm gonna end up exactly like him. Might as well give them what they expect."

"Or you could prove them wrong," I say firmly. "You've got so much going for you, Tommy. Don't throw it away for some vodka at a school dance. You know it's not worth it. You can choose to break the cycle."

For a minute, Tommy doesn't say anything. Just stares at the floor between his feet while a single tear escapes down his cheek. Then he nods. "I'm sorry," he mumbles.

"Don't tell me. Show me," I say to him. "You have the rest of this year before you graduate. I don't want to see you in my office again for anything less than a celebration. You got it?"

"Got it," he says, more firmly. "So what about tonight?"

"Well, it doesn't appear you really drank anything from that flask, so how about I call your mom and explain the situation to her? Let her know we talked. Avoid getting the police involved. You take time over break to get your head on straight, and then come back afterward ready for a fresh start. Deal?"

"Deal," he says. And I see an appreciative smile tug at his mouth. "Thanks, Dr. D."

"Don't make me regret this," I tell him.

He shakes his head. "You won't," he assures me. Leaning in closer, he continues. "You know, I don't even really like Carter? I'm not sure why I was hanging out with him."

I shake my head and laugh. It doesn't surprise me. Unlike Tommy, Carter's redeeming qualities are few and far between, and they come from completely different backgrounds. Carter's parents are still married and are very, very wealthy, and he's an entitled brat who thinks if his parents yell loud enough, he can get away with anything.

"I'm not sure why either, bud," is all I say. Then I pick up the phone to call his mom.

Chapter Twenty-Nine

♫ *"You Should Probably Leave" — Chris Stapleton* ♫

PAISLEY

As Briggs deals with the delinquents, I decide to swap out the lemonade. The kids are apparently feeling rebellious tonight, and I wouldn't be surprised if one of them spiked it before they got caught. I grab the jug and walk toward the concession stand to mix a fresh batch, just to be safe.

When I get there, I empty the contents of the pitcher into the sink and look around for more powder, but there's none in sight. Only a few cans of soda and a half empty pack of water bottles. Shit. I'll have to come up with something else. Maybe I should have actually *tested* the lemonade before dumping it down the drain. But still, better safe than sorry. The last thing we need to do is send a bunch of teenagers home from the dance drunk for Thanksgiving break.

I spot a door at the far end of the room marked storage and walk toward it, hesitating for a second before pushing it open. I'm not sure if I'm technically allowed in here, and some of the coaches get *really* territorial about their things for only God knows why, but what other choice do I have?

The smell of stale popcorn wafts toward me when I shove the door open. The space is small. *Super* small. There's hardly enough room for me in here with all the boxes haphazardly scattered around, but it shouldn't take long to find what I'm looking for. Hopefully.

I walk further into the closet and hear the door slam shut, and my heart lurches. Hopefully this isn't like those horror movies where the door locks behind me and I'm trapped in here. I'd hate to be the poor custodian who finds me after an entire week off from school. Now *that* would smell bad.

I pull on the cord to the light, but of course there's no bulb. Let's just add to the horror movie setting, shall we? Luckily, the lights from the dance illuminate the space through the small window in the middle of the door, and my eyes adjust quickly.

I push aside a few bags of pretzels and dodge a stray popcorn bucket that comes tumbling off the shelves above me, which are overloaded with chips, candy, and hotdog buns. Seriously, can't someone take time to organize this shit? Who's in charge of this space, anyway?

I'm about to give up looking when I spot some cases of lemonade way in the back on the top shelf.

"Ah-ha! Gotcha!" I say to the lemonade, as if we were playing a game of hide-and-seek. If we were, I just won. Sucker.

I lean over a box to grab a small step stool from the corner when the door behind me creaks open. Creepy, but at least I'm not locked in here after all.

"Paisley?" The voice is warm and all too familiar, and of course when I turn my head to look, Briggs's silhouette is in the doorway.

Betraying me immediately, my heart rate skyrockets the minute I land my eyes on him. Goddamn it. I shouldn't feel excited that it's him. I shouldn't feel relieved, or giddy, or whatever the hell this fluttery thing that's happening in my chest is.

"Ye-yeah?" I say distractedly as I attempt to not topple anything else over.

"Charlie mentioned you were looking for more lemonade. Thought I would come see if you needed any help," he says, stepping farther into the space and letting the door swing shut behind him.

"Oh, thanks," I say, my eyes flicking up to meet his. "Sneaking in vodka, huh? What happened to the good ol' days of kids getting drunk *before* coming to the dance? These kids have no class."

Fortunately, he laughs. "Oh? Is that what teenage Paisley used to do?" he asks, a hint of curiosity in his voice.

I continue reaching for the step stool as we talk. It's a little further in the corner than I anticipated, but I almost have it. "I was always more of a UV-Blue girl back in the day." I smirk. "What about you? What is your drink of choi—"

My foot catches the edge of the box, and suddenly my stomach plunges, my heart jolting as I'm thrown forward. My arms fly out, fingers grasping for leverage. For a moment, everything feels like it's happening in slow motion until suddenly hands grip my waist, pulling me upright. I attempt to steady myself, and my breath catches sharply when I realize Briggs and I are now mere inches apart, so close that I can feel the warmth radiating off his chest. My pulse skips, a mix of relief and embarrassment.

"UV-Blue, huh?" he asks, continuing our conversation as though nothing happened. "I'm more of a tequila guy myself." He leans in just a little, his eyes never leaving mine. Even with the darkness of the room, the ocean blue of his irises is piercing—intense—like he's waiting for me to be the one to break this spell between us.

I swallow. "T-tequila, really?" My voice is much quieter than before, trying to keep things casual, but the way his gaze is locked on mine makes my pulse quicken even more.

"Yeah, well... I hear it makes clothes fall off." His voice drops an octave, and a spark of heat runs through my body.

Did he really just say that?

"That's... just a song lyric," I mutter, shifting ever so slightly, which only makes me lean further into his grip. He still hasn't taken his hands off my waist, and he's so close now that his breath brushes my ear.

"Maybe." His lips twitch into a smirk, and my stomach flips again. "But it's still true. Tequila has a way of making you do things you wouldn't normally do."

His gaze flicks back to mine, his eyes darkening.

I should say something. Say *anything*. I should break out of his hold, but I can't. I don't even want to. Instead, my gaze falls to his lips, plush and slightly parted, that are basically begging to be kissed. And God, they look so soft, so fucking kissable, that warmth spirals from my chest down to my stomach and all the way to between my legs.

Every single part of me is turned on right now. Everything about him, every inch of space between us, feels like it's pulling me in further, and the thought of kissing him makes every part of my body ache.

"Briggs..." I whisper, my voice trembling.

"Yeah?" He leans in a fraction more, and I swear his lips almost brush against mine.

I can barely breathe now, the tension so thick I could cut it with a knife. My heart's pounding so loudly I wonder if he can hear it, too. I swallow, trying to fucking contain myself, but I feel like I'm seconds away from something I might not be able to come back from.

"Briggs... this is a slippery slope," I say cautiously, pulling back a fraction of an inch.

He watches me for a moment and then closes his eyes briefly, like he's having similar conflictions. His voice is low and almost apologetic. "Yeah... I know." He looks back at me, his eyes softer now. "I'm sorry, Paisley. I didn't mean to make you uncomfortable."

He takes a slight step back, and a small knot forms in my stomach. Uncomfortable? No. If anything, I'm feeling *too* comfortable. That's entirely the problem.

I lean in further, closing the recent space he created between us. "I'm not uncomfortable. It's just..." I pause, biting my lip as I figure out what I'm trying to say. Maybe this is something he does all the time. Maybe this is nothing new for him. But I can't help feeling that this—whatever *this* is between us—is real. Different. *Right.* "Is this a slope you've ever been down before?"

"No," he says immediately. "Never. This is all new for me, too." He trails his hand up from my waist to the crook of my neck, his gaze following as it moves, like he's trying to memorize every inch of me. "I don't know what's happening to me. I know we're crossing a line, and I know we should probably keep our distance, but you have no idea how much I'm drawn to you, Paisley. How much I fucking *crave* you."

I inhale sharply, feeling the heat of his hand on my skin, and then allow myself to relax into his touch.

"I know. I feel it, too." My voice shakes slightly. "But Briggs..." His name comes out of my mouth like a plea, and it hangs in the air between us, heavy.

"Paisley..." he says, so close now I think he might kiss me. Part of me hopes he does.

I close my eyes for a second, taking a shaky breath to steady myself. When I open them, he's even closer. In this moment, I want nothing more than to feel the weight of his lips on mine.

"You're married..." I force myself to whisper.

"This is true." His voice is a hushed murmur, deep and full of desire. The space between us is practically nonexistent now, and my body is begging me to lean in and close the gap.

"And I'm married…" The weight of those words makes my stomach sink.

"Also true…" He moves his finger beneath my chin, tilting it up ever so slightly. My hand finds his waist, and I pull him closer without me even realizing it. "But I don't want to stay away from you, Paisley. I'm not sure I even could if I tried."

His breath hitches, and my chest tightens. "Me either," I say softly.

He's so close now that I can't think, can't focus on anything except the way his lips move when he says my name. I'm about to give in, about to cross that line, about to—

"Mrs. Hamilton!" The loudspeaker crackles to life, Charlie's voice booming through the school, and reality comes crashing down around us like tidal waves. "Please report to the gym!"

I freeze and my eyes fly open, my heart pounding in my ears, and the distance between us grows, not just physically but emotionally. The weight of the moment slips away as Briggs exhales, his breath ragged. He steps back slowly, and I can see the same combination of frustration and guilt and desire in his eyes that I feel.

He clears his throat, his gaze dropping to the floor before flicking back up to mine. The heat between us a minute ago has been replaced by our cold, stark reality.

"I guess you've better get back out there." His voice is rough. "I can finish getting the lemonade."

I nod, trying to regain some semblance of control. "Duty calls," I agree, awkwardly, already missing his body pressed against mine.

I side-step him, careful not to touch him, even though every part of me wants to. Before I leave, I glance back over my shoulder and catch him watching me.

"Thank you for checking on me."

"Anytime." He offers me a sad smile.

I pull the door open and let it slam shut behind me as I saunter toward the gym. I let out a deep breath and straighten my dress, but my mind races, trying to pull itself together after what just happened—or what just *almost* happened.

Either way, the moment's over, and it's hard to tell whether I'm relieved or disappointed.

I think maybe a little of both.

Chapter Thirty

♫ "Numb" — Linkin Park ♫

BRIGGS

The sound of pins crashing barely registers over the thoughts racing through my mind. I might be at the bowling alley with the guys, but my head's still stuck in that damn storage closet with Paisley. It's all I've been able to think about for the last twenty-four hours, and it was definitely all I was thinking about when I was taking care of myself in the shower when I got home after the dance last night.

Her scent was clinging to me, and I tried to scrub it away, but the way her voice cracked when she said my name, with so much innocence and yearning, kept playing in my mind on a fucking loop. I had one hand against the slick tile of my shower wall to brace myself while the other was wrapped around my cock, begging for relief. The water pounded against my back, but it didn't drown out the thought of those big, brown doe eyes staring up at me. Every stroke echoed the rapidness of my breathing in that closet last night, and my body chased a release I knew was both wrong and inevitable.

But fuck, she was so beautiful. The way her breath hitched when I leaned in closer, her chest rising and falling from the struggle of trying to stay in control.

And that dress... that fucking *dress.*

The next thing I knew, a low groan escaped my throat, and I gritted my teeth as I rubbed my cock like I was trying to punish it. But when the release finally hit, it wasn't the relief I was searching for. Instead, it left me empty and unsatisfied, knowing it would never compare to what it would feel like having her perfectly plump lips wrapped around me instead.

Even now, the mere fucking thought of her has me gripping my bottle of beer a little tighter and my pulse picking up again.

"Davenport, you're up!" Aaron says as he walks over to where I'm sitting and raises his bottle of Busch Light to me.

I blink, pulling myself out of my haze, and shift slightly in my seat to adjust the ache that was starting to build. I clink my bottle against Aaron's, giving him a smile before taking a long swig of my beer, allowing myself an extra minute to get my body in check.

I stand, roll my shoulders, and grab my ball from the rack. I toss it down the lane, not even pretending to care where it lands. It ends up clipping the edge of the pins, leaving four standing.

Lance laughs behind me. "Guess all that thinking you were doing over here still didn't help your aim, huh?"

I give him a half-laugh and shake my head. "Just a little distracted tonight."

"Distracted by what? Bethany texting you about Thanksgiving dinner?" Aaron huffs, leaning back in his chair.

The mention of Beth's name causes a weight to form in my chest, so I abruptly change the subject. "Man, feels like it's been forever since we've all been able to make it out here." I grab my beer from the table and take a seat across from Aaron.

Lance nods. "You're tellin' me. But I'm glad we all found the time. It's been a hell of a week."

He grabs his ball and throws it down the lane, knocking down eight of the pins and leaving a 7-10 split.

Aaron glances to the lanes, laughing as he sets his beer down. "You know, my kid might only be three, but I think he's got more skill than half the bowlers in here tonight. You two included."

"Yeah." I roll my eyes. "I'm sure he'll start his own league in Kindergarten."

"I'll start saving for lessons now," Lance mocks. He knocks down another pin but isn't able to pick up the spare. "Maybe by then I'll be recovered from having another baby. You know, sleep deprivation, diaper duty, all that fun stuff will be behind me."

"I'm pretty sure you're already sleep-deprived, bud. I can't believe you guys are having a third," I say, half smiling and half serious.

"Ah, it's not that bad," he counters. "You get used to the chaos. At least there's an end in sight once they get older."

Yeah, eighteen years from now, when you're too old to enjoy life. I try to hide my thoughts and lean back in my chair.

"Yeah, you're gonna be fine, man," Aaron says, patting Lance on the back. "What about you, Davenport? Any little bowling stars on the way yet?"

I pause for a moment, taking a sip of my beer, and then shake my head. "Ah, not exactly. Beth has been bringing it up more lately, but... we're not quite there yet."

"Why not? You've been together for how long? It's gotta be in the cards soon, I'm sure."

I shift uncomfortably in my seat, for a much different reason than before, and look down at my near-empty bottle. "I don't know, man. I just... don't think we're on the same page lately."

Aaron raises an eyebrow, and Lance leans forward. "What do you mean? You and Beth have been solid for years."

I sigh, my fingers tapping against the table. I've had this conversation with myself a hundred times, but putting it into words is a challenge.

"I don't know. It's just... we've been together so long, it's like we've settled into this routine. Things are fine. Good. We're comfortable, but there's not really any excitement, you know? Sometimes it feels like we're more roommates than anything else."

I'm not used to opening up and being so vulnerable with the guys, but the issues between Beth and me coupled with these damn incessant thoughts about Paisley Hamilton have left me with no other options.

"That's just marriage, man," Lance insists as I knew he would. "You've been together so long the honeymoon phase wears off. Don't overthink it. Happens to everyone."

"Yeah, Briggs. Maybe you guys need to, I dunno, find some time to reconnect? Go on a date night or something," Aaron comments. "It'll work itself out."

"Yeah, maybe." I look at my drink again, my thoughts drifting elsewhere. "It's hard when... I don't know. It's just... I haven't ever felt like *that* before. With anyone."

"What do you mean?"

"Nevermind," I say, shaking my head and brushing it off. "It's just been different lately. I've been feeling... restless." My mind flashes briefly to Paisley in that closet last night. "I guess that's the best way to put it."

"I get it. But listen, you've been with Beth too long to not have it work out. You guys just need to find your rhythm again. You'll get there. Trust me," Aaron reassures me and claps me on the back.

"Yeah, man. Marriage is like bowling. You hit a few gutters now and then, but you always find a way to bounce back," Lance says, grinning at his own analogy.

I chuckle. "Yeah, you're right. That's life, I suppose. And nothing a few beers with my buddies can't fix, right?"

But no matter how much I laugh along and put on this facade, I know that beer, bowling, and friendly jabs at the guys can only distract me for so long. Because every spare moment I have, my mind drifts right back to her.

And the worst part is I'm starting to not feel guilty about it anymore.

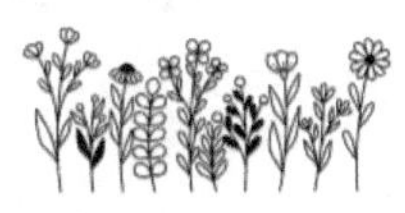

I stumble through the door of my garage, my vision blurry and my head spinning. Maybe I shouldn't have had that last Captain Coke. I probably shouldn't have had the three before that, either. It's a good thing Aaron's wife brought us home so none of us had to drive. I might feel like shit in the morning, but I know Aaron and Lance won't be feeling any better.

As I drag my feet over to the door into the house, a sudden rattle of metal snaps me into high alert, and I jolt upright. The fuck?

I spin around, and my eyes land on the raccoon trap in the corner of the garage.

"Ah-ha! Gotcha, you sneaky bastard."

For weeks, this little shit has been knocking over our garbage cans and ripping into our bags of trash. Yeah, I could have probably shot him, but I wanted to do the humane thing of catching him and releasing him somewhere far away from our house. I've never caught a raccoon before, but I thought, how hard can it be? And looks like I finally got the fucker.

I rush over to the trap, only tripping a few times on the way, and fumble with the lock on the cage. Excited to finally come face to face with the menace, I swing the door open, my hands shaking with anticipation.

But to my own horror, and also to my amusement, I end up looking straight into the eyes of... a cat. What?

"Bruce?" I let out a loud laugh. This isn't a fucking raccoon—it's Aaron's damn tabby.

Before I can react, Bruce scurries out of the cage as fast as a rocketship. He bolts past me, almost knocking me backward, and another laugh escapes me. Catching Aaron's cat may not have been my goal, but it feels like a win regardless, and it will make for great fucking story.

"Briggs?" Beth's voice cuts in behind me. "What are you doing? It's one o'clock in the morning."

I turn slowly. She's standing in the doorway in her pajamas, her arms crossed tightly over her chest. I've clearly woken her, and remorse bubbles in my stomach.

"Oh, hey. Sorry. Just checking the trap," I mumble, gesturing vaguely at the empty cage.

Bethany watches Bruce dodge the rest of the way out of the garage and then gives me a skeptical look, clearly not as entertained by the situation as me.

"Briggs, you're drunk. How do you think Amber will feel about you trapping her cat?"

"Beth, it's fine. It's just a cat, and it didn't get hurt or anything. It was a harmless mistake." I shrug and attempt a casual smile.

Beth sighs and crosses her arms. "That's not the point. Do you realize how this looks?" she snaps. "You stumbling home from the bar drunk? Trapping people's pets? It's a small town, Briggs. People talk."

And there it is again. The concern for our appearances, for how we look to other people, for me not playing the part she wants me to.

"People will always talk, Beth. Who gives a shit?" The liquor flowing through my system has given me some courage to apparently speak what's been on my mind, and she flinches slightly at my bluntness.

"This isn't like you. Drinking. Staying out late. Acting reckless—"

"*Reckless?*" I echo. "Jesus, Beth. Catching a cat by mistake isn't *reckless.* Going out once in a while isn't reckless. It's called being *human.*"

She sighs, louder this time. "I don't mean just tonight. You're not yourself lately. Thinking about quitting your job, this whole idea you have for the bar—"

"You know how much I hate my job! I've been telling you for *years* how much I hate it. But every time I bring it up, you dismiss it. Like my happiness doesn't matter as much as how we look on paper." I pause, trying to focus on her and not the dizziness I'm starting to feel. "And besides, I never said I was going to *quit* my job. I just wanted to see if this bar was feasible or not."

She shakes her head slowly, disappointment lacing her features, but she doesn't say anything.

"Look," I continue, trying to soften my voice. "Can we talk about this tomorrow? Let's just go to bed."

"Fine," she says quietly, turning back into the house and leaving me alone in the garage.

I exhale, slumping heavily against the garage wall. She's probably right. I'm not acting like myself. But maybe that's because the person she expects me to be isn't who I am anymore.

I'm not sure it was someone I ever truly was.

Chapter Thirty-One

♫ "Brave" — Sara Bareilles ♫

PAISLEY

I grab my maroon sweater off the hook in the bathroom, glancing at my reflection in the mirror one last time before heading to Charlie's for some girl time. Because let's face it, after that little incident in the storage closet with Briggs last night, I definitely need it. I smooth down a few straggling hairs and then flip off the light and walk toward the living room where the faint sound of some sports commentary emits from the TV. Ethan's usual Saturday night routine. Normally I'd be cuddled up on the couch next to him, lost in a book, but these past few weeks, being at home has started to feel almost suffocating.

As I step into the living room, Ethan is sprawled out on the couch with Cheeto lying next to him. Fittingly, Ethan is eating Flamin' Hot Cheetos, and her head keeps darting toward the bag trying to steal one—the very habit that inspired her name. When we adopted Cheeto last year, her name was actually Donna. *Seriously? Who names a cat that?* But it took us a few days to come up with a new one. One night, we had a bag of Cheetos sitting between us on the couch, and she came up and shoved her entire head in the bag before snagging one and sprinting away. It didn't take us long after that to decide what we would call her.

I lean over the back of the couch and start scratching under her chin. "Hi, baby," I say in my cat-mom voice before giving her a kiss on the head. "Now you save some Cheetos for your dad, okay?"

She purrs in response and immediately tries to shove her furry face into the bag again. Damn cat.

"I'm heading out soon," I tell Ethan.

He nods in response, one hand tucked behind his head and the other grabbing the remote. "Have fun. Will you be home late?"

I hesitate, hearing the detachment in his voice. Or maybe there isn't any, and I'm just imagining it. Hoping for it?

"No, not too late. Charlie is making dinner and we'll probably only have a glass of wine or two." I walk around the couch and sit beside him, close enough that our knees touch. "How was work yesterday?" I ask, resting my hand on his leg. When I got home from the dance last night, he was already asleep, and we haven't had much time to talk today since he was out on the land getting things ready for season opener this week.

He shrugs. "Same old, same old. Bunch of guys who never want to do any work. Things are getting a little harder to do now that the ground is starting to freeze. Not getting as much done in a day. How was the dance?"

"Yeah, that makes sense. Well hopefully you can get a few more weeks in before lay-off season." I rub his leg gently as I continue. "It was... good." I pause as my mind flashes to the moment Briggs and I shared in the closet, guilt trying to claw its way through my chest. "Couple of kids tried to sneak in some alcohol, but we got it handled before they got too far."

"That's good," he grunts in response, his focus still on the TV. I let my hand slide down to his, hoping he'll take it, squeeze it, *something*. Instead, he pulls his arm away to grab his water bottle from the coffee table.

I let out a slow breath, trying not to feel disheartened. I shrug it off and lean in closer and brush my lips against his for a soft kiss, hoping it will ignite the same feelings I experienced with Briggs last night. For a second, I hope he'll respond, lean into it, pull me closer, show me that whatever I've been feeling toward Briggs is all in my head.

But he doesn't. His lips barely move against mine before he pulls back.

"Have fun tonight, babe."

Still wanting to ignite some passion between us, I try again, leaning in for another kiss. I linger a little longer this time, deepening it just enough to see how he's feeling. His hand settles on my shoulder, more of a push than a pull, and his lips part slightly before he shifts back.

"You're gonna be late if you don't get going," he says lightly, smiling.

A weight settles in my chest and a lump begins to form in my throat. This is nothing new. He's not being entirely dismissive or cold toward me—he's just not... *anything*. There's no fire between us. Not even a tiny little glowing ember. And lately, I'm wondering if there ever has been. At least not to the extent that I felt with Briggs. That was different from anything I've ever experienced before.

How can that be?

With Eth, it's been the same for the past seven years. At first, I hoped his intimacy would grow and that passion between would develop, but it hasn't.

Pushing the thought aside, I force a smile and stand up. "Right, yeah. I'll see you later tonight then."

I turn on my heel toward the kitchen, but I can't let it go without saying something.

"You know what... no," I address him. "Why don't you ever want to kiss me?"

He looks taken aback, his eyes widening slightly and his brow furrowing as he turns his head toward me. "What are you talking about? We kiss all the time," he says, brushing it off.

"No. We don't," I counter, my tone a little sharper now. "You give me pecks on the cheek or quick goodbyes. *Sometimes*. But there's no... connection. No excitement. No *eagerness*. It feels like you think it's a chore to kiss me. To touch me," I say, a little quieter now, my emotions welling inside and tears building in my eyes.

"That's not true," he says defensively, sitting up straighter and crossing his arms. "We've been together forever, Pais. It's normal."

"Normal?" I ask, incredulous. "Well what if I don't want to accept this as my *normal*? Look, Ethan. I'm not asking for some Hallmark movie romance every single day, but I can't even remember the last time you kissed me—I mean *really* kissed me— like you actually wanted me." My voice breaks slightly on the last word, and I hate the way it sounds. Weak and desperate. "And it's not for my lack of trying."

He sighs heavily and rubs a hand over his face, clearly already tired of this conversation. "I don't know what you want me to say, Paisley. I'm just not a super affectionate guy, okay? That's not how I'm wired. It doesn't mean I don't love you."

I chuckle softly at his words. Truthfully, I know he loves me. I've never doubted that. I just wonder if he will ever love me the way I've always wanted to be loved.

"I know you love me, Ethan. I just... I wish you would show it more sometimes."

The room grows unbearably quiet after that, and he watches me for a moment before standing. "Well, you know we could... if you want, before you go," he offers, gesturing toward the bedroom.

My heart leaps for half a second, hoping for a chance at the intimacy I've been craving. But it's not desire in his voice. It's obligation.

I hesitate, unsure if I'm in the right mood or headspace to take what he's offering. After a few seconds, though, I nod. "Okay, sure."

He motions for me to walk toward the bedroom. There is no build up, no foreplay leading into what's about to happen. No touching, no kissing, no anything.

He follows me into our bedroom and signals for me to get on the bed. I strip off my clothes on my own and lie face down, knowing he never likes me looking at him when we are intimate.

I hear a zipper from behind me as he takes off his jeans and boxers, and I don't have to look at him to know he's left everything else on. As if he can't be bothered to take the time to undress completely or to feel our skin touch.

Once he enters me, it's the same as always. Predictable. Mechanical. Over in a few minutes. He does what he thinks is enough to please me, and I pretend that it does so it's over faster.

When we're done, he dresses quickly and then leans down to kiss me lightly on the forehead like I've just helped him check an item off his to-do list.

"That was great, babe."

He walks back to the living room while I lie on the bed for a moment longer and stare at the ceiling, wondering how much longer I can tell myself this is enough.

"Ugh, you guys, I don't know if I can make it two more trimesters. This first one was exhausting enough," I complain to Charlie and Leah.

We're sitting near Charlie's fireplace, and the flames flicker against her brick accent wall in her living room. Her coffee table is cluttered with kids' books from her two daughters who are at their grandma's tonight, and blankets are strewn across the couch next to some dirty dishes sitting on the end table. The room kind of resembles my brain lately: a complete and utter fucking mess.

"I knowwwww!" Leah agrees, dragging out the word for emphasis. "I don't know if I'm going to survive. I love my seniors, but they're driving me freaking nuts already. I'm so glad we have this week off to recover."

"You're telling me," chimes Charlie. "I have juniors and seniors in the library all day taking college classes, but because all of their classes are virtual, the shitheads just sit on their phones and gossip all hour. David came in one day this week and got mad at *me* because they weren't doing anything. But like, hello? Are you or are you not the one who put them in there with nothing to do?"

"Sounds like David," I chuckle. "And I bet he didn't even talk to the kids when he came in."

"Or even say hi to them for that matter. I'd be surprised if they even know his name," agrees Leah.

"Or that he's the principal! Davenport basically runs the school. I never see David in the hallway. And if he is, he always has that scowl on his face," Charlie comments. "And not the broody kind of scowl that can be sexy. It's more like a 'I hate this fucking place and all these people in it and would rather me and my tiny dick be out on the golf course' kind of look."

"Don't forget the hands on his hips! With all those power poses, he *has* to be over-compensating for *something*," Leah adds as she stands up to imitate his stance. "But speaking of Davenport," she continues as she sits back down, "he's the one who supervised the dance last night, yeah? How did it go?"

I force a casual shrug and reach for my glass of wine, hoping my face isn't as red as it feels at the mention of Briggs's name. "It went well, I think. The usual—kids trying to sneak in some Vodski—but at least Charlie didn't start a fire this time." I wink at her.

Charlie gasps. "That was *one time!* And it wasn't even a fire. Just a little smoke. Besides, I'm not the one who tried cooking fucking burgers in her classroom." She gives Leah a pointed look.

Leah snorts, causing her to spit out some of her drink. "God, I forgot about that! Damn, David *really* didn't like that, did he?"

"You're never gonna live it down, babe." I grin.

"Anyway, back to the dance," Leah says, waving us off. "Vodski, huh? Who was it this time?"

"Carter and Tommy," I say, swirling my wine like I'm unbothered, although the memory of Briggs from last night has me anything but.

"They weren't exactly subtle about it," Charlie adds. "I literally saw them pull out the flask and then walk into the bathroom together."

"Tommy? Dierks?" Leah asks. "What's going on with him lately? He used to be such a good kid."

I shrug. "I'm not sure, but Briggs handled it. Pulled him aside. Probably had one of those 'let's discuss where your life is going' talks to intimidate him."

"That's kind of hot," Charlie smirks. "Gotta love a dominant man. I bet half the moms who come to parent-teacher conferences fantasize about him. Fuck, I might, too, if I hadn't heard him tear into a kid running down the hallway last week. What a buzzkill." She rolls her eyes.

Leah grins, taking a sip of her wine. "Really? That whole grumpy vibe he has going on kind of does it for me."

My face heats up so fast I can't even try to hide it. "Oh, please," I blurt. "He's not even close to your type."

"So? Doesn't mean I don't have eyes. And that sexy professor thing he has going on with his glasses sometimes... it's pretty hot." She shrugs and raises her eyebrows at me. "Besides, he's not *your* type either, so what's with the sudden defense?"

"I'm not defending anything!" I say a little too eagerly, which makes both of them stare at me with huge smirks. Shit. Nice one, Pais. Way to be obvious.

"Oh my God," Charlie says, pointing her glass toward me. "I knew it! You totally have a crush on Davenport!"

"I do not," I lie, trying to hide my embarrassment.

"Holy shit, Paisley," she says, learning forward. "Spill. Did something happen that we don't know about?"

"No! Nothing happened." I wave them off, trying not to think about what almost *did* happen. My stomach does somersaults just thinking about it. What the hell is going on with me? I can have sex with my *husband* and hardly feel a thing, but Briggs's *hand* touches me and I almost combust?

"Okay, sure," Charlie says, giving me a knowing look. "But let's be honest. You, my dear, were disoriented the entire night."

I groan, sinking deeper into the cluttered couch. "I was not. It was just a weird night, okay?"

Leah gives me a look. "Weird how?"

I bite my lip, trying to think of a way to dodge the question without sounding like I'm hiding something. "I don't know. Just... a lot of emotions. End of the trimester, the stress of the dance, being around so many kids all night... that's all. It's not a big deal." It's also not a good cover, and I know they aren't going to buy it.

"Uh-huh," Charlie says, unconvinced. "And I'm sure all of that has nothing to do with Davenport? Or should I say *Briggs...*" She raises her voice an octave when she says his first name, clearly mocking me.

"It doesn't." My voice comes out a little sterner than I intend, but I need to shut this conversation down before it goes any further. There is nothing going on between Briggs and me. There can't be. We're both married for God's sake.

"Whatever you say, girl," Leah comments, and she shifts the conversation to something different. Thank God.

I stand up and walk to the fridge to refill my wine glass, glancing over my shoulder at Charlie and Leah. Maybe I should tell them about what's going on with Ethan and me. I can just leave the part about Briggs out.

I pour more Risata into my glass, and my Apple watch vibrates with a notification. When I sit back down on the couch, I slide my phone out of my purse to look at the text.

I nearly choke on my drink when I see the message on my screen, which doesn't go unnoticed by Charlie and Leah.

"You good over there, Hamilton?" Charlie asks me, her eyebrow raised.

Heat crawls up my neck. Seriously, can't I take something for that?

"Um yeah," I mumble, swiping out of the message like it's a virus. "Just a little caught off guard, that's all."

"By what?" Leah asks incredulously.

Think, Paisley, think. Why would you be looking at your phone? What could have been so shocking that you nearly spit out your wine all over Charlie's couch?

"Oh, um, nothing," I say quickly, trying to sound much more casual than I am. "Was scrolling on Facebook and saw someone from high school just got married."

They both nod, accepting my lie as the truth. "Who got married?" Leah asks.

I shrug, keeping the story vague. "Just some girl I used to hang out with. I didn't know she was engaged, so it surprised me is all. Looked like a cute wedding, though." I try to sound nonchalant and hope they don't ask to see the pictures. I've never been a very good liar. Remind me to never play cards in Vegas.

I'm not sure why I haven't told Charlie and Leah about my growing attraction toward Briggs. Or even about any of my interactions with him lately. It's not like they would judge me, especially since nothing has *happened* between us, but telling them about it would mean admitting to myself that whatever these feelings are is real enough to warrant a conversation.

I think I've been trying to push the memory of our interactions—and any thoughts of him completely—out of my mind. But since last night, that's been much harder to do. And this fucking text sure as hell doesn't help.

Luckily, Leah and Charlie move on and start talking about something else, and I excuse myself to use the bathroom, taking my phone with me. When I swipe open my lock screen, his message is still there, taunting me.

Why can't I stop thinking about you?

I swipe out of the message quickly, willing it to disappear entirely. It's eight o' clock on Saturday night. He must be drunk, right? Why else would he text me? Yeah, definitely drunk. He probably won't even remember texting me in the morning, so it would be awkward if I replied. I totally shouldn't reply.

But for some reason, I just can't fucking help myself.

Chapter Thirty-Two

♬ *"Stone" — Whiskey Myers* ♬

BRIGGS

Fuck, that's bright.

The sharp sunlight pierces through the open blinds in my room. I must have forgotten to close them last night. Or maybe Beth intentionally opened them to get back at me for making an ass of myself when I got home from the bowling alley. Who the fuck knows.

What I *do* know is my head's pounding and my throat's scratchy, so I reach for my water bottle on my nightstand. My phone is lying next to it, and the sight of the small, black rectangle instantly brings a memory to surface.

Fuck. *Did I text Paisley last night?*

I sit up in bed far more quickly than I should, and the room tilts on its axis. I place my hands on the bed on either side of me and pause for a moment, waiting for the sudden dizziness to subside. Yep, I *definitely* should not have had that last Captain Coke. Looking around, I notice my room is a disaster—pillows have fallen on the floor, my shirt from last night is draped over the bed post, and my phone isn't even plugged in.

God, I'm too old for this shit. We took shots last night, didn't we? Fucking Lance. That son of a bitch.

Once I gather my bearings, I grab my phone off the table to confirm my suspicions. Sure enough, Paisley's name is at the top of my messages, and I scan through our conversation, which luckily appears to be brief, to see how much of an ass I *really* made of myself.

Why can't I stop thinking about you?

> *I don't know, but I wish I didn't know what you mean.*

Can we talk about last night?

> *There's nothing to talk about. Nothing happened. Nothing can happen.*

I know.

Fuck. Why couldn't I have met you sooner?

> *I've been asking myself that same question...*

Fuck me. I'm not sure what's worse—the fact that I stopped texting her after she was so vulnerable, or the fact that I texted her at all in the first place.

I look at the timestamp of my last message and notice it was from a little before I got home and found Aaron's cat in the raccoon trap.

That fucking cat. I better text Aaron this morning and make sure Bruce made it home all right. Though I know Aaron will get a kick out of it, Amber might feel a bit differently.

Looking back down at my phone, I debate my next move. I should probably just let it go and chalk it up to some drunken conversation that we never speak of again.

But for some reason, there's a pull to text her. To let her know I didn't send that message last night simply because I was drunk, not that she even knew I was.

I begin typing a message and stare at it, hovering my finger over the send button. Is this a good idea? I don't fucking know anymore.

Instead of hitting send, I toss my phone to the side and lie back down for a moment, which causes the room to shift once again. I drag my hands over my face, my stubble scraping my palms. I roll over to my left, and the scent of Bethany's shampoo lingers on the pillow next to me, faint and floral.

Lance and Aaron said this is normal. That marriage isn't all fire and lust forever. It's comfort. Stability. Partnership. They're probably right.

But damn, wasn't there supposed to be some excitement somewhere along the way? Have we ever had that?

I try to bring myself back to the early days of my relationship with Beth. Studying for finals together. Getting our first apartment. Chinese takeout in the living room. It was good. We were good. Happy even. But... there was no *heat*. Not the kind that keeps you up at night, needing more. Not the kind that has you acting like a damn teenager relieving himself in the shower just from the thought of her. Not like the thoughts I've been having about...

Fuck.

Is whatever this is between Paisley and me just because it's something new? Or is there potential for something real, something I've never had? Paisley does something to me that I can't explain, and it's making me crazy. This *is* crazy. I barely know her.

But I *feel* like I do.

I drag myself out of bed, the hardwood cold under my feet, and trudge downstairs. The smell of coffee fills the air, springing a little bit more life into me. Beth is sitting at the island scrolling on her phone.

The guys are right. Marriage is about showing up for each other, day in and day out, even when it's hard. And I owe it to Beth to at least try.

"Hey," I say softly as I walk toward the coffee pot. My voice is hoarse, a testament to the amount of alcohol I consumed last night. "I was thinking... it would be nice to spend some time together this weekend before the craziness of Thanksgiving. Want to see a movie later?"

Bethany looks up, her face softening from my suggestion. She sets her phone down on the countertop.

"A movie?" she asks, a hint of surprise in her voice.

"Yeah," I answer, pouring myself a cup of coffee. "Might be fun. There's a new sci-fi film that came out last night, and I know you like those. We could go to the five o'clock and grab dinner after if you want."

She smiles, and her shoulders relax. "Sure, that sounds nice. It's been a while since we've gone out just the two of us, hasn't it?"

"Yeah." I nod, taking a sip of my coffee, the dull ache in my head finally beginning to subside. "Guess we've both been busy."

Chapter Thirty-Three

♫ *"So Good" — Halsey* ♫

PAISLEY

The smell of butter and artificial cheese floats through the theater lobby, a combination that shouldn't be appealing but somehow oddly is. Ethan nudges me gently toward the concession stand after purchasing our tickets.

"Popcorn and Sour Punch Straws?" he asks, already reaching for his wallet.

I nod, distractedly looking at the menu that hangs above the workers. "And a Sprite?"

He grins and approaches the cashier. As he orders, I slide my phone from my pocket again, quickly looking at the screen. Just to check the time, I swear. Why else would I be looking?

I tuck it away before Ethan notices, and my gaze lands on the wall of movie posters to the side of the lobby. I attempt to read the titles to distract myself from the tightness I've felt in my chest for the past few days.

I thought a date night would be a good idea. Something totally normal. Something couples do. Dinner and a movie—the most vanilla, marriage-saving hack out there, which is exactly what I need.

"Here." Ethan hands me the soda and candy. "You good?"

I turn toward him and flash a smile. "Yep," I say more cheerfully than probably needed. "Just tired. Excited that it's finally break."

He leans closer, lowering his voice. "You know it's not too late to turn around and go home and lounge on the couch instead."

"Nice try," I tell him with a light chuckle. "You promised me a rom-com, and a rom-com I shall get."

He laughs, and I relax a little. But then, from the corner of my eye, I see the doors to the theater swing open. I glance toward the entrance reflexively, and suddenly the Sprite in my hand feels ten pounds heavier.

Briggs walks in first, his jacket dusted with snow that finally decided to come this year, and Beth follows close by his side. She's smiling and brushing snowflakes from her perfect golden hair. Her arm is linked casually through his, and he leans toward her, seemingly engrossed by something she says.

My grip tightens on my cup and my teeth clench, but luckily Ethan is too busy putting his wallet back into his pocket to notice.

"Ready?" he asks.

I blink, dragging my attention back to him. "What?"

He motions toward the theater hallway with the popcorn bag. "Ready to go find seats?"

"Oh, right," I say, trying to brush off my discomfort. I don't move right away, and instead, my stupid eyes drift involuntarily back towards Briggs and Beth. They are in line for tickets, still chatting, completely oblivious to my gaze.

He never texted me back last night, and now, it's like that conversation, or that moment in the closet, never even happened.

And while I know that's probably for the best, I still can't help the ache in my chest.

I don't know what even possessed me to reply to him in the first place.

Okay, yes I do—two glasses of wine, my stupid fucking feelings, and my lack of willpower. Not a great combination. When I saw that message from him come up on my phone, my stomach instantly fluttered, and I knew right away that it was a feeling I shouldn't have for anyone except my husband.

But I did. I do. What the fuck is wrong with me?

But then he stopped replying, and I instantly felt... exposed. And embarrassed. Our conversation was *mainly* harmless, but when I woke up this morning, I immediately chastised myself for saying the things I did.

I'm sure he regrets saying anything at all. But he could have said *something*. Even if it was *hey, I regret everything I said and didn't mean any of it.* Even if it was him telling me how much he wishes he could take back what almost happened in that fucking closet. But instead, all I got was silence.

And now here he is, completely unfazed, on a date with his wife.

Why the hell does that bother me so much?

I glance quickly back toward Ethan, who's already halfway across the lobby, his eyes trained on the glowing screen that lists the movie times and theaters, completely unaware I'm not trailing behind him.

I swallow the lump forming in my throat, and my eyes yet again flick unwillingly back to Briggs. Beth reaches up and adjusts the collar of his jacket, and the gesture seems painfully familiar for them. My stomach twists.

Briggs turns slightly, like he can feel me watching, and his piercing blue eyes immediately connect with mine. Time seems to slow and everything around me blurs. My breath freezes and my chest tightens even further.

"Paisley?" Ethan's voice from across the room jolts me back to reality.

I tear my gaze away, my face burning. "Yeah, sorry. Coming."

Turning quickly, I walk hurriedly in Ethan's direction. I can feel Briggs's eyes still on me, on *us*, and the heat and intensity that's radiating from his stare seeps straight through my entire body—through my clothes, my skin, and all the way down to my fucking bones.

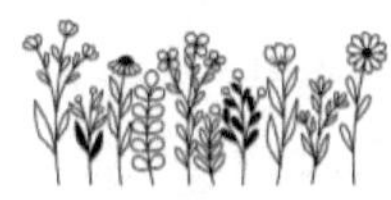

Ethan's hand rests casually on my thigh as the movie plays on the big screen above us. Normally, this would make me feel comfortable, but tonight it's making me restless. The theater is unbearably hot and the material of my sweater is making me feel suffocated. I shift in my seat, gently removing his hand and giving it a reassuring squeeze.

"Bathroom break. Be right back," I whisper.

I navigate past legs and feet blocking the narrow aisle as I beeline for the door. As soon as I step into the hallway, the cool air washes over me, and I take a deep breath of relief.

Lost in thought, I rush down the hallway toward the bathroom, and as I turn the corner, I immediately crash into someone.

Hands fly up and grab my shoulders to steady me, and the electricity that floods my body as a result tells me who it is before I even have to look.

I peer up, my heart slamming annoyingly against my ribs. Briggs stares down at me, his glasses sliding slightly down his nose. "We have got to stop meeting like this," he says, attempting a smile.

But I'm not in the mood. Not after last night. Not after seeing him with her. Not after all these stupid fucking feelings came to surface all over again in the lobby.

I shrug out of his grip and take a step back. "No kidding."

He blinks, clearly caught off guard by my clipped tone. "Sorry. I didn't see you coming."

"Yeah." My voice is flat, void of any emotion. "I bet."

He stiffens slightly and adjusts his stupidly sexy glasses. "What's that supposed to mean?"

"Nothing." I cross my arms defensively, suddenly aware of how we're alone in the dim hallway. "Enjoying your movie?"

Briggs exhales slowly. "It's fine. Beth's more into sci-fi than I am."

"She looked happy," I say sharply, the edge of my jealousy sneaking into my voice. "The two of you seemed awfully cozy."

His jaw tightens, and his eyes narrow. "Funny. I could say the same about you and Ethan. Seemed like you two were enjoying yourselves."

"Yeah, well, guess we're both getting pretty good at pretending, huh?"

He steps forward slightly, voice lowering as his eyes bore into mine. "Is that what we're doing now? Pretending everything is fine when we're both clearly unhappy?"

I scoff. "From where I was standing, you and Beth seemed perfectly content. You didn't exactly seem unhappy when she was straightening your collar and laughing at whatever you were saying." I know I sound like a jealous teenager with a crush, but I can't help it.

His expression falters. "Paisley, that's not—"

I cut him off, suddenly not wanting to hear whatever he's about to say. "Look, about last night—"

"Forget about last night," he interrupts, his tone sharp. "You want to pretend there's nothing between us? Fine. But don't you dare stand here and act like I'm the only one who feels whatever this is."

My chest tightens painfully, and I let out a deep sigh. "I just think it's best we avoid each other outside of school. Clearly we're not good at... boundaries."

Briggs steps even closer, his voice low. "You think I haven't fucking tried that?"

His hand reaches out, his fingers lightly brushing my cheek, and it sends another jolt through my body. I draw in a sharp breath and lean into it, my defenses slipping for a moment.

"Briggs..."

But then I look into his eyes, and panic floods back into me just as quickly as my vulnerability. I quickly step back, out of his reach. "We can't. It's not fair. To Ethan. To Beth. To anyone."

Briggs nods slowly. "You're right. But it's going to be difficult to keep our distance considering we're both going to the PBIS conference next week."

I groan softly, pressing my fingers to my temples. I had forgotten all about Briggs going to that conference. "Shit."

"My thoughts exactly," he mutters, a humorless smile tugging at his lips. "Two full days pretending we barely know each other."

"We *do* barely know each other," I say bitterly, even though I know it's not completely true.

Because even though it's only been a couple of months since we set up my damn furniture together, I *do* know him.

I know how every morning at exactly seven forty-two, he stands in the commons area to greet the kids, hands tucked casually into his pockets, nodding at each one as they pass. I know how he makes an additional effort to specifically say good morning to the students who have a rougher home life so they know someone is excited about them being there. I know he drinks his coffee black from the same chipped Stonebrook High mug every single day, refilling it precisely at the start of third hour. I know that during staff meetings he tucks himself in the corner to avoid getting overly involved, sitting with his arms crossed and pretending not to care, but lightly taps his pen against his notebook every time someone says something that irritates him. I know how he rolls his sleeves halfway up his forearms whenever he's deep in thought and how he runs a hand through his hair when he's stressed. I know that even though he's mastered looking calm and stoic in front of everyone else, he's reserved a softer, more playful look he gives only to me.

"That's bullshit and you know it," he says, clearly exasperated. "I *know* you, Paisley. I know how your cheeks flush when you're nervous or embarrassed. I know that you bite your lip when you're unsure about something or are trying to hold back how you really feel, how your shoulders tense every time you're stressed, and how you roll your eyes whenever you receive a compliment. I know how you light up talking about books and how much you care about your students. I know how you make me feel like my dreams aren't stupid, how you somehow breathed passion back into a job that has felt fucking pointless for years. I know that you're the only one in my life right now who doesn't think my speakeasy idea isn't just some crazy dream, but that it's a goal worth chasing. You make me feel seen, Paisley, like the things I want aren't trivial."

I look away quickly before he can see the moisture pooling in my eyes. I can't deal with this right now.

"I need to get back to my movie. You should do the same."

I start to turn when he grabs my arm. "Paisley, wait. This doesn't have to be—"

"It does," I snap, snatching my arm away. "It really does, Briggs. Because whatever this is, whatever is happening here, can't fucking happen." My voice is loud and weak at the same time, and I push through the bathroom door and let it swing shut behind me, sealing us apart once again.

Chapter Thirty-four

♫ *"Beautiful Mess" — Diamond Rio* ♫

BRIGGS

I turn my key in Paisley's classroom door handle and slowly creak the door open. The lights are off, but the early sun is bleeding through the windows, and the place still smells like her coconut shampoo even though it's been over a week since she's been here.

I slip into the room as quietly as I can, latching the door behind me without a sound. Heart hammering in my chest, I make my way toward her desk and set the box of granola bars and bag of salt and vinegar chips, carefully arranging them so she will see them as soon as she walks in. I contemplate leaving a note but opt not to in case someone else happens to come in here and see it first.

After our run-in at the movies over break, I had to stop myself from texting her probably a dozen times. Seeing her there with Ethan rattled something inside of me, even worse than the night I ran into her at Shooters or when I helped jump her car or when I was in that closet with her during the dance.

Because it was different this time. With him, it looked like she *belonged* there. Like she was someone who had chosen that life and was doing her best to stay in it. And I hated how much that twisted inside me. It took everything I had not to stride across that lobby and say something.

But what would I have even said? *Leave him? Choose me?* I can't even say that out loud without sounding like a goddamn lunatic. And what right do I have to barge into her life when I haven't even figured out the shit going on in mine?

I'd gone to the movies that night trying to do what Aaron and Lance said—trying to be present, to show up for Beth the way a husband's supposed to. To rebuild our connection. I thought maybe if we just had one good night together, it would jog something in me. But sitting in that theater next to her, all I could think about was Paisley.

So now I'm here, standing in her classroom at seven o'clock in the fucking morning the first day back from break. I don't know what I'm expecting. For her to walk in here, see the granola bars and chips, and what? Suddenly realize that I'm the guy she wants? That she's ready to blow up her entire life for me?

Is that even what I want?

By the time the bell rings a half an hour later, I have convinced myself that this whole thing was a terrible fucking idea, but when she sidles up next to me in the corner of the hallway, I know it's too late to take it back.

"I didn't realize snack delivery was part of your job description," she says casually, her eyes fixed on the lockers in front of us.

Damn, she didn't waste any time calling me out. "What are you talking about?" I ask, doing my best to sound clueless.

Her eyebrows arch. "Oh, really? That's how this is gonna go? I guess I should believe that the exact same brand of granola bars I hide in my bottom drawer just magically appeared out of thin air, then."

"Someone brought you snacks? Lucky. Guess I'm not on Santa's nice list this year." A slow smile spreads across my face.

"Oh, don't play dumb, Briggs," she says, rolling her eyes. "I know it was you."

I take a sip of the coffee I'm holding, a weak attempt at hiding my smile, and shrug. "Could've been anyone."

"Uh-huh. Sure." She leans in a little closer, her voice dropping to a whisper. "You know I have hidden cameras in there. I'll just check the footage."

I scoff. "You don't have cameras in there. That's illegal."

"Okay, fine. I'm bluffing. But I'm still right, aren't I?"

I roll my eyes and step closer, leaning closer to her ear, my voice lowering to match hers. "Maybe. You're welcome, by the way." I wink at her so she knows I'm only giving her a hard time.

"Thank you. That was very kind. But I'm surprised you even had time to do something like that, what with all the movies you've been seeing." She's not looking at me when she speaks; she's still peering down the hallway, watching as students slowly begin to emerge.

I blow out a breath. "Beth and I were trying to... I don't know. Reconnect, I guess." I run a hand through my hair and notice her face fall slightly. I bring my eyes to meet hers. "But it didn't work."

"Oh?" she asks, her tone slightly unreadable. "Why not?"

I glance around again, making sure no one is near us. "Because I can't stop thinking about you."

She finally turns my way and stares at me, shifting on her feet. My breath picks up in anticipation while I wait for her response.

"You shouldn't say that," she whispers finally.

"I know."

"Briggs..."

I rub the back of my neck, wishing I could stop, wishing I could walk away. But I can't.

"I couldn't stop, Paisley. Not during break, not when I was trying to convince myself it was all in my head, and not even when I was at the movie with Bethany. You're—" I pause, making sure no one is in earshot. "You're in my fucking head. And no matter what I do, I can't get you out."

Her cheeks flush, and she looks down, her fingers fidgeting with the edge of her olive green cardigan. "You... you can't say things like that," she murmurs.

"But it's true."

I can see her calculating what to say next, and she looks almost physically pained from the war breaking out in her mind. "Briggs," she whispers, "nothing can happen."

I swallow hard and nod my head. "I know."

But why not? I know things are messy. Complicated. But what if they weren't?

Holding her gaze, I don't move, and neither does she.

"You all packed?" she asks, changing the subject.

"For?"

Her mouth lifts into a half-smile. "PBIS?"

"Ah." I smile back. "Yeah. Threw some button-ups in a bag. Figured I'd wing it once I got there tomorrow."

She smiles slightly. "Are you leading any breakout sessions this year?"

"God, no." I chuckle. "Once was enough."

She smiles, but it falls quickly. "You know this is gonna be weird, right?"

"Weird doesn't even begin to cover it."

The bell rings overhead, and the hallway fills with noise and movement from the students.

She starts to step away but then pauses and turns toward me. "Briggs?"

"Yeah?"

"I think about you, too, you know," she says quietly. "Every second of every day, I think about you. And it's breaking me apart."

Chapter Thirty-five

♬ "Hands to Myself" — Selena Gomez ♬

PAISLEY

"Can we please go get drinks now?" Charlie groans from my hotel bed, sprawled out with her legs crossed at her ankles and one arm flung dramatically over her forehead.

Honestly, I'm surprised she didn't spike her water bottle this morning and bring it to the damn seminar sessions with her. But let's be real: if she did, I wouldn't even judge her. Having time off school to attend a conference is like a vacation and should be treated as such.

Damn, now I'm kind of bummed I didn't think of that idea earlier.

"I'm almost ready," I say, tilting my head to the side as I add a final swipe of blush to my cheek. "Don't you think it's a little early? The piano bar downstairs probably isn't even open yet."

She peeks at me from under her arm. "It's after five, and we sat through *six* sessions on instructional strategies and behavioral interventions today. I deserve vodka." She sits up farther and hoists herself up on her elbows. "And also, don't act like you're not getting all dressed up just in case a certain assistant principal shows up to the bar tonight."

My hand freezes mid-air, mascara brush suspended in front of me. "I—what? I'm literally just putting on mascara."

"Mmhmm," Charlie hums unconvinced before dropping back onto the bed and laughing. "Relax, Pais, I'm kidding. Mostly. I just think you look suspiciously cute for a conference bar."

She picks her phone up off the bed and starts scrolling, clearly not giving it too much thought. I roll my eyes and try to laugh it off, but deep down, I know she's right. I look at myself in the mirror and fix the hem of my white crop-top. It shows just a sliver of skin between the bottom of it and the waistband of my mid-rise jeans. Add the heeled booties I packed for tonight and the curls in my hair, and yeah—maybe I am trying a little harder than usual.

I just didn't realize it was that obvious.

Charlie and I drove to the conference this morning and got here late—because duh, you can't survive hours of professional development without caffeine—and ended up walking into the ballroom right as the keynote speaker started. We had to grab a couple seats in the back, and even though I knew Briggs was already here, I didn't see him anywhere.

But I could feel him.

I don't even know how to explain it, and it probably makes me sound crazy, but it's like there's this invisible thread tugging somewhere in my chest whenever I'm in the same vicinity of him. Like the universe is actively trying to push us together.

So yeah, the thought of seeing him tonight, hours away from Stonebrook and all our responsibilities there, both terrifies me and makes my stomach do that stupid flipping thing it's been doing nonstop lately. Especially after yesterday when he sneaked into my classroom and left my favorite snacks in there. What the hell is he trying to do to me, anyway?

"Who else is going down to the bar?" Charlie asks as I step into my boots.

"I told Tami and Beckah to meet us there if they're up for it. Not sure if they will, though." I shrug.

Charlie groans again and stretches before standing from the bed. "Ugh, I hope they do. It's so much more fun at these things when everyone's drinking and no one is trying to pretend they're still in teacher mode."

I laugh as I grab my wallet off the dresser. "You're not wrong. Meet you down there in ten? I just need to use the bathroom quick."

She narrows her eyes. "Don't you dare bitch out on me, Paisley Hamilton."

I roll my eyes. "I won't. Pinky promise."

And I mean it. She's not far off—normally, after a long day, the idea of curling up in bed and watching trash TV sounds way more appealing than making small talk and sipping overpriced cocktails.

But tonight, there's a chance I'll get to see Briggs, and that alone is reason enough for me to go.

When I walk into the bar, Charlie is already making best friends with the bartender. Although she's madly in love with her partner, John, she's always been gregarious and maybe a little over friendly toward everyone. But it usually benefits me when we go out together—free drinks are always a nice perk.

"Drink up, bitch!" she yells from across the room, holding a gin and tonic toward me. Because it's still somewhat early, there are only a couple people in here, and her booming voice echoes across the bar. Laughing, I sit on the wooden barstool next to her and let the first sip of my drink hit my lips.

By the time an hour passes, we're on our third round, and I'm starting to feel a little hazy. My back is turned to the door, and suddenly the energy shifts in the room. I refrain from turning around, but Charlie's green eyes shift from me to the entrance, a smile pulling at her lips.

"Guess who just walked in here," she says, teasingly. "Looking hot as fuck, by the way. Damn, that's what he's been hiding under that grumpy exterior?"

Not being able to resist, I turn and see Briggs walking to a table near the bar with Nate. He's wearing dark-washed denim jeans with a tight black henley, and holy *fuck*. I've never, in my entire life, seen a man look as delicious as he does right now.

Well played, universe, well played.

Flipping back around to face Charlie, I shrug nonchalantly as convincingly as I can.

"Wow, that's a look I've never seen on you before," she says, taking a sip of her drink. "Spill, Hamilton."

"What?" I ask, trying my best to sound oblivious. Damn, I really *would* be a bad poker player.

She eyes me, scrutinous. "Don't even give me that. There's something different about you lately, Pais. And judging by the look on your face the minute you saw Davenport, it seems pretty obvious it has something to do with him."

I suddenly have the urge to tell her more about what's been going on with him and me, probably thanks to the fucking alcohol. But I've been feeling so alone and conflicted in this, and having someone to talk with about it might help.

"Actually... I kind of lied," I continue. "Briggs and I have been talking a lot more, and it's gotten kind of... intense?"

"Okay, we'll circle back to you lying to me later. But what do you mean by intense?"

"Shut it," I groan. "It was totally innocent at first. He stayed late one night to help me put some furniture together in my classroom that Sunday before school started, and then he had to help me jump me car, and then—"

"Okay, well, first of all, the hell? You never told me about *any* of that. What the fuck, Pais?"

"I know, I know. I'm sorry. I didn't want to make a big deal out of it. It was nothing. We were just getting to know each other, like as friends." I take another sip of my drink. "But lately our interactions have become a little more... sexual?" I say quietly, so no one around us can hear. "And there's so much tension between us. It's crazy, Char, but I don't remember ever feeling like this with anyone."

"Not even with Ethan?"

I shake my head. "I know that sounds insane. But the more I get to know Briggs, the more I realize that he's everything I've ever wanted. And I know I don't know him that well. But when I'm with him, things are just... different."

"Okay..." she treads lightly. "Well have you and him—"

"No, no, of course not. We haven't acted on anything. Although we did have a moment at the Fall Ball where things got awfully... heated. I don't know. I guess more than anything, I've kind of been questioning things lately."

"What do you mean?"

"With Ethan. Putting everything with Briggs aside, you know what my relationship with Eth is like. Things are good. They've always been good. But I have kind of always wondered if they could be... better?" I take a deep breath to collect my thoughts. "Especially now that I've been talking to Briggs more, I'm realizing I kind of pushed some of my wants and needs aside when I married Ethan. I'm not saying that I necessarily want to be with Briggs, or if that's even a possibility, but I'm starting to feel like maybe, I don't know—" I pause, twisting my hands in my lap. "That maybe I settled with Ethan? And I feel terrible saying that because I made the decision to marry him. And we've only been married for two years—"

"But you've been together a lot longer than that,' she points out.

"Still. How many people start to question their marriage only two years after saying 'I do'?"

"Probably less than who should. Seriously, so many people settle, and then they stay stuck because they feel like they made a choice, and they have to live with it. But people change, Paisley. *Relationships* change. And sometimes, one person changes and the other person doesn't. As far as you and Ethan are concerned, it's obvious that you two aren't on the same page anymore. You want to grow, and seize opportunity, and potentially move out of Wisconsin, and he—"

"Is fine staying where he is," I finish her sentence for her, defeated.

"Exactly."

"Okay, yeah, that's all true. But it doesn't mean I should be talking to Briggs behind Ethan's back. Yeah, it started out as nothing. Completely innocent. But even then... it's like I *knew* where this was going to lead, and I kept talking to him anyway."

"I understand that, but you haven't acted on it, and maybe this is giving you some much needed perspective that you've been overlooking for a while. But if you feel like you're going to cross a line, come talk to me. Don't do anything you'll regret. K?"

"I know. I'm not going to. Besides, just because Briggs has been a little more flirtatious toward me doesn't mean that he would act on anything."

I peer across the bar. The sun has set now, and the Edison bulbs are projecting an amber light throughout the room. Briggs is sitting at a table with Nate, a drink in his hand that looks like a rum and Coke. He must feel me looking at him, because before I have a chance to look away, his eyes catch mine. He gives me a onceover, his steel blue eyes scanning my entire body, and a serious look crosses his face. It's darker, heavier, like he's barely holding himself together.

I bite my lip in frustration and force my attention back to Charlie, who has now changed the subject to something I can't even register. My phone sits on the bar next to me, and it lights up with a notification.

*Are you trying to torture me coming
in here looking like that?*

Heat crawls up my entire body, spreading like wildfire. I quickly flip my phone over, hoping Charlie doesn't notice. Torture? He thinks *this* is torture? The past two months have been torture.

I try to focus on Charlie, but I can still feel the weight of his gaze on me from across the room. I exhale a shaky breath and sink back onto my barstool, ignoring the way my hands tremble as I pick up my drink.

After one more round, I told Charlie I was calling it a night and headed up to my room. It's almost nine o' clock, and although our first session isn't super early tomorrow, I still don't want to be hungover, and I knew if I hung out downstairs any longer, that would be the case. I learned my limit a long time ago, and after four or five drinks, I start to teeter the line of buzzed and cross over into the line of drunk, which always brings a hangover with it.

Most of our colleagues were still having drinks when I left, including Briggs. As I sashayed my way across the bar, his gaze lingered on me a little longer than what is deemed acceptable, but no one else seemed to notice.

After I ignored his message, he didn't text me again, and he never made his way over to where Charlie and I were sitting at the bar. I shouldn't feel disappointed about that, but of course, I do.

Shrugging it off, I walk into my room and kick off my shoes. I sit on the bed and let out a deep exhale as if I've been holding my breath all week. But as soon as I do, there's a knock on the door.

"Charlie, I told you I was g—" I start, swinging the door open, but it's not Charlie. "Oh—h-hi."

"Hi," he says, that infuriatingly adorable smile plastered across his face.

"What are you doing here?" I poke my head out into the hallway to see if anyone is with him.

"Well, you just looked so damn beautiful downstairs that I couldn't convince myself to go to bed without doing this."

"Without doing wh—"

I don't get to finish. The door slams behind him, and suddenly he's on me, pinning me against the wall, his lips crashing into mine.

Everything inside me explodes. A fleet of emotions slams into me all at once. Confusion, desire, guilt, passion. A dizzying mix of right and wrong.

I've imagined this moment a dozen times, but nothing— *nothing*—could have prepared me for this. His lips are soft but urgent, and his hand curls around the back of my neck while he presses his body further into mine. Hunger radiates off him.

I part my lips, letting my tongue meet his, and I swear I might fucking combust on the spot. I wrap my arms around his waist, pulling his body flush with mine. His weight against me is like a puzzle piece I didn't even realize was missing, finally falling into place. It's all too fucking much and yet not enough at the same time.

And then suddenly, everything makes sense. This is what I've been missing, what I've been *craving*.

He pushes into me further, and his hand travels down my back, slipping beneath the waistband of my jeans. His hand cups my ass, and he lets out a groan—like he's finally able to touch me the way he's been dying to. I kiss him harder, like I can't get enough, savoring the moment in fear this will be the only time I'm able to.

My hands roam under his shirt, across the warm skin of his back, desperate to sear the feel and taste of him into memory.

And then he pulls away suddenly, his forehead still pressed against mine. "You have no idea how long I've been wanting to do that." He's still so close to me that his words vibrate between our lips.

But before I can respond, before I can even *think*, he slips from my touch as quickly as he came, and he turns and walks through the door without another word, leaving me alone in my quiet hotel room.

I collapse against the wall behind me, its surface jarringly cold on my skin, and get swallowed up by the silence.

So much for not crossing the line.

BRIGGS

Fuck.

I can still taste her. The gin on her tongue and a hint of vanilla chapstick on her goddamn perfect lips. It's driving me mad.

I've been back in my hotel room for five minutes, and I haven't stopped replaying that fucking kiss in my head. How her body felt pressed against mine. How she pulled me closer like she couldn't get enough. How her breath hitched when she felt my hand slip under her jeans and grab her ass. How she leaned into the kiss deeper, like she wanted me, too.

And God do I want her. I want her more than I've wanted anything in a long time. But then I walked away, right out the door without a single fucking word, leaving her all alone in that damn hotel room.

Why the fuck did I do that?

Right. Because I'm trying to be the person both my brain and body are desperately rooting against.

So instead, I'm sitting on the edge of this shitty bed, staring at the shitty beige walls and shitty hotel flooring, wondering what the hell I'm supposed to do now.

Because there's no questioning it anymore. I know what I want. *Who* I want. And I want *her*.

No. I fucking *need* her.

I've been lying to myself for weeks. For months. For *years*, telling myself that what I had with Beth was enough. That what I feel for Paisley is just a harmless attraction, something that would fade over time. But that kiss showed me everything I didn't know I had been missing.

I drag my hands down my face, trying to calm the storm raging inside me. I shake my head, as if it will let go of the guilt, the desire, the overwhelming sense of foreboding that my life is about to change in ways I can't prevent or undo.

This is so fucked up. I know that. So why the hell is my body urging me to walk back up to that room and finish what we started?

I stand and pace the small space like it's going to help, but it doesn't. I squeeze my eyes, but it only heightens the memory of her a few minutes ago. My mind flashes back to that surprised look on her face when she opened the door and saw me standing there, her beautiful brown eyes staring up, as if she was expecting anyone but me. I couldn't even let her finish her sentence before I pressed my lips to hers. And the way her nails dug into my back... like she didn't want to let me go, like if we didn't taste each other immediately, we'd fucking snap.

Just like I'm about to now thinking about it again.

"Fuck," I mutter and flop back down on the bed, letting out a deep breath.

And before I can stop myself, my hand slides under the waistband of my pants with a will of its own.

I shouldn't.

I *really* fucking shouldn't.

But that image of her is branded into my memory, and my body is begging for release.

I slide up to the headboard and unbutton my jeans, shoving them down barely enough to free my aching cock. I lean my back against the cool wood behind me and wrap my hand around my length, letting out a shaky breath. I'm hard as fuck already solely from the memory of *kissing her.* I can't imagine what it would be like to fully take her as mine.

I shouldn't be doing this—not here, not now, not with *her* in my head—but just like that moment in the shower a few weeks ago, I can't fucking stop myself. The thought of her is too much to ignore.

And I don't even think I want to anymore.

I stroke myself slowly, my thumb tracing over the tip of my cock, spreading the pre-cum down my shaft. The more I think of her, the faster I pump my fist. Her voice plays in my head—the way she always says my name, that slight moan that escaped her lips when I pressed her against the wall tonight.

I move faster, chasing my release, my free hand gripping the sheets harder as my body starts to tighten. I need this so badly it's almost painful. I rub my cock faster and faster, and when it finally hits, it's like the world explodes behind my goddamn eyes.

"Oh, fuck," I groan, the orgasm rocking through my body like nothing I've experienced before. Jets of cum fall onto my stomach, and I collapse against the headboard, shaking and breathless.

I lie there for a moment, waiting for the guilt to come.

But it doesn't.

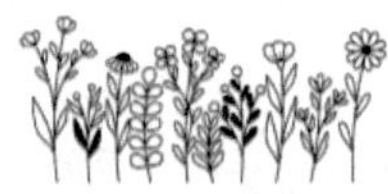

The obnoxious blare of my phone alarm jolts me awake. As I roll over to turn it off, I'm instantly hit with the memory of what happened with Paisley last night. Again, I wait for the shame to surface at the thought of her, to rise within my chest, but excitement about seeing her today comes instead.

Unfortunately, I have to sit through three sessions before that, and because I'm in administration, the chances of being in the same seminars as her, or any of the staff, is low.

I groan, running a hand over my face, and stare at the popcorn ceiling above me. With being so wrapped up in my own thoughts, I haven't even had a chance to consider how Paisley is feeling about last night. It *seemed* like she wanted me back, but what if she's racked with regret this morning? What if, in an attempt to see whatever this is between us, I ruined any chance of us even being friends now? What if I've just made things worse for her?

The thought of causing her any pain instantly makes my stomach twist in knots. Fuck. I need to talk to her.

I hop out of bed and jump into the shower, letting the warm water penetrate my skin to relax my nerves and lessen the tension in my shoulders.

Once I get out, I throw on a pair of khaki chinos and a black athletic pullover. Luckily, I probably won't see her until a little later today, so I have some time to think about what I'm going to say.

By the time I make it down to the hotel lobby, there are already dozens of people shuffling around and walking to their first sessions. Instead of going right toward the meeting rooms, though, I veer left and head toward the coffee shop near the check-in desk, needing some caffeine to survive the seminars today.

And there, standing in line with a thick brown braid trailing down her back, is Paisley. Charlie is next to her, ordering her coffee, and Paisley walks in my direction to wait for her drink at the opposite end of the counter.

Fuck. So much for having time to think about what I would say to her. Maybe I should walk the other way. Pretend I don't see her before she sees me? But it's too late. Before I know it, I'm standing only a few feet away.

She grabs her iced coffee from the counter and turns around, her brown eyes locking with mine immediately. For a split second, her eyes widen, a look of panic crossing her features, before they soften a bit. I take a few steps toward her cautiously.

"Hey," I manage.

She glances over her shoulder at Charlie, who's now waiting for her drink and is too busy scrolling on her phone to even notice I'm here.

"Hi," she says softly. Her voice is light, like she's as unsure of what to say as I am.

The air between us feels heavy as it always does, and there's a slight flush in her cheeks. I love how I always know how she's feeling just by the sight of her.

"About last night—" I start, but she cuts me off with a shake of her head.

"Not here," she whispers, her eyes darting back to Charlie.

I nod, swallowing hard. "Right. Does Charlie—"

"No," she says quickly. "I didn't tell her. I wouldn't. Not until you and I can…"

"Yeah," I interrupt, knowing what she's going to say. "I guess we should probably talk about it."

She nods her head emphatically. "Right." She looks back at Charlie again, who is now grabbing her drink and will be joining this conversation any second. "Anyway, we should probably get to our first session. See you at the closing remarks later today?"

"Yeah, sounds good," I say, my voice sounding distant.

She offers a slight smile, and that alone causes my pulse to beat rapidly. She turns on her heel to walk away, but I softly grab her arm, a bolt of electricity shooting through my hand.

"Oh, and Paisley?" She turns, and her eyes meet mine again. "Just so you know, I don't regret anything."

A soft sigh escapes her lips. "Good. Because neither do I." She walks away without saying anything more.

The rest of the day passes in a blur. The sessions fly by, and my focus is shit all day. I move from room to room without even knowing how I get from one place to the next, my head too wrapped up in what the hell I'm going to do.

At the closing session, Paisley and I both sit at the same table as the rest of the staff, but she barely looks at me. Instead, she keeps her sight trained on the speaker, only losing focus when Charlie whispers something in her ear.

If there is a Hell, I think this might be it.

How do I move forward from here? How do I go on acting like every single part of me isn't on fire simply being in the same room as her? How do I act like I don't want to pull her to me and kiss her and tell her how amazing she is every second?

I don't know how I'm supposed to go through each day, being so close to her and not being able to touch her or claim her as mine.

But I do know one thing: there's no way I'm going to be able to stay away from her now.

Chapter Thirty-Seven

♫ *"Stay" — Rihanna ft. Mikky Ekko* ♫

PAISLEY

The bell echoes loudly through my room at the beginning of my planning period. And thank fucking God because I am exhausted. When I got home from the conference yesterday, Ethan was still at work, and then he stopped at his parents' and didn't get home until late. By the time he did, I was already in bed. I told him I was exhausted from the seminars—which wasn't a lie, exactly—and needed to get some rest.

But mainly, I didn't know how to face him after what I had done. When Briggs kissed me the other night, it felt like the moment I've been waiting thirty years for. The moment you read about in books and see in movies but don't think will ever actually happen in real life. His lips—his body—felt like they were curated specifically for mine.

But once he left me alone in that hotel room, the guilt started to sink in. What kind of person does that? What kind of *wife* does that? I know Ethan and I have our problems, but he doesn't deserve this.

And yet I can't stop fucking thinking about it. I thought about it all night, and all morning during my work out, and during my entire drive to school, and every second during my classes today.

I sit down at my desk, leaning back in my chair and closing my eyes. The afternoon sun shines through my window, and I allow its warmth to cascade over my entire body. I attempt to clear my mind, but my thoughts keep trailing back to Briggs and that fucking kiss.

Then before I know it, my hand grabs my phone and opens our message thread. We haven't talked since our brief interaction at the coffee shop yesterday morning. I thought about texting him a million times since then—no, that's not an exaggeration—but I couldn't find the words. What would I even say? With the way he bolted from my doorway that night, I have no idea how he's feeling. He said he doesn't regret it, but how *does* he feel?

My phone buzzes in my hand and startles me. There's a new message from Briggs, and my stomach flip-flops upside down and jumps up into my throat.

Are you in your room?

I stare at the screen for what feels like an eternity, though it couldn't be longer than three minutes. I start typing my response when my body stiffens as it senses a change of energy in the room.

I look up and find Briggs, looking handsome as fucking ever, barreling through my doorway. He's wearing black dress pants and a grey button-up dress shirt that emphasizes his biceps. As he steps over the threshold, he swings the door shut behind him and closes the window curtain.

"Come here," he demands as he motions me to stand.

As if my brain is wired for his commands, I stand and walk toward him without question. He's still striding my way with determination, and before I can register what he's about to do, both of his hands are on either side of my face, and he's pulling me into him. His lips find mine hungrily, and he kisses me with a fervor that surpasses the fleeting moment in the hotel room.

I expect him to pull away, but he does the opposite. He pushes me against the whiteboard, and I stumble back and try to catch myself, sending Expo markers clattering to the ground around us. I grab his waist and pull him toward me, and the world around us fades into a blur, leaving only the heat between us and the intoxicating scent of his mint and bourbon cologne.

My heart pounds in my chest, and every touch, every movement, sends a shock of electricity through my veins.

In this moment, time stops and nothing else exists. It's just him and me, tangled together in a whirlwind of temptation and passion. There is no room for hesitation or restraint, only the overwhelming need for each other, our bodies guided by a primal need that's bigger than either of us.

But within a matter of minutes, realization dawns, and I'm jolted back to reality. We are in my classroom. At school. Where his wife works. Where we could get *caught*. Where we most definitely should not be doing this.

I pull away, breathless, and gaze up into his blue, lust-filled eyes.

"We shouldn't be doing this," I whisper, though it comes out as more of a question than a declaration.

"I know," he agrees, surprisingly. "But I just couldn't stay away. I thought about you all night. About that kiss. About how I needed more. About how *I need more*," he adds with certainty.

Taking a deep breath, I put some distance between us and walk away from the whiteboard and the sea of markers on the floor. I know what we are doing is wrong, on so many levels, but being near him clouds my judgment, and all of those reasons seem to disappear. All I can think about is how he makes me feel everything I've been wanting to feel for years.

"You're trouble, Briggs Davenport," I say, attempting to tease him, but defeat comes through in my tone.

A hint of sadness crosses his features, and I can tell he's feeling the same way I do. For the past few weeks, I've been so focused on the confusion I've been feeling that I sometimes forget he's in the exact same position as I am.

"I know," he says, some playfulness returning to his demeanor, "but so are you." He raises his arm and runs his finger through his brown tufts of hair, and I notice that he's not wearing his wedding ring.

Does he usually wear it? I could swear that he did.

Maybe forgetting it this morning was an innocent mistake. Or is it symbolic that this thing between us is more than what we've been allowing ourselves to believe?

"Forget your ring this morning?" I hear myself ask, the words slipping out of my mouth before I have a chance to even think about if I want to know the answer.

He glances at his hand. "Something like that," he says, and my mind instantly jumps to Bethany, wondering if she also noticed the gold band missing from his finger.

I'm sure she would just assume he took it off to work on something in the garage and forgot to put it back on. The fact that I know she probably wouldn't think anything of it brings that familiar sick feeling to my stomach.

"Briggs—" I start, but I'm cut off by someone jiggling my door handle to my classroom.

"Who is that?" he whispers, and my heart freezes. Who could be trying to get into my classroom? I'm about to tell him not to worry about it and that it's probably just a student trying to turn in a missing assignment, but then a key jangles in the lock.

I'm not sure who could be opening my door—the only people with keys to my room are the other teachers in the English department and other administrators—but I am sure that whoever comes in will be confused to find Dr. Davenport and Mrs. Hamilton alone in her classroom with the door shut and the lights dim.

Before I have a chance to go into full blown panic of how bad this must look, the door opens and Catherine peaks her head in, a look of surprise and confusion plastered across her face.

"Oh," she exclaims. "Sorry, um, I didn't think you were in here..." she trails off, her eyes darting between Briggs and me. "I saw your door was closed, so Amy let me borrow her key. I just... wanted to drop this paperwork off for you. It's for PBIS."

"Oh yeah, thanks," I chuckle awkwardly. Forget about my face being flushed—it has to be fire hydrant red.

"We were just talking about a student," Briggs interrupts, a little too eagerly. Smooth, dude, smooth. "Which is why we had the door shut," he adds, making it even more awkward.

"Oh, okay. Sorry to interrupt." She sets the paperwork down on a nearby desk and closes the door, rather uncomfortably, as she leaves.

With her no longer in the room, my heart returns to a normal rhythm. Luckily Briggs and I were only talking when she came in. But what if we weren't? What if she had come in a couple minutes earlier?

And by the uneasy look on Briggs's face, I can tell he's asking himself the same question.

Chapter Thirty-Eight

BRIGGS

"What are we doing, Briggs?" Paisley asks solemnly as she hops up on a student desk.

"I think what we've been wanting to do for a long time." I close the space between us and lean against the desk beside her, our shoulders almost touching. After our little run-in with Catherine a few minutes ago, I don't dare get too close, but my body is still urging me to anyway.

"But... what is this to you? You say you've never done this before, but—"

"I haven't," I say sternly. "Never. This isn't just some fling for me, Paisley, or some way for me to pass the time. Whatever this is between us—it's real. More real than anything I've ever felt before."

"Even with Bethany?" She looks up at me, and it's hard to discern whether it's fear or hope in her voice.

I nod, turning to face her fully, standing between her legs but not touching her. "Even with Bethany."

She looks down at her hands, so I continue.

"This isn't just about you and me, Paisley. It's more than that. There are a lot of aspects of my relationship with Beth that haven't been what they should be for a very long time. I think part of me always knew, deep down, that she wasn't the person I was meant to be with, but it was easy to ignore. And for a long time, that's what I did."

"So what's different? What made you realize it now?"

"You."

Her brown eyes lock with mine, and for a moment, she's silent.

"Do you believe in soulmates?"

Her question catches me off guard, and I take a minute to think about it. She waits patiently, not rushing me to answer.

"I'm not sure," I finally say. "I don't think life is about finding your perfect, predestined match that the fates have aligned just for you. I think it's about finding the person you can fully be yourself around, the person who makes you feel comfortable but also challenges you to be better. The person who ignites a fire inside of you that you didn't know needed kindling."

"Yeah," she says, her voice barely above a whisper. "I used to think love was a choice. That you wake up every day and choose to be with someone, even if it's hard. That no matter how good the relationship, there would always have to be sacrifices. But..."

"But what?"

"But what if that isn't true? What if we've been conditioned by society to accept good as good enough?"

I frown, unsure where she's going with this. She looks back down and traces the seam of her pants as if she's trying to collect her thoughts.

"I love Ethan," she says, almost as if she's reminding herself, and the mention of his name is like a punch to the gut. "He's good to me. He doesn't hurt me. He makes me laugh. He *loves* me. We have a good life together." Her eyes lift to mine, and there's fear and vulnerability in them. "But what if 'good' simply *isn't* enough? What if I stay with him, and in twenty years, I realize I spent my whole life settling? What if I wake up one day and wonder what it would have been like to have something fucking *great?*"

My throat tightens. I want to speak, to tell her I understand exactly how she's feeling, but I can sense she's not done yet.

"You don't throw away a good thing to chase something better," she continues, her voice slightly breaking. "That's what everyone says, right? That's what we've always been taught. Be grateful for what you have. The grass isn't always greener. All those stupid fucking clichés that are supposed to mean something but don't." She takes a deep breath, steadying herself. "You don't ruin a stable life for a *feeling*, Briggs. But what if this is more than just a feeling? What if *you* are exactly what I've been looking for? What if we miss out on something real, something extraordinary, because we're too afraid to leave something that's *good*?"

I step closer, now completely eliminating the space between us. Probably not a good idea, considering what just happened with Catherine barging in, but I can't help myself.

"Paisley." My hand lifts, and I trace her cheek with the back of my fingers.

"I don't want to be reckless, Briggs. Or selfish. That isn't me," she pleads. "But I'm scared as hell thinking about the possibility of waking up when I'm fifty and realizing I made the wrong decision."

Her words validate me in a way I didn't know I needed, because I've been feeling the exact same for weeks. I take her hand, rubbing her knuckle.

"I get it."

Her eyes search mine, waiting for more. Waiting for reassurance. Waiting for the same vulnerability she offered me. I swallow hard and continue.

"I've spent years convincing myself that stability is the same as happiness. That just because Beth and I get along and don't fight, just because we have a life that looks good on paper, it means we should be happy. I've been lying to myself, trying to convince myself that it was enough. But it's not. And I'm so fucking tired of pretending that it is. And I think you are, too."

She lets out a slow breath and nods. "I'm scared, Briggs."

I pull her to me and wrap my arms around her. She rests her head on my shoulder, and I softly kiss her forehead.

"I'm scared, too, Paisley. But we're not crazy for wanting more. It's okay to want more."

Chapter Thirty-Nine

♫ "Starving" — Hailee Steinfeld & Grey ft. Zedd ♫

PAISLEY

There's nothing worse than finding the person who sets your soul on fire after you're already married. That's all I can fucking think about as I sit across from Charlie and Leah at the bar tonight.

I successfully avoided Briggs all day. Not that I *wanted* to, but I thought putting some distance between us would help me clear my head. After that second kiss in my classroom, I need to figure out what this is, what I want, before having a deeper conversation with him. So I purposely stayed in my classroom between periods, and I took the long way around the school to the prep room hoping I wouldn't run into him. I avoided the main office like the fucking plague, and I pretended to be busier than I actually was all day.

But it was no use. I still fucking thought about him every second of the day. He had texted me once, asking if everything was okay, saying he was worried he hadn't seen me. I didn't reply.

Instead, I asked Charlie and Leah if they wanted to grab drinks after school, and now I'm here, feeling way tipsier than I should, and the alcohol still isn't doing what I'd hoped it would. It's not making the thoughts about Briggs disappear—it's just making them harder to ignore.

"Pais, are you listening?" Charlie's voice snaps me back to the moment, and I realize I've totally missed the last five minutes of our conversation. What were we even talking about?

"Sorry, yeah," I mutter, rubbing my temple. "I'm listening. Just trying to determine if I'm going to die of liver failure before I turn thirty-one."

Leah laughs. "Eh, I think you'd die of something more dramatic than that."

I take a sip of my water, figuring I probably don't need to finish the gin and tonic sitting in front of me. "You're right. Knowing me, I'll be teaching one day and spontaneously explode on the spot. Poor kids will have to run and tell Nicole about it, and then the janitor will have to come clean it up."

"Um, okay," Charlie snorts. "Fucking morbid, Pais. No more alcohol for you." She grabs my half-full drink and slides it in her direction, taking a sip.

"All yours, babe," I tell her. "I think I've hit my quota for the night."

"Well good thing you aren't the one driving."

She's right. I don't have my car here, and Charlie was going to bring me home. But maybe...

"I need to use the bathroom," I mutter, pushing up from the booth before either of them can respond.

I stagger my way there, my vision a little hazy and my head spinning slightly. I push the door to the bathroom open and catch a glimpse of myself in the mirror. My hair is in a long, fishtail braid tonight, and my brown eyes are more dilated than usual. After fixing the smudged mascara under my eyes, I lock myself in a stall and pull my phone out of my pocket, knowing exactly what I'm about to do even though I know I shouldn't.

What I *should* do is call Ethan. I should go home and curl up in bed, pretend like everything's fine, and keep going on with the routine I've built myself into.

But instead, my thumb hovers over the screen, and I scroll until I find Briggs's name in my call log. I shouldn't call him. I know that. What if he's with Bethany? What if she sees?

But the overwhelming desire to hear his voice wins, thanks to the liquor coursing through my veins, and my thumb presses down on his name before I can stop myself. The line rings, and my heart thumps so hard I can hear it in my ears.

This was a bad idea. Oh, fuck, fuck, fuck, what am I doing? I'm such an idio—

"Paisley?" he answers, his voice rough and laced with concern.

"Can you come get me?" I blurt, my words slurring slightly.

There's a pause, and for a moment, I want to crawl inside myself and die. Yep, this was *definitely* a bad idea. And the worst part is I can't even blame Charlie for this one. This was all me.

"Are you okay?"

"Yeah, I'm fine. Ugh, I'm so sorry. I shouldn't have called you. I just—"

"Where are you?"

"The Tavern. But it's fine. Charlie can bring me home. Don't worry about it. I shouldn't have called. I don't know what I'm—"

"I'll be there in ten minutes," he clips, and the call ends before I can respond.

I stare at my phone as if it will have all the answers, which it doesn't, before I eventually walk back to the table where Charlie and Leah sit.

"Okay, don't hate me, but I'm having Ethan come get me." The lie slides off my tongue easier than I'd like to admit.

"Probably a good idea," Leah says as she nods. "Go home and get some sleep."

I slide my purse over my shoulder. "Are you two going to stay for a bit?" I ask, trying to feel out the situation. The last thing I need is for them to walk out at the same time Briggs arrives to pick me up. Now *that* would be hard to explain.

"Yeah, I think we'll stick around for a bit. It's still early, and there's plenty of night left."

I release an audible sigh, some of the worry I had a moment ago leaving my body. I give them each a hug goodbye and tell them I'll see them on Monday.

Once I'm outside, I let the crisp night air wash over me, cooling my flushed skin and clearing some of the haze from my mind. The temperature is barely above freezing, and the air bites at my exposed legs in my dress, but the sharpness against the heat of my body is refreshing.

I close my eyes for a moment, and as I do, the rumble of a car pulls up next to me. When I open my eyes, Briggs is already getting out of his car and walking around to the other side.

"Come on," he says as he opens the passenger door. "Let's get you warmed up. It's freezing out here."

He grabs both of my shoulders and helps me into his Dodge Charger. The warmth of the car causes my skin to flush again, so I slide my jacket off and toss it into the back.

"I'm sorry," I say immediately as he climbs into the driver's seat. "You didn't have to come."

"You really think I wouldn't?" He lets out a humorless laugh.

I swallow hard and look down at my hands. "Ethan doesn't know I called you."

I peek up through my lashes and see his jaw tense. He doesn't answer at first. Instead, he puts the car in drive and pulls into a spot at the back of the lot. Once the car is in park, he looks over at me.

"Yeah. I figured."

I turn to face him. "I can't fight this anymore," I say abruptly. "I need you, Briggs. Every part of you. I don't care about the repercussions."

His hands find the steering wheel again, and the muscles in his arms strain as he grips it tightly. He doesn't answer right away, but when he does, his voice is hesitant.

"Paisley, we can't. Not tonight."

"Why not? We both know we want this. Why are we pretending we don't?"

"Because you're drunk." His gaze flicks to me. "And this," he motions between us, "is more than just a drunken hookup for me."

I laugh, but it's empty. "You think I don't know that by now? Briggs, I…"

I freeze, trying to collect my thoughts as I look at him. His hair is tousled, evidence that he's been running his hand through it, and his blue eyes are dark, almost grey. He looks tired. Exhausted, even. Yet still so handsome. Looking at him now, I'm not sure how much longer I can resist the temptation that's been haunting me for fucking weeks.

My body trembles with need as I inch closer to him, and I place my hand on his thigh, sliding it up closer.

He doesn't shove me away immediately. Instead, his hand captures mine.

"Paisley," he warns, his voice strained. "Don't."

It sounds more like a plea than a command, and his pulse pounds against my wrist, his body betraying him. His jaw is set, his lips slightly parted, and his breathing is ragged, his body trembling with restraint.

"I want you, too," he admits. "But not like this. Not when you're like this."

I look into his eyes and nod slowly. "I get it. It shouldn't be like this. No matter how badly I want to, this isn't the way."

He closes his eyes for a moment as he lightly trails his finger down my arm. "So we wait. But Paisley," he says, his voice firming up. "I do want to know what it's like. Even if I only get one night with you, at least I'll get to live out the rest of my days knowing what it's like to be yours."

I swallow hard, my throat tightening. "When?" I whisper.

"Beth is going away at the beginning of winter break for a girls' trip to Nashville. Do you think you can get away for a day?"

I meet his gaze. Guilt creeps up my spine, but desire drowns it out. "I should be able to. Where would we go?"

"I'll take care of it."

His words sink in slowly. This is no longer an *if*, but a *when*. This is no longer harmless. No longer hypothetical.

My pulse skids, fear and desire colliding in my chest, and we sit in the silence of the car for a few minutes before he lets out a deep sigh and pulls out of the parking lot.

If we're going to do this—like really do this—I need to know everything I can about him, so I better use this time to my advantage. I need to know it's everything I want. That it's worth risking everything I have.

I swallow, pressing my palm against my thigh to keep from reaching for him again. "So... you're a psychologist. You overanalyze everything, right?"

His lips twitch, but he doesn't take his eyes off the road. "That's what I've been told."

"Okay. Then let's analyze this. Us." My voice sounds more confident than I expect, and the effect of the alcohol has slightly started to wear off, leaving me a bit more steady and grounded. "I don't want to make a mistake."

His eyes flash in my direction, his expression hard to read. "I think it's a little late for that concern. Don't you?"

"Maybe." I shrug. "But if we're going to risk everything, I need to know it's worth it. That we're not just two people who got caught up in the moment. With Ethan…" I pause.

"Yeah?"

I take a deep breath. "With Ethan, I feel like that's where it went wrong. We didn't take the time to truly *know* each other. We had fun together, and we were comfortable around each other, but I don't think I truly knew him—the deeper parts of him—until years down the road. We didn't take the time to have the tough conversations. Views, beliefs, morals, goals… and that's where we struggle now. I don't want that to happen again."

"Fair point," he says. "I can relate to that. What do you want to know?"

I shift in my seat, turning toward him. "Are you religious?"

His eyebrows lift slightly, telling me he wasn't expecting such a forward question right away, but he answers without hesitation.

"I believe in something. I grew up in the church because my dad is extremely religious. He had a rough life and claims that God saved him. We were in the pews every Sunday and Wednesday, but once I turned eighteen, I stopped going. A lot happened around that time that made me question whether what I was learning there was true or not." He pauses for a moment and lifts one shoulder. "I think there's something bigger than us, but I don't think being a believer has to be tied to a church. What about you?"

"That makes sense. My parents were never very religious, so I didn't go to church growing up. I agree, though, that there has to be more than just us. Humanity is such a small speck of the universe. Like, for example—" I pause and grab his free hand he has resting on the gear stick. "Here. If your palm represents the entire history of the universe, then human existence would only be this tiny freckle. I think it's quite egotistical for us to believe there aren't more powerful forces at play."

"Huh," he says, gazing down at his palm. "I've never thought about it that way."

"Me either. I heard it mentioned on a TV show a couple weeks ago." I shrug and give him a coy smile.

He laughs and shakes his head. I let go of his hand, assuming it will find its way back to where it was, but he rests it on my thigh instead. The warmth of his palm sends a shiver up my spine.

"Anyway," I continue. "How about politics?"

Briggs sighs, rubbing my thigh with his thumb. "You really want to go there?"

I smirk. "I told you. If I'm going to potentially blow up my life for you, I need to know you're not a total asshole."

He laughs. "But a little bit of an asshole is okay?" he teases.

"If it's in the right context." I wink. "But seriously. Politics. Lay it on me."

He lets out another soft laugh. "Fair enough. I would say I'm in the middle. I don't vote straight ticket—I vote for the candidate I align with most in each election. Historically speaking, though? I would say financially, I lean a bit more right. Socially, probably more left." He shrugs. "I don't really like to put a title on it. I think both sides are too extreme these days. For me, I believe people should have the right to make their own choices. I want better education funding, more awareness around healthcare, and I think the world would be a better place if we just let people live how they want. Do I relate to everyone's choices? No. But if your choices don't affect me and aren't hurting anyone, then who am I to judge, you know?"

It feels like a weight has been lifted off my chest, but I don't show it. Politics is one area that has caused a lot of contention between Ethan and me over the years. I'm similar to Briggs, but Ethan leans very heavily in his views, and he doesn't always think before he speaks.

"Good answer."

He smirks. "Your turn."

"I'm about the same," I admit. "Grew up in an insanely conservative town, but I started questioning a lot as I got older, especially being in the education field. I think people deserve kindness, no matter who they are. Sounds naive, probably, but I just want everyone to feel loved."

His lips part slightly, like he wasn't expecting me to say that. "Yeah. Me too."

"Okay, what about kids? Do you want them?"

Briggs shifts in his seat. "Beth does." He pauses, and when he speaks again, his voice is more solemn. "I thought we were on the same page, but it doesn't seem like it anymore. I like kids. I like mentoring them, coaching them, helping them. But having my own?" He sighs. "It's not something I've ever really wanted."

I nod, looking out the window. "Ethan wants them. Eventually. I always said I did, too, but..." I trail off, my throat tightening.

Whose idea was it to have this damn conversation? Especially after one too many drinks? Damn, Past Paisley. Scheming against me once again.

"But?"

"I don't know if that was true. Or if I just said it because I thought I was supposed to."

"What do you mean?"

"Like, it's always been this unspoken expectation. The amount of kids in my family—it's insane. Most of my cousins had children before they were even twenty-five. All of them have at least two. Fuck, my sister has *five*. At every family gathering, people are always asking when it's my turn, what I'm waiting for. But truthfully, the more I think about it, the more I've kind of been the black sheep in that regard.

"People think that because I'm a teacher, I must love children. But I always *hated* babysitting. Never did it growing up. People say it's different with your own, but I just don't particularly *enjoy* being around kids, especially young ones—hence why I teach high school." I smirk. "But society tells us that's the natural next step, right? Find a job, get married, buy a house, have kids." I shake my head. "But when does that leave time for ourselves? When does that leave time for *me* and what *I* want to do? When the kids are grown and I'm retired? When I'm too old to enjoy it?"

Briggs looks over at me, and his eyes soften. "And what is it that you want to do?"

"I want to travel. To see the world. To know what it feels like to grow somewhere I wasn't planted, I guess."

He doesn't say anything, so I continue. "I know it sounds selfish. But isn't it more selfish to have kids when you know you don't really want them?"

He shakes his head. "I don't think you're selfish. I think you're honest. And I think about that a lot. About how much of my life I'd have to give up. About how much of my life I haven't even *lived* yet. Beth has brought up the idea more and more lately. But honestly..."

"What?" I ask, my voice soft.

"I'm not even sure if *she* wants them, or if she just thinks it'll fix whatever is missing between us. As if having a kid will make everything better. But every time I try to picture it, I just... can't."

I glance at him and place my hand on his. "You can't picture being a dad?"

Briggs exhales sharply. "No. At least not in a way that makes me feel... excited. Or fulfilled. I can picture going through the motions, you know? Holding a baby, teaching someone how to ride a bike... but when I envision that future, there's no excitement attached to it. Instead, I feel—" He hesitates, then shakes his head. "Trapped."

I let the words hang in the air between us for a few seconds as I trace my finger along his hand.

"I don't want to resent my own life," I whisper.

He flips his palm over, fully taking my hand in his and interlacing our fingers. "Exactly."

"I hate how people act like not wanting to have kids means there's something wrong with you. But I don't want to be stuck in the same fucking lifeless cycle everyone else is. There's so much I want to do, so many places I want to see. But I know if I stay with Ethan... none of that will happen. And what if I'm meant for something else?"

Briggs pulls my hand up to his lips and gently kisses it, and my heart plummets into my stomach. "What if we both are?"

I train my eyes back on the road and notice we are turning onto my street already.

"You can drop me off at the end of the driveway, and I can walk the rest of the way," I say, a hint of shame in my voice. "Ethan doesn't know what Charlie drives. But if he's awake, he might see you through the window.

He lets go of my hand and nods. "Okay."

He slows the car and brings it to a stop. I reach for the door handle, but I don't open it right away. Instead, I look back at him one last time, my heart beating rapidly in my chest. What would it be like to spend my life with him? To park this car and go inside together, spending the rest of the night wrapped in his arms?

"Thanks for coming to get me," I murmur.

His blue eyes flick to mine, dark and unreadable behind his glasses. "Anytime, babes. Anytime."

Chapter forty

♫ *"Mr. Brightside" — The Killers* ♫

BRIGGS

Dropping Paisley off at her house, knowing she was going inside to *him,* was the hardest thing I've ever had to fucking do.

It took everything in me to put my car back in drive and leave her there. Because it's not him she should be falling asleep with and waking up next to. It's *me.*

But I know that's not possible. Not right now, not without blowing up the entire fucking foundation we've built our lives on.

And yet the thought of her being in bed with him right now, the thought of him *touching* her, sets my body on fucking fire, and I involuntarily clench my fists as I approach my front door.

I step inside, closing the door quietly behind me. The house is dark except for the soft glow of the lamp next to the couch in the living room. Beth is sitting there in her pajamas, typing away on her laptop. The sight of her causes my stomach to knot.

"Hey," she says when she hears me come in. "How was Lance?"

I hesitate for half a second before forcing a shrug. "He's good. Just needed to talk some stuff out." The lie slips from my lips easily.

My mind races back to the car, to Paisley's hand on my thigh, to how badly I wanted to give in to the temptation. But I knew that wasn't the way I wanted it to happen. Not when she was drunk. Not in a car in some bar parking lot. She deserves better than that.

Beth nods, unaware of my internal turmoil. If I get too close to her, will she smell Paisley's perfume on my shirt? Or is she too wrapped up in her own mind that she wouldn't even notice? "That's good. I just submitted the final payment for the Airbnb. Nashville with the girls over winter break is officially happening!" She sounds excited, and I smile. It's half fake, half not.

Because her being gone means a night, a *chance,* with Paisley. Just the two of us.

Beth sets her laptop down on the coffee table and walks into the kitchen where I'm still standing in the dark. I'm leaning against the counter, and she reaches out to touch my hand. It's meant to be simple, easy, loving, but my body reacts instinctively, and I pull my hand away.

Her face flickers with confusion. "Briggs? Is everything okay?"

"Yeah," I lie again. "Just tickled my hand. But I'm beat. Been a long couple of weeks with the conference and basketball and all that. I think I'm gonna crash," I say, and I walk upstairs before she can protest.

Bethany must choose to stay downstairs for a while because she doesn't follow me up. After showering to wash Paisley's scent off my body, I crawl into bed in my boxers and pull up a list of hotels nearby on my phone.

If Paisley and I are going to do this, then we'll need a place that isn't too close to spend the day together. And it needs to be somewhere nice, somewhere that feels like an escape. My eyes scan my screen, and a quaint hotel about an hour away from Stonebrook pops up. It's modern, private, and endearing, It's perfect.

I book the hotel for the Saturday night Beth will be out of town, hopeful that Paisley meant what she said tonight. If she changes her mind, I can always cancel, but I'm going with the odds that she won't. Once I'm done securing the hotel, I pull up my message thread with her.

Got us a place. Two weeks from now.
Just say the word, and I'm yours.

I set my phone down on my bedside table and close my eyes, but as soon as I do, I picture her with him. Does she kiss him the way she kisses me? With the fucking fervor and hunger that makes me lose my goddamn mind? Does she touch him the way she touches me? Does her hand grope his body like she owns it, making him ache for more? Are they in bed together now, her legs wrapped around him, her body against his, giving him what should be mine?

I'm not sure I can wait two weeks. Each night without her, thinking about her with him, is going to be a slow, sadistic form of torture. My body aches for her—it craves what my mind knows is wrong but what feels so fucking right.

Chapter Forty-One

♫ *"Bad Things"* — mgk & Camila Cabello ♫

PAISLEY

I'm yours.

I stare at Briggs's message from the other night, and I'll be damned if those two words don't turn my brain into an even bigger fucking mess.

Because he's *not* mine. And unless we're willing to blow up everything we have, he never will be.

Walking inside my house the night he brought me home felt like walking into a prison I didn't know how to escape from. My body was racked with guilt, but I also felt so... *alive*. I assumed that once I was away from Briggs, I would come to my senses, but even after I walked into my house, I longed for his hands to be on me again.

Once I got into bed—after a guilt-ridden shower of scrubbing away the lingering scent of mint and bourbon—Ethan tried to cuddle up to me, but it felt all wrong. Almost like I was living someone else's life, or like I was somewhere I wasn't supposed to be. Every time his hand touched my body, Briggs came to the forefront of my mind. And how fucked up is that? Lying in bed with your husband, thinking about another man? I always swore I would never be that woman. So how did I end up as her?

Years of telling myself that what I have with Ethan is enough while deep down knowing that it wasn't, that's how.

I didn't respond to Briggs's text, wanting time to mull it over and be absolutely sure this is what I want to do. But standing in my bathroom now, thinking about how I get to see him at school today, I couldn't be more sure.

I *want* him to be mine. Even if it's only for one day, I need to know what that would be like.

I walk through the bedroom after my shower, towel-drying my hair. Ethan is awake, getting ready to leave for work, and his eyes follow me.

"You look beautiful," he says, his voice soft and almost hesitant, and I have to keep from jumping at the startling sound of it.

Excuse me, what? I can't remember the last time he said something like that to me out of the blue. And now, when I'm more detached from him than ever, he says shit like that? My stomach twists with guilt.

"Thanks," I mumble, turning toward my dresser.

He stands and walks up behind me, pressing a kiss to my bare shoulder. The contact makes my skin crawl.

I close my eyes, trying to focus on the warmth of his lips and the way his hands settle on my waist. But it doesn't feel how it's supposed to. His touch doesn't make me lose my breath. Instead, my body tenses, and my mind drifts back to somebody else.

I swallow hard. "You're gonna be late," I say with a smile as I shift out of his grasp.

"Have a great day, baby," he says, and the use of the pet name makes my stomach churn.

"You too."

He walks out of the bedroom, and I rush into the bathroom, locking the door behind me. When the front door clicks shut a few minutes later, relief washes over me, and I feel like I can breathe again.

And then, just like that, it flips. My chest tightens with anticipation and excitement. Because I get to see him today.

And not just *see* him.

I have plans for something even better.

When the final bell rings, I basically charge down the hallway, not caring who I topple over in the process. I hardly saw Briggs today, and I've been impatiently awaiting this moment all day.

I head straight to the office, knowing I'll need to be quick to catch him before he goes to the gym for basketball practice. Ideally,

David and Helen would be gone, but I know better than to hope for that.

And just as I expected, as I walk through the doors, Helen is still sitting at desk, staring at her computer screen.

"Oh, hi, Paisley. What's up?"

"Hi," I say as innocently as possible. "Is Br—um, Dr. Davenport—still here? I need to talk to him about a student."

"I haven't seen him leave yet. You can head back and see if he's still in his office."

I smile nervously. What I'm about to do is risky, and my body is already sweating. "Thanks."

Luckily Briggs's office isn't far down the hall, so I'm at his door before I have a chance to overthink it.

The door is slightly ajar, and he is standing at his desk, sliding paperwork into his school bag. His khaki chinos hug him perfectly, and I swear, if I look hard enough, I can make out the outline of his cock beneath the fabric. A black, Under Armour sweater stretches across his broad shoulders, and he has the sleeves pushed up far enough to reveal the ink sketched down his arm. I need to remember to ask him to see it in all its glory, but I have other plans right now. The darkness of his shirt brings out the tan complexion in his skin, and his steel-blue eyes are even more piercing than usual when he gazes up at me after I softly knock.

"Excuse me, Dr. Davenport?" I say sweetly. "Do you have a minute? I have a question about a student." I talk loudly enough so if David and Helen are still in earshot, they can hear.

"Sure, Mrs. Hamilton." There's a glint of suspicion in his eye as he looks me up and down.

"Um," I say before walking further into the room, "would you mind if I shut the door? Confidentiality and all that." A mischievous grin plays at my lips.

"Absolutely." He clears his throat. "Privacy is best."

I shut the door behind me, clicking the deadbolt into place. My heart thumps in my chest, and my palms are already clammy, but I try my best to hide my nervousness and to feign confidence instead.

"So, there's this student," I begin, pacing the space in front of his desk, "and she's having a really hard time concentrating lately. There seems to be a major—" I stop and turn toward him, scanning his body up and down flirtatiously. "Distraction."

"Oh, yeah? What kind of distraction?"

"Well, you see…" I continue, walking my way around his desk. I push on his shoulders slightly, signaling him to take a seat in his desk chair. "She keeps daydreaming, and it's making it awfully hard for her to concentrate."

"Oh? And what is she daydreaming about?"

"I'm not sure how to say this, but she keeps wondering what it would feel like to get fucked by her assistant principal?" The words surprise me as they slip out of my mouth. I've never been so forward before. Usually, I'm too shy to voice what I want, but something about Briggs makes it easy to say exactly what I'm thinking. "In fact, it's all she can think about."

Briggs's eyes darken more, his gaze intensifying. The corner of his lips lift into a small smirk. "Hmm. That is quite the predicament." He brings his hands in front of him, fingertips pressed together like he's brainstorming ideas. "And what do you think will help this student focus again?"

I put my hands on the armrests on either side of him and slightly push the chair back, leaving enough space for me to stand between him and the desk. I turn around and slowly clear a spot on his desktop as I continue talking.

"Well, you see... that's what I was hoping you could help me figure out." I spin around and hoist myself up on the desk, leaving me sitting in front of him with one leg crossed over the other. I bite my lip slightly as I look into his eyes, and the heat between us builds.

"Well then, I guess we better brainstorm. Do you have any ideas?"

I methodically uncross my legs and slowly spread them apart to allow him a view of my black lacy panties. When he glances down, he inhales sharply.

"I think she... well, I think she really needs to get it out of her system. I think she needs to *taste him*, Dr. Davenport." My voice is breathy, a mix of tease and urgency.

My body is already reacting to the thought of having him in my mouth, my nipples hardening beneath my dress. Briggs leans back in his chair, his eyes locked on the area between my legs.

"Is that so?" he murmurs. "And you think that will solve the problem?"

My eyes scan down to the outline of his hardening cock. I nod and lick my lips. "Oh, definitely. In fact, I think it's the only thing that will," I whisper back, my hands now gripping the edge of the desk.

He stands from his chair and positions himself between my parted legs. His fingertips brush against my inner thigh, and the contact makes my heart beat even harder.

"Then perhaps," he says, his voice now a husky whisper as he leans in closer to my ear, "we should do what we can to help her concentrate."

I spread my legs a little wider, welcoming the contact. "Yes, please."

His hand moves up, tracing the inside of my thigh, his touch both gentle and possessive. "But we need to be very quiet, don't we, Mrs. Hamilton? I would hate for anyone to hear us."

I lean back to look into his eyes, and then my lips find the corner of his mouth in a teasing kiss. "Very quiet," I agree. "I promise I'll be a good girl, Dr. Davenport."

My panties are now soaked. I know the risk of somebody hearing us should make me nervous, but it's only heightening my arousal. His fingers travel further up my legs, dangerously close to where I'm aching for him to touch me, making me squirm on the desk.

I can't wait any longer. I reach for his belt, my hands shaking with need. He helps, just as desperate for this as I am, and as soon as his pants are undone, his cock springs free, hard and ready.

I push myself off the desk and drop to my knees in front of him, my mouth already watering. I lean forward and take him in, the contact on my tongue eliciting a small moan.

I wrap my lips around the head, my tongue swirling, and Briggs makes a guttural sound. I pull back slightly and use my hand to work my saliva down his shaft, squeezing him just tightly enough to spark another subtle groan. After stroking him a few times, I place my hands back on his thighs and grip for balance as I take him deeper into my mouth.

I move my head slowly at first, savoring every fucking inch as I taste him. As I move faster, his breathing starts to quicken and his legs begin to tense, so I ease up slowly to ward off his orgasm. I swirl my tongue around the tip of him before I slide down further again, taking him as deep as I can, the head of his cock hitting the back of my throat.

I gag slightly but don't pull back; instead, I let the muffled sounds of me choking on his cock fill the quiet room. His hands find my hair, and he guides my head to bob up and down faster, my saliva coating him and running down his leg.

I look up at him through my lashes, our eyes locking, and I know that does him in. His jaw clenches, and his eyes begin to close. His breathing becomes more ragged. My cheeks hollow as I suck harder, my head moving even faster now.

My panties are fucking drenched, and I'm eager to taste him—all of him. I want it. I want to feel him lose all control because of me.

His hands tighten in my hair and his body stalls for a moment, and then his cock pulses in my mouth, his come coating the back of my throat. I keep my lips tight, and I swallow his entire release, my eyes never leaving his. His groans are muffled as he clearly refrains from making too much sound. I lick him clean, savoring every last drop. Once he's finished, I pull back and stand up, wiping the sides of my mouth clean.

Before either of us can speak, his phone rings loudly through the room and causes us both to jump. We look over to see Joe's name on the caller ID.

"Fuck," he mutters under his breath, his voice rough from the intensity of the moment. Ignoring the call, he pulls up his pants and readjusts his shirt. He palms his hair in frustration as he checks his watch on his opposite wrist. "I've got to get to practice. I was supposed to be there ten minutes ago."

Conflict flashes in his eyes. I can tell he wants to stay, that he doesn't want to leave after what just happened, but that he knows he needs to go, especially so no one gets suspicious and wonders where he is.

"It's okay," I reassure him.

He quickly rebuttons his pants, his movements a bit hurried, but his eyes never leave mine.

"I'm so sorry, Paisley," he says, his tone filled with remorse. "I promise to return the favor, but I have to go."

I straighten my dress and start combing my fingers through my hair to lessen my disheveled appearance.

"Don't be sorry." I step closer to him and put both my hands on his chest. "We'll have another chance, remember?"

He nods and leans down to kiss me. It's soft and gentle, much different than the hungry, fervent kisses we've experienced, yet it somehow feels even more intimate.

"I'll make it up to you. Soon," he promises.

I watch him as he heads for the door, his body heavy with reluctance to leave. Before he opens it, he looks back at me, a playful smile plastered on his face.

"I hope that was helpful for your student." He winks. "And by the way, she gets an A fucking plus. Best student I've ever had."

Chapter Forty-Two

♫ *"The Great Escape" — BOYS LIKE GIRLS* ♫

BRIGGS

"You gotta admit that was a damn good shot, Coach D." Tommy's voice cuts through the uproarious laughter and blaring music in the locker room.

We just finished a buzzer-beater game, with him taking the winning shot, and the team is now running around whooping each other with towels while "Remember the Name" by Fort Minor blasts through the speakers.

I pat Tommy on the shoulder. "Hell of a shot, kid. But don't let it go to your head. I still expect to see ya at practice on Monday."

"You got it, Coach." He laughs and shakes his head before jogging over to the showers. I lean against the locker as Joe walks toward me.

"Man, I swear this is the loudest I've ever heard 'em after a game. You'd think we won State."

I chuckle, crossing my arms. "True. But buzzer-beaters don't happen every day. Better let 'em enjoy it."

"Tommy's gonna be riding this high all weekend."

"Hey, as long as he comes back Monday ready to run drills instead of rewatching his highlight reel from tonight's game, we'll be all good," I say, grinning.

"Speaking of highlights." Joe nods toward the food splayed out on a table in the entry way of the locker room. "I'm gonna go grab some of those snacks Carli and Beth made for the team. We really outkicked our coverage with those two, didn't we?"

I laugh, trying to cover my discomfort. "Yeah, we definitely have the most well-fed team in the conference."

Joe shuffles over to the food, and my phone buzzes in my pocket.

*Good game, Dr. Davenport. If
you have a few extra minutes, I'd
love to celebrate with you ;)*

Hmm... what did you have in mind?

Slipping my phone back into my pocket, I leave the locker room to find Bethany. She and Carli always come to our home games together, and we always drive separately since I usually have to stay late to make sure all the team members get home and everyone else clears out of the school. No need for us both to suffer. Tonight, it seems that will work in my favor, but I should still find her and let her know she can take off without me.

Teenage body odor slams me in the face as I walk into the gym, and Bethany is standing near the bleachers, talking with a group of the players' moms.

"Hey. I have a few things I need to take care of here, so it might be a bit before I make it home."

"Like what?"

I force a small shrug. I hate lying to her, again, but the idea of getting to spend a few minutes with Paisley overrides the guilt brewing in my chest.

"Just some game reports, checking in with a few players. The usual."

She sighs and rolls her eyes slightly. "Briggs, you know you don't have to be the last one out of the gym every game night."

I let out a low chuckle. "Actually, I do. Kind of comes with the job."

"Okay," she says, studying me for a second. "See you at home." Then, without another word, she turns back to her conversation.

As I walk away, my phone vibrates again in my pocket. I pull it out and glance around me, making sure no one will see it.

Guess you'll just have to come
see for yourself...

*Consider me intrigued. Give
me 10.*

I walk to the coach's office to put away the film equipment before walking to the other wing of the school to see Paisley. She's all I've been able to think about this entire week since that moment in my office the other day. And fuck, was that good. The best goddamn head I've ever gotten, that's for sure. The way her lips moved around my cock... just the thought of it has me stiffening already.

But between student meetings and her working at Tumbleweed after school most days this week, I haven't been able to see her, or even talk to her, much since. I'm still waiting for an opportunity to return the favor. Instead, I've had to rely on stolen glances between classes or walking by her room while she's teaching just to get a glimpse of her. It's been torture.

I have to have her again.

And I *have* to get myself under control before I start rocking a hard-on in the middle of the school hallway.

Once I'm done haphazardly putting everything away, I walk toward her room in a daze. By the time I reach her door, the tension brewing inside me is nearly unbearable. I knock softly, knowing she's expecting me.

She opens the door almost immediately.

"Oh, good! You're here," she says, pulling me inside. "Okay, the celebration will commence momentarily, but first, I have something to show you."

"That's kind of what I was expecting," I say, cheekily, and she rolls her eyes.

"Yeah, yeah, in due time." She waves me off. "But I'm being serious!"

"So am I." I grin at her, and she leans into me with her hands on my chest, offering me a kiss. It's quick and gentle, but it feels natural.

"You're ruthless." She smiles into my lips before pushing me away. She claps her hands together and grins. "Okay, so you know how I tend to be a little over the top when it comes to my organization…"

I raise an eyebrow. "A little?"

"Shut up." She laughs, and then she walks over to her computer monitor and pulls something up. "Anyway, I figured I'd draw up a potential floor plan for that space we looked at. You know, just in case you decide to go for it. I know you haven't made a decision yet, but I thought this might help you visualize if it would actually work or not."

I lean over her desk, peering at the diagram on the screen. "Wow. That's extremely detailed. How long did this take you?"

"Not long." She shrugs. "A couple hours, maybe."

"Not long? Paisley, you didn't have to do this for me."

"Duh," she points out. "I wanted to. Your idea of fun is analyzing data reports. This is mine."

"Paisley, we've been over this. I don't *actually* do that for fun."

She eyes me suspiciously. "Sure you don't."

I shake my head and grab her hand, pulling her closer to me. My hands land on her waist. "You're ridiculous, you know that?"

"Oh, trust me, I know. But if you *do* get the space, just promise me you'll name a drink after me. Something fun and flirty. Dangerously strong but deceptively sweet."

"Deceptively sweet, huh?" I tease. "Sounds about right."

"Damn right. And it better have a name that's as ridiculous as I am."

"You've got it," I say, mulling it over. "Maybe something like... The Hot Hamilton?"

She laughs. "How about The Davenport Downfall?"

I mock a grimace. "Sounds ominous."

"Fitting then, don't you think?" She winks.

I smile back at her. "The place is perfect, though, isn't it? You did a great job making my vision come to life."

"I can't wait to see what you do with it." She bites her lip and shrugs. "I mean, if you end up getting it, that is. No pressure or anything."

"Stop overthinking. I love how excited you are about it."

She places her hands around my neck and pulls me even closer. "Are you excited?"

"Yeah," I admit, pressing my forehead to hers. "But not just about the bar. About everything."

"Me, too," she says softly. "I think it's time for that celebration I promised you." A playful smirk pulls on her lips. "And if I recall, you still need to return my favor from Monday?"

"That sounds right." I put my finger under her chin and lift her face up to kiss her.

Then, without warning, I move my hands down to her ass and hoist her up, her legs wrapping around me instantly. I turn around and place her down on one of the classroom desks, and her thighs part even more, causing her dress to ride up and expose more of her. I lick my lips at the sight.

"You've done so much for me, Paisley," I tell her, my fingers tracing the hem of her dress. "It's time for me to show you how grateful I am."

She bites her lips, nodding slightly, and her eyes darken with lust. My hands travel farther up her thighs, pushing the fabric higher until it bunches around her waist, leaving her red, silky thong fully exposed.

I lower myself to the ground and kneel before her, sliding her panties down her legs before she rests each thigh on my shoulders to give me full access. She trembles under my touch, and her breathing quickens. I press a kiss to the inside of her leg, and she shivers in response. I move higher, my kisses becoming more deliberate, more demanding.

When my lips finally meet her core, a soft moan escapes her, and my cock twitches at the sound.

Fuck, she's sexy. And I'm the luckiest guy in the world to get to worship her right now.

Her hands reach down and tangle in my hair, pulling me even closer to her center. My tongue goes to work, feeling how fucking wet she is and reveling in the taste. I explore her for a few minutes, listening as her body reacts to what she likes. When I begin circling my tongue on her clit faster, her hips buck up and grind against my mouth.

"Briggs," she gasps, her voice dripping with need, and I move faster, determined to feel her come apart on my tongue.

When I sense she's getting close, I let up a little and slow my pace, heightening her arousal even more. I work my tongue slowly, and her thighs tighten around my face.

Feeling her close to the edge again, I push her over it. I slip a finger inside her, feeling how ready she is. God, I wonder how it would feel if it were my cock sliding into her instead.

She moans, trying to be as quiet as possible, but the sound vibrates through her entire body. I add another finger, curling them to hit that sweet spot inside of her, while my tongue keeps its rhythm on her clit.

"Holy fuck, Briggs," she cries out, her voice hoarse. Her hips move, riding my fingers, chasing her release. I thrust them in and out, matching the pace of my tongue, imagining it's me inside of her instead of my fingers.

My cock strains against my pants as her body tenses and her orgasm builds. I don't relent, my fingers fucking her harder, my tongue lapping at her clit, until her body shudders and her pussy clenches.

"Oh my God," she breathes out. "Yes, don't fucking stop," she orders, and I keep my pace until she rides the wave of her orgasm completely.

As she comes down from her high, I slowly withdraw my fingers and raise them to my mouth. I look her in the eyes while I lick them clean, savoring her taste.

"Fucking delicious."

"Now *that's* fucking hot," she tells me. "I want a taste."

She grabs my shirt and pulls me up toward her, her mouth crashing into mine and her tongue forcing its way between my lips. She kisses me deeply, tasting herself on me, her hunger matching mine. Her hands roam down to my waistband, attempting to pull it down with urgency.

"I want to feel *all* of you," she insists, and fuck, it's hard to resist. But I know this isn't how I want it to happen. Not here. Not now. Not when I can't spend hours exploring her body and worshipping her the way she deserves.

I begrudgingly break the kiss and pull back. "Next weekend," I remind her.

"Why not now?"

"Because Paisley. You deserve more than this. More than a quick fuck in your classroom before we both have to go home," I say, my voice softening. "I want to take my time with you. To savor every fucking minute I have with you. To learn every curve of your body. To spend hours discovering it."

She pushes me back softly. "Dr. Davenport," she teases, "who knew you were such a romantic?"

"I mean it," I continue, taking her hand in mine. "I've never felt like this before, Paisley. With you, it's not just about being physical. It's more than that for me." I kiss her hand.

"Next weekend?" she asks.

"Next weekend," I promise. "Hotel is already booked."

She smiles, leaning in to rest her forehead against mine. "Alright. Next weekend. But you better make it worth the wait," she whispers, her tone playful.

"You have my word."

I lean back in a chair in Paisley's classroom the next morning, arms crossed, watching as she moves through the rows of desk. Technically, I don't need to observe her again for a few months, but nobody needs to know that. Being in her room, watching her teach, allows me to see her. And besides, the kids just think one of their classmates is on thin ice and that I'm keeping a close eye on them. It's a win-win.

I love seeing Paisley in her element, and as I listen to her now, her voice is animated and enthusiastic as she reads a passage from the novel her Honors 11 class is currently studying. *The Great Gatsby*, I think? It's been decades since I've read it, but the characters' names sound familiar. Students follow along in their own books as she reads, post-it notes and pencils in their hands.

I've seen plenty of teachers go through the motions since becoming an assistant principal, but Paisley doesn't do that. She's meticulous in her planning, making sure every lesson, every activity, has a purpose and is relevant to the teenagers sitting in front of her. And what I love most is that she makes sure to *tell* them that. She welcomes them questioning why they do anything they do in class because she always has an answer for them. She truly is one of our best, and I'm not only saying that because I'm falling in love with her.

Shit. *Am I falling in love with her?*

"Alright," Paisley says to the class and pulls me from my reverie. "Let's break this passage down." She sets the book on her desk as she turns to the whiteboard to jot down some notes. "What's going through Daisy's mind here? Why do you think

Fitzgerald chose for her to say this? What does it reveal about her character—about how she's feeling at this moment?"

She taps the Expo marker against her chin, acting as though she's thinking just as hard at the students even though she's probably taught this lesson a dozen times.

Some of the students near me begin discussing the question, and although it's been years since I've read this book, the storyline sounds ironically familiar. Uneasiness washes over me as I consider how difficult it must be for Paisley to teach this unit right now.

A student's hand shoots up, and Paisley calls on her. "I think Daisy is really conflicted. She *does* love Gatsby, but she also loves Tom... just in a different way. Gatsby wants her to completely erase her past with Tom, but it's not that simple. Tom's a part of her life. He always will be. So she's stuck between what she wants and what she thinks is safe. I think Fitzgerald wanted us to see how afraid she is of making the wrong choice."

I can tell this is an honor's level class with upperclassmen based on this student's answer. That, or Paisley is really fucking good at getting them to think critically about the texts they read. Probably a mix of both.

"I disagree," another student chimes in. "I think she's realizing she doesn't actually have to choose. Sure, Gatsby is offering her romance, but Tom offers her stability. Maybe she just wants both."

Paisley mulls over the two answers, taking a beat to respond. "Well, what's more important? Love? Or stability?"

Her eyes scan the room and instantly soften when they meet mine, but she looks away quickly. I take my phone out of my pocket and fire off a text in her direction while she's distracted.

"Avery," she continues, "we haven't heard from you yet today. What do you think?"

"Ah, I don't know, Mrs. H.," he says begrudgingly, rubbing the back of his neck. "Does it really matter? In the end, she's not gonna leave Tom. But she doesn't want to let Gatsby go, either. Seems selfish if you ask me."

Paisley nods. "That's a fair assessment. Anyone else care to add?"

A girl beside me speaks next. "She might be selfish, but isn't it society that made her that way?" She sounds offended as she talks pointedly at Avery. "This is the 1920s. She's *expected* to behave the way she does, and she's trapped in a system where marriage is more about status than it is above love. To me, it seems she's just conforming to what's expected of her rather than breaking free. So is that considered selfish?"

"That's a great question." Paisley glances at the clock. "And is exactly where we will pick up tomorrow. Great conversation today. I appreciate all of you and your hard work. Take the last five minutes of class to just hang out and decompress before third period." She smiles at them and walks over to her desk while they immediately begin chatting with each other.

When she reaches her desk, she glances at her phone and must notice her new notification. She picks it up and immediately stiffens for a second as her cheeks redden.

You look so damn fuckable

right now.

Quickly flipping her phone face down, she clears her throat before turning to talk to the students approaching her desk. As she speaks with them, her eyes scan past their bodies and in my direction, a slow smile spreading on her lips. She knows I'm watching her every move.

The bell rings a few minutes later, and the students shuffle out of the room.

"Don't forget to finish the reading for tomorrow!" she calls out after them, but most of them are already gone.

I wait until the last student disappears before walking up to her. She glances at the door, then back at me, shaking her head with a smirk. "You *cannot* text me things like that while I'm teaching."

I lean against the student desk behind me and cross my arms. "Why not? It's true. You *do* look fuckable when you're teaching. And besides, you liked it."

She rolls her eyes but doesn't deny it. "That's not the point."

Chuckling, I peer around her classroom. There are cozy Christmas lights strung around, posters of inspirational quotes all over her walls, and drawings and thank you notes from students hanging above where her laptop sits. A stack of assignments sits on her desk, and the top of each page reads "Mrs. Hamilton believes in ____" rather than having a simple name spot. Fuck, this woman is something else.

I move a little closer to her, wanting to eliminate the space between us but still acknowledging that her door is wide open. "You're a damn good teacher, Paisley. You know that?"

"Thank you," she says sheepishly. "I love what I do."

"That much is obvious." I look back down and fidget with a paper on her desk, leaning in even closer to her while my eyes glance toward the door to make sure no one's in the hallway. Her fingers skim the edge of her desk, moving closer to mine, like she's trying to resist the urge to touch me.

"You should probably delete that text," I tell her in a low murmur.

She gazes up at me through her thick, black lashes. "You think?"

"Maybe." I smirk. "Unless you plan on reading it again later when you're alone."

Her breath hitches when I wink at her, and just as her fingers are about to graze mine, I push off of the desk. I turn and head for the door, forcing myself not to look back.

Because I know if I do, I might just say fuck it and lock the door instead.

Chapter Forty-Three

♫ *"Daylight" — Maroon 5* ♫

PAISLEY

This is a terrible idea. An absolutely terrible idea.

And yet here I am, dragging myself out of bed like it's completely normal to willingly do things I know I'll regret. Or things I know I *should* regret.

Will I regret this?

I still don't know the answer to that, even though Ethan left for work an hour ago and left me alone with my stupid thoughts and feelings and a ceiling I've stared at for way too long.

Sunlight streams through the trees outside my window, mocking me with its calm, peaceful, perfect morning while my stomach twists with anticipation, and I think I might hurl.

God, I can't believe I'm actually going through with this.

I stumble to the bathroom, rubbing the sleep from my eyes, and catch my reflection in the mirror. I stare at the person looking back at me.

This isn't me. I'm not a woman who would do this. Hell, I've spent my life judging the women who would. But here I am anyway. I guess that's how life works—it's easy to judge from the sidelines until you find yourself in a situation exactly like the one you've always scoffed at.

I've been with Ethan since college, and I've *never* crossed this line before. I've never even got close to it. Never even considered it.

But with Briggs, the line feels... blurry. If this were just about wanting him—the physical part of him—maybe this would be easier. Easier to dismiss. Easier to shut down.

But it's not. Because he *sees* me. He knows how I'm feeling before I find the words, and when I finally do, he listens. He makes space for me to be exactly who I am, and isn't that what I've been searching for?

I rummage through my closet, searching for the dress I picked out for today. My eyes flick to the clock on my nightstand. Thirty minutes stand between now and the moment I step into that hotel room.

When I finally do pull into the parking lot, it's 7:59 exactly, but I sit in my car for a few minutes attempting to calm my nerves. My legs and hands are visibly shaking, and I'm pretty sure I'm sweating.

Yep, definitely sweating. I'll need to reapply deodorant before heading inside.

It's not that I don't want to go in there; I really, *really* do, but what if he changes his mind after this? What if this takes away all of the excitement and he realizes I'm not what he wants afterwards? What if this is all for nothing?

Or worse. What if it's not?

Steadying my breath, I open my car door and cross the parking lot, butterflies flying chaotically in my stomach. My floral dress whips around me in the wind. It's fucking freezing in Wisconsin, but I know how much Briggs loves me in dresses. Or maybe it's not so much the *dress* he loves, but rather the thought of how easily he can take it off me.

I push through the doors and glance at the reception desk. Do they know? Can they see the guilt that has to be written all over my face?

I wonder if this happens a lot—people finding love in the most unexpected places. Or people falling out of the love that's expected of them.

I saunter through the lobby, and suddenly I don't know what the hell to do with my hands. I read an article in *Cosmopolitan* once that said awkward hand placement is one of women's biggest concerns on a first date, and I remember laughing at how ridiculous that seemed.

But now, as I awkwardly walk with one hand dangling at my side and the other swiping my hair behind my ear, I totally get it. Well played, *Cosmo*. Well played.

The ride up the elevator feels like it takes eleven years, but eventually I'm standing outside the hotel room.

Room 214.

I slowly raise my hand and knock. I barely hear his footsteps on the other side over the thrumming of my heart, and when he opens the door and I see him, I swear said heart tries to lurch out of my fucking chest.

"Hey," he says hungrily, his eyes scanning down my body, and now I'm not even aware I *have* hands, much less thinking about what they're doing. Because *my God,* is he beautiful. I always seem to forget the effect he has on me until my body betrays me as soon as I see him.

He's wearing a bright white tee and black chinos, both of which hug him perfectly in all the right places. For fuck's sake, this man's got it going *on.* I didn't even know men like him existed, much less in our small ass town. But I'm lucky—or maybe unlucky? Depends who you ask, I suppose—that he ended up in the same place I did three years ago.

As soon as he sees me, he gathers me into his arms and spins me around, the door slamming shut behind us. I wrap my arms around his neck and take a deep breath, inhaling the scent of him.

"God, I missed you," he whispers into my ear.

I beam up at him, and the space between us shrinks. Our lips crash into each other, and a jolt shoots straight through me.

We force ourselves to separate long enough for him to fully lead me into the hotel room. His strong, soft hand tugs me along, and I pull him toward me to hug him again, this time less willing to let go. We stand here for a few minutes without saying a word, just breathing each other in.

Before Briggs, I never realized a connection could feel like this—like we're moving to the same beat without even trying. I thought it was normal to settle, to go through the motions and call it enough. To feel satisfied but not truly *fulfilled.* That's just life, right?

But it's not like that with Briggs. With him, it's all spark and heat and everything I didn't even know I was missing until he came blasting into my life. With him, everything else fades away. All the monotony and the doubt and the guilt. Nothing exists outside of us.

And right now, I want to show him how much he means to me.

I pull on his hand and lead him to the bed, pushing him down so he's sitting in front of me. I climb on his lap and straddle him, and I can already feel his length rubbing against me. He's obviously equally excited to see me.

I caress his face, feeling the stubble on his cheek all the way down to his chin. I lift his face so he's looking right at me.

"You're so fucking perfect, you know that?" I whisper.

His eyes light up at me beneath his dark brown lashes, and he presses his lips to mine. I rock my hips back and forth, building the friction between us.

I lift his shirt over his head, and my eyes widen a fraction while I drink him in. He's... strong. Like seriously strong. And the stubble running across his chest is impossibly sexy.

My gaze drifts to his bicep, landing on the tattoo that I can finally see in its entirety for the first time, and then I push him onto the bed and trail my lips all over his body.

Before I have a chance to do anything more, he flips us around so I'm the one lying on the bed. He reaches for the hem of my dress and lifts it over my head, exposing my entire body for the first time. He pulls away and looks at me. I mean *really* looks at me. And for a second, I think about how I am completely exposed, about how I should feel self-conscious, worried about the sunlight streaming through the window and how it's making my body look. But I don't.

His finger trails from my cheek all the way down my side, sending shivers through my spine.

"You are so beautiful," he whispers, and he leans down to press his lips to mine once more while he runs his fingers between my legs. "And already so wet for me," he says, his voice raspy.

"Briggs, I need you," I beg desperately.

"So impatient," he teases. "But I think I'll make you wait a little."

He slips off my red panties and brings his finger to my clit, rubbing it in gentle circles. It's only been a few seconds, and I could already explode. But as soon as I'm close, he moves his finger away, relieving the pressure. He does this over and over until I almost can't take it anymore.

Finally, his thumb lands on the spot that makes my legs tremble, and I know I'm about to lose it. Slowly easing a finger inside me, he thrusts it in and out while rubbing my clit at the same time. Within an instant, I'm experiencing what might be the most intense orgasm I've ever experienced.

Once I come down from my high, my hands instinctively reach up to find his belt, and I eagerly begin to undo it.

His pants drop to the floor, and he stands before me in his black Calvin Kleins, looking the sexiest I've ever fucking seen him.

The outline of his cock beneath the material shows he's hard already, and I grab his waist to pull him down on top of me.

"You drive me fucking crazy," I whisper in his ear. "And I want you to be mine. All mine."

Emphasizing that last point, I trail my lips down his neck, and he flips us again so I am straddling him fully. I continue my kisses down toward his cock, lingering on his inner thighs to tease him a bit. I pull his boxers down and his cock springs free, allowing me to stroke him gently, rubbing the head with my thumb. Slowly, I bring my mouth to him and drag my tongue along his length, watching it twitch in response. I've never been one to want to go down on a man, but something about Briggs's dick makes me want to shove it down my throat every day of the fucking week. I'm goddamn addicted to it. To him.

I twirl my tongue around his tip while he lets out an impatient groan, and I finally give in, sliding the rest of him into my mouth.

I slowly lower my mouth farther, feeling him hit the back of my throat, and move my head up and down before releasing him to drip spit all over him. He shoves himself back into my mouth and holds my head in place until I'm gagging and tapping his leg to let me come up for air.

"Look at me," he commands, and I peer up, eager to feed the hungry look in his eyes. "Good girl," he tells me, and my clit throbs at the praise.

I take him back in my mouth, this time more aggressively. Opening up my throat, I let him fuck my face until he's close to coming and has to pull himself away. When he does, I lower myself and take one of his smooth balls in my mouth, gently sucking on it and swirling my tongue around, causing him to moan in pleasure.

"Stand up. Now," he orders, and I get even wetter at the demand, my pussy still begging for the pressure of him inside me.

He flips me around, and I hear the rustling of a wrapper as he positions himself behind me. He places his hands on my waist as he bends down and kisses all along my neck and back. A surge of desire watches over me, and my pulse races faster. The space between my legs pulsates with a deep ache that is desperate to be satisfied. Without a word, he slowly eases himself into me, and I moan as he makes my body come alive.

"Goddamn it. You feel so fucking good," he whispers, his voice rough with desire. "And I'm not even all the way in yet."

He unhooks my bra and brings his hands up to cup my breasts as my nails dig into the mattress. He deepens himself inside me, and as we move together, the heat between us rises. But before I can fully let go, Briggs pulls out of me, leaving me with a feeling of emptiness that instantly makes me cry out for more. He flips me around and pulls me toward him at the end of the bed.

"I want to look at you, Paisley. You're too fucking beautiful not to."

He positions himself between my legs again and enters me in one smooth thrust. He starts moving his hips in a slow rhythm and brings his mouth to my nipple and circles his tongue around it. A ripple of pleasure washes over me, and I rest my head as I let out a low moan, my body trembling with pleasure. His thrusts pick up speed as we fall into a rhythm.

"Do you see what you do to me, Paisley?" he asks breathlessly while pounding into me. "You drive me fucking mad."

We continue this pace for a few minutes, taking each other in as if it's the last time we'll see each other. With every thrust, I get closer and closer to the edge. He leans down to kiss me and brings his thumb to my clit again, and that single motion is enough to send me flying. A moan escapes my lips, but Briggs brings his hand over my mouth to keep me quiet.

"Be a good girl," he says, his voice filled with a hungriness I haven't experienced before, and he lets out a guttural groan.

I didn't even know this kind of dominance was something I wanted, but my orgasm becomes even more euphoric as a result. His cock tenses inside me, and I can tell he's on the brink of his own ecstasy. When he begins thrusting with everything he has, his head falls back, letting me know he's about to come. I push my hips toward his and tighten myself around him to send him over the edge.

"Oh, fuck," he growls, and his cock swells inside of me, leaving us both panting and satisfied.

He collapses next to me, turning his head towards mine. And at this moment, I feel completely and utterly alive for the very first time.

I lean over and kiss him once more. "Now *that* was a nice hello."

My head is nuzzled into Briggs's neck while the sun, now high in the sky, shines through the curtains in the dim room. Briggs is lying with one arm draped over my shoulder, his other hand softly trailing my arm that lies across his stubbled chest. His touch sends shivers down my spine and butterflies into my stomach.

"Briggs," I murmur, breaking the silence.

He turns his gaze toward me, a slight smile on his lips.

I find his hand that was trailing down my arm and bring it to his chest, intertwining his fingers with mine. I take a deep breath and press a soft kiss to his knuckles.

"Do you ever wonder about us?"

Briggs's gaze shifts slightly, the familiar turmoil of emotion churning inside him. A feeling I know all too well.

"Every day."

I study his face, searching for the answers that I have been so desperately seeking, but I know it's not that easy. For either of us.

"What are we going to do, Briggs?" I whisper, the weight of our situation pressing heavily on my chest, suffocating me so hard the words can hardly escape.

He sighs, his breath matching mine in the stillness of the room. "I wish I had an answer to that," he admits. His voice is heavy. "I have no idea how this will turn out. All I know is that when I'm with you, nothing else matters, and truthfully, I can't imagine my life without you."

Tears threaten to escape as I think about his answer. I've never been one to believe much in fate, but at this moment, I can't find any other way to explain it. Briggs Davenport was destined to be in my life. I just have no idea how I'm going to keep him in it.

"Hey, no tears," he says, pulling my attention away from my thoughts. "Let's not worry about that right now. I know we need to figure it out, and we will, but right now, I'm just happy I get to spend the day with you. And if this turns out to be the only day we get together, then I will live the rest of my life a happy man knowing I got to know what it was like to be yours. No matter what you decide—what *we* decide—I'm here for you, okay?"

"Okay," I nod, wiping the tears from my cheeks.

"Now, we have all day for me to learn every possible thing I can about you before I have to let you go," he continues. "So, tell me about yourself, Paisley Hamilton."

I chuckle softly. "What do you want to know?"

"Everything. I want to know what makes you... *you*. Because you, Paisley Hamilton, are the most incredible woman I have ever fucking met." He pauses, like he's trying to find the right way to say whatever he's thinking. "I want to know what drives you. What dreams keep you going every day. I want to know the moments of your life that have shaped you, the ones that have broken you, the ones that have made you into the intelligent, empathetic, and charismatic person you are."

His words hang in the space between us, and for the first time in my life, I understand what it's like to have someone who truly wants to know me, to unravel me.

"But I also want to know your fears," he adds, his voice soft but determined. "I want to know the parts of you that you've been too afraid to show anyone else. The demons that keep you up at night. The worries you think make you too much for others to handle, or the ones that make you think you're not enough.

Because every part of you, every fucking part of you, is beautiful, Paisley. And you deserve someone who sees how amazing you are. Every single day." He brushes his hand lightly against my cheek. "I want to know the *real* you. Not the watered down version of yourself you think you have to be. Because every time you let me in just a little bit more, I find parts of *myself* that I never knew existed."

"Well that definitely did not help stop the crying," I say with a laugh before he pulls me in to kiss him again.

And then we talk about everything—about our childhoods, where we grew up, where we went to elementary school. I tell him about the time I went on vacation to Mexico with my family, and he tells me about the days upon days he spent at the bowling alley as a kid. We share everything it would normally take a month of dating to discover, both of us knowing our time together is limited.

But as we begin to approach more serious subjects, dread creeps into my chest. I want to tell Briggs everything about my past, but some things are harder to talk about than others. Whenever I bring this topic up to Ethan, the mood instantly shifts, and an awkward blanket drapes over the entire room. He never really says much, and we usually move past the subject pretty quickly, which is why I've reserved the topic for my family for the most part. But if I truly want to see that what I have with Briggs is different, then I need to see if I'm able to completely open up to him like he says he wants me to.

"There's something I don't really talk about much," I confess, my voice hesitant as my gaze shifts away.

"Okay," Briggs replies, sensing the shift in my tone. "You can talk to me about anything."

Taking a deep breath, I dig for the strength to continue. "My brother... he passed away when I was fourteen. He was twenty-eight, so there was a bit of an age difference between us. But my family has always been extremely close, so it still was really hard to take, especially as a teenager. I don't talk about it often because I know it always makes other people uncomfortable, but there isn't a day that goes by that I don't think about him." I pause, taking in the pained expression that crosses his face.

"I'm so sorry, babes," he murmurs, his voice filled with genuine empathy. "Can I ask how you lost him?"

"Drinking and driving. It was a Saturday night, and he was out having drinks with a friend. At some point, they decided to leave the bar, and he must have thought he was okay to drive." A tear slides down my cheek, and Briggs wipes it away for me. "But he never made it. Somewhere along the way, his car hit the shoulder of the road. He overcorrected, flipping the car, and he was ejected through the windshield. His friend was wearing a seatbelt, so he survived, but my brother wasn't as lucky."

Briggs grabs my hand in his. "That's horrible, Paisley. What is your brother's name?"

It doesn't go without notice that he says "is" and not "was." I squeeze his hand a little tighter.

"Steven. I remember being so... void of emotion when my mom told me. She got the call around three in the morning, and she had to come get me from a friend's house. When I got in the car, I was convinced we were going to the hospital. I'm not sure if it was that I was half asleep or just so in shock, but it wasn't until we turned the opposite way on the road that I realized the severity of the accident. I looked around the car, to my mom, dad, and sister, and they were all crying, but I didn't feel... anything. My mind was blank. My cheeks were dry."

"I'm sure you were in shock."

"Oh, definitely. But my fourteen-year-old self didn't know it at the time. I had lost family members before that—grandparents, aunts, uncles—but never anyone so close. I remember my sister asking my mom if I had heard her, which broke me out of my reverie. For a long time, I thought there must be something wrong with me for *not* feeling how they were feeling. It wasn't until years later I learned my response was completely normal."

"Everybody grieves differently, and there's not a right or a wrong way," Briggs reassures me.

I nod. "I know that now. Anyway, we found out later that at least he wasn't in any pain. After he was ejected from the car, he died on impact. Knowing he didn't suffer brings me a little bit of comfort. I felt—*feel*—so bad for his best friend, though. He blamed himself for the accident for a long time. Sometimes I think he still does. But we don't. It was an accident, and both of them made the decision to get in the car that night, not just Steven. Still, I can't imagine the pain he must go through each day knowing he was the last one to see him alive."

Briggs's body language shifts. "I can understand," he says quietly. "Although our situations are completely different, I also lost someone close to me when I was a teenager." His words are laced with emotion and vulnerability. "My best friend. We were inseparable ever since we were kids. Like brothers. And then, he was just... gone."

I squeeze his hand in mine again, offering whatever comfort I can. "That must have been incredibly hard for you," I whisper.

He swallows. "We were both teenagers when it happened. We grew up together, spent every summer together, spent most weekends at the bowling alley with our dads. Our moms were best friends ever since we were born, so it was natural that we would be, too. He was the kind of person who always had a smile on his face, but..." he pauses, his words trapped by his grief. "But I didn't realize how much pain he was hiding."

A shadow crosses Briggs's face as he recounts some of the signs that he missed, signs that I'm sure would have gone unnoticed by anyone.

"I remember the day I found out. It felt like the ground had been ripped from right under me."

"How... did it happen?" I tread lightly, not wanting to press too hard.

"He had been struggling for a long time, I guess. Battling demons none of us saw. I guess in the end, he couldn't take it anymore. His mom found him on a Sunday morning. She went to his room to tell him to come eat breakfast, and that's when she saw the rope."

My heart drops, and a wave of sympathy hits me not only for Briggs, but for that poor boy and his mom. Tears line Briggs's eyes.

"I blamed myself for a long time, you know, for not being there when he needed me. But as teenagers, we get so wrapped up in our own problems that we just kind of become oblivious to everyone else around us," he admits, his voice breaking slightly. "But no matter how many times I would replay the days leading up to his death, I couldn't shake the feeling that it was my fault. That I had failed him."

"You couldn't have known," I assure him. "Unfortunately, people who are determined to take their lives are often good at hiding it. As a teenager, you didn't know what signs to look for. You saw what he wanted you to see. It's not your fault."

Briggs falls silent for a moment. "I know that now. But it took years for me to forgive myself."

His words hang in the air between us, both of us reflecting on the loss we've experienced.

"He's actually why I went to college for psychology. I wanted to learn more about human nature, about how our brains work."

"That makes sense." I nod. "My brother is actually why I went into teaching. After it happened, I had some really supportive teachers at school, and having such a great support system really taught me how to be resilient. Obviously, if it was possible, I would want my brother back, but over time, I've been able to find some silver linings and see how much stronger it's made me. I quickly realized there are some kids who don't have any of those systems in place. Kids who struggle with things every day, and they have no one rooting for them. I wanted to be able to provide that support and encouragement for them if they ever needed it."

"You do a great job at that. I've seen you work with the kids, Paisley, and you're an amazing teacher. I've been in education for ten years, and you're the best teacher I've ever worked with. It's part of what drew me to you in the first place. You have such a big heart, and it shows."

"Thank you," I respond, a blush passing over my cheeks. I've never been good at receiving compliments. "So your friend—what is his name?"

"Camden. But everyone called him Cam."

I trace the shape of the tattoo on his bicep, my fingers lightly following the cracked, shadowed bowling lane. Up close, I can see the way the design fades into darkness at the end, leading into an old clock with no hands. Like time has stopped. Realization dawns on me.

"That explains the tattoo."

His lips twitch into a soft smile. "Yeah. I don't talk about it much. I actually try my best not to think about what happened anymore." His thumb brushes over the inside of my wrist. "I guess... I guess I've gotten pretty good at blocking a lot of shit out," he admits. "But..."

"But what?"

He lifts his gaze to mine. "But with you... I feel everything."

I lean in to kiss him, and as our lips meet, I realize I have no idea how I am ever going to let this man go. He gently slides his finger under my chin, tipping my head up to look into his steel blue eyes that always have a way of peering directly into my soul.

"Paisley..." he whispers, his voice soft and delicate. "I think I'm falling in love with you."

I swallow, my brain calculating whether or not it's a good idea to say what's been running through my mind for weeks now.

"I think I'm already in love with you," I say, and then I get lost in a kiss with a man who isn't my husband.

Chapter forty-four

♫ "Chasing Cars" — Snow Patrol ♫

BRIGGS

"So," Paisley says casually as she plops a grape into her mouth. "What is it that you really want? What's your end game?"

After spending multiple hours tangled up in the sheets together, I laid out the blanket I brought for us on the hotel bed. I considered rolling it out on the floor, but I can only imagine what has been left behind on a hotel carpet. Yeah, no thanks.

So we opted for the bed instead for our makeshift picnic. I told her that ideally I would take her on a proper date to get to know her, but since we are confined to the space within these four walls, this will have to do.

She was happy just the same.

"You." I look her directly in the eyes, so she knows I'm serious. "*You* are my end game."

Her cheeks flush with the familiar shade of pink I've come to love. "But how would that work? Do you plan on leaving Bethany?"

Her question makes my stomach constrict. Not because I haven't thought about it—I have, more times than I can count—but because I haven't fully thought out *how* that conversation is going to unravel.

I decided weeks ago that Paisley is who I want. My marriage with Beth was over long before she even came into the picture. Paisley just helped me realize it.

Still, I know it's going to come as a shock to the person I've spent the last decade of my life with when I tell her that.

I swallow and nod hesitantly at Paisley. I know where I stand, especially now, but I'm still not entirely sure where her head is at. Has she even considered leaving Ethan?

"I do." I say firmly. "No matter how this plays out between you and me, I know it's for the best. I can't be the person she wants. The person she deserves. And even if you and I..." I stop, not sure how to phrase it, ultimately deciding not to even go there. "Regardless, I know I need to leave."

She grabs my hand and squeezes it in hers. "That's really scary, Briggs. Where will you go?"

"My family has a cabin right outside of Stonebrook. It's vacant most of the time, unless it's summer, so I can stay there until I get my shit sorted out."

"You've thought about this."

"Yeah. I have. It needs to happen. And probably soon. This—how I'm feeling, what I'm doing—isn't fair to her." I take a deep breath to prepare myself for what I'm about to ask next. I know it needs to be discussed, but that doesn't mean I'm prepared for the answer. "What about you? Where are you at with... all of this?"

She looks away from me, shifting her gaze to a painting on the wall. It takes her a beat to respond, and I can tell she's calculating what to say.

"I don't know." She sighs. "I know that's not what you want to hear, but it's how I'm feeling right now." She squeezes my hand even harder. "Today has been... ugh, amazing doesn't even begin to describe it. You make me feel ways I've never felt before, and that's equally exciting and terrifying. But when I think of leaving Ethan, of him being out of my life completely..." She blinks, and a single tear escapes down her cheek. "I don't know what to do. I don't know how to go on with my life as if this—as if *you*—never happened. But how do I tell a man I love, a man I care so deeply about, that I found someone... what? Better? How can a person say that to someone? It will completely break him. I don't know if he would ever recover."

"But what's the alternative?" I say, hoping it doesn't come off insensitively. "Staying in a marriage that doesn't make you one hundred percent happy because you *feel* bad? That's no way to live, Paisley."

Her hand slips free from mine, and she wrings hers together in her lap. "I know that. But how would this even work? We leave Bethany and Ethan, and what? Skip off together into the sunset? We live in a small town, Briggs. There are too many factors. Too many obstacles."

She's not wrong. I've had this exact conversation with myself a million times already. The reality is we would probably have to get new jobs. Start over. Move away. Leave everything else behind.

But would that really be so bad?

"I would leave Beth," I tell her, a plan forming in my mind. "Then after a while, you would have a similar conversation with Ethan. There's no need to mention there being someone else. We both had our own share of issues in our relationships prior to falling for each other."

"Okay... and then?"

"Then we 'bond' over our mutual divorces. We get closer. Confide in one another. Eventually, we realize we have feelings for each other, and then we casually start dating. No one will have to know it started before."

"I guess." She shrugs, deflated. "I know that would be the best case scenario. But that's going to take *months*. Months of pretending you're nothing to me when..."

More tears stream down her face now, and she doesn't finish her sentence. She doesn't have to. I pull her to me.

"I know, babes." I rub her back gently and kiss her forehead. "I know. But we will figure this out. If you're serious about this, about *me*, we will figure it out."

She nods against my shoulder, but she doesn't speak.

"You know that episode of *Friends* where Ross and Rachel get back together, and Phoebe starts saying she knew they eventually would because he's her lobster?"

She chuckles against me and pulls back to look in my eyes. "That was random. But yes. I didn't know you were a *Friends* fan." Her eyebrows raise in curiosity.

I eye her back. "I don't live under a rock, Paisley. Anyway, it was on the other day, and I heard Phoebe talking about how lobsters mate for life. How even if people struggle to find each other, once they end up together, that's it. Game over."

"Okay... what is your point?" She's full on laughing at me now, but I grab both her hands and look her in the eyes with a serious expression.

"My point is, Paisley Hamilton, that *you* are my lobster."

Her eyes brim with tears, for a much different reason than a few minutes ago, as her lips pull into a smile. "I thought you didn't believe in soulmates or anything like that?"

"I didn't. But that was before."

"Before what?"

I tuck a stray piece of hair behind her ear and look into her eyes. "Before it was us."

She smiles even more at that. "Well if that isn't the most romantically cheesy thing I've ever heard."

She kisses me then, and my hands find their place on either side of her face, trying to deepen it, but after a few seconds, she breaks free.

"You do know that's not true, though, right?"

"What do you mean? It's not?" I ask, actually surprised. Phoebe Buffay lied to me?

She shakes her head as she laughs. "No, honey. Actually, I'm pretty sure lobsters are anything *but* monogamous. The female comes and gets knocked up and then dips out to have the kids, and the male moves on to the next one." She pats my leg in a futile attempt to comfort me. "But the thought was still really sweet."

"Fuck." I laugh. "Well, either way, I'm still going to call you my lobster."

She smiles at me then, and I swear my heart grows three sizes. "Oh, I fully expect that, lobster boy."

After finishing our picnic, Paisley and I spend the rest of the afternoon wrapped in each other's arms. The time goes way too quickly, and before either of us knows it, she has to leave.

Beth is out of town, but Ethan isn't, and she said it would be suspicious and out of character for her to spend an entire night away from home. But the thought of her having to go back home to him drives me crazy.

She sits on the edge of the bed now, already dressed, her hair still tousled from where my hands ran through it earlier. She reaches for her earrings on the nightstand, putting them in with ease, and I can't stop fucking staring at her. Watching her. Drinking her body in and memorizing every feature, in case this is the last time we...

No. I don't want to think about that. It can't be.

She exhales slowly, shaking her head. "This feels impossible."

I'm still laying in bed, and I shift up onto my elbows. "What does?"

She looks toward the door, toward the world outside of our oasis we've spent the last eight hours in. "Walking out of here and pretending like none of this happened. Going home, to *him*, as if everything is normal. Spending the next two weeks of winter break without even being able to see you. Returning to school and acting like you're nothing more than my assistant principal."

She turns and looks at me while biting her lip. She knows how sexy I think she looks when she does that, and if she didn't look so damn distraught right now, I would pull her to me and claim her body all over again.

But reality quickly sets in. I hadn't fully thought about how it's the beginning of winter break. How she's going to be home, with him, for the next two weeks, and how I'll be home with Bethany.

Fuck.

"How do I possibly do that, Briggs? How do I go home to him now?"

I sit up higher, scooting to the edge of the bed so I can place my hand on her thigh.

"When I see Ethan tonight, he's going to ask me about my day with Charlie. He'll talk to me about his day as if everything is normal. And I'll just have to stand there and act like I didn't spend all day here with you. That I wasn't just..." She trails off, shaking her head.

I don't know what to say. Because as much as I want to comfort her, to tell her it will be okay, I refuse to lie to her. I won't tell her this isn't fucked up and messy and complicated and painful. Because that's exactly what it is.

Instead, I run my hand up and down her thigh, trying to comfort her through my touch. "Then don't do it forever." I say flatly. "Don't keep going back to a life that doesn't make you happy."

She sighs, and lets out a soft, humorless laugh. "It's not that simple."

"I know it's not. And I need to listen to my own advice, too. But..." I hesitate, choosing my words carefully. "You said it yourself. What we have... it's different. It's something we've never felt before." I swallow, my throat tightening. "Can you really go back to a life without that? Without *us*?"

She glances away from me, speaking so quietly I barely hear her. "I don't know."

I reach for her hand and thread my fingers through hers. "I do."

She squeezes my hand and is quiet for a moment. Then she shakes her head again. "I can't just blow up my whole life overnight."

"I'm not asking you to," I say gently. "I just... I just need to know you're at least considering it. That this wasn't—"

"Stop." She cuts me off. "Don't even go there. You know this wasn't nothing."

I bring her hand up to my lips and softly kiss her knuckles. "Okay," I say quietly. "Then what *do* you want?"

"I want you," she says with certainty. "But I don't want to hurt him, either."

I nod. "Then we'll figure it out."

"We'll figure it out," she repeats, but she doesn't sound convinced.

Instead, she stands and straightens her dress, grabbing her keys from the nightstand. My chest tightens, and my stomach lurches. Because for all of our talk today about wanting to be with each other and figuring things out, she's still walking out that door. Still walking away from me and back to him.

And I still have to fucking let her.

Chapter forty-five

♫ "Torn" — Natalie Imbruglia ♫

PAISLEY

Walking into my house tonight, I feel like a stranger. The kitchen counters are the same minty green that I hated when we moved in, and the throw blanket on the couch is still folded the way I left it this morning. Cheeto and Sebastian are swarming my feet as usual, and Ethan's Old Spice cologne faintly lingers in the air. Nothing has changed. And yet, everything has.

I slip off my shoes and hear a rustling coming from the bedroom. Rounding the corner, I find Ethan loading the clothes from the hamper into a basket, a sight I've sure as hell never seen before. He looks up when he hears me enter the room, and his expression softens.

"Hey, baby," he says, setting the basket down, and the use of his usual pet name almost makes my skin crawl right off of my body. He crosses the room and wraps his arm around me, and I instantly tense. Fuck. Can he smell Briggs on me?

I shift uncomfortably. His body against mine should feel comforting, welcoming, *normal*... but it doesn't. Instead, it feels suffocating. I force a smile as he kisses my forehead.

"Hey."

"How was your day with Charlie?"

My heart clenches, but I don't hesitate. I was prepared for this question.

"It was good," I say as nonchalantly as possible, hoping I don't sound as nervous as I feel. "We just hung out at her house. Pretty lowkey day."

He pulls back slightly and studies me, his hands resting on my hips. "You okay?" he asks, searching my face. "You seem a little off lately."

I nod quickly. "Just tired. Long week leading up to break, and the change in routine is already throwing me off."

It's not a lie. At least not really. I *am* exhausted. Just not from sleep deprivation.

"Well, I did laundry," he says, motioning to the half-folded pile on the bed. "I know I don't help as much as I should, so I thought I would start trying more."

My breath hitches in my throat, and my eyes begin to burn.

He did laundry? Are you fucking kidding me?

After years of me asking—no, *pleading*—for help, for balance, for him to see me drowning under the weight of all the fucking things I do for us, *now* he decides to try? After I've already crossed a line I can never come back from? After I've already given my heart to someone else?

Tears press the edges of my eyes, hot and unforgiving, and I have to turn away before he sees them. If he does, he'll probably think they're happy tears, that this is what I've been waiting for. And in some cruel, fucked up way, it *is*, isn't it? Isn't this the version of him I've *begged* for? For the man who notices I'm struggling? For the man who listens to me? For the man who makes an effort?

It should be enough. *This* should be enough. God, I wish it were enough.

But it's not.

Not anymore.

Standing here, looking at the pride on his face and at those fucking clothes lying on the bed, it's like the universe is mocking me, punishing me, torturing me. Dangling everything I've wanted for *years* right in front of me after I've already begun to let go.

I can feel Ethan watching me, waiting for me to say something, to acknowledge his tiny act of effort like it's some grandiose gesture. And the thing is, for him, it probably is. Maybe he can sense me pulling away. Maybe this is his way of showing me he's trying, of showing me he cares. Of showing me it's worth staying.

But it's too late.

And God, that breaks me more than anything else. Because for the first time, I realize that even if he were to become the exact version of himself that I've been wanting him to be, to become the *husband* I've been waiting for him to be, there's still one thing he isn't.

Briggs.

I press my lips together, forcing down the bile rising in my throat, and plaster a smile across my face. "That's great, Eth. Thanks."

His shoulders drop a little, like he was expecting something more. And maybe if I was still the Paisley I was a few weeks ago, or even a few hours ago, I would give him that. I would wrap my arms around him and offer him a kiss, showing my appreciation. But I'm not her anymore. I'm not sure I ever will be again.

"You wanna watch something tonight?" he asks, hopeful. "Maybe a movie?"

I shake my head slightly. "I'm really tired. I think I'm just gonna shower and read for a bit tonight."

He hesitates, then nods. "Okay. Maybe tomorrow?" His voice drops an octave, and the sound of it breaks me even more.

"Yeah. Maybe tomorrow."

I hate to see him so deflated. I offer him a slight smile before slipping into the bathroom. I shut the door before he can say anything else, and his footsteps retreat to the living room. The second I know I'm alone, a breath shudders out of me. I turn the shower faucet on and let the water heat up as I grip the edge of the sink, staring at someone I no longer recognize in the mirror.

"Who are you?" I ask her.

I peel off my clothes, the smell of Briggs still on my skin. The smell of the hotel sheets. Of our sweat. His cologne.

The scalding hot water hits my skin as I step into the shower, and I welcome the burn. Using more force than necessary, I scrub myself clean as if I can erase him, erase the pain, erase the turmoil brewing inside me.

My heart is tearing in two, and I swear I can actually *feel* it, like something is ripping me apart from the inside. Trying to claw its way out of my fucking chest. The last time I felt like this much pain was when Steven died, and I don't know if I'm strong enough to survive it twice. It's unbearable. Obliterating. Paralyzing.

But this time, I'm grieving something that isn't even gone yet. And the worst part is I don't even know who I'm mourning.

My head, my heart, and my gut are all telling me something different, and I'm not sure which one to listen to.

I suck in a sharp breath, and my ribs tighten. I can't get enough air, and my body trembles under the weight of a choice I know I have to make but that feels impossible. A sob rips through me before I can stop it, and I crumble to the shower floor.

I curl my knees into my chest as the water continues to run over me. My arms wrap around my legs as if that will hold me together. But it doesn't. Another sob escapes me, so I press my forehead against my knees, hoping the shower is loud enough to drown out the sound and keep Ethan from hearing me fall apart.

Because if he does, if he sees me like this, what would I even say?

That I love him, but it's not enough anymore?

That I love him, but I want to be with someone else?

That I love him, but I don't know if he's the person I'm meant to be with forever?

My hands fist my hair as I rock back and forth, trying to breathe through the pain. Another gut-wrenching cry rips through me, and then another, and another, until I am gasping for air through my tears, my body convulsing.

When I finally feel like I have no tears left and the water has run cold, I force myself to stand.

I step out of the shower and wrap a towel around me, my hands finding my phone that's sitting on the bathroom counter.

*You're everything I didn't know
I was looking for, lobster girl.*

*You're everything I have been looking
for but didn't think I'd ever find.*

I hit send before I can think twice. Before the guilt can creep back in. Before I look into the mirror and see myself standing in a home I built with someone else.

Slipping into sweatpants and an old Stonebrook Eagles hoodie, I grab a book and head out to the couch where Ethan sits watching TV.

"Mind if I join you?" I ask quietly, hoping he can't see the swollenness of my eyes.

"Sure," he says softly.

I grab a blanket from the ottoman and sit next to Sebastian, pulling my knees toward my chest and cracking open the book.

I try to focus on the words in front of me, to fill my mind with fictional characters and their problems rather than thinking about my own. But my mind keeps drifting—to all my memories with Ethan, to the moment in the hotel room with Briggs, and to the text that just cracked me even farther apart.

Chapter Forty-Six

♫ "Happier" — Marshmello & Bastille ♫

BRIGGS

I swing the axe down hard, splitting the log clean in half. The two pieces scatter apart and land in the snow with a soft thud. My breath clouds in the cold air, but I barely feel it.

I put the next log up and swing again. I don't need this much firewood. I've already stacked enough to last us through the rest of the winter, but I keep going anyway. The movement keeps me from thinking, from spiraling. It keeps my body busy, and my mind quiet.

But it's not fucking quiet enough.

It's been a week since I've seen Paisley. Since I've been able to kiss her, to hold her, to see her smile. A week since I let her go.

We've texted a few times, but not often. Beth returned a few days after our tryst in the hotel, and Paisley was back home with

Ethan. Between the holidays and her shifts at Tumbleweed, neither of us has had much free time. Her texts have been short and sporadic, and at this point, I really don't know what she's thinking. Has she been lying in bed with Ethan at night, staring at the ceiling and wondering how the hell she's going to move forward? Has she been avoiding his touch, the way I have been with Bethany?

I fucking hope so. The thought of him having his hands on her... I can't even think about it.

I reset another log and swing as hard as my body allows me.

After a few more pieces, I bring the axe down once more, and it sticks into the wood. Rather than yanking it free, I leave it there and wipe the sweat from my forehead with the back of my hand before pulling my phone out of my pocket.

I open our text thread and stare at it for a minute, debating. I really shouldn't text her, especially when Ethan could see it. But I'm going fucking crazy over here, so I do anyway.

I miss you.

Three dots appear almost immediately. Then they disappear. Then they appear again. I wait with baited breath, watching as her message comes through.

I miss you, too. So much. But I need some time to think.

I frown at the screen. That is not what I wanted to hear, though I'm not completely surprised given our conversation at the hotel before she left.

A sharp exhale leaves my lungs. I shove my phone into my pocket and walk back toward the house, contemplating my response. I should tell her I understand. That I'll give her all the time she needs. That I won't pressure her.

That's what I *should* do. But I've never been one to follow expectations, so instead, I say none of that.

I have to know. Now that she's had a few days to think about it, I have to know.

There's a pause even longer than before. My heart thumps in my chest as I step onto my deck.

I close my eyes and run a hand through my hair.

Okay.

That's all I can get myself to say. What else is there? Paisley might not know what she wants yet. She might need time to figure it out.

But I don't. And although that hurts like hell to admit, I know what I need to do. Regardless of what happens between us, I can't keep living a lie.

Beth deserves better. *I* deserve better.

My chest tightens even more as I walk into the house and hang up my coat. The Christmas tree still stands in the corner of the living room, and red and green lights are strewn over the top of the cabinets in the kitchen. Beth got home from Nashville the day before Christmas Eve, and the majority of the past week has been spent with our families.

I'm fucking exhausted, and this is the last conversation I want to have right now, or ever, but it needs to happen. Putting it off longer isn't beneficial for anybody.

Beth is sitting at the counter, working on something on her laptop. Her eyes flick up to me as I step farther into the kitchen.

"Hey," she says. A smile pulls at her lips. She looks happy to see me, which makes this so much fucking worse.

"Hey." My voice is hoarse. I clear my throat. "Um, can we talk?"

Beth eyes me suspiciously. She can tell by my tone that it's serious, and the smile slips from her face.

"Okay..." she says slowly.

I motion for her to follow me into the living room, and we sit side by side on the couch. I take her hand in mine, not exactly sure how to proceed. I've broken up with women before, sure, but ending a fucking marriage? This is new territory for me. And this is a conversation I never envisioned myself having. How do I even start?

I look down at our hands, searching for the right words. But are there any in this situation? I don't think so. So instead, I just tell her the truth. Why drag it out?

"I don't... I don't think this is working anymore."

Beth's eyebrows pinch together, and she blinks. "What?"

I exhale slowly, my breath coming out shakily. "Us. This. Our marriage. I... I don't think it's working anymore."

Her breath catches. She shakes her head, and a tear instantly falls onto our still conjoined hands. "Briggs. What are you talking about?"

"I think..." I pause. "I think maybe we don't love each other the way we're supposed to."

She flinches. "That's not true. I *do* love you. How could you think I don't?"

I shake my head and close my eyes. "Not the way we should, Beth."

She's crying already, her tears staining her cheeks. She tries to wipe them away, but she can't stop them. Pulling her hand from mine, she asks, "Why are you saying this? Where is this coming from?"

Her voice is louder now. Angry. I can't blame her.

"It's been coming for a long time. I—*we*—haven't been happy. I think we both know that. We want different things, and—"

"Is there someone else?" She stares at me, eyes wide, searching my face.

I hold her gaze, and my throat tightens. I should have expected this.

"No."

She scoffs, angrily wiping at her cheeks. "I don't believe you."

All I do is look down and shake my head. I don't argue. Because she's right—but she doesn't need to hear that.

Beth exhales sharply, turning to face me, her mascara smearing down her face. "Briggs, *please*. Don't make a rash decision. Whatever this is, we can work through it. Please don't do this. We can fix it."

My stomach twists, but I don't respond. I'm not sure I would be able to if I tried.

"If this is about the bar," she continues, "If it's what you really want, we can figure it out. You can quit your job. You can do something else. I just can't lose you. *Please*."

"It's not just about the bar, Bethany," I say gently.

"Briggs, if there's—" she pauses for a moment. "If you've made a mistake, we can work past it. I can forgive you. Just please don't do this. Please don't leave me."

She grabs my face in her hands, and it feels foreign. But when she leans in to kiss me, I let her. I allow her lips to press against mine, and I wait to feel the spark I've been wishing was between us. The heat I feel when I'm with Paisley. Because this *would* be easier, wouldn't it? Staying. Fixing what's broken. Pretending I didn't already make up my mind.

But you can't fix something that's never truly worked in the first place.

I shake my head and pull away from the kiss. "I can't, Beth. I'm so sorry." I wipe at my face, noting that my cheeks are now also wet.

She lets out a quiet, broken whimper. Then she stands from the couch and storms out of the room, disappearing into the bedroom and slamming the door shut behind her.

I stay on the couch for I don't know how long, letting her have the time she needs. I at least owe her that.

Eventually, the door creaks open, and she saunters back out to the living room and sits across the room from me on the other couch.

"So now what?" she whispers so quietly it's as if she's afraid of the answer.

"I'm going to stay at the cabin for a while. We can figure out logistics later with the house and everything else. For now, I'll pack a bag with essentials and come back in a few days for more things."

"So you're serious."

It's not a question.

I slide over to where she's sitting and take her hand in mine. "Yes. I'm so sorry, Beth. I love you—I really do. It's just... something's not right. Something's missing. I've tried. For so long I've tried." I shake my head in desperation. "I *wish* I could make myself feel the way I want to feel. The way you deserve for me to feel."

She doesn't say anything, so I slowly stand from the couch and walk to the bedroom. Beth follows me in and sits on the edge of the bed. As I grab a bag from the closet, her shoulders shake, and she cries so hard, she struggles to breathe.

I hate myself for being the reason why. I want to comfort her, to tell her it will be okay—but who am I to say that when I'm the one who's tearing her apart?

I throw clothes into my bag hastily, taking only what I need to get me through the next few days. I'll come back for more once our conversation isn't so fresh and we've each had time to settle our emotions.

Before I leave, she walks over to me and gives me a hug, and I squeeze her hard, offering as much comfort as I can without breaking her even more.

The drive to the cabin is a blur. I should feel relieved, lighter, happier. I finally did what I should have done years ago.

But all I feel is empty.

The cabin is freezing when I walk in, having been unused for weeks now. I flick the light switch and drop my bag at the door, exhaling.

This is what I wanted, right? So why does it feel like the world is caving in around me?

I crank the heat up on the thermostat and sink onto the couch, staring into the emptiness of the cabin. I did the right thing. I *know* that. This is what needed to happen.

But that doesn't mean it doesn't hurt.

And God, does it fucking hurt.

Chapter forty-Seven

♫ "Numb Little Bug" — Em Beihold ♫

PAISLEY

"Watch out!"

I barely hear the voice before I see someone in an apron flying past me with smoking hot fajita skillets in her hands.

"Jesus, Jade!" I shout from behind her. "You nearly took me out!"

Jade throws a glance over her shoulder, calling back to me. "Sorry, P! It's crazy out here tonight."

She's not wrong. Holiday break always brings a new wave of customers to Tumbleweed with the mix of school being out and adults taking extended PTO from work. Plus, I swear everyone is always more willing to blow money around the holidays. Especially on food. Who wants to cook after preparing a big Christmas dinner and having the chaos of Santa at their house?

The smell of steak, peppers, and fresh tortillas floats through the air, and while normally that would make my stomach growl, it does nothing for me. I haven't had much of an appetite lately. Or one at all, for that matter.

"Paisley, did you take table twelve's drink order yet?" Parker, our shift lead, asks as he rushes by me.

Fuck. What is it that they wanted? I shake my head, trying to clear some of the fog. It's far too busy in here tonight for me to be off my game.

"Uh, yeah, just haven't put it into the POS. The girl wanted a margarita on the rocks, and the guy wanted a Pepsi. I was on my way to grab them some water."

"Get it into the system. They've already been here for too long to not have any drinks in front of them." He doesn't say it rudely, just as a reminder that I need to pick up my pace.

Normally I don't have an issue with busy nights, but I've been in a weird, foggy haze for days now.

This last week has been fucking brutal. It's been nine days since I spent time with Briggs, and it's been agonizing. Not only because I miss him—and I miss him *so* damn much—but because my guilt grows more and more every day. Pretty soon I'll have to charge it for rent.

But as much as I dream of being with him, I also cannot fathom being without Ethan. I keep trying to envision what that life would look like without him in it, and I can't. The other morning, he walked out the door for work, and I was a pile of snot and tears before he was even gone from the driveway just thinking about never seeing him again. And that's what would happen, isn't it? There's no world where I could be with Briggs and also keep Ethan in my life. I might be an optimist, but even I know that isn't a possibility, which makes this choice fucking impossible to make.

And the worst part is that me being in this position is no one's fault but my own.

Since break started, Charlie has invited me to go out a few times, but I haven't been able to find it in me to see or even speak to anyone, especially someone like Charlie who would immediately read through my bullshit façade of having my life together.

I haven't been able to sleep. I haven't been able to eat. I haven't even been able to look in the damn mirror. And yet, as guilty as I feel, I still can't get myself to regret what happened.

"Paisley, drink orders?"

Shit. "On it!"

I walk over to the POS and enter the order before I can get distracted again. Then I drop some water off at their table and jot down what they want for food.

Once I'm finally caught up and all my customers are happy, I break into the kitchen to breathe for a minute. It's a fucking zoo out there, and we've been rushing nonstop, but there's finally a bit of a lull now that it's nearing eight o' clock.

"What's with you tonight?"

I spin around to find Jade staring right at me, her hands on her hips and an accusatory look on her face.

"What do you mean?"

"You're off your game tonight, bia. Don't think I can't tell something's going on." She brings her finger up and points it in my face.

"I'm fine." I force myself to smile. "Just out of my routine with break and everything. No need to worry about me, *mother*."

She rolls her eyes and narrows them slightly like she doesn't believe me, but she doesn't push. "Uh huh," she says instead, taking a sip of her Pepsi. "You all caught up on your tables right now?"

"Yep. Just waiting for their food to go out."

She jerks her chin toward the back of the kitchen. "Go take five. I gotchu."

"Jade, I'm—"

"Don't you dare argue with me, bitch. Something's obviously bothering you, but I'm not going to push you to talk about it... yet. So go take a breather, clear your head, and then come back out here like the badass server I know you are."

I give her another smile, and this time it's genuine. "Thanks, babe." I blow her a kiss as I turn on my heel.

I slip past the kitchen and into the back storage area to grab my phone before stepping outside. The frigid air bites my skin, and goosebumps instantly erupt on my arms, but it's refreshing. I lean against the wall of the building and close my eyes, sucking in a deep breath.

Once some of the haze lifts, I pull my phone out and swipe through my notifications, and my heart plummets into my stomach when I see Briggs's name on my screen.

Great, there goes all the air I just got.

Fuck.

He *left*? As in *Bethany*? As in *his marriage*?

Fuck, fuck, fuckity fuck.

My pulse hammers, and my hand inadvertently flies up to my face and covers my now gaping mouth.

I read the messages again. And again. And again. And again. And then one more time just to be sure... as if something will change.

Because oh my fucking God. He actually did it. He *left* her.

I should respond. I should say something. *Anything.* But my fingers don't move.

Because now, this is real.

Now, everything is *real*.

Sebastian hops up onto the couch next to me and nuzzles his head into my arm. I scratch behind his ear absentmindedly. I remember when we found him on the street two years ago, alone and scared, with no one around him.

Kind of like how I'm feeling now.

He was in a storm drain sleeping in a bed of leaves, covered in fleas, and we brought him home with every intention of bringing him to the humane society. Before we knew it, though, he became a part of our family, and he never made it to shelter.

"I could never leave you, baby. Could I?" I ask him as he climbs into my lap.

A tear escapes before I can catch it, and it drips down my cheek to the tip of my chin before landing on Sebastian's black and orange fur. He looks up at me lovingly, completely unbothered.

I wish I felt that way.

I know what I'm doing is wrong, and if I was an outsider looking in, I would hate me. I *know* that.

But the people on the outside don't know what it feels like to have your heart ripped in two.

If only I had a reason to leave. If only Ethan were a bad husband, it would be easier. If he neglected me, hurt me, betrayed me… I wouldn't have to wrestle with this decision. I would no longer be the person I hate. If only he did *something* to push me out the door without the guilt that leaving brings with it.

But that's not the case. Ethan doesn't do any of those things. He loves me.

Yet it's not enough. Fuck. Why isn't that enough?

God, what kind of fucked up person *wishes* their husband would give them a reason to leave?

I squeeze my eyes shut, inhaling sharply. I lift Sebastian off my lap and place him gently on the couch before pushing myself up. I need to get ready. Today is the first day back to school after break. The first day I'll see Briggs. And while part of me *aches* to see him, the other part of me—the part that's still grappling with the possibility of leaving this life I've built with Ethan—is terrified.

And the second I step through the doors of Stonebrook High, he's exactly where I knew he would be: standing at the end of the hallway, broad shoulders tense, hands in his pockets, and my eyes latch onto him instantly. He's talking to Miranda, nodding along to something she's said, but I can tell—no, I can *feel*—his mind is elsewhere. And I can sense the moment the energy in the room changes, and he turns to face me.

Fuck, I want to look at him. I want to soak up the way he's looking at me. I want to go to him, to fucking run to him. It takes everything in me to do the opposite, and instead, I spin on my heel and walk down the hallway to my classroom.

Because I'm a damn coward.

I never responded to his text the other day. When he told me he left Beth, I read the message five hundred times—probably more—but I couldn't find it in me to reply.

I wanted to. But what would I have said? *Oh, that's great! I still have no idea if I'm going to leave my husband even though I can't stop thinking about you?*

Yeah... right.

I squeeze my eyes shut, willing myself to get my shit together before kids start showing up for class.

But I'm not even in my room for two minutes when Charlie comes charging through my door, Leah at her side.

She rips the expo marker I'm using out of my hand, forcing me to look her way.

"Nice to see you, too, babe," I say, grabbing the marker back. "Now, can I help you?"

"Tell me you heard."

My stomach sinks. Jesus, word travels fast. "Heard what?"

"About the Davenports. Beth and Briggs. They split up over break."

I swallow hard but force my expression to remain neutral. "I, uh," I start to say but stop myself. "Do you know why?"

They both shake their heads. "No idea. We just heard Gabby talking about it in the staff lounge."

"Gabby?" I scoff. "That girl gossips even more than you two. You can't believe anything she says."

I'm not sure why I'm trying to act like this news isn't true when I know damn well it is.

"You have a point," Leah chimes in. "And normally I would agree, but she was talking to Carli, and you *know* she would know."

Carli. Beth's best friend. Of course she knows. And if *she's* talking about it, that means *everyone* is going to be talking about it soon. My heart aches for the pain and turmoil I know Briggs must be feeling. Pain that *I've* made worse by avoiding him all break.

I roll my eyes. "Jeesh. What a nice friend to be gossiping about it already."

"Oh, come on, Pais," Charlie groans. "You can't tell me you're not the least bit curious." She eyes me cautiously, no doubt thinking about our conversation at the PBIS conference.

I force a laugh because I can't possibly tell her the truth. That I'm not curious because I *know* exactly what happened and why.

Turning back to the whiteboard to continue writing, I shrug. "It's really not my business."

From my peripheral, I notice Charlie narrowing her eyes at me, but I keep mine trained on the board. Because if she looks hard enough, if she gets a chance to read my face, she'll see.

See that I already knew.

See that it one hundred percent *is* my business.

See that I've been lying to her for weeks.

And see that I've fallen in love with Briggs Fucking Davenport.

Chapter Forty-Eight

BRIGGS

It's been two weeks since I've spoken to Paisley. And it's been the longest, most excruciating two weeks of my entire fucking life.

I've seen her at school, but I can tell she's avoiding me as much as she can. It's only when I walk past her room while she's teaching or when I supervise the hallway by her door that I'm able to catch a glimpse of her. Other than that, it's like we're two ships passing in the night.

I've thought about going to see her during her prep. I've thought about texting her. I've thought about waiting by her car after school to tell her the silence is fucking killing me.

But I haven't. Because she said she needed space, and that's what I'm going to give her.

Even if I feel like I'm drowning without her.

The heat from the fire washes over me as I sit on the couch in the cabin. I take a sip of my whiskey, and the liquid burns as it coats my throat.

I drop my head and swirl the ice in my glass. How much have I even had to drink tonight?

I was hoping the alcohol would drown out the thoughts of her—of her at home with *him*—but it has only made them stronger.

It's only made me think more about what the hell she's been doing these last two weeks and if she's even thought of me at all.

She said she loved me, and I believed her. But what if that isn't enough?

The logs in the fire shift, and the flames crackle. I stare into the glowing embers.

Is this my life now? Spending my nights alone in this damn cabin, waiting for something, someone, that may never come?

Did I make a mistake?

I thought leaving Beth was the right choice, but what if Paisley never chooses me? What if she stays with him?

I pick up my phone, and my thumb hovers over Paisley's name. I could check in, ask how her day was. See if she's doing okay.

But would that change anything? Or would that make things even worse?

I don't want to be the man who has to beg someone to choose him. That's not who I am. That's not who I want to be.

So I shut my phone off completely and toss it on the cushion next to me, and then I down the rest of my drink instead.

The drive to my house the next morning is long and quiet, and pulling onto the gravel driveway brings a sense of familiarity and foreignness at the same time. As I slow my car to a stop, Aaron is outside of his house shoveling snow, and I take a deep breath before stepping out of my vehicle. I walk in his direction, and when he sees me, he leans on his shovel and lifts his hand to wave at me.

"Well, well, well, look who it is."

I smirk at him and shake my head. "Don't start."

Once I get closer, I give him a pat on the shoulder, and he pulls me in for a hug.

"Missed seeing you around here the last few weeks. Amber told me. About you and Beth. Surprised I didn't hear it from you."

A sting of guilt starts to rise. I know I should have told him. He's my best friend. But with everything going on with Paisley—or everything *not* going on with Paisley—I haven't been able to bring myself to talk to anyone much lately.

"Where you been hiding out?"

"The cabin. Sorry I didn't tell you, man. Just haven't felt up to talking much. I needed some time."

He gives me a skeptical look. "Two weeks of time? Look, Briggs, I'm sorry. I know this can't be easy. But you sure you made the right decision?"

I look down at the snow-covered ground and shove my hands into my jacket pockets. "No," I answer honestly.

Aaron nods and shovels another pile of snow off his driveway before turning back to face me. "You thinking about going back?"

I let out a shaky breath. That's the same question I asked myself the entire drive over here. It would be easier to go back. To start over with Beth. To work on things. But that would only work if Paisley was the sole issue in our marriage, and I can't pretend problems weren't there far before Paisley Hamilton came along.

"No," I finally say. "I don't think so. I've been thinking about it, but I can't."

Aaron sighs. "Why not?"

"Because I'm not sure I was ever truly happy. At least not like I wanted to be."

"So what's different? What made you figure this out now?"

I give him a pointed look but don't answer.

"Ah," he replies, knowingly. "Does Beth know?"

I shake my head. "There's not much for her to know about now. Besides, I don't want her to think I'm leaving because of that. I would have gotten to this point eventually." I pause, thinking about what to say next. "At the end of the day, this is about me."

"Alright, man. Well, I'm here if you need to talk. You know that right?"

I nod. "I know that."

After talking with Aaron for a few more minutes, I walk over to the door and ready myself to head inside.

Do I knock? Technically this is still my house, but Beth doesn't know I'm coming today, so I suppose that would be the right thing to do. Before I have a chance to, though, the door creaks open, and Beth is standing on the other side. She seems surprised to see me, but at least she doesn't look angry.

"I'm, uh... just here to grab some more of my things."

She nods and opens the door a bit more, signaling for me to come inside.

"How have you been?" she asks as I take my coat off and hang it on the rack. "I haven't seen you much at school."

"Yeah." I look at her, and my shoulders get heavier.

She looks tired—her usual sleek, straight hair is pulled into a messy ponytail, and she's wearing leggings and an old, oversized sweatshirt with the name of our college on it. She's not wearing any makeup, and her blue eyes look duller than I remember. Still, she looks beautiful. Beth has always been beautiful—but it's never sent a spark through me the way it does when I look at Paisley.

"I've been spending a lot of time in my office, I guess."

Beth crosses her arms and leans against the kitchen island. "You didn't answer my question," she says, tilting her head slightly. "How have you been?"

I shrug. "Fine. Been better, obviously."

"Then come home, Briggs," she pleads, a hint of desperation in her voice.

Fucking shit. I hate watching what I'm doing to her.

"Beth—"

"Don't do this. Don't act like it's already over between us."

"B—" I start, but she interrupts, stepping closer to me.

"Just listen. I know we weren't perfect. But we were *something*, weren't we? How can you so easily throw us away?"

My jaw tenses, and my eyes start to burn, so I look away.

"Of course we were," I say softly. "I loved you Beth. Hell, I still fucking love you. It's just…"

"What? Whatever it is, we can fix it. Can't we?"

I shake my head solemnly. I don't want to hurt her. I don't want to do this. I wish it were that easy. I *want* to say yes, to tell her we can make it work.

But then I think about Paisley—about the way she *cares*, the way she encourages me to pursue my dreams, the way it feels being with her. That day we spent together—it was like I was finally able to breathe after years of fucking suffocating.

And although I don't know where the hell I stand with her, or if I'll ever get to be with her, that doesn't matter. Because I know *this* isn't what I want anymore.

I turn to Beth and speak softly. "I think it's past fixing."

She looks down in understanding but doesn't say anything.

"I'm just going to grab a few things. Shouldn't take me long. Then I'll be out of your way."

"Take all the time you need. I'll be in the living room."

She walks away from me, and I spend a moment taking in the space around me before heading upstairs.

The cabin might be quiet and lonely, and definitely not where I'm meant to be, but this place doesn't feel like home anymore, either.

Chapter Forty-Nine

♫ "Breathe (2 AM)" — Anna Nalick ♫

PAISLEY

Another shitty day at school is over. Another day of going through the motions, trying to put on a happy face for my students, when I'm crumbling inside.

Avoiding Briggs for the last month has been fucking torture. No, actually, torture would be better than this. I think I must have been sent to Hell and didn't even realize it. Who would have thought it would be so cold here?

Life has been moving in slow motion. Every day feels longer than the one before it, and if Ethan can tell something is off with me, he's been trying his damn best not to show it.

When I walk in the door, both Sebastian and Cheeto rush to my feet and nuzzle into my legs. I swear cats have a sixth sense when knowing something is wrong. The two have hardly left my side for the last month.

If I leave, will I get to take them with me? They're as much Ethan's as they are mine, but I can't imagine not having my fur-babies in my life. I may not think I want children, but you can bet your ass I would have a whole hoard of cats if I had the money and space for them.

I bend down to scratch Cheeto behind the ear, and something on the counter catches my attention. I set my school bag down and walk into the kitchen, seeing a bag of peanut butter M&Ms and a pack of Sour Punch Straws. Both of my favorites. Sitting beside it is note with Ethan's handwriting.

I love you more than anything. I'm sorry if I don't show it enough.

I stare at the paper, and all of my breath dives out of my lungs. This is what I've wanted. I've wanted Ethan to notice when something is wrong, to notice *me,* to fucking *care.* To do something to show me that he sees me.

And here it is. My favorite candy, a handwritten note, and a big-ass reminder that he loves me.

I should feel warmth spreading through my chest. I should be filled with relief. Instead, I think I'm going to fucking vomit.

I pick up the note, my fingers trembling. I can picture him writing it, probably in a rush before heading out the door for work today. Ethan isn't one for big displays of affection. He shows his love in smaller ways. A touch to my back here and there, watching our favorite shows together, telling me he loves me. And I always thought that was enough. That it *could* be enough. But this? This is a big deal for him. This is a sign that he's trying.

And I fucking wish it was enough now.

I *wish* this made my heart swell instead of ache. I wish I was giddy right now, texting him something playful and flirty, telling him to bring his fine ass home early so I can properly thank him. I wish I felt the way I imagine I would feel if this note were from someone else.

But instead, it's only remorse. Because the only person I want to get a note like this from... is Briggs.

It hits me like a wrecking ball to the stomach, and biles rises in my throat as I clutch the note in my hand, squeezing my eyes shut.

Shit. Shit. Shit.

I cover my mouth and rush into the bathroom, dropping to my knees in front of the toilet. I empty the contents of my stomach until there's nothing left, leaving me dryheaving and gasping for air.

I thought if I had space from Briggs, I'd get the clarity I needed. That if I just distanced myself long enough, I'd be able to figure out how to make things right with Ethan. But here he is, doing the things I've been begging him to do, and it doesn't change a damn thing.

I don't want Ethan.

I *love* him, but I'm not *in love* with him anymore.

That realization sends me hurling over the toilet once again, my whole body shaking as the tears start falling.

Cheeto wanders into the bathroom and lets out a small, confused meow and nudges my side, but I can't stop the sob that rips through me.

I have to leave.

I have to fucking leave.

Not because of Briggs. Not because of an affair or a fantasy or a fleeting moment of passion.

I have to leave because *I can't stay.*

I can't keep pretending this is enough when I know, in my fucking bones, that it's not.

But how the hell do I do that? How do I walk away from a man who has never hurt me, never abandoned me, never made me feel unloved?

How do I *stay* in a life that doesn't feel like mine anymore?

I walk back to the kitchen and grab my phone to shoot a text to Maddie.

Hey. Last minute, I know... but any chance you're free this weekend? I need to get away.

Pack a bag, girl. The guest room is already made up.

When Ethan gets home, I try to act as normal as possible, knowing I'm doing a shit job at it. I mindlessly make dinner, and we eat while we watch an episode of something I couldn't even tell you the name of because my mind is somewhere else entirely.

As we get ready for bed, I broach the subject of this weekend carefully.

"So," I say as I pull back the covers. "I think I'm going to spend the weekend at Maddie's. Take some time away, go off the grid."

"What does that mean?"

"I just need to get away for a little bit. I probably won't have my phone much."

"You need to get away from what? Me?" The offense and hurt in his voice makes my chest ache.

"No... I just need time to think." I realize too late that's probably not the best way to phrase it.

"To think about what? Leaving me?"

His directness startles me. Maybe he's been paying more attention than I've realized. After all, I *have* been completely consumed with my own emotions and problems that I haven't taken time to notice how much he must be hurting, too.

"What? No," I say, taking a bit too long to answer. "I'm not feeling like myself. I need time with a friend, time to decompress and get my head on straight."

He crawls into bed beside me and turns off the lamp. He doesn't say anything for a few minutes, and then he cuddles up next to me and wraps his arms around me. I let him.

"Please don't leave me, Paisley," he whispers, so quietly I barely hear him, and I know he's not just talking about this weekend.

Chapter fifty

♫ *"Iris" — The Goo Goo Dolls* ♫

BRIGGS

"Congratulations, Mr. Davenport," Jo says as I finish crossing the *t* on my signature. "The place is officially yours." She drops the keys into my hand and smiles warmly. "I know this is just a lease agreement for now, but I assure you that once I'm gone, it'll be all yours. No fuss, no probate. I'm in the process of finishing up the Transfer-on-Death Deed, so should the Lord come-a-knockin', it'll automatically go into effect."

"I still can't believe you're willing to do that." I pick up my copy of the agreement and give it another onceover. "This is an insane deal. Are you sure this is what you want?"

"I'm sure, honey," she reassures me. "I want this place to go to someone who's going to care about it the way I do. It might not look like much now, but back when my Henry was alive, this place

413

was really something." She looks around at the space, and I can tell she is reliving her memories all over again. "We met here, you know." She turns to face me. "Back when Henry's dad ran the place. He was working as a mechanic, and I was only twenty. I had an issue with my car and decided to bring it in. Just so happened he was the one who was working that day. I knew from the first moment I saw him that he was the one."

"How long were you together?"

"Fifty-six years. He was my first and only. Lots of people said I was crazy, that we didn't know each other well enough to get married after only six months. But when you know, you know. But you already know all about that, don't you?"

"What do you mean?"

"I saw the way you looked at Paisley when you two were here, dear. It reminded me of the way my Henry used to look at me." She pauses. "How long have you been in love with her?"

"Oh, I'm... we're not—"

She waves me off. "I saw the way she looked at you, too."

A lump forms in my throat. Is she right? Does Paisley love me? Is it that obvious?

Jo softly touches my arm with her hand. "Don't rush it, dear. Sometimes the heart is a few steps ahead. Love like that is rare. If it's meant to be, she'll come around when the time is right." She starts to walk away and then adds, "I'll get this paperwork taken care of. You have my number if you need me."

"Thanks, Jo."

She gathers her purse and puts the lease inside of it before hiking it onto her shoulder. As she's walking toward the door, she stops and turns toward me.

"Oh, and Briggs? There's one more condition for this agreement."

"What's that?"

"Promise me you'll never give up on your dreams."

I nod at her and smile. "I promise."

Once Jo is gone, I put the lease into the folder and drop it onto the concrete countertop. The space definitely needs some work, but it will serve as a welcomed distraction.

I slide my phone out of my pocket and scroll down to my messages with Paisley. I want to text her, to tell her this place is officially mine. She's the one who found it. If it wasn't for her, this wouldn't be happening. If she hadn't believed in me, I wouldn't be here.

But I don't want to force her decision, so I tuck my phone back into my pocket, pick up the industrial-size broom next to me, and start sweeping.

Chapter Fifty-One

♫ *"Hold My Hand" — Lady Gaga* ♫

PAISLEY

"Thank you so much for letting me stay here for a couple days, Mads." I place my bags on the floor of her guestroom and take a seat on the bed.

"Oh, stop. You literally do not have to thank me. I'm happy to have you." She leans against the doorframe. "But Pais, what's going on?"

I shake my head and look down at my hands in my lap. "Drinks first. Then we can talk about it."

"You know I already bought the wine, babe." She winks at me and turns to walk into the kitchen, grabbing the bottle from the fridge along with two glasses.

"Alan is out with the guys tonight," she hollers from the other room, "so we'll have a couple hours just to catch up!"

As soon as the bell rang for the weekend, I drove down here so I could spend as much time away as possible. I even took a personal day on Monday to avoid the Sunday scaries as soon as I get home.

I change into sweats and head out to the living room where Maddie is already waiting, full glass of wine in hand and another sitting on the coffee table.

"You get two glasses to unwind. Then you're spilling whatever is going on in that brain of yours."

I sink into the couch, grabbing the glass from the table and taking a good, long sip. "Fair enough."

Maddie eyes me closely. "Pais, you look fucking drained. And not just *I'm a teacher in February and my kids are driving me nuts* kind of drained. What's going on?"

"Hey," I say, swirling the wine in my glass. "You said I got two glasses first." I smile weakly, followed by a long exhale. "I don't even know where to start."

Maddie leans back on the couch and takes another sip. "Then start with what made you come here this weekend. What are you trying to get away from?"

I take a beat before answering. "I feel like I'm drowning, Mads. Every day, I wake up, and I have to pretend everything is fine when it's not. And I don't even know when or *how* this started. I just woke up one day and... realized I wasn't really happy anymore."

"Okay..." she treads lightly. "Well, have you talked to Ethan about it?"

"Kind of," I admit. "I tried. Probably not hard enough. But I feel like I can't really talk to him about it."

Maddie frowns. "Why not?"

"Because… because he wouldn't understand." I push my hair out of my face as I continue. "Fuck, *I* don't even understand. I think I'm losing my mind. Like I'm in this life I'm supposed to want, that I *thought* I wanted, but I just… don't anymore."

"Do you mean in regard to Ethan? Or everything else?"

I bite my lip, afraid to speak what I've been feeling into existence. "I think… just with Ethan. Teaching is good. I still love what I do, and I love my job. But that's kind of, um, part of the problem."

"What do you mean?"

I open my mouth but then close it. Saying these words out loud makes them real, and I'm terrified of what will happen once I'm not able to take them back.

"I… uh…" I pause, swallowing the lump in my throat. "There's kind of… someone else…"

Maddie leans forward abruptly, her wine sloshing in her glass. "Wait, what? *Who?*"

"Someone at work." The words slip out more easily than I thought they would. "It wasn't supposed to happen. I didn't go looking for it. I'm not even sure *how* it happened. But it did." My voice shakes slightly as I speak. "And it's not just an attraction or a crush or anything like that. It's… more. So, so much more." I groan as I lean back onto the couch.

Maddie leans back with me, processing this new information. "How long?"

I shrug. "Since the start of this school year, basically. But it wasn't until a month ago that we…"

Maddie's eyes widen. "You mean you—?"

I nod, not letting her finish her question. "Once. And it was the best and worst day of my life. I thought it would give me some clarity, and it did, but it also made things so much harder."

"Holy shit." Maddie blows out a slow breath. "Pais, I had no idea."

"How would you? I didn't tell anyone. Not even Charlie, and she works with us. I've been carrying this alone. For a while, I thought I could push it away and ignore it. That it would just... go away. But that hasn't worked. Which is why I'm here. I need time to process, to figure out what I truly want."

"I'm assuming Ethan doesn't know?"

"Of course not. And I hate myself for that. But there's more to it, Mads. I know I'm a terrible person, and I made a horrible decis—"

"You are *not* a terrible person, Paisley," she interrupts sternly.

I wring my hands in my lap, and my eyes burn. "It's not just about Ethan, either. This is about me, and what I want. Ethan and I are so different, and I just... I don't know if I can stay in this marriage for the rest of my life."

Maddie takes another sip of her wine, mulling over what I've said. Shrugging, she answers nonchalantly. "Then don't."

My head snaps up. "What?"

She gives me a knowing look. "Paisley, by the way it sounds to me, you've already made your decision. I think you're just afraid to admit it to yourself."

"But it's not that simple. I love Ethan. He's my best friend. He hasn't done anything to deserve this."

"And? That's not a reason to stay in a marriage. Listen. You can love someone and still know they're not your forever. It doesn't make you a bad person. It makes you human."

I set my now empty glass on the table in front of me. "I don't know how to leave," I whisper.

Maddie reaches over and squeezes my hand in support. "We can figure that out. Together. I'm here for you, Pais. No matter what."

I squeeze her hand back. "Thanks, Mads. So you don't think I'm despicable?"

"Never, babe," she reassures me. "I'm a little salty I'm only hearing about this now, and it hurts my heart you've been going through this alone, but I could never think less of you. Now fucking spill. Who's the guy?"

I shift in my seat, and heat moves up my cheeks. "Um, his name is Briggs. He's my assistant principal."

"Briggs? Wait. Isn't that the dude in the Giggle Squad?"

I groan, dropping my face into my hands. "Oh my God, I forgot you knew about that."

Maddie cackles and slaps her own knee. "I *knew* that name sounded familiar! Holy shit, Paisley. I thought you guys said he was an asshole?"

"Not an asshole. Just kind of... grumpy? Turns out it's only because he's been stuck in a job he hates," I mutter, laughing slightly. "But there's a lot more to him than I originally thought."

"A lot more to him, huh?" she asks with a mischievous smirk.

"Jesus, that's not what I meant." I roll my eyes. "Seriously, Mads. He's smart, and driven, and thoughtful, and—"

"Hot?"

I smile and then bite my lip again, my face now full on burning. "Devastatingly so."

She lets out a dramatic sigh. "Ugh, of course he is. It's always the hot ones who ruin lives."

I laugh and swat her arm. "Okay, too soon."

She grins, but then her eyes go wide again. "Wait, wasn't he also married?"

I purse my lips and nod. "Ergo, part of the problem. But..."

"But what?"

"He left. Moved out."

"Wait... for *you*?"

I shake my head. "For *him*. I mean, I think I probably played a role in that, but he wasn't happy. He hadn't been for a long time."

"Okay, that makes it *slightly* less scandy. But still—Jesus, Pais." She lets out a breath. "So is he getting divorced?"

"I honestly don't know." I grab the bottle of wine and refill my glass, topping Maddie's off, too. "He texted me that he left a few weeks ago, but I haven't talked to him since. I don't even know if he's still waiting for me."

"Please, Pais. Have you seen your ass? He's definitely waiting."

"Okay, can we be serious for like two minutes, please?" I laugh.

"That's hard for me." She smiles. "But okay, seriously. If he makes you feel something—like really feel something—then you owe it to yourself to see where that leads."

"I know. But Ethan—"

"Will be fine. It's going to suck. And you're right, he doesn't deserve that. No one does. And truly, I feel bad for the guy. But *you* are my priority, Paisley. So you need to do what makes *you* happy and to put yourself first for once. This maybe isn't the most traditional way of doing that, and sure, people are going to talk, and yeah, it's going to be really fucking hard, but you have a support system, and we will be here for you. Whatever you decide."

"Thank you. I really needed to hear that," I say softly.

"And you don't have to decide anything right now," she reminds me. "So for tonight, let's just drink until we forget all about it." She raises her glass.

I clink mine to hers, and a small smile forms. "Deal."

"Just one more question. Then we can stop talking about it." She pauses and drops her voice an octave lower. "So... how was it?"

I take a deep breath and let out a long exhale. "Honestly? Mind-blowing."

"I fucking knew it," she squeals.

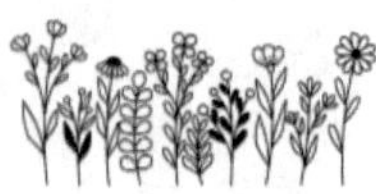

My fingers glide over the spines of the books lined on the shelves, and I stop and pick one up, tracing the embossed letters with my index finger. The cover is dark but soft, decorated with delicate wildflowers winding around the title. I tilt it in the light, watching the gold script catch and shimmer.

Flipping it over, I skim the summary. The main character is young and falling for someone she shouldn't. It's a story of temptation, about something unexpected turning into something that feels inevitable. My stomach twists.

I glance at the wildflowers again. Resilient things, blooming where they shouldn't, thriving in places they have no business being. My pulse stutters. I shove the book back onto the shelf and continue walking.

"So, hear me out," I say to Maddie. "What if we... got tattoos today?"

She turns and looks in the direction I'm staring, which is through the window and at the dark building across the street from us, and then swivels her head back toward me, wide-eyed. "Say fucking *less*, girl. Let's do it."

"Well damn, that was easier than I thought." I laugh.

"Um, do you even know me? I'm surprised I'm not the one who came up with the idea first. Nothing says mid-life crisis like getting a tattoo."

"Wow," I say playfully, "Thanks, babe."

"Well, it's true." Maddie shrugs her shoulders. "So, what are you going to get?"

"I'm not sure yet. Guess I'll have to think about it a little more. Or just decide when I walk into the tattoo parlor." I laugh. "What about you?"

"Something witchy, for sure. Maybe a ghost reading a book or something."

"That's so you. I love it."

"What the hell are we waiting for? Come *on*! Let's go before you chicken out on me." She grabs my hand and tugs me along the carpeted flooring, straight out onto the sidewalk and into the crisp air. I pull my jacket tighter.

Maddie swings our hands like we're giddy teenagers, and it relaxes me a bit.

"Eeeeek!" she squeals. "I can't believe you're getting your first tattoo today!"

"Right? Me either," I admit. "I'm actually kind of terrified."

The hair on the back of my neck stands, not from the cold but from the thought of a needle digging deep into my skin to leave a permanent mark. But I shake it off as we run across the street, trying not to overthink it.

As Maddie opens the door to the tattoo shop, my watch buzzes with a text notification.

*Hope you're having a good
time. Love and miss you.*

My heart stops for a brief moment at the sight of Ethan's name. Maybe this is a sign. Of what, I'm not sure, but the coincidence of him texting me right now makes me sick to my stomach.

I am about to pull out my phone and text him back when the door to the shop jingles and a burst of warm air floods around me. I take that as an excuse to leave my phone in my pocket and follow Maddie inside.

The shop is exactly what I expected—black walls, loud music, and tons of artwork hanging on the walls. I've only been in a tattoo shop once before when I got my belly button pierced for my sixteenth birthday, and *that* needle was bad enough. How the hell am I going to sit through getting a whole fucking tattoo?

The place smells like a mix of ink and disinfectant, and I cannot believe I'm here to permanently mark my skin with a decision I made less than fifteen minutes ago.

Man, Past Paisley *really* screwed me over this time.

Just as I'm about to beeline for the door, a tall man with rich brown skin and dreads pulled into a pony greets us. Both of his arms are covered from wrist to neck in ink. "You ladies got an appointment?"

"Nope." Maddie grins. "But she's having a mid-life crisis, so we figured, why not? Think you could hook us up—" She leans over the counter to get a look at his business card. "Marquis?"

He laughs under his breath. "I'll see what I can do. You girls take a seat here for a minute while I check things out. And by the way, most people just call me Q."

"Thanks, Q," she says in an overtly flirty tone.

"Jesus, Mads," I whisper in her ear. "Are we here for tattoos or for you to hit on the tattoo artist?"

"Why can't it be both?" A laugh escapes her lips. "Relax, Pais. This is going to be good for you." She picks up an artist's portfolio sitting on the table and begins flipping through it. "It's like a literal symbol of you reclaiming your life. A big *fuck you* to anyone who tries to tell you who you should be and what you should do."

I huff out a laugh. "Sure. That, or it's just proof I'm going through some shit. I might as well chop off my hair next."

She shrugs. "I think you could rock a bob. You'd look hot."

Before I can respond, Q reappears from behind the curtain that leads to the back. "Alright, ladies. I gotchu."

He gestures for us to follow him, and I realize that this is actually happening. Shit. I can't back out *now*. That would be worse than the time I was at Valleyfair and was in line for the Wild Thing and chickened out as soon as I got to the front. I'll never forget the nine-year-old kid who was waiting behind me with his dad and roasted me for being afraid of a rollercoaster.

Nope. Not again. I'm doing this.

Q leads me to a chair and signals for Maddie to sit in the other one, where another tattoo artist sits. "First tattoo?"

"Is it that obvious?" I ask, settling in. "Be gentle with me." I smile.

He smirks. "No promises."

Maddie snickers.

He asks me what I want to get, and we take a bit of time talking it over while he drafts up a few sketches. Once I'm happy with the result, I stretch my arm out and Q slides on some black, latex gloves.

"Nervous?" he asks.

"Yeah. But not just about this," I mutter.

He nods like he's heard that before.

"You sure you want it facing you?"

"Yes," I say immediately.

"You know most people get it—"

"I know. But it's not for them. It's for me."

He holds my gaze for a beat and then nods. "Respect."

Q wipes my arm with disinfectant and then starts with the stencil. My stomach knots as I glance at the faint outline of the image and words. Words I chose. Words I need.

Then he pulls out the needle. It doesn't look as scary as I thought it would, but I'm sure it's deceiving.

"You ready for this?"

"Not even a little bit." I shake my head. "But go for it."

"Fair enough." He smiles again. His teeth are even and bright, contrasting his smooth, dark complexion. His dark eyes are focused, but his smile is warm and comforting. My shoulders relax slightly.

The machine buzzes to life, a sharp electric hum that makes my skin prickle before it even comes close to touching me.

"Try to stay as steady as possible," he reminds me.

I close my eyes in anticipation, hoping that by not looking, it will make it hurt less. But the first press of the needle stings like what I imagine a wasp would feel like, though I've never actually been stung by one. It's sharp, sudden, and shocking. My whole body tenses on impact.

"Fuck," I breathe out.

Maddie laughs beside me. "You good, Pais?"

"Yeah, yeah," I manage to say through gritted teeth.

The pain deepens as Q moves, dragging the needle in slow, deliberate strokes. It's not unbearable, but it is relentless, like being scratched with a razor blade over and over and over again. After a few minutes, I glance down, assuming he *has* to be at least halfway done, but he only has the first two letters finished.

Jesus fucking Christ.

I try to focus on my breathing, letting out a steady, controlled exhale, but all I can focus on is the painful sensation of the needle dragging across my tender flesh. The way it feels like it's digging through my entire arm. The way my entire body vibrates with the motion.

And then I realize, I'm so wrapped up in the pain, that I quite literally can't think about anything else.

Damn. This is exactly what I needed.

No stress. No guilt. No overanalyzing every single fucking decision I've made in the last two months.

Just this. Just the pain I *chose*.

Q looks up at me through his dark lashes. "You're handling this better than most, especially for your first time."

"Really? Because it hurts like a bitch."

He laughs. "Really. Some people sweat somethin' terrible, then look like they might pass out. Hell, some of them actually *do*."

"Well, I can't look *ugly* while getting my first tattoo," I deadpan.

Maddie snorts from the chair next to me. "Obvi. Priorities."

Q shakes his head, clearly amused, and keeps working. "You two girls are something else."

I look over at Maddie, who is sipping her iced coffee and scrolling on her phone as if we're casually hanging out on the couch and she doesn't have a literal needle shoved into her skin right now. There's not an ounce of pain sketched across her face.

I let my eyes drift closed for a second, focusing on the rhythm of the needle and the buzzing of the machine.

"How's it feel?" Maddie's voice interrupts my thoughts.

"Like therapy." My voice comes out steadier than I expect.

"That's good." She laughs. "And it's cheaper, too."

By the time I pull into my driveway Monday afternoon, I feel like I've been gone for weeks instead of just a couple of days. The weekend with Maddie was exactly what I needed—some space, some time to think, and a couple too many bottles of wine to drown out the noise in my head.

When she left for work this morning, I packed my bag and headed to a coffee shop for a bit. I got some work done for school, like grading papers and making sure my lessons were ready to go for the rest of the week, before driving home. My head felt clearer when I left, and I knew what I needed to do.

But now that I'm here, it all feels real again. The weight of what's coming sits heavy on my chest, and I'm not sure I'm ready for it.

Ethan isn't home yet, so I unlock the front door and am immediately welcomed by Sebastian's familiar meow followed by Cheeto's prancing footsteps. I toss my purse onto the couch and take a deep breath.

"Hi, babies," I murmur as Sebastian winds himself around my legs.

Cheeto hops onto the back of the couch, stretching her legs in front of her in the adorable way cats do. I scratch behind her ears and let out a shaky breath. I might know what I need to do now, but that doesn't make it any easier.

The cats are a reminder of everything I'm about to change. It's not just about losing Ethan, which is still partially unimaginable, but also all the other small things I'll lose along with him. Family. Friends. Our house.

I plop down on the couch and sit there for what feels like hours. Eventually, the door creaks open behind me, and Ethan's voice fills the room.

"Paisley? You home?"

I turn around, still sitting on the couch, to face him. I know there's no hiding how I'm feeling. He's going to sense something is wrong.

"Hey." I give him a small smile, but it feels fragile, like I'm going to break any second. "How was your weekend?"

"Long." He walks into the living room and pulls me up into his arms, and the scent and feel of him is so familiar I almost wish I could let myself sink into it, let myself pretend everything is okay. But I can't. Not anymore. That much I know.

He pulls back slightly to look at me and searches my face with concern in his eyes. "What's going on, babe?"

I swallow hard. This is going to be even harder than I thought.

"It's... I just..." I pause, trying to find the right words. "Ethan, I don't know what I'm doing anymore."

His face falls, and the space between us feels like it stretches for miles. "What does that mean?" His voice cracks, telling me how badly he's been hurting. How badly *I've* been hurting him—and he doesn't even know the half of it.

"I—I don't know," I stammer. My hands shake as I step back from him, not knowing where to look or what to do with them. "I've been thinking about things all weekend, and I—I just don't know."

Tears brim my eyes, and I can't seem to stop them as they streak down my cheeks. I look up at him quickly, and he looks so confused, so hurt, that all I want to do is make him understand, to comfort him and make him feel better.

He takes a step toward me, closing the distance between us again, but I pull away, my heart pounding.

"Paisley. What's going on? I love you. You know that, right? I love you. Always."

I nod, my throat tight. "I love you, too." The words taste bitter on my tongue. Unfamiliar. Untrue.

"Always?" he asks, his voice hopeful, pressing his forehead gently to mine.

I open my mouth to answer, but the words don't come out. I want to say yes. I want to tell him that everything will be okay, that I'll stay and we can fix this.

Always. Forever. That's what I used to say.

But now it feels like a lie.

I step back, needing air. "I don't know," I say quietly, and my tears flow even harder.

His face drops even more, the color draining from his cheeks. He reaches out for me again, and this time, I let him pull me into his chest while I crumble.

"I thought we were happy," he whispers into my hair.

A sob rips through me. "I thought I was, too," I murmur against his chest. "But—but something's changed. And I can't keep pretending anymore. I'm so sorry, Eth." I gasp for air between sobs. "I'm so, so, so sorry..."

Chapter Fifty-Two

♫ *"You and Me" — Lifehouse* ♫

BRIGGS

The wind picks up in slow, creeping increments, rattling the trees and whipping against the screen door of the cabin. The air is thick and heavy, the kind that suggests a major storm is coming. It has been an unusually warm winter, and the snow has already melted, leaving the dead grass exposed and muddy. But still, this kind of storm isn't common this time of year in the midwest.

I look out the window. The rain hasn't started yet, but there are dark clouds starting to gather in the distance. I swirl the amber liquid in my glass and open the window to allow some fresh air into the cabin.

I take a sip of my whiskey and let the burn settle into my chest as I sit at the counter and stare at the plans I've drawn up for 18th Amendment. I should be focusing on next steps, like permits, renovations, and timelines, but my mind keeps circling back to the same brown-eyed brunette it always does.

Give it up, Briggs. She isn't coming.

I slump into my chair and connect my Bluetooth to the speaker in the living room, hoping the sound of someone else's voice will drown out the volume of my own inside my head.

Knock, knock.

My heart basically lurches out of my fucking chest, both in hope and startlement.

It's her. It has to be her.

I rise to my feet before my brain even has a chance to process, the chair scraping against the wooden floor as I move.

She's here. After all this time, after all the waiting, I finally get to see her, to hold her, to feel her lips on mine again...

I yank the door open, and my stomach drops to the floor. I let out a loud, disappointed exhale.

"Davenport," Joe says from the other side of the threshold, his usual smug grin in place. "We need to talk."

The sky behind him is a deep gray, and the first drops of rain splatter on the red porch.

"Joe."

"You're a bit off the grid out here, huh?" He steps inside without an invitation, shaking the rain from his sleeves. His eyes flick around the cabin, subtle judgment crossing his features. "Living like a bit of a recluse, I see."

I don't acknowledge his question. Instead, I lean against the counter and cross my arms. "Didn't expect you to drive all the way out here to check in on me."

It's been over a month since Beth and I separated, and this is the first time anyone has come by to see me. Hell, it's the first time anyone other than Aaron has even talked to me unless it's related to school or coaching. Guess when you fall from your pedestal, absolutely no one is there to give a damn.

He lets out a laugh, but it doesn't meet his eyes, and something tells me he's not just here to see how I'm holding up. He steps farther inside the cabin, glancing at the bar plans splayed out of the counter but not saying anything about them.

"So, it's true, then? You're really doing this. Walking away from everything."

I shift my gaze to the fire and take another sip of my drink. "Yep. Really doing this."

He clicks his tongue, and I can see him shake his head out of my peripheral vision. "Look, man. I get it. You're going through something. What, I'm not sure, but people are starting to talk. They've *been* talking."

"And?" I clip. "You think I give a shit what anyone is saying?"

"Maybe you should. You know how this town is. People see things. Make their own assumptions." He tilts his head. "There are... rumors circulating about why you left. About who you left for."

I clench my jaw, my fingers tightening around my glass. Who the hell does this guy think he is, coming to *my* property, to tell me shit I already know? I don't fucking *care*.

"I don't owe anyone an explanation. And quite frankly, it's none of their fucking business."

Joe sighs, stepping closer. "Maybe not. But you're the assistant principal of that school. You're a *coach*, man. You really think this is a good idea? Parents aren't gonna like it, Briggs. You don't want to be the guy everyone whispers about from the sidelines."

I let out a dry laugh and down the rest of my drink. "Again, you think I give a damn about what people are going to *say*? It's *my* life, Joe. I made my choice. And aside from Beth, it doesn't affect anyone else."

Joe shoves his hands in his pockets, studying me, his expression hard to read. "I think maybe you should reconsider. Beth—"

"I'm not going back," I cut in.

He holds my gaze for a long moment, then exhales. "Alright. But when it comes to coaching next year, I think we may need to make some changes, then. We can't be having the community talk. That's gonna look bad for the school. For the team. You probably shouldn't—"

"Are you telling me I'm not going to be able to coach?"

"Nothing's been decided yet. I just think..."

Another dry laugh escapes my lips. "You're a real piece of work, Joe." I walk back over the door and open it, signaling it's time for him to go. "But don't worry about it. Not even sure I'll be in Stonebrook next year, so I wouldn't be around to coach, anyway."

"You thinking about leaving?"

"I'm thinking that's none of your fucking business. Now if you would..." I tip my head toward the porch.

He steps back onto the deck. "Hey, no hard feelings. Just thought you should know what people are—"

"Noted." I cut him off. "Drive safe. Rain's coming down pretty hard out there now."

Without another word, I close the door behind him, the wind catching it slightly and slamming it shut. Water pelts against the roof, and I stand there for a moment, staring out the window. I take a deep breath, attempting to steady my pulse, and lock the door behind me.

I watch as Joe leaves, his headlights disappearing down the dirt road, but I don't feel the relief that I should.

Because Joe's right. People talk. And there's a reason why they're talking. I haven't heard much of what they're saying—no one would dare say anything to my face—but Beth has asked me again if there's someone else. I told her no. Because that's the truth, isn't it?

Yeah, I'm in love with Paisley Hamilton, but there's not a damn thing I can do about it. She's with Ethan. And from where I'm sitting, it looks like she's going to stay with him.

Am I okay with that? Not even a fucking little bit. But I still don't regret my decision to leave.

I walk into the kitchen and pour myself another drink, turning the music up louder. After throwing a few logs onto the fire, I turn down the lights and sink into the couch, allowing myself to get lost in the song playing. The lyrics spill into the space—a song by Lifehouse I've always liked, but tonight it hits differently.

Face it, Briggs. She's not coming. She's not changing her mind. She's not choosing you. If she wanted to, she would have by now. It's too late.

I'm not sure how long I sit here, lost in my thoughts, as the storm rages outside. The rain hammers harder against the cabin, and thunder rumbles in the distance. Every once in a while a crack of lightning flashes through the window.

It doesn't matter anymore. I'll figure it out. One way or another, I'll be okay. Whether or not she comes back, I will be okay.

Another bolt of lightning illuminates the room. The wind picks up even harder, and something knocks against the cabin door so loudly, it makes my pulse jump.

I freeze, and my chest tightens, but only for a second. It's just the storm. The wind. But what the hell is it knocking around out there?

The sound comes again, so I push myself up and shuffle toward the door. A gust of wind must have knocked down some branches that clattered onto the porch. I pull on the handle, expecting a loose piece of debris to come flying inside, and as the door creaks open, the wind howls in and slaps me in the face with the cold, damp air.

But when I squint through the dark night, it's not a piece of wood on my porch.

It's Paisley.

Drenched from head to fucking toe, bags at her sides, hair soaked and plastered to her face, cheeks streaked with mascara.

She lifts her gaze to meet mine, her brown-eyes shining brightly beneath her lashes, a tired smile tugging at her lips. My stomach tightens as my mind tries to process if she's actually here.

We stare at each other for a moment, and after what seems like an eternity, she finally speaks.

"I'm sorry it took me so long."

Epilogue

PAISLEY

5 YEARS LATER

The clock is *crawling*. No, actually, I think it might be moving backward. Either that, or I've fallen into some kind of black hole like in *Interstellar*, and the last two minutes of class are going to stretch on for the rest of eternity.

At the front of the room, I lean against my desk and close the book with a decisive thud.

"Alright, my wonderful earthlings, that's it for today. Seeing we still have a minute or so left of class, I *could* leave you with some deep, thought-provoking words about how learning never really stops even when you're on break—"

I'm interrupted by the collective groan of the students sitting in front of me, most of whom are already halfway out of their seats and headed for the door.

"But I won't," I finish. "Because I've been teaching long enough to know better. So instead, I'll just say this: enjoy your week off, make good choices, and please, for the love of God, don't make me see you on the news."

A few chuckles fill the room.

"Wouldn't dream of it," one of them tells me. Though with this particular student, I'm not so sure that's true.

The bell rings, and the students spill into the hallway, hooping and hollering about spring break officially beginning. I let out an exhale and grab my bag, slinging it over my shoulder and walking toward the door.

When I go to turn off the lights, my eyes catch a glimpse of my forearm, and I smile at the words staring back at me.

Lebe zwischen den Wildblumen.

My fingers absentmindedly brush over the inked wildflowers that accompany the phrase, and my smile grows larger as I flick off the lights and step into the hall.

The drive to 18th Amendment is second nature to me now, considering I stop there most nights after school on my way home, other than Tuesdays and Thursdays when I go to a 4:30 hot yoga class. I was never much of a yogi, but when we moved to Willowhaven four years ago, there was a studio only twelve minutes from our house. Turns out, the breathing exercises and meditative classes have done wonders for my mental health, and God knows I needed it.

The winding roads to the bar are familiar but not weighed down with memories the way Stonebrook's used to be, and when I pull up to the old brick building, the faded 1918 Automobile lettering stares back at me. The 18 is slightly darker now, telling people this is the right place, but someone random driving by wouldn't give it a second thought. The upstairs cafe lights are dimly lit, but I circle around back where a discreet door stands in isolation.

I step inside and press the button on the small panel along the wall, and a low, dark voice crackles through the speaker.

"Password?"

"Seriously? I know you can see me through the camera."

"House rules," he says, and I know there's a smirk on his face on the other side of this damn intercom.

I smile and roll my eyes. "Wildflower Whiskey."

The lock clicks open, and as I walk down the dark corridor, I'm welcomed by the smell of aged bourbon and a mix of tobacco and patchouli.

Right as I am about to slide onto a barstool, Briggs approaches and swoops me into his arms. He wraps his arms around my waist, and mine find their way around his neck as I pull him closer to me. Even after all these years, just the simple feel of his arms around me makes my stomach flip.

I pull back and stare into his deep blue eyes before pressing my lips to his, and for a second, I forget we're in the middle of the bar.

"I love this dress on you," he growls in my ear as he brings his hands down to cup my ass, telling me he also doesn't remember there are others in the bar around us.

Either that, or he just doesn't care. Knowing Briggs, it really could be either.

Eventually, we separate, and he walks to the other side of the bar. His sleeves are rolled up, exposing the tattoo I've now memorized every inch of—the ink I've traced hundreds of times with my fingertips while lying in bed at night.

"How was school?" he asks like always.

"Insane," I tell him as I pick up a cherry from the garnishes and plop it into my mouth. "I swear, the minute spring break is in sight, teenagers forget how to function. I had to stop a kid from submitting an essay in *Comic Sans* today." I mock shudder to show my disgust.

Briggs raises his eyebrows at me, a grin pulling at the corners of his mouth. "Oh, the horror," he says dryly.

"Seriously! Quite frankly, I'm worried about the future of our society."

"Well, it's a good thing they have you there to teach them, then." He leans across the bar and kisses me on the cheek, causing them to immediately flush. You would think by now that I would be used to all the attention he gives me, how loved and valued he makes me feel, but my body still hasn't caught up, apparently. And I *still* haven't gotten my blushing under control.

"Right? Good thing." I huff out a laugh. "Anyway, you almost ready to go?"

He studies me for a moment, as if he's tracing the features of my face with his eyes and memorizing them all over again. Then, without a word, he grabs a glass, pours something into it, and slides it across the bar to me.

"One for the road?" he asks.

I feign suspicion. "Briggs Davenport. Are you trying to get me drunk before our flight?"

He smirks. "Obviously."

"Well, lucky for you, I'm easily persuaded. But tread lightly. If you get me too tipsy, I might just try to convince you to join the mile high club."

He laughs and rolls his eyes. "As if it would be the first time. We've been over this, babes. I'm way too tall for us to fit in an airplane bathroom together."

I take a sip of the drink, which is fruity and fucking delicious, and shrug. "Still worth a shot. Eventually you'll give in."

He shakes his head and laughs again. "I just have a few things to finish up here. You finish your drink, and I'll be back out in a bit. I have to check in with Wes and make sure he's good to go for next week. Can't have the place falling apart without me here." He winks and turns to walk through the doors behind the bar.

I take a minute to drink in my surroundings; I've sat in this very bar stool dozens—*hundreds*—of times now, but every time I do, I'm in absolute awe of what Briggs has created over the past five years.

Damn. *Five years.* How has it been that long?

Five years of learning and unlearning, of finding our footing together, of making mistakes, having tough conversations, and continuing to choose each other every step of the way.

The first two years after I showed up at his cabin were excruciating. It wasn't some fairytale ending where we could immediately be together and everything else just disappeared.

No. It was hard. It tested us. But we came out stronger as a result.

The rest of that school year, we kept our distance as we navigated ending our own relationships, relying solely on stolen glances and evening rendezvous together. I moved out of my house and got an apartment of my own, and Briggs spent the remainder of spring and summer at the cabin before he moved in with me for a year. Every moment we got to share felt both like a gift and a risk. When the world didn't understand—when people whispered behind our backs and assumed they knew exactly what had happened—it was easier to keep things quiet. We didn't have the luxury of living in the open for a long time, having to drive at least an hour or two away from Stonebrook that entire summer to go on dates just to avoid the whispers and the stares of the community.

So, we spent most of our time here at 18th Amendment. Renovating. Talking. Learning everything we could about each other. Arguing over paint colors and tile choices only to make up by having sex in every nook and cranny in this space. (Sorry, Jo! Though I have a feeling she would be proud of that, anyway).

This place was something that was not only his, but *ours*—something that didn't have anyone else's judgment attached. It became our sanctuary, our refuge, especially when the weight of everything outside of here felt like it was almost too much to bear.

By the time fall rolled around, we were both—begrudgingly—back at Stonebrook High for one final year. I hadn't applied anywhere else after everything went down. I was worn out, exhausted—emotionally, mentally, and physically—and looking for a new job on top of a divorce, a new relationship, and a new place to live seemed like too much to handle. So I stayed, and Briggs stayed, too.

When the school year started, it felt like every day was a fucking test, like God or whatever higher power exists was testing not only my own strength but the strength of our relationship. We dealt with judgmental community members, unsupportive admin, and gossiping teenagers. There were more days than not that I questioned if I even wanted to teach anymore. The accusations, the assumptions, the sideways glances, the constant reminders that people *thought* they knew everything about us... was fucking relentless. The rumors weren't just whispers. They were being shouted from the goddamn rooftops, and *everyone* was listening.

But I would do it all over again if it meant I would end up here. Because it was worth it. *He* was worth it.

Luckily, by the following spring, a teaching position opened up thirty minutes from the bar, even farther in the opposite direction of Stonebrook. It was a saving grace, our escape, and I applied for the job without a single second of hesitation.

Briggs, on the other hand, was on the fence about what to do. He thought about going back into administration, especially when the bar was still a pipe dream and not yet fully functional. But with his money saved up, along with the sum of money he got for his half of his house, he decided to take the risk and go all in on 18th Amendment.

Briggs felt bad Beth had to sell, but she insisted she needed a fresh start and didn't want to stay in a place with so many memories. She never asked for the mess we made, but she handled it with more grace than we probably deserved. She stayed in Stonebrook for a while but eventually moved closer to family. We've heard she's doing well. Sometimes that's all you need to know.

Jo, who sadly passed away two years ago, was extremely helpful during the process of renovating the bar, and through her connections in Willowhaven, it took off quicker than either of us expected. As promised, he kept the upper level staged as an old automobile shop, an homage to Jo and Henry, but decided to run it as a cafe during the day. At night, when the coffee shop closes, the speakeasy opens, and the only way to get in is with the monthly password, which, of course, is usually something extremely ridiculous.

As for Ethan, he sold the house a few years ago and moved to another state where he could start over. He's remarried with two kids now. Ironically, Ethan never wanted to leave Stonebrook when he and I were together. Maybe that means our relationship was holding him back in its own way, too. At first, I wasn't sure whether that was comforting or if it was a stark reminder of how little we had truly had together, but it didn't matter. That chapter ended when it needed to so another one could begin—for both of us.

And through it all, Briggs and I continued to choose each other. To fight through the hard. To love and appreciate each other every step of the way. Because, as Briggs would say, that's what lobsters do.

I finish the last sip of my drink—The Closet Confession, according to the board hanging above the bar—just as Briggs emerges from the back room. His hair is slightly tousled, and he's wearing a gray henley that brings out the gray specks in his eyes. The sight of him causes my heart to nearly lurch out of my chest.

"You ready to go?" he asks as he approaches, his voice low.

I nod, setting my glass down on the counter. "Yeah, just... one more thing." I bat my eyelashes at him the best I can.

He raises an eyebrow. "I know that look. What is it?"

"So, I know we need to get to the airport, but... do we have time to stop by the house first? I, um, need to say goodbye to the cats one last time before we go."

Unfortunately, in the divorce, Ethan got to keep Cheeto. Leaving her behind was one of the hardest parts for me, as theatrical as that sounds, but in the end, I think it was the best. Ethan needed her more than I did at that point in our lives, and it was the least I could do after, well, everything. At least I got to keep Sebastian, and the first year Briggs and I moved in together, we adopted another kitten from the humane society. We call him JT.

His laughter booms through the room, which causes a few heads to turn. "Goddamn. I should have expected that." He reaches for his jacket. "Or maybe I already did, which is why I told you our flight was thirty minutes earlier than it actually is." He winks.

"You did not!" I swat his arm playfully. "You lied to me?" I pretend to be offended, though I fear the huge grin on my face gives me away.

Bless this man and him knowing everything I need.

Briggs slings his arm around my shoulder and pulls me close to him. "Only for your own good, lobster girl. Now let's go! We have a plane to catch!" He leans over and kisses the top of my head, and I can feel him smile into my hair.

We step out into the cool evening air, and I reach for his hand, threading my fingers through his. I squeeze his hand a little tighter, a flood of warmth rushing through my body.

It wasn't that long ago that the future felt suffocating. But now, finally, I can breathe easily.

Because that was before it was us.

PAISLEY'S PLAYLIST

"Landslide" by Fleetwood Mac
"Can't Stop The Feeling" by Justin Timberlake
"The Middle" by Zedd, Maren Morris, & Grey
"Unwritten" by Natasha Bedingfield
"Autumn Leaves" by Ed Sheeran
"Boot Scootin' Boogie" by Brooks & Dunn
"Shallow" by Lady Gaga & Bradley Cooper
"Dreams" by Fleetwood Mac
"I Wanna Dance with Somebody" by Whitney Houston
"Slow Dancing in a Burning Room" by John Mayer
"Collide" by Howie Day
"Feel So Close" by Calvin Harris
"Fast Car" by Tracy Chapman
"Kiss Me" by Sixpence None the Richer
"You Should Probably Leave" by Chris Stapleton
"Brave" by Sara Birellies
"So Good" by Halsey
"Hands to Myself" by Selena Gomez
"Stay" by Rihanna ft. Mikky Ekko
"Starving" by Hailee Steinfeld & Grey ft. Zedd
"Bad Things" by mgk & Camila Cabello
"Daylight" by Maroon 5
"Torn" by Natalie Imbruglia
"Numb Little Bug" by Em Beihold
"Breathe (2 AM) by Anna Nalick
"Hold My Hand" by Lady Gaga
"Let Me Go" by Hailee Steinfeld ft. Alesso, Florida Georgia Line & watt

BRIGGS'S PLAYLIST

"Against the Wind" by Bob Seger
"Something Just Like This" by The Chainsmokers
"Simple Man" by Lynyrd Skynyrd
"How's It Going to Be?" by Third Eye Blind
"9 to 5" by Dolly Parton
"MakeDamnSure" by Taking Back Sunday
"Dream On" by Aerosmith
"Wicked Game" by Chris Isaak
"Wonderwall" by Oasis
"Witchcraft" by Frank Sinatra
"In Too Deep" by Sum 41
"Over My Head (Cable Car)" by The Fray
"Yellow" by Coldplay
"Scared to Start" by Michael Micargi
"Numb" by Linkin Park
"Stone" by Whiskey Myers
"Beautiful Mess" by Diamond Rio
"Stargazing" by Myles Smith
"Dreams" by The Cranberries
"Mr. Brightside" by The Killers
"The Great Escape" by BOYS LIKE GIRLS
"Chasing Cars" by Snow Patrol
"Happier" Marshmello & Bastille
"Here Without You" by 3 Doors Down
"Iris" by The Goo Goo Dolls
"You and Me" by Lifehouse

First of all, I cannot believe I am actually writing this right now. Three years ago when I first put pen to paper, this book was just a pipe-dream—something that I thought I would work on here and there and that would never actually see the light of day. But thanks to the support of my family and friends, along with lots and lots of iced coffee, it's now something you are holding in your hands, and *that* is absolutely wild to me.

Before It Was Us would not have been possible without the endless support of my very own lobster—Barnaby, without you, I would have given up a long time ago. Thank you for always encouraging me to at least get one word down when I said I was going to work on my book and did everything possible to procrastinate actually working on it. Thank you for always bringing me a blanket to cuddle up on the couch with my laptop, for answering the countless questions I had about getting into the mind of Briggs, and for listening to me read scene after scene just so I could hear it out loud. But most of all, thank you for being a real-life book boyfriend, which made the vulnerable and romantic parts of this story the easiest parts to write.

Thank you to my two besties who received endless video and audio messages from me in our group chat about whether something worked or not and for being the very first two people to read this book in its entirety, encouraging me and cheering me on while also providing constructive feedback. You made this story what it is today, and I couldn't have done it without you both. You know who you are.

Thank you to my beta readers who gave me feedback that helped me with the—albeit grueling—revision process and who helped the storyline progress *so* much better in the end, and of course to my ARC readers who helped with the final touches.

Thank you to the other indie authors and members of the Writertok community who constantly hyped me up and motivated me to write even on the days I didn't want to. You all continue to inspire me.

And last but most certainly not least, thank you to my readers, to all the Paisleys and the Briggs in the world, for giving me a reason to write this story in the first place.

Author's Note

When I first started writing *Before It Was Us*, I wasn't sure I was going to finish it. And then once I did, part of me wanted to stick it on a shelf and let it live there without another living soul ever seeing it.

Not because I didn't love the story or the characters, but because of *what* the story is about. I knew as a fellow reader that infidelity is one of the most hated tropes out there. And believe me, I get it. I felt the same way before meeting Paisley and Briggs. So every time I sat down to work on their journey, I worried about how this book would be received. About whether people would read the back cover and instantly write it off as a story that "glorifies cheating" or "romanticizes bad decisions." But that was never what this book was about.

This story was born out of the quiet, gut-wrenching question so many people carry but are too scared to say out loud: *what if I did everything right, everything I was supposed to, and still ended up in the wrong life?*

Because the truth is, stepping outside of a marriage is far more nuanced than most people want to admit. It doesn't always come from a place of malice or selfishness. Sometimes it's born from deep loneliness, from years of disconnection, from the quiet realization that you've built a life that doesn't even feel like yours.

The point of Paisley and Briggs's story isn't the cheating itself—it's *how* they got there. It's about the slow unraveling, the moments that led up to it, and the gut-punch of guilt and desire that overwhelmed them while trying to navigate their feelings.

Paisley and Briggs aren't perfect. They're flawed and impulsive and tangled up in their emotions—but they're also deeply human. They've spent years trying to be who they're *supposed* to be, being happy with what they've been told is enough, and what they find in each other isn't just romance or lust. It's clarity. It's the terrifying realization that maybe love isn't always easy or convenient or well-timed... but that doesn't make it any less *real*.

Writing this story was harder than I thought it would be. I wanted readers to root for Paisley and Briggs, but not at the expense of Ethan and Beth. I didn't want clean-cut villains or perfect victims. I wanted readers to feel conflicted, just like our narrators do. Because that's what real life often is—layered, complicated, and nearly impossible to figure out.

I know this book isn't for everyone, but it *is* for those of you who have ever felt stuck in something that looks good on paper but still doesn't feel in your bones how you wish it would. It's for the people who've silenced their intuition to keep the peace. For the ones who've stayed when they knew they were meant to go.

For those who have lain in bed at night and asked themselves, *is this really all there is?*

So if Paisley and Briggs's story made you feel seen, or understood, or even just a little bit validated, I'm so glad it found you. Because you're who their story was meant for.

xo, Marie